Her Reluctant Groom

ROSE GORDON

D1525707

HER RELUCTANT GROOM

Published by Parchment & Plume, LLC
www.parchmentandplume.com

Other Titles Available

Prologue

London
March 1815

Emma Green's eyes shot open as her feather mattress dipped under the heavy weight of a man sneaking into her bed. Her body stiffened in fear as he settled in close beside her.

"Emma, wake up," a masculine voice whispered.

Emma clenched her eyes shut as tightly as she could, willing this vile man to go back to his own bed. Or at least to go bother her sister, his wife.

Gregory Thorne, Duke of Hampton and her brother-in-law, placed his clammy and calloused hand on her shoulder, sending chills down her spine. "Wake up, girl." His voice was a bit louder than before as he fiercely shook her shoulder.

"Get away from me," she hissed, swatting at his hand.

He grabbed her wrist. "Not this time. You've put me off long enough. Not anymore."

Bile rose in her throat and she kicked at his legs under the covers, only tangling the sheets around her legs more. "Get away from me," she yelled, trying her best to break the hold he had on her.

Gregory made a *tsk, tsk* noise. "Now, now, Emma. It won't be so bad. Just lie there like a good girl. It'll be over soon enough. And who knows? You might like it."

"Never," she spat, hitting his forearm with as much force as she could with the heel of her left hand.

His other hand came up, and he roughly closed his fingers around her wrist, stopping her from hitting him again. Rolling his heavy body on top of hers, he shoved her hands high above her head and held them down. Transferring her left hand into the same hold as her right, Gregory tightened the fingers of his left hand around both her wrists and used the fingers of his right hand to roughly stroke her face. "Oh, Emma," he whispered. "How I've longed for you since the day I married your sister. And now, after thirteen years, you shall be all mine." He lowered his head to place a wet, sloppy kiss on her lips.

Emma moved her head just in time to cause his repulsive kiss to land on her cheek rather than her lips. She cringed at the sensation of his slug-like lips on her skin and tried to yank one of her hands free from his bruising grasp. "Let me go," she said, squirming under him.

The weight of his disgustingly naked body kept her pinned to the bed as his hand brutally squeezed her breast so hard she winced. "So soft. So luscious. So firm. So unlike Louise's." He sneered in distaste, then squeezed again, sending sparks of pain shooting through her.

Catching him somewhat unaware due to his current interest in her aching breast, she jerked her elbows forward and very nearly knocked him on the top of his head.

He tightened his grip again, almost crushing the bones in her wrists. "Don't do that again," he said sharply, adjusting his body so more of his weight was on the top half of her. "I know you've spread your legs for Sinclair. You can do the same for me."

He repositioned himself to put more weight on her upper body in an effort to hold her wrists steady. Taking advantage of that small bit of fortune, in one quick motion, Emma brought both knees up to connect directly with Gregory's groin.

A loud cry escaped Gregory's throat, and his hands immediately released their grasp on her body and flew between his legs as he rolled off her and to the side.

Emma wasted nary a second and scrambled out the other side of her bed. She threw on her dressing robe and started for the door, only to be halted by her sister.

"What is the meaning of this?" Louise snapped; her arms across her chest. Her dark green eyes darted from her escaping sister to her husband, groaning in pain on the bed. "What have you done, Emma?" Her tone was full of bitter hatred, and not for her husband. No, all that bitterness was directed straight at Emma.

"Nothing, Louise." She knew her sister wouldn't care one way or the other what went on in that room tonight. Louise only cared about herself. She didn't care if her husband had affairs, only that he kept them discreet. For as long as Louise had been married to the duke, he'd tried to make amorous advances toward Emma. She'd never given him any indication she was interested in an affair with him, but that didn't matter. He continued to make advances all the same. She cringed.

"Good," Louise said crisply.

"Get out," Gregory wheezed.

Louise pursed her lips. "Very well."

"Not you." His icy stare moved to Emma. "Her."

Emma's heart raced. She'd always hated coming to London and staying with them. But the fact remained she had nowhere else to go. After her parents had died in a carriage accident eight years ago, Louise and Gregory were the only family she had left.

"Very well," Louise said with an annoyed huff. "I'll show her to a different chamber for the evening."

"No," Gregory said tightly, still clasping his privates as if he were afraid they'd fall off if he let them go. "She's not to spend another night in my house. Ever."

Emma sucked in a hard breath. Was she actually being thrown out? She had nowhere and no one to go to. They knew that. At seven-and-twenty, was her virtue really worth anything any longer? She'd long ago passed the marriageable age. She was a firmly-on-the-shelf spinster now. Did such things as virginity and purity matter any longer? She glanced at her naked brother-in-law and knew the answer instantly. Yes. Yes, it all still mattered. She may never marry or have true love or any of that other stuff that was only meant for fairy tales, but there was no way she'd give her virtue to him. Not even if it meant she'd have a bed to sleep in, food in her mouth, and a roof over her head. He was not worth it.

"Well, you heard him," Louise chirped, grabbing whatever she could get her hands on from Emma's vanity and tossing it into her reticule. "Out with you."

Emma stared at her sister in shock. They'd never been close as children. Then, nearly thirteen years ago, the last threads of a sisterly bond had been snipped when they'd gotten into a string of quarrels involving Louise's treatment and eventual jilting of their long-time friend Marcus Sinclair. Emma knew her sister didn't like her and never would, but seeing her so happily humming as she carelessly tossed Emma's belongings into her reticule with the intent of throwing her out at nearly midnight caused her heart to ache anew. "Louise," she whispered, praying her sister wasn't truly going to throw her out this way.

"Suck in that lower lip," Louise said coldly. "You brought this upon yourself. Now, I'd advise you to put on your fanciest gown so when you leave here and go straight to Marcus—like we all know you'll do—you'll look nice. Then he'll start to pay you for the favors you've been freely giving him."

Emma's lower lip quivered, and she bit down on the inside of her mouth to make it stop. She wasn't going to give them the satisfaction of seeing how upset she was at their cold words and harsh treatment. "Louise," she said again. "I truly have nowhere to go." She hated admitting such a thing, even if it was true.

Growing up in the country, she'd never had an abundance of friends. Marcus and Olivia Sinclair and their cousin, Caroline, had been her only friends over the years. Olivia, however, was unfit company for a dog, and she'd actually left the country not long ago, or so Emma had heard. Caroline had married a year before, and though Caroline and Emma were still close, it felt different somehow. That only left Marcus, the man she'd spun romantic daydreams in her head about since she was practically still in leading strings.

She'd always fancied herself in love with him, even when he became engaged to her sister, and even continued to feel the same after his horribly disfiguring accident. She couldn't seek refuge with him though. He'd been nice enough to her in the past thirteen years when she'd gone to his house to visit Caroline or put up with Olivia's dreadfulness as an excuse to see him. But now that he lived alone, he'd probably not let her past the front door. Nor had she tried. The contempt he must feel for her being the sister of the woman who had jilted him, and brought him a lifetime's worth of embarrassment and misery. Surely, he would always keep her at arm's length.

Louise handed Emma her excessively heavy reticule. "Here." She smirked. "I advised you to change, and as usual you didn't heed my instructions. Too late now. Out."

"Louise, be rational. It's barely midnight. I can't go out there like this." She gestured down to the dressing robe she wore over her nightrail.

Louise shrugged. "Go to Marcus. He's only a few hours' ride from here. He won't care what you're wearing. I imagine he'll have it off you in less than a minute anyway," she added flippantly.

Emma ground her teeth. "Despite what you think, I've not been carrying on any type of affair with Marcus."

"I don't believe you," Louise said flatly. "But that matters naught. What matters is that you leave now." She sighed. "If the problem is you lack the funds to hire a ride to Dorset, then perhaps you could take a hack a few blocks over to Watson Townhouse and see if your friend Caroline will loan the money to you."

Emma's hand tightened on the strap of her reticule as she glanced into the menacing eyes of her sister. "You really want me to leave?"

"Yes."

That was all it took, just one word.

Emma put the strap of her reticule on her shoulder, and without a backward glance to either of the two beings who had done their best to make her miserable these past eight years, she left the room, walked down the hall, descended two flights of stairs, and walked straight out the front door.

Chapter 1

One Week Later

Dear Marcus,

I am writing to you to prevail upon your lasting kindness one more time, dear cousin. Emma has come to stay with Alex and me for reasons I am not at liberty to disclose. And while I love her dearly and enjoy her company more than just about anyone else's, I have gotten myself into a predicament and need your help.

Later this week, I shall be hosting my first house party! It is only for close friends and family, but Emma has declared she has no interest in participating and plans to spend the ten days secluded in her room. Now, Marcus, do not put the paper down! I am not asking you to attend. I know you'd sooner gouge your own eyes out than attend a social event, which is why I would like you to convince her to stay at your estate for the duration of the house party. She currently doesn't have a chaperone, but I trust that shall not be an issue as I know you think of Emma the same as you think of me and will take care to make sure she is safe and her reputation well-guarded.

We both know she'd never come to you to ask for any sort of favor, so please do this for me, Marcus. I am the one asking, not her.

I will be sending her to Ridge Water on an errand Wednesday afternoon. That should give you plenty of time to think of a viable excuse for her to stay.

I thank you so much.

Yrs,
Caroline

Marcus, Earl of Sinclair, looked down at the missive in his hand and fought the urge to crumple it and then see if he could remain sitting in his chair and throw it directly into the rubbish bin thirty feet from his desk.

"Bad news?" Patrick Ramsey, Viscount Drakely, asked from the other side of his desk.

Marcus twisted his lips. "Not bad exactly. But not good, either."

Patrick reached forward for the missive, and Marcus made it easy for him by sliding it across the desk. He had no problem feeding the younger man's curiosity. The two had been close friends for thirteen years. Patrick knew all about Marcus' past with Louise and Emma. In fact, he knew more than anyone else since the two had met the day of Marcus' horrific accident. Marcus was convinced if not for his friend's interference that day, he would not be alive.

Patrick's lips moved and his eyebrows rose as he scanned Caroline's missive. "Are you going to let her stay?"

Marcus scrubbed his scarred face with his equally scarred fingers. Caroline had said she didn't have a chaperone, and heaven knew between the three female staff members he employed, not a one had the time—or suitability—to act as a proper chaperone. "I shouldn't."

"Ah, but you will anyway. I can see it in your eyes."

Marcus jerked his gaze away. "Caroline has never asked me for a favor before."

"Mmmhmmm," Patrick said slowly. He idly tapped the missive from Caroline on his thigh. "So your agreement to invite Miss Green to stay is only because Caroline asked it of you? It has nothing to do with your attraction to Miss Green, and this being the perfect opportunity to spend time with her?"

"Don't I owe Caroline a favor for all the hell my family put her through?"

7

Patrick put the parchment back on Marcus' desk. "I suppose so," he said casually. "But what if it were Miss Green asking?" His eyes held an unusual sparkle. One that gave Marcus pause. Patrick had been nearly expressionless since his wife died in childbirth almost five years ago.

Marcus shrugged. "I supposed I'd let her stay then, too," he said, annoyed.

"Of course you would," Patrick agreed jovially, the gleam in his eye still present. "You're probably just irritated she's been staying with Caroline and her husband and didn't come here in the first place."

Dropping his head to hide his scowl from Patrick and his eerie perceptiveness, Marcus pretended to take a sudden interest in his ledger. He'd be lying if he said he wasn't a mite disappointed she hadn't seen fit to come to him if she were in trouble; but he couldn't blame her for not seeking his assistance, considering his past engagement with her sister.

Patrick chuckled. "Why do you fight it so?"

"Stop," Marcus snapped, piercing his friend with his gaze.

Shrugging as if to say he really didn't care one way or the other what Marcus said or did, Patrick turned to look at his three young daughters who were playing together on the floor with whatever little trinkets they could find to entertain themselves with in Marcus' study. "I have an idea." He turned back to Marcus and flashed him a brilliant smile.

"No," Marcus said, eying the girls. "They're all very sweet, well-behaved children, but I'll not use watching your children as an excuse to keep her here during Caroline's house party."

"And why not?" Patrick countered, his voice laced in mock indignation. "As you said, they're very well-behaved. I have to go to London for a series of meetings to get ready for when parliament sessions begin in a few weeks. At least this way they wouldn't be stuck with that horrid woman they call a governess."

Marcus shook his head. "Emma may like them as much as the rest of us, but it's not fair to anyone to do that."

"How so?"

"First, it's not fair to Emma to ask her to take care of three little girls without any help for such a long time. Second, it's not fair to me to have my house suddenly overrun by the female species. And third, it won't be fair to the girls when it's time for them to leave."

"I see your point," Patrick conceded solemnly. "They would miss her something terrible."

"Exactly." Marcus smiled at Patrick. "Just think how difficult it would be when they cry and refuse to leave her to return to your tedious care."

Patrick scowled then bent his head to look at the floor. He rested his palms against his temples, scratching the sides and top of his head as he thought. Suddenly he sat up straighter than a sword. "That can be fixed."

"How?" Marcus asked with a scoff. "Do you plan to request Emma act like more of a dullard than you so they're actually excited to return home when you come back from London?"

"No, no." Patrick shook his head for emphasis. "She can be as entertaining as she wishes. She could be a one woman Astley's act, for all I care. Actually, it's encouraged. My plan is that I could ask her to marry me. That would solve everyone's problems."

Marcus' heart constricted in the most painful way. Patrick was a good man. He'd make an excellent husband. Just not for Emma. No, actually he would. He'd treat her right and take care of her in a way she'd never been cared for before. The problem was Marcus. He'd always known Emma would marry, but the thought of her marrying his closest friend was the cruelest fate of all. "I suppose you could," he said flatly, refusing to meet Patrick's brown eyes.

Patrick leaned back in his chair, crossing his arms, head cocked in contemplation. "This would work out well for all of us. Miss Green could finally have a true home, and the girls would have the mother they lack."

"And you would get another chance at your heir," Marcus put in, trying to disguise the bitterness he felt by forcing a thin smile to his lips.

Shaking his head, Patrick's eyes went wide. "No. This would

be a marriage of convenience only. Those girls having a mother is far more important than producing an heir. My cousin isn't a bad sort. He can inherit."

The quill in Marcus' hand snapped and, ignoring the keen look of interest from his friend, he put the bottom half of the quill back into the stand as if nothing were amiss. "She deserves better than that. I cannot stop you from asking her. Nor can I advise her one way or the other about whether to accept your suit or not. But I'm asking you as my friend to do what's right and explain to her she'll never have children of her own if she accepts your suit." Those were the hardest words he'd ever spoken aloud.

Patrick sighed. "You're right, deuce take it." His lips twisted in irritation. "No woman wants to marry knowing she'll never get to be a true mother."

"Just so," Marcus clipped, staring at his desk.

"Maybe I should just marry Mrs. Jenkins," Patrick mumbled.

Marcus grinned and met his friend's eyes. "Sounds like a much better arrangement. She's what, fifty? She'd probably be relieved you have no interest in frequenting her bedchamber."

Patrick shuddered. "More than one kind of fear would keep me out of that room."

A picture of the ancient, crotchety old woman flashed in Marcus' mind.

"What if you ask Emma to watch the girls for a few hours during a couple of the days?" Patrick suggested hopefully. "Remember when Caroline still lived here, they'd come over and Caroline and Emma would let them take tea and try on their hats, and all that other female nonsense?"

Marcus closed his eyes. That might actually be a good way to go about convincing her to stay with him for the duration of the house party. Emma was almost too stubborn for her own good sometimes; she'd need a good reason to stay.

"You agree," Patrick said smugly. "I can tell by your face."

Marcus opened his eyes and stared at Patrick, bewildered. His accident had left his face so scarred that those who hadn't been around him very much couldn't decipher most facial expressions aside from a smile or outright anger, or so he'd been told. Most of the time people had no idea what he was thinking or feeling due to his scars.

"Your lips curl up only on the left side when you're smiling in agreement," Patrick explained.

Unconsciously, Marcus brought his fingers up to his lips and ran his fingers across them. He cleared his throat. "Right. Well, you might have said something I *might* agree with." He sighed. "I'll ask her if she'd be interested in entertaining them for a few days during her stay."

Patrick nodded. "Very good. They'd like that."

"I know." He could empathize with the little girls who only had themselves for playmates. For the past thirteen years, he'd lived a life of solitude except for a few close family members and even fewer friends.

"Excellent." Patrick got up, walked over to the three motherless girls, and allowed them each a chance to make a fool of him by having him rock their doll or wear their fanciest tea hat for a few minutes. Then he informed them it was time to go home.

Marcus said goodbye to the three girls, and as always, let them each pick two candies—one for each hand—from his tin of sweets before seeing them out.

"I'll let you know what she says," Marcus murmured to Patrick as he helped his daughters into the carriage.

Tipping his hat, Patrick climbed up into his carriage, leaving Marcus to go back into his empty estate and prepare for Emma's arrival.

Stubborn Emma may be, but he'd persuade her to stay. He was sure of it.

Chapter 2

Emma stared blankly at Caroline. "Me?" she squeaked. She hated it when her voice sounded that way and her eyes nearly popped from their sockets, but just now she couldn't help it.

"Yes, you. I just need you to bring these things over to Marcus." Caroline gestured to an array of things Emma considered beyond trivial. Why in the world did Marcus need an embroidery hoop? Or what about the mismatched, heeled slippers? He was a man. What did he need this junk for? Did he, like Olivia, have a strong need to keep everything he'd ever touched? Still, when would he have touched an embroidery hoop or mismatched slippers?

"Why?" she asked, staring at Caroline.

Caroline grinned. "Hmm, how interesting. Just a minute ago you were squealing that you didn't want to be the one delivering the box, and now it seems you want to know why? Does that mean you've accepted the task?"

"No." Emma picked up a blank and slightly yellowing paint canvas. "Why do you need to send this rubbish to him? He probably doesn't even know any of it's gone."

Shrugging, Caroline Banks, Lady Watson, Emma's dearest friend, tossed a magnifying glass with a hairline crack running the length of the glass into the wooden crate. "Whether he knows it's gone or not, it belongs to him. Well, to Olivia," she amended, sneering. "Olivia kept all sorts of bizarre things, and these all belong to her."

Emma stared at her highly intelligent friend as if she were a simpleton. "And your reason for returning it is?"

"They're hers. She has a right to have them."

"But she's in America," Emma pointed out, inspecting a comb that was missing more teeth than it had.

Caroline sighed. "I know, but somehow I ended up with all of this, and I don't want it and she does. Since it's hers, I'm sending it back."

Emma blinked as she tried to make sense of her friend's unusual sentence. It wasn't typical for Caroline to be acting this way. Something was off. "Caroline," she said slowly. "Say I do take this crate of detritus over to Ridge Water. What good is it really going to do? Olivia isn't there to know if you have it, if her brother has it, or if it's at the bottom of the Thames. Why does it matter? Find the closest rubbish bin and deposit it there."

"I can't," Caroline said adamantly as she scrunched her nose and picked up a lone stocking with a giant hole in the toe.

Emma could no longer contain her curiosity about a little book she'd seen at the bottom of the pile that looked oddly like a diary and picked it up. "How exactly did you acquire this unusual lot of rubble?"

Pursing her lips, Caroline flung a candle stub that couldn't have been longer than a quarter of an inch into the box. "She gave it to me over the years."

"Then it's *yours*," Emma exclaimed.

"No, it's hers." Caroline plucked Olivia's moldy, half-used diary from Emma's fingers and tossed it back into the box. "She gave me a piece every time a gift was necessary: my birthday and Christmas mainly. Anyway, these are all the things I accumulated from her as gifts. I shoved them into a box in case I needed to give them back. If there's one thing Olivia is, it's predictable. She wrote me about a month ago asking for a few of these items back."

"No, she didn't," Emma said, her voice full of disbelief. Although she didn't know why she was questioning Caroline's word. Olivia had more than once given her something and asked for it back.

"Yes, she did. She even described in exact detail the three

things she wanted back."

Emma shook her head. "All right. I'll take it over. Although I still don't understand why you can't just send a footman to deliver this. It's not like any of it is valuable."

"I quite agree." Caroline tossed the last of the objects—a tarnished ear scoop—into the box then closed the lid. "But I want to be sure this arrives, and I trust you far more than any of the servants. Who knows what might happen if it doesn't arrive? Olivia might come back and insist on searching my house in hopes of finding her long lost carving of a duck-billed platypus." She rolled her eyes. "Thank you, Emma. I appreciate it far more than you know."

"You'd better," Emma mumbled. Her stomach knotted at the idea that in less than an hour, she'd be standing at the door of Ridge Water. A chill ran up her spine. She hadn't seen Marcus but maybe three or four times since Caroline's wedding last year; and she hadn't seen him at all since Olivia decided to go to America, of all places. The irony of Olivia willingly living in the place she'd talked so nastily about for years was not lost on Emma. However, the excuse of visiting Olivia in order to glimpse Marcus was. Now she wasn't sure what she'd find when she saw him. He'd always treated her nicely when she'd been there to visit his sister or cousin, but she didn't know how he'd act when she came to him this time.

"Hmm." Caroline tapped her index finger against her cheek. "Would you like to change your gown? Perhaps something a bit more comfortable for traveling?"

Emma glanced down at her gown. It wasn't anything special. Just a simple frock, really. When she'd left her sister's that night in London, all she'd had was her nightrail and dressing robe. Caroline had been staying at Watson Townhouse, her London residence, and had taken her in without a second thought. Since then, Caroline had been lending her gowns. Caroline offered on several occasions to have gowns made up for her, but Emma had refused. Living off her friend's generosity was one thing; she'd not go so far as to take advantage. Not that she enjoyed borrowing her friend's gowns any better, though. "I think this one shall be all right."

Caroline shook her head. "No, no. That gown is already wrinkled. It will look like it's been balled up at the bottom of your wardrobe by the time you arrive. Let's go find something else."

Ten minutes later, Caroline had Emma in a gown that was far too fancy just to travel to Ridge Water and back. "I don't think this is going to be any more comfortable," Emma protested, willing herself not to look at her image in the mirror. It had been eight years since she'd worn a dress this nice.

"All right, let's get that box of Olivia's trinkets and you can be off," Caroline said, abruptly ending Emma's woolgathering.

Emma walked over to pick up the wooden box off Caroline's secretary.

"Put that down," Caroline exclaimed, trying to take the box from Emma's newly-formed grip on the sides of the crate. "You just put on a new gown, and you'll wrinkle it if you try to carry that heavy box. I'll go get Alex to carry it."

Alex, Caroline's husband, was an interesting man to say the least. He was a baron who couldn't get two things off his brain, one of which being science. The man loved science and anything science related. He even had an odd ability to take anything non-science and somehow make it into science. For instance, his courtship with the number two thing that was always on his brain: Caroline. Emma had never met a man who openly loved his wife more. The night Emma first saw Alex and Caroline in the same room together, she knew something was different. The second time she saw them together, she realized what it was. They were in love.

Her heart ached a little knowing she'd never have what her closest friend had, and yet, she didn't begrudge Caroline her good fortune to love and be loved back.

A minute later the object of her thoughts and Caroline's affections came in and took the box from Emma. He kept his face turned down to hide his scowl. It was no secret Alex detested Olivia. Nor was it a mystery as to why. Emma bit the inside of her cheek, trying not to smile.

"Emma, would you be opposed to bringing something to Marcus for me?" Alex asked hopefully, ignoring the strange look his wife was shooting him.

Emma shrugged. "Why not."

"Excellent." Alex beamed at her. "He lent me a pair of his boots once, and he might like them back."

Caroline swatted his shoulder. "Stop it. You know he'd never give you something and expect it back. Especially a pair of stinky old boots." She made a face that made both her husband and Emma grin.

"Are you sure?" Alex knit his brows together. "Just to be safe, I brought them." He put the crate down and dug one hand into each of his trouser pockets, bringing out two boots that couldn't have been worn by anyone past the age of four.

Emma laughed. "I take it you feel the same way about this as I do."

He nodded. "I think it's ridiculous she'd ask for the things back, but I think it's more ridiculous that Caro's actually going through the trouble of sending them back."

"Think what you want," Caroline said, smiling. "Just think it while carrying this box down to the carriage."

Alex tossed the little boots inside the box, then carried it to the carriage. "Is Annie going with you?"

"No!" Emma and Caroline said in unison. Emma didn't know why Caroline hadn't insisted on her bringing a maid with her, nor did she care. She had an important stop to make after going to Ridge Water and didn't want the servants at Watson Estate speculating any more on her situation than they already were.

"Does he know I'm coming?" Emma asked before the carriage door was closed. "I don't wish to surprise him."

"He knows. I sent a note," Caroline said, an unusual spark in her blue eyes.

Emma nodded and let Alex close the door.

Fifty minutes later, Emma stood outside the door of Ridge Water, staring at the brass door knocker and biting her lip.

It had been a long time since she'd been here to see him. Perhaps her feelings had changed and she'd be able to look at him without her heart racing, palms sweating, and knees weakening.

Just then the door swung open, and Emma knew she possessed no such luck. As soon as her eyes fell on Marcus, all the old feelings came flooding back. Most would find him undesirable with his heavily scarred face and highly pronounced limp. But that was because they were unable to see him the way she did. People were often so shallow their eyes only landed on his eye-catching attributes, and missed the subtle things such as his slate grey eyes which were full of unreleased humor, or his flawless grin that only came out when he was truly amused, or his light brown hair that curled up at his collar.

"Emma," he greeted with a wide grin that took her breath away.

She swallowed. Hard. Flushing with embarrassment, she broke eye contact and cleared her throat. "Car—Caroline sent some things," she stammered, gesturing to the carriage.

"She did?" he drawled, glancing to the carriage. "What did she send?"

"You don't know?"

He shook his head. "Afraid not. She just said you were coming, she didn't say you would come bearing gifts."

Emma smiled weakly. "These aren't the kind of gifts any normal person would like."

Cocking his head to the side, his eyes swept her from head to toe. His lips twisted in what she knew to be contemplation. "I've seen that dress before."

Emma shook out her skirts and inclined her chin an inch. "You had it commissioned for Caroline before she married the baron. Since the birth of her child, she can no longer wear it," she said smoothly. She had a suspicion Caroline had made that up. Caroline was just as thin now as she had been before Edward's birth, but Caroline knew Emma would have never put the dress on without Caroline claiming it no longer fit. Besides, Caroline still had a few more weeks left of mourning, she wouldn't need this dress for a while yet.

"Hmm. Well, don't tell Caroline this, but it looks much prettier on you."

Her cheeks burned at his words. He'd never complimented her before. He'd been nice, of course. Just never the kind to pay compliments. Particularly ones that weren't true. He'd never seen Caroline in this dress as far as she knew. No matter though. She was flattered nonetheless. "Thank you, Lord Sinclair."

His lips twisted a little at her words. "You've known me for years, Emma. You may call me Marcus. You did when we were children."

"I know." But that had been so long ago. Before his accident. Before her sister's engagement to him. Before he was jilted. Before she'd had to feign a friendship with his sister just to see him. And all during those years, she'd avoided calling him anything. Everything had seemed either too personal or too formal for what they were to each other.

"Would you like to come inside?"

She glanced at the carriage. "I can't." Caroline's houseguests were due to arrive in the next hour and a half. She'd like to have this crate dropped off and be on her way soon so she could be firmly out of the way before they arrived.

He frowned. "Why not?"

"I need to get back to Watson Estate soon," she said as if that explained anything.

He pushed off from where he'd been leaning against the doorjamb and limped to the carriage, Emma trailing close behind. He opened the door of the carriage and picked the box up off the seat. He held it in his hands and gave it a small shake. "Hmm. I wonder what could be in here."

Emma slid the lid off. "Wonder no more." She couldn't stop herself from grinning at the way his lips contorted when he saw the contents.

"What *is* this?" He set the box down on the steps of the carriage.

Shrugging, Emma willed herself to keep a straight face. "Gifts Olivia has given to Caroline over the years. Apparently she wants them back."

Marcus groaned. "Why did she even keep this nonsense?" He

picked up a stained miniature of an old woman with a blue wig atop her head and squinted at it.

"Probably because, unlike us, she's been wise to Olivia's habits and knew Olivia would one day ask for all this rubbish back."

"I always knew she was smart," Marcus said, shaking his head. "Come inside, Emma."

"No, I really must be going," she said, casting a quick glance into the carriage.

Marcus followed her gaze and she inwardly cursed when his eyes, followed by his fingers, landed on the bundle of papers she'd left on the seat. "What's this?"

"Nothing," Emma said, trying to grab the papers from his hand.

He held them over his head. "I take it these were not from Caroline, were they?"

"No," she said, making a fool of herself by standing on her toes and trying to grab the papers.

He grinned. "What are you hiding?"

"Nothing. Just go on and read them," she said with a sigh, resigned. "You'll know soon enough, I expect."

Marcus lowered the little bundle of papers, but instead of reading them, he shoved them into his breast pocket. "Come have tea with me, and I'll give them back."

"Promise?" she asked, chastising herself for looking forward to the prospect of tea alone with him.

"Promise." He picked up the box Caroline sent.

Emma waited by the front door while he gave instructions to the coachman. Chapman, Ridge Water's butler, came out to greet her like he always had when she came to visit. She politely greeted him back and inwardly commanded herself not to smack him upside his head for not being the one who had come to the door. That was his job. He was the butler. He was supposed to have greeted her at the door, not Marcus.

"Blue room," Marcus said, coming up the steps.

Emma nodded and placed her hand on his proffered arm,

19

allowing him to set the pace. He stopped off for a second to leave the box in his study then continued down the hall to the room known to them all as the blue drawing room.

A tea service was already set out with two cups and a giant plate of biscuits. She smiled up at him. "Either your servants are excellent at eavesdropping or you planned this."

"Which would you prefer to believe?"

"The truth," she said, letting go of his arm and going to sit on the settee closest to the teapot.

Marcus sat down across from her, shocking her to the core. Usually Marcus sat in the corner where he'd be covered by shadows. "I planned it."

"Oh." Her traitorous heart beat out of control.

He leaned back against a giant pillow. "Gets lonely around here, thought I'd make the most of a visitor."

"I see." Disappointment washed over her. Apparently anybody would have sufficed to provide him his afternoon entertainment.

He accepted the cup of tea she'd poured for him and brought it to his lips to blow on it before taking a sip. He made a sour face. "That stuff is terrible," he said, putting the cup down so indelicately half of it sloshed over the side then onto the saucer and table.

She took a sip and swallowed it just as fast as she could. "Seems your cook forgot to drain the leaves out," she said, pulling a tea leaf off her tongue.

Marcus suddenly looked away, crossed his arms, and shifted on his chair. "I apologize. Don't drink anymore."

Emma pushed her tea and saucer away from her then grabbed a biscuit and took a bite. "The biscuits are good."

His eyes were fixed on her in the oddest way. "You've a bit..." He trailed off and brought his finger to his lips.

She blushed and licked her lips as quickly and thoroughly as possible, not wanting to leave a single crumb on her lips. She was a grown woman, for pity's sake. She should be able to eat without making a mess. "Better?"

"Yes," he barked roughly, shifting once again.

She pushed the plate toward him. "Try one."

Stiffly, he leaned forward and snatched a biscuit. He broke it in half and placed half into his mouth, nodding his approval. "Good," he remarked. "Quite an improvement over that bitter tea."

Emma looked around the room, not sure what to say. She hadn't been alone with Marcus since she was twelve and he was sixteen and he took her to fish in the stream.

Marcus stared right back at her, seeming equally uncomfortable.

"I should be going," she burst out, standing. "May I have my papers back, please?"

Marcus blinked at her and slowly dug into his pocket to grab her papers. His eyes left hers and his fingers unfolded the bundle. "What's this?" He glanced up at her after he'd read the first few sentences.

She crossed her arms. "None of your business," she snapped. "Just give them back."

His eyes continued to travel the lines of the first page before flipping to the second. "A governess?"

"Yes," she said sharply, plucking the papers from his fingers.

"But why?" He blinked at her.

Fury bubbled inside her. Marcus reading those shaming papers was the last straw. It was bad enough she'd have to seek a position as a governess due to her situation, but to have him question her about it was going too far. "I owe you no explanations," she said in a tone that could freeze water in the desert.

"I know that," he said softly. "I just don't understand."

"And you don't need to." She turned to go, but he reached for her wrist to keep her from leaving.

"You're right, Emma. It's not my place to ask you about your personal life. I'm sorry. But what if I happen to know of someone who is in need of a governess? Can I ask you a few questions then?"

She stared at him in disbelief. He was the definition of a recluse. She doubted he'd been beyond an hour's radius of Ridge Water in the past five years.

"Patrick," Marcus said after a minute. "Viscount Drakely is in need of a governess for his three girls."

She blinked again. She'd nearly forgotten Viscount Drakely. Besides Alex and Caroline, Lord Drakely, or Drake as he was most commonly known to everyone except Marcus, was the only other person Marcus ever saw. Lord Drakely was a decent man, if not a bit withdrawn at times. She'd met him many times over the years, and had even come to think of him as a friend. But that didn't exactly mean he'd be willing to hire her on as a governess for his little girls.

"Are you sure?" she asked weakly. The lady at the employment agency hadn't seemed too optimistic about Emma being able to find a position. Drake may not live in the shire, but that didn't matter so much to her. Just now, her desperate need of employment meant she was game to live almost anywhere.

"I'm fairly certain," Marcus said. "Currently he doesn't have one at all. He still employs Mrs. Jenkins."

Emma shuddered. The woman wasn't awful, but she was a nursemaid, not a governess. Those girls needed the instruction of a governess or they'd never succeed in finding a husband. "Can you ask him?"

Marcus leaned his head back and closed his eyes. "I can," he said at last. "Or you can."

She shook her head. "No, I can't."

"Why not?"

"Because that would be awkward. I cannot walk up to his house, knock on the door, and say, 'Pardon me, Drake, I've noticed your girls lack a suitable governess, would you be interested in hiring me for the job?'"

Marcus chuckled. "Sure you could. You could say it just like that, and he'd probably hire you on the spot."

"Or toss me off his estate," she muttered.

"He wouldn't do that. He'd probably hire you for your nerve alone." He held out his hand. "Can I see the papers again?"

She clutched them tighter to her chest. "Why?"

He shrugged. "If I'm to recommend you, I need to know your

qualifications."

"You know as well as I do that I don't have any."

"Sure you do," he countered, reaching for the papers once more.

She handed him the papers and sat down. "I'm not qualified," she said dully, staring at the oak tree just out the window. She wasn't qualified for much of anything, it seemed.

He ignored her and read over the pages. "Emma," he began softly, handing her back the leaflets, "is this what you want?"

Emma's gaze locked with his. What she wanted didn't matter. She had no money and no family to speak of. This was the only option left to her, aside from becoming someone's paid mistress, that is. "Yes."

"Then I'll talk to Patrick."

"You think he'll hire me?"

His left shoulder lifted in a lopsided shrug. "I don't know for sure. But I imagine he'd be willing to allow you a few days to act as their governess to see if it would work."

She couldn't ask for much better than that. "All right. When will you see him again?"

Marcus drummed his fingers on his knee. "Soon, I expect."

Excitement coursed through her. "How soon?"

He grinned. "How soon is good enough for you?"

"I don't know."

He took out his pocket watch. "Hmm, it's too close to dinnertime to go just now, but what if I send off a messenger and you wait here for his reply?"

"Of course," she said quickly before he changed his mind. Drake only lived an hour or so away, and Caroline would be too busy with her house party tonight to care if Emma was late.

"Excellent. I'll just run to my study and dash off a note."

Emma nodded and tried to rack her brain for something she could do to busy herself for the next few hours. Surely Marcus had no intention of keeping her company. "I'll run upstairs and see if there's any mending to be done," she said, feigning excitement.

Marcus turned around. "Why?"

"I need something to do."

"And you want to sew?"

"Well, no, I don't *want* to."

"Then don't. Read a book. Go for a walk. Ride a horse. Take a nap. Do whatever you want, Emma."

"Perhaps I'll go for a walk to the creek."

"Good choice," he said, resuming his steps. He reached the doorway and stopped. "There are a couple of poles in the shed if you'd like to fish."

"Will you be joining me?" she asked hopefully.

Chapter 3

"No, not today," he said quietly, as disappointment flooded him. He'd love to spend time with her but wasn't sure if her invitation was issued in earnest or only out of politeness.

"Just as well," she said with a sigh. "I'll just go for a walk then."

He nodded and left to dash off a somewhat lacking note to Patrick. He wasn't truly planning to arrange for Emma to be the girls' governess. She might be getting on in years and feel she needed to seek such a position, but she didn't. She was still stunningly beautiful, with her golden blonde hair and emerald green eyes. She could find a husband yet.

He plopped down into the chair behind his desk and grabbed his quill and piece of parchment. Pondering only a minute, he scribbled a letter to Patrick.

Patrick,
She said she'll be available to entertain your girls on Thursday and Friday this week and Tuesday, Wednesday, and Thursday next.
Marcus

Before Emma could unexpectedly come into his study, he folded up the missive and went to the main hall to give it to one of the two liveried footmen he still employed. After Olivia left for America, he'd reduced Ridge Water to a skeleton staff of two footmen, the butler, two maids, the housekeeper, and a temporary cook who was only here until Mrs. Masters could return from Yorkshire. In his stables, he still employed several grooms, one who even acted as a coachman on the rare occasion Marcus decided to go somewhere.

From the side windows, Marcus glimpsed Emma walking down the path that led to the creek. He longed to go after her. Even though she had the ability to render him speechless, just being with her would be enough. Tea had not gone as planned. The tension between them had been enough to choke a man. He scowled. How would these ten days work if he couldn't think of what to say to her? Returning to his study, he picked up his ledger and made some quick calculations. He hated settling accounts and doing the math involved in running an estate, but for as much as he hated it, it would keep his mind on what it should be on, and off Emma.

Two hours later, he glanced up at the wall to the clock that had been annoyingly ticking off the seconds like it did every single day. He sighed and shoved to his feet. It was time to go to the drawing room and wait for dinner. With any luck, Cook would have made a better dinner than she had a pot of tea. He cringed at the memory of that tea.

"How was your walk?" he asked Emma as he entered the drawing room.

"Nice. Peaceful." She smiled wistfully. "Marcus, I'm sorry about earlier. I didn't mean to be so short with you."

He flicked his wrist. "You couldn't be impolite if you tried."

"Nonetheless, it wasn't nice of me to speak to you that way. You've been nothing but kind to me."

"Please, forget about it, Emma. We've all been in situations we wish we weren't. If you need help, all you need do is ask."

She nodded, and he took a seat across from her, wishing she would confide in him. "You are helping me," she said a moment later. "The governess position, remember?"

"Right." He glanced at the clock on the mantle. "I think Walters should be there by now, or within the next ten minutes at the latest. Perhaps an hour or so after dinner we should know something."

Hands folded primly in her lap, Emma blinked at him. "When do you think he'd allow me to start?"

"Tomorrow," he said honestly. Tomorrow was Thursday; one of the days he'd told Patrick she'd be willing to watch the girls.

She bit her lip. "I hope I'm able to organize a lesson tonight. No matter. Between Caroline and Alex, I've learned enough scientific facts the past few days to fill an afternoon if I need to."

Marcus chuckled. "Please make sure I am not within earshot when you start your science lecture. I heard enough scientific nonsense from Alex during our years of school together." He shuddered. Science was a dandy interest for others, just not for him.

"And don't forget all the knowledge you shoved into your head while copying Caroline's experiments and submitting them to *Prominent and Avant-Garde Horticulture*," she teased, a smile spreading across her lips.

He shuddered again. "Don't remind me. Although, I do feel I need to make a confession about that. When I copied her work, I copied it literally one word at a time. It took forever to look at one word, write it, then glance back at the sheet for the next. But it was much less painful to do that than to read an entire sentence and duplicate it."

"It couldn't have been *that* bad." Her green eyes were full of mischief. Their utter dislike for the subject of science was one thing they'd always shared. Another had been their ability to disguise their dislike in front of Caroline, who liked science nearly as much as her husband.

"It was torturous," he said, scowling. "The first time I copied it, I nearly fell asleep three times while doing that tedious task."

Emma giggled. "Then why didn't you just have a servant do it?"

He blinked at her. Why hadn't *he* thought of that? For nearly four years he'd made himself miserable copying Caroline's dreadfully boring biology notes. "I have no idea."

She shook her head. "It was a nice thing for you to do. I hope you know she really appreciated it."

"I know she did," he said uncomfortably. Praise was something he'd never been fond of accepting. "Tell me, Emma, how long have you been staying with Caroline and Alex?"

"A while," she said, dropping her gaze to the floor.

He sighed. "You're not going to tell me anything, are you?"

"No."

Marcus bit back a grin and ran his hand through his hair. Emma had always been stubborn. She had been the day they met when she was three and he was seven, and she still was now at seven-and-twenty. "It's of no account. I'll just write to Caroline and ask her," he said as casually as if he were talking about the weather.

She snorted. "She won't tell you." Her voice was strong, confident.

"I think she will. She owes me a favor, you know?"

Emma shook her head ruefully. "And you'd use your favor asking something as ridiculous as that?"

Marcus nodded.

"You're cracked." A devious grin took her lips. "Anyway, she won't tell you."

"And why are you so confident?"

"Because I know you won't really ask her."

He crossed his arms. "What makes you think that?"

Shrugging, she looked him straight in the eye. "You don't care enough about me to bother to ask."

You have no idea how wrong you are. "You never know, I just might ask."

She frowned at him. "Ask if you wish, but she still won't tell you. Her promise to me trumps any favor you might ask of her."

He scowled. Caroline was so loyal it was nearly sickening. "I wager I'll get it out of you yet."

"And how do you propose to do that? Withhold Drake's response until I tell you?"

"If I must," he agreed. "But that wasn't my first choice."

"And what was your first choice?" She licked her red lips in the most innocently seductive way.

"You'll just have to wait," he said huskily. "My plan won't work if I tell you what it is."

She rolled her eyes. "You're wasting too much energy on something frivolous."

"To you, perhaps," he allowed. "To me, it's not so frivolous."

"Why's that?"

He stretched his legs out and casually crossed his ankles, simultaneously willing the butler to announce dinner before he revealed too much. "I find it curious you're not with Louise and Hampton in London."

Emma's long, slender fingers pinched the fabric of her skirt so tightly that when she let it go, she'd left dozens of little creases in her skirt. "I just decided I needed some time away." Her tone gave nothing away. Unfortunately for her, her stiff body language gave away enough.

"Emma," he said slowly, softly. "Does your need for time away have anything to do with your sudden interest in becoming a governess?"

Her green eyes sparkled, and not in a good way. "Please, leave it alone, Marcus." Her voice could only be described as a harsh whisper.

"All right. But please remember if you need anything, you can come to me." He'd told her as much earlier, but he knew his words had been in vain. He'd have to tell her again and again with the hope that eventually it would take root in that thick head of hers.

She didn't acknowledge his offer of help, not that he'd expected her to. Instead, she glanced down to inspect the hem of her gown and sat quietly until Chapman came in to announce dinner.

Standing, Marcus offered her his arm. "May I escort you down?"

"Always." Emma lightly placed her fingertips in the crook of his proffered arm. "It smells good," she commented as they neared the dining room.

He inhaled. "Yes, it does. Although, after our tea this afternoon, I'll be cautious about what I drink tonight."

"How could she possibly ruin lemonade?"

"Trust me, *she* could."

"Do you know this from experience?"

"Yes. As the bitter tea we had this afternoon can attest, she's fairly new to the trade of cooking. I don't think her former employer asked her to do much besides make biscuits, roasted chicken, kippers, and coddled eggs. I'd wager our dinner will have all four of those dishes. Oh, and custard with a strawberry on top for dessert."

She eyed him askance. "That's not what you ordered, is it?"

"No. But I ordered her to make the best meal she could. And since those are the only dishes she can make that are decent, I wager that's what we'll be eating."

"All right, my lord, I'll take your wager," she said cheekily. "I honestly doubt she'll be serving biscuits and coddled eggs at dinner."

Marcus stopped walking. "And what shall we wager?"

"What can you stand to lose?" she asked, grinning.

"What do you want?"

She twisted her lips and tapped a long, slender finger against her cheek. "I don't know," she admitted at last.

"Would you like a new gown?"

Her green eyes went wide like he knew they would. "No! Nothing so valuable."

"Why not?"

"I have nothing nearly as valuable to offer you," she explained, breaking eye contact.

He placed his free hand under her chin and tipped it up toward him. "Does that matter? You seem confident you're not going to lose, so wager anything you wouldn't mind giving me."

"I don't have anything," she said with a hard swallow.

In her eyes, he read the truth. Something terrible had happened between her and Louise, and she truly had no real possessions. None of the tangible variety, anyway. That must be why she was so willing to accept a gown from him, even if it was the furthest thing from proper for an unmarried lady to accept such a gift from a man who wasn't her father, brother, or protector.

"What of a kiss?" he asked suddenly, the tips of his ears burning as unease settled over him. She'd never be willing to kiss him. He was a fool to have asked. "Never mind," he mumbled, trying to hide his slip. "Just forget the whole thing. I forfeit. Tomorrow, I'll send for the village seamstress."

"No," she said adamantly, shaking her head. "I accept your wager, Lord Sinclair. If you lose, I'll have a pretty new gown, and if I lose, you'll get your kiss."

He stared at her. Unable to respond. Unable to move. Unable to think. She was willing to kiss him if—no, *when*—she lost. "That's quite a bargain, Miss Green."

"Shall we?" she asked, gesturing to the open dining room that was less than four strides away.

He nodded. "Of course."

The dining room at Ridge Water was gigantic by anyone's standards. When Marcus ate alone, he'd sit on the end seat. It felt like it was a mile between him and the chair across from him at the other end. He hated it. He hated the solitude and loneliness that came with it. He'd attempted to rejoin Society several times since his accident. But every time he tried, he was met with either queer looks and disparaging remarks, or snide and mocking comments about how he'd ruined his entire life when he was barely eighteen. Thus, he continued to live as a recluse and hadn't ventured to London for anything other than urgent business for more than five years.

Before Caroline married and Olivia left, the three of them would take their meals at one end of the table. He'd sit on the end and they'd sit on either side of him. Occasionally Emma would stay for meals and would sit next to Caroline.

Tonight there would be a bit of a different seating arrangement. He'd ordered the footman who'd laid out the table to put the two place settings right across from each other. He just hoped the man understood he meant across the table widthwise and not lengthwise. If not, they would both be eating their meal in solitude or have to shout to be heard by the other. He grimaced.

Neither of those options sounded particularly appealing.

Blessedly the footman had understood Marcus' directive, and two settings were across from each other near the end of the table closest to the door. "Let me get your chair," Marcus murmured, shooing the slightly shocked footman away.

Emma sat down and waited while Marcus took his seat and nodded for the footman to serve up the first course.

John, the recovering footman, stepped out from the corner and brought over to them a small platter with a big, shiny silver dome on top. He held it out between them and slowly lifted the top to reveal a warm plate of biscuits.

Marcus shot Emma a triumphant smile and swiped a biscuit.

Emma stared at the plate of offending biscuits.

"Go on, take one," Marcus encouraged, grinning.

"I just can't believe it," she muttered, picking up the one closest to her.

John put the serving plate back on the sideboard and brought over two little dishes. One dish was filled with butter; the other contained strawberry jam.

Rolling her eyes and mumbling under her breath, Emma picked up her knife and slathered some strawberry jam on the top of her biscuit.

Three bites later, Marcus motioned for the serving of the second course.

John walked back over to them. This time with a much larger dome-topped platter. He removed the lid to reveal two bowls filled with what looked to be salad.

Emma smiled sweetly as she took her bowl and set it down in front of her.

Marcus slipped his off the tray and peeked at Emma as she stared blankly at her salad. He tried to keep his grin in check as he picked up his salad fork and speared a piece of slimy, brownish lettuce. A minute later, she pushed the bowl away. "I believe I'll wait for something a bit more nourishing." She glanced at the remaining five covered dishes.

Next, John brought coddled eggs, followed by turtle soup,

then kippers, which was chased by broiled duck breast.

"Hmm, what do you suppose is under the last dome?" Marcus asked an impatient-looking Emma.

She shifted in her seat. "Roasted chicken," she said flatly.

He frowned. Did she find the thought of kissing him to be that repulsive? "Do you want to cry off?"

"No." She exhaled. "But what about a double or quits?"

"I'm listening." He put his elbows on the table and leaned forward.

She wet her lips. "No matter what that last dish is, if I'm able to drink this entire glass of lemonade I'll get two gowns, and if I can't—" she shrugged— "I'll give you two kisses." She held up two fingers and shook them for emphasis.

Marcus glanced at their lemonade. Neither of them had so much as touched their glasses. Judging by how bad the tea was earlier, coupled with how terrible every other dish served tonight was, neither of them had wanted to hazard a sip of their lemonade. And a hazard is what it would be, he was certain. More than three times in the past week alone, he'd snuck down to the kitchen to make his own lemonade.

"Sounds interesting," he mused, pushing his glass closer to her. "But if this is to be a true double or quits, then everything is to be doubled and you should have to drink both glasses."

"I accept," she said with a gulp. She looked at the glasses of lemonade, then to the last course that was still under the dome. "Do you mind if I drink this now? I'd like to use the roasted chicken to get the taste out of my mouth afterward."

He crossed his arms and chuckled. "Whenever you're ready, Miss Green."

She picked up the first glass and brought it to her parted lips. She paused for a second, then tipped her head back and guzzled the liquid torture in the most unladylike fashion he'd ever witnessed. She brought the empty glass down with a hard *thwack* and glanced at the other while she wiped her sourly twisted mouth with the edge of her napkin. She glanced up at him and smiled weakly, blinking back the tears that had formed in her eyes from the sour lemonade. Without looking away, Emma picked up the second glass and proceeded to drink every drop in another long, continuous, guzzling gulp.

"You win," he conceded with a dim smile, motioning for John to bring over the chicken.

Emma put her glass down and allowed John to serve her some of the chicken breast. "I'll not cost you too much," she said quietly.

He put his fork down. "I'm not concerned about the cost of the gowns. You may have any type of gowns you'd like."

"Thank you for your generosity," she said solemnly, stabbing a piece of her chicken.

Marcus nodded and ate his chicken. There weren't many dishes his temporary cook could make, but roasted chicken was certainly one of them.

After dinner, Daniel, the footman Marcus had sent to Patrick's, still hadn't returned. Marcus pulled out his pocket watch. "We have at least half an hour before the messenger will be back. Shall we discuss those new gowns?"

Emma shook her head. "Marcus, you don't have to—"

"Nonsense," he said, cutting her off. "You won that wager. You're getting the gowns."

She frowned. "That's not what I was going to say. I know I won that wager, and I'd hold your nose and force you to drink two glasses of that awful lemonade if you so much as thought of reneging on buying me those gowns. But what I was going to say was that you don't have to make small talk with me while we wait. I know you're probably itching to get off that stiff chair and prop your leg up on the ottoman you keep stored under your desk."

"You're right. I'll just be on my way." He scooted his chair backward and stood up. He'd been building castles in the clouds, thinking she'd want to talk to him while they waited.

"Wait, Marcus." She gained her feet and came to stand in front of him.

He looked down at her. She wasn't tall, but she wasn't short, either. Right at six foot, he was what most would consider above average. Next to him, the top of her head barely reached his chin.

"Yes?"

She blinked at him then an unusual, almost nervous smile spread across her lips. She cleared her throat. Then again. "Marcus," she began, her voice terribly uneven for having cleared her throat twice before speaking. "I just wanted you to know the reason I drank all that dratted lemonade wasn't because I didn't want to kiss you, but because I *need* those gowns." She came up on her toes and softly pressed her supple lips against his rough cheek.

Chapter 4

Emma's cheeks burned with embarrassment. She had no idea what had come over her and moved her to kiss him like that. Not that she regretted it; she didn't. However, that still didn't change the fact that she was standing inches in front of him and his big body was blocking the only exit, making it impossible for her to run down the hall and hide.

She chanced a quick peek at his grey eyes. They were staring straight at her, making her cheeks burn more. "I—I'll be in th-the drawing room," she stammered, hoping he'd let her by.

He sidestepped to the left and she hastily quit the room, mentally chastising herself for kissing him. Her sister had caused him a lifetime's worth of grief and embarrassment with all her female games years ago. He must think her no different now that she'd kissed him like that. But, oh how she was different. Unlike Louise, Emma truly loved Marcus. She always had. She hated that her sister treated him so poorly. Not just for jilting him—for everything. For all the stupid games she'd played with him before jilting him. Louise had treated him horribly, and Emma had no doubt he'd always hold her at arm's length because of it. Kissing him would likely result in his complete avoidance of her.

She sighed. Did it really matter? He'd never wish to marry her anyway. She needed to stop hoping that he'd one day notice her and accept the reality of becoming a governess.

Being a governess was not what all little girls dreamed about for themselves for when they became adults. No, little girls dreamed of marriage to an honorable man—it was a boon if he was titled, of course. Young ladies also dreamed of marriage, otherwise they wouldn't attend endless balls and musicales and routs in order to find a husband. Spinsters dreamed of being governesses. Those were the unfortunate young ladies who had passed their prime and saw they had no place on the marriage mart. They didn't wish to become a rich man's mistress; nor did they wish to knit and embroider with an old woman while she yelled, stomped her cane, and made them do everything for her because they were her "companion".

After Emma's parents died eight years ago, Gregory, Louise's husband, had become Emma's guardian until her twenty-first birthday. What she didn't realize was Gregory freely dipped into the account that was to be her dowry, and by the time she was one-and-twenty the money was gone. She had continued to live with Louise and Gregory because she had nowhere else to go.

Following her parents' deaths, Gregory had inherited the small cottage near Ridge Water in which she and Louise had grown up. Most of the year, Emma lived there and kept it running smoothly in exchange for a paltry allowance. Now that Gregory and Louise had made their intentions of disassociating with her clear, the hope of ever seeing that cottage again was gone, let alone living there. That only left being a governess.

Compared to how she'd been treated by Louise and Gregory, she'd gladly embrace life as a governess.

Now all she had to do was wait for Lord Drakely's reply.

Emma kicked her slippers off and propped a pillow under her head. Living in the country for so much of her life, she'd never been one to stay up too terribly late. She closed her eyes and thought to take a quick nap while she waited for Marcus to let her know Drake's decision.

A little while later, the door creaked open, followed by Marcus' uneven steps. Emma smiled. The poor man couldn't sneak up on anybody with how loud his footsteps were.

"Emma," he whispered, leaning down to smooth back her hair.

She opened her eyes and looked at him. The few candles she'd lit before lying down had burned out, and the only source of light was the moon flooding in from the open window. She struggled to sit up. "What did he say?" she asked, bringing one hand up to hold the top of her hair while her other hand groped around on the settee to find the hairpins that must have slipped out while she was sleeping.

Marcus' fingers found her wrist and pulled her hand away from her hair. "Let it fall," he said, his voice husky and uneven.

She met his eyes and let him bring her hand away, half her hair following suit. Marcus reached up and slipped out the remaining pins, then handed them to her.

"What did he say?" she forced herself to ask.

Ignoring her, Marcus ran his fingers through her silky blonde locks. "I had no idea your hair was so long." He twisted a lock between his thumb and forefinger. "It's very soft, too."

"I wash it with lavender oil," she blurted.

He brought the lock between his fingers up to his nose. "Indeed."

"Marcus," she whispered as his hand dropped her hair and caressed her cheek.

Marcus didn't answer. Not with words anyway. He bent his head and captured her lips with his. His kiss was gentle and sweet as his lips moved on top of and in between hers.

She wound her arms around his neck. She loved having his big, powerful body so close to hers. His kiss became more demanding as he focused his attention on her bottom lip and drew it between his lips where he nipped and soothed her sensitive flesh. She sighed, intoxicated. He continued his delightful ministrations on her lip, and she sighed again, forcing the faint creaking noise she heard far from her thoughts.

"Emma?"

Emma's whole body jerked at hearing her name and her eyes snapped open, landing right on Marcus. Except, instead of it being dark, several candles were lit. She reached up and touched her hair. It was still perfectly pinned. She blinked at Marcus' grinning face and sighed.

"Good dream?" he asked, still grinning.

She grabbed the pillow behind her and flung it at him. "Yes. And then you had to go and ruin it."

"Care to tell me what you were dreaming about?" He ducked from the pillow she'd just hurled at him.

She grabbed another. "No." She blushed and hurled that pillow at him for good measure.

He caught it against his chest. "Must have been a terribly good dream," he mused.

"I don't think terribly and good should ever belong in the same sentence." She sat up on the settee and put her feet back into her slippers.

Marcus took a seat next to her. "Perhaps not." He reached his hand up and smoothed back a stray lock of her hair. "But all the same, would you care to tell me what has stained your cheeks such a fetching pink and made you sigh so sweetly?"

"No, I wouldn't care to," she retorted, grabbing at the missive in his hand.

Marcus didn't try to move the paper away, he let her have it and leaned back to watch her as she read it.

"Here?" she squeaked. "He's having them brought here tomorrow morning at nine?"

"That's what it says." Marcus' voice reminded her of Louise talking to her three-year-old son. "He probably just wants to make sure it'll work out before you move into his house. Think how upsetting it would be to the girls if it didn't work out."

"That is the most convoluted thing I've ever heard."

He shrugged. "That may be. But that seems to be his offer. Accept it or don't."

She nodded and swallowed, then started wearing a hole in the rug. Did she have a choice? If he was to be her employer, she needed to heed his commands. No matter how asinine they may be. "All right. If I start at nine, that means I'll need to leave Watson Estate by eight at the latest. Which means I need to get up—" she bit her lip— "no later than five if I want to wash my hair. Hmm, if I don't wash my hair, that takes off the forty-five minutes it takes for it to dry. But I'll still need to bathe and—"

"Emma?"

Her eyes flew to Marcus and she blushed fiercely. "Oh, sorry, I forgot you were still here."

"I don't give a hang that you were discussing personal bathing in my presence," he said. "I just wanted to offer a solution."

She raised her eyebrows at him. What solution could he possibly offer? He wasn't a woman. He didn't have long hair to wash or a gown to get into. When he still hadn't shared his ill-suited solution, she asked, "Yes?"

"Stay here. If you stay here, you'll have an extra hour."

Her eyes couldn't decide whether to blink at him or go wide and bulge out. In the end, they did a bit of both. "I can't stay here," she burst out. "That is most improper. Everyone will think I'm a...a...strumpet."

"Who exactly is everyone?" Marcus placed a throw pillow behind his head.

Her mind raced and she couldn't think. "Umm...Caroline. I'm supposed to be staying with her. She'll know I'm staying here. And don't forget Alex." Her eyes grew larger. "All their guests will know, too." She shook her head wildly. "I cannot have it so widely known that I've even been here so long without a proper chaperone as it is." Panic filled her as she started thinking of all the guests at Caroline's party who had likely already arrived and might already be speculating on what she was doing. "I need to go. I'll be back in the morning before Drake drops his daughters off, I promise." She snatched up her reticule and started for the door.

"Emma!" Marcus grunted as he pushed to a standing position and hobbled across the room. "Stop running," he ground out as she flew down the hall. He was following her as fast as his leg would allow, which was surprisingly quick considering how pronounced his limp was.

"No, I really must be going," she said over her shoulder, not slowing her pace.

"Emmaline Green, stop." Marcus reached for her wrist. "You're not going anywhere. I doubt Caroline or Alex are going to care you've been gone so long. As for you continuing your stay at

Ridge Water, I'll send them a discreet note letting them know you'll be acting as a temporary governess for Patrick's daughters. Don't worry, I'll conveniently leave off where you'll be staying, and naturally they'll assume you've gone to stay at Briar Creek. Will that suffice?"

She swallowed. "But what of all their guests?"

"Emma, since when have you ever cared what others thought of you?"

Inclining her chin, she said, "Since I accepted the post as governess to Drake's daughters. It might hurt my employment if everyone thinks I'm a fallen woman." That was a lie. She'd started to care what others thought about her a split-second after Gregory had accused her of having inappropriate relations with Marcus, not that she'd ever tell Marcus that.

Marcus nodded. "I understand that. But nobody is going to know, I promise. I'll send a discreet note to Watson Estate." His voice softened to a near whisper. "Surely you know Caroline and Alex are not going to tell their guests where you're staying or what you're doing. Caroline cares too much about you to do that."

"I know that," she admitted. Caroline would never do anything to intentionally shame or embarrass anybody.

"Then who are you afraid of finding out? Her guests? By my guess, they're all Alex's cousins, which means you have nothing to worry about. That bunch is as scandalous as they come. And it's not as if any of them are planning a trip here, so they'll never know."

"I know that, too," she said, shifting her gaze. "But Drake will know I stayed here, and he'll terminate my employment on the spot when he realizes I stayed the night alone with you."

"No, he won't," Marcus said flippantly. "When he gets here tomorrow, he's going to be so relieved to get those girls off his hands; he's not going to want to sit around for tea and chitchat. He's going to leave, and the last thing on his mind will be where you spent the night."

She stared at him. Actually, staying here might be a good idea, after all. At least if she was here, she'd have a valid reason not to be attending any of the games, dinners, or other nonsense Caroline had planned. Nor would she have to have an uncomfortable conversation explaining where she was going and why if she were caught sneaking out of Watson Estate in the morning. Not to mention, and perhaps this was the most compelling reason, she'd get to spend time with the man she loved. "But I brought nothing with me," she protested weakly.

A hint of a smile bent his lips. "And what exactly do you have over at Alex and Caroline's that is so important you can't live a day without it?"

Emma lowered her lashes and looked at the floor. There wasn't anything at Watson Estate she couldn't live the rest of her life without. The only things Louise had tossed into her reticule were miscellaneous vanity items and a few books. Fortunately, she'd always kept what she considered to be her most prized possessions in her reticule anyway. "I suppose I'll stay."

"Excellent. The bedchamber next to the one Caroline used to occupy is vacant and aired. I'll go see if I can find you a brush and comb." He turned to walk away before she could form another protest.

***

Marcus shook his head as he walked down the hall. This was proving to be more difficult than he originally thought. He'd known she was stubborn, but she seemed to be fighting him more now than ever before. He stepped into his study. In anticipation of Emma's stay at Ridge Water, he'd instructed one of the footmen to go up to the attic and bring down his grandmother's trunk. The clothes inside would be well out of fashion, but he knew a silver brush and comb set was also stored in that chest. He'd always kept it hidden away from Mother and Olivia. Who knew what they'd do with the contents if they knew how valuable they were.

He lifted the lid and pulled out a ball gown that had diamonds sewn into the netting overlay. Carefully, he laid it across an empty chair and pulled out the matching diamond encrusted slippers. Just one slipper alone was worth a small fortune. He dug deeper into the trunk to where he knew the vanity items had to be. He pulled out a silver brush and comb and placed them side by side on his desk, then turned his attention back to the inside of the chest.

Looking down, his eyes caught on the reflection of his face in the bottom of the trunk. He flinched and jerked his eyes away before pulling out the hand mirror that had so brutally shown him his mien. He knew what he looked like. His fingers told him when he touched his face. His skin reminded him when he used any of the muscles in his face to smile or laugh or frown or sneer or scowl or make any other facial expression. The tight skin would pull and he was once again reminded of his folly. He didn't need a mirror to tell him, and had long ago gotten rid of any and all of those dreaded objects in his path.

He set the offending mirror next to where the brush and comb were already resting on his desk before returning his eyes to the inside of the chest and searching for anything else Emma might like. He could have gone down the hall and borrowed the items from where his mother had kept extras for forgetful guests, but for a reason he couldn't explain, he didn't think community vanity items were good enough for Emma. To his mind, she deserved only the best, and he would make sure she had it.

Marcus found a few hair combs and set them aside. Down at the bottom was a little wooden box wrapped in what appeared to be a deteriorating chemise. Trying not to think of what the fabric was and where it had once been, he unwrapped the box and swallowed. It was a jewelry box. He set it down and used the edge of the trunk to help push himself back to standing position.

He scooped up the tarnished hair combs, brush, mirror, and large comb, and brought them to Molly for polishing.

Marcus waited while Molly went about her task. She offered to bring the things upstairs when she'd finished. Marcus declined her offer; he wanted to see Emma one more time before bed. He was only torturing himself by going to see her, but he just couldn't help it.

He climbed the stairs, grimacing in pain each time his booted foot made contact with yet another stone step. Though he'd actually broken his left leg in two places at the time of his accident, his right leg could hurt just as badly, and sometimes worse, when climbing stairs. His right knee had been twisted in a painful, unnatural way causing lasting damage.

Reaching the outside of her door, he took a deep breath and softly knocked.

She didn't answer.

He tightened his grip on the freshly polished silver items in his hands. He didn't wish to just leave them on the floor outside her door, and she'd need them when she got up in the morning. She was probably asleep already. That wasn't a problem. He'd just go in and set them on her vanity for her to find when she woke. He'd already learned she was a heavy sleeper. A smile took his lips. She'd been having one excellent dream earlier. Too bad he didn't know what—or should he say *who*—she'd been dreaming about. His smile slipped at the thought, and he shook his head to clear his thoughts.

He stuffed the hair combs into the pocket of his coat and placed his hand on the doorknob. With a quick exhalation, he opened the door as slowly as he could so it wouldn't creak too much. As soon as he got the door open all the way, his eyes widened, his heart raced, and his throat worked convulsively.

"You can just put the towel on the stool," Emma said, not turning to see who she was talking to.

Marcus' brain tried to tell his hands to close the door and his feet to walk away, but they didn't listen. Instead, he stayed rooted to the floor with his eyes fixed on the Emma's back as she leaned forward and continued to wash her shapely legs. Her long hair was pinned on top of her head, giving him an unobstructed view of her slim neck, flawless shoulders, and upper back.

He swallowed again. "Emma," he whispered, making her freeze. "I'm sorry, I didn't mean to startle you. I knocked, but I didn't hear anything. I thought you might be asleep, so I opened the door and well, there you are." He clamped his mouth shut. He was rambling. He cleared his throat. "I brought you up some things for your hair. I'll just leave them here outside the door."

"No need. You can bring them in. Just put them on the vanity."

She still hadn't turned to face him, and she'd stayed leaning forward, blocking his view from anything he hadn't glimpsed already.

The vanity table was only ten feet away from where he stood at the door. He forced himself to walk over to it and set everything down for her. "I couldn't find any hairpins, but I'm sure we have some. If you'd like me to ask a maid to go look for some, I can."

She shook her head. "I think I have enough. I carry extras in my reticule in case I lose some during the day."

He nodded even though she wasn't looking at him. "All right. I'll leave you to your bath, then."

"Marcus," she called as his feet reached the threshold.

He paused. "Yes."

"Thank you."

"You're welcome, Emma. Is there anything else you need?"

"No."

He accepted her reply and left the room, shutting the door firmly behind him. A sharp bark of laughter passed his lips. He'd wanted one more glimpse of her before he went to bed. That's exactly what he'd gotten. The problem? Now he'd never be able to sleep.

Chapter 5

Marcus threaded his fingers together behind him and leaned his head back. The past two days had gone rather well, all things considered.

At Marcus' suggestion, Emma worked with the girls on their letters and numbers on Thursday and Friday, only interrupted when Marcus took note of the girls' glazed-over eyes at luncheon. He decided to rescue the girls from Taskmaster Green for a bit to play with a few old instruments. It was to everyone's great relief that today was one of the days the girls would stay at Briar Creek. He shook his head ruefully. Those poor girls had no idea what their days would hold when they'd been bounded into their carriage those mornings. He'd be rather surprised to see them visit without their father again after next week.

During dinner last night, Marcus had told Emma he had two pieces of excellent news for her. The first, he'd found another cook to take over until Mrs. Masters returned; and she would begin her post on Sunday. The second, the village seamstress would be bringing patterns and material to Ridge Water in the next few days to fit Emma for her new gowns. He took a measure of satisfaction in the sweet smile that took her lips at the announcement. The dress she'd come wearing on Wednesday was very nice, but it wasn't hers. Neither were the ones she'd worn Thursday and Friday; they'd been borrowed from the housekeeper. It was time she wore her own.

A startled female shriek from the hall jolted Marcus from his thoughts. In search of a distraction, Marcus limped to the door of his study to poke his head out and see what was causing the commotion.

Peering down the hallway, Marcus' breath caught and his lungs expelled nearly every bit of air they'd been holding.

"What happened?" he asked harshly, moving down the hall as fast as he could to where Emma was standing clad in a soaked chemise with a steady current of blood running down her leg.

Molly, who was standing next to Emma fanning herself with her hand, looked like she was about to faint. Emma's face flushed red as she continued to hold the front of her chemise away from her so the blood wouldn't stain it.

"I slipped," she said weakly. "I went for a swim in the creek, and when I was getting out of the water, I didn't realize how slick the rocks were and I slipped."

He nodded. He'd done that once or twice himself as a boy. Several of the large rocks surrounding the edge of the creek became very slick when they got wet. Marcus glanced at Molly. She was clearly in no condition to help Emma. "Molly, go get some strips of clean linen, a basin of fresh water, and the salve from the pantry, then bring it all to my room." He turned to a wide-eyed Emma. "I want you to wrap your left arm around my neck, then when I pick you up, put your right one around me, too."

"But your leg," she exclaimed. "You can't carry me."

"I assure you, I can." Putting her left arm around his neck for her, then placing one of his arms around her lower back and the other around her knees, he lifted her up.

"Marcus, put me down," she squealed, kicking her legs and squirming.

"Stop that," he ground out. "If you keep doing that, I might drop you. Then you'll have a bruise on your derriere in addition to the cut on your leg."

She turned her flaming face away from him, presumably because she was embarrassed at his words. "All I need is a wet cloth," she said as he carried her down the hall. "It's just a small scrape, really. I would have gone in the servants' entrance and straight to the kitchen, but it was locked."

"A small scrape?" He raised his eyebrows and cast a glance to the lower half of her leg. It was covered in blood. "I shudder to think what you consider a major scrape. A lost limb, perhaps?"

"Stop teasing. It's truly not that bad. I don't know why you're making such a fuss."

He reached the door to the downstairs room that had become his bedchamber for the past thirteen years. "Could you open the door, please."

She shook her head. "No. If I open the door, then I'll have to let go of my chemise and it will fall in the blood."

"And if you'd put your other arm around my neck like I instructed it would have already been ruined," he retorted. "Just open the door. I'll buy you a new chemise."

"It's not mine. It's Caroline's," she said as if that explained everything.

"I'm sure Alex will buy her another one. Now open the door before I drop you."

Reluctantly, she let go of her chemise and opened the door so he could carry her inside and put her on his bed. "No, not on the bed. I'll stain all the linens."

"They're dark so it won't show." He swiped the towel hanging over his dressing screen for good measure then walked back to her and positioned it under her legs the best he could without exposing more of her than he dared. "And if it does, believe it or not, I think I might have enough blunt to buy another set of sheets."

She rolled her eyes. "I've never doubted the state of your coffers."

"That's reassuring. Now stop worrying about them. I can afford to buy you a new chemise and another set of bed sheets if I must, in addition to your two new gowns."

Frowning, Emma clenched her legs together. "Perhaps you should wait in your study while Molly attends me."

He snorted. "Molly will not be attending you. Judging by her shriek and chalk-white face, I find it hard to imagine she's not passed out in the kitchen just now."

"Then I'll just take care of it myself when the supplies you ordered are brought in. That's what I'd intended to do before you got involved."

Shaking his head, Marcus went to the doorway and took the items he'd ordered from a shaking Molly. He turned back to Emma and carried the basin of water in one hand and the salve in the other, the strips of linen resting over his arm. "Dearest Emma, you'll not be taking care of yourself. Not in my house, anyway." He placed the basin on the small table next to the bed. "As long as you're a guest at Ridge Water, you shall receive only the best care."

Her green eyes didn't move or blink. "And who do you have in mind to tend to me if you just sent the only available female servant off? That awful cook of yours?"

"No," he said, shaking his head. "I will attend you."

Now her eyes did do something. They bulged. So much so he was fairly certain they just might pop from their sockets. "I think not." She crossed her ankles to hold her legs even tighter together.

Marcus dipped a cloth into the warm water and wrung out most of the excess water before bringing it to her legs. So much blood had trailed down her legs; he really didn't know exactly where the cut was or how large it was. "Emma," he said softly. "You're going to have to trust me. Please." He took the cloth and began to wipe the blood off the parts of her calves he could see. Gently, he grabbed her ankle that had crossed over the other and pulled it off so he could clean the inside of her calves. He dunked the cloth and squeezed it out again, tainting the water pink. This time her legs were relaxed and separated, allowing him easy access to wipe the blood off. Once they were clear of the dark red blood, he frowned. He'd assumed she'd gnashed the side of her knee judging by how much blood was on her calves.

He looked up to her face. She'd turned to face the far wall and he could only see a profile of her face. Her jaw was clamped and her eyes were shut. Her usually pale cheeks were tinged pink with what he presumed to be embarrassment. His gaze slipped. Her body was trembling violently covered only by her soaked, translucent chemise. He swallowed. Her chemise offered as much covering as spider web. His eyes caught on her hard pink nipples and his body instantly hardened in response. Jerking his eyes away, he cleared his throat. "Emma, take your chemise off," he commanded more harshly than he meant to.

"No. I believe you've seen enough already."

He sighed. "I'm not trying to make up excuses to see you naked. Your body is shaking and you'll get sick if you keep it on. Take it off."

"Just finish, please," she said, gesturing to her thigh.

He frowned. Her thigh? Why would she gesture there? He gripped the edge of her chemise and raised it a few inches. Before he could think better of it, a low whistle passed his lips. "This isn't a minor scrape," he said sharply, grabbing a fresh piece of linen and holding it against her leg to put pressure on it. "I'll be right back. While I'm gone, you take your chemise off then hold pressure against this." He turned to walk out of the room and stopped by the door. "I mean it, Emma. That chemise had better be off and you'd better still be in that bed holding pressure on that cut."

"Or what?"

He turned around. "If you don't have that chemise off, I'll take it off for you. And if you leave this bed, when I catch you—and don't doubt I will—I'll tie you to the nearest one, cut that chemise off you, and tend to your wound."

"You're just like all other men. You'll do anything you can to try to see a pair of breasts."

"No, I'm not," he said with a slight frown. "As I explained earlier, your health demands you get out of that wet chemise. I'll not have you catch the ague because of your pride, Emma." He sighed, and raked a hand through his hair. "If your concern is that I'll glimpse you naked, dismiss it. If that's all I wanted, I wouldn't bother to insist you take off your chemise since leaving it on reveals just as much as taking it off."

She looked down at the transparent fabric clinging to her breasts like a second skin. A noise of frustration sounded from her throat, and her arms crossed over her clearly visible breasts. "Have you been looking?"

Heat crept up his face. "I'd tell you no, but we both know that would be a lie." He shifted to take his weight off his injured leg. "I'm not asking you to lie there naked, Emma. Use a sheet or my dressing robe to cover up." Not allowing her another protest, he left the room in search of more medical supplies.

When Olivia had lived at Ridge Water, so had Mr. Thompson, their physician. Or so it seemed. He was here often enough that he left a small supply of medical goods for Marcus on the occasion he couldn't rush right over for one of Olivia's ailments. Marcus kept them in a crate on the bottom shelf of his library. Considering how much blood Emma had already lost and how big the cut was, he wouldn't be surprised if she'd be weak for the next few days. He picked up an almost empty bottle of brandy so he could clean her wound and a few pieces of suture. With all the blood around, he couldn't tell exactly how deep or wide it was, but he wanted to be prepared to sew it up if need be.

He walked back into the room and frowned. Emma was still wearing her blasted chemise. Before he could say something to her about it, she met his eyes. "I couldn't get it off," she said with a swallow. "I'm sitting on it and when I tried to pull it up, I couldn't get it off without falling over."

Marcus put the medical supplies down and walked over to her. Her skin felt like ice and her blue lips were quivering so rapidly her teeth chattered. He took hold of the hem and dragged it up her legs as far as he could. "Let go of the cloth, and use your hands and feet as leverage to push your bottom a few inches off the bed so I can pull this up." His voice came out broken and ragged, and perhaps a bit nervous.

She glanced at him a second and his face flushed. Letting go of the linen, Emma put her hands palm-down on either side of her and used her palms and the heels of her feet to push herself about two inches off the mattress, giving Marcus just enough room to move the chemise out from under her.

"You can sit back down now," he murmured, peeling the chemise off her wet skin.

She shivered and raised her arms up so he could take it

51

completely off. As soon as it was off, she collapsed against the pillows, offering him a complete view of her deliciously naked body. The crimson blush on her cheeks was the only telling sign of embarrassment.

Marcus tore his eyes away from where they had no business looking and stalked across the room to his dressing screen. A second later, he found what he was looking for: his navy blue dressing robe. He carried it back to her and laid it across her, covering her from her collarbone to just below her dark blonde triangle of feminine curls.

"Thank you," she said uncomfortably, bringing her hands up to rest against her covered upper half.

"I didn't mean to cause you embarrassment. I should have gotten that for you before removing your chemise," he admitted with a swallow. Marcus peeled off the blood-soaked cloth stuck to her thigh and tossed it on the table beside him. Then he wiped the area clean with a fresh piece.

Fortunately, her cut wasn't as deep as he'd thought a few minutes ago, and not too wide, either. But it wasn't just a little scratch, and it would likely leave a scar about five inches long on her thigh. He picked up the bottle of alcohol and uncorked the top. He set the stopper down and picked up a clean strip of linen, folding it into a small square. He knew from experience this was going to sting and burn in the worst way. He needed to distract her. "Can I ask you something?"

She swallowed and nodded, still clutching onto his dressing robe as if it were a life preserver she'd been tossed while drowning in the ocean.

He put the folded square of cloth over the top of the open alcohol bottle and turned it over to saturate the cloth. "Why were you really staying with Caroline?"

She sucked in a breath and twisted his dressing gown between her fingers in such a way that the fabric spiraled. "I wanted to," she answered with a shriek as he touched her cut with the cloth.

"Is that so?"

She bit her lip and nodded frantically, two tears slipping out the sides of her eyes.

He slowly ran the cloth up her cut and winced each time she flinched. "Emma, be honest with me," he said slowly. "Does the reason you've been staying with them have anything to do with the bruise on the bottom of your left breast?"

She gasped. "That's none of your business, Marcus," she snapped, leaning forward to sit up and swat at his wrist with her right hand, her left hand doing its best to keep her covering from slipping. "Let go! Just leave me alone." She wrapped her fingers around his wrist and tried to push his hand away.

"No," he said calmly, shaking off her grasp. "Answer my question, Emma."

Her fiery eyes met his. "What makes you think that bruise has anything to do with my going to live with Caroline? Perhaps I got it today when I slipped."

He shook his head. "Don't lie to me. I know better. That bruise isn't new. If it was, it would be red and purple. Seeing as it's a brown and greenish-yellow color, I'd say it's more than a week old."

She slapped at his wrist and tried to push his hand away again. "Get out."

Marcus set the cloth on her leg and put his hands on her shoulders. "Emma, stop. I only want to help you. But I can't do that if you won't tell me what happened."

"I'm not going to tell you, so stop asking," she responded evenly, keeping his gaze.

His heart ached at hearing those words almost as much as it did when he'd first seen the bruise a few minutes ago. He wasn't the most intelligent man on the planet, but he knew how she'd gotten the bruise; he just wanted her to trust him enough to tell him. He'd do anything he could to help her. She just had to ask. "I won't ask you any more questions," he said flatly. "Now lie still and I'll finish."

Emma sighed and fell back against the pillows, then relaxed her legs again for him to finish cleaning her cut with the alcohol and rub the salve on it.

"It's going to scar," he told her flatly as he put a piece of gauze over the cut. He wrapped the biggest piece of clean linen he had over the gauze and around her thigh. "But not too badly, I shouldn't think."

"Thank you, Marcus," she said quietly while he was cleaning up the medical supplies.

He turned his head around to smile at her and assure her there was no need to thank him, but as soon as his eyes met her form, he scowled instead. "What the devil are you doing?"

"Leaving," she said, using her violently shaking fingers to attempt to tie a knot in the front of his dressing robe.

He dropped the things in his hands and took hold of her just in time to keep her from collapsing on her wobbly legs. "Where do you think you're going?"

"Upstairs," she said, not meeting his eyes.

"No, you're not. You're going to get in that bed and stay put. If you start walking around, that's going to start bleeding again."

She shrugged. "Then I'll take care of it. As I said, it's just a minor scrape."

He snorted. "No, it's not. You're lucky I didn't have to stitch it up. Now, get into bed before I have to clean it again."

"Marcus, I don't need you to care for me. I'm old enough to do things for myself."

"I know that. But I want to help you."

"No," she countered, crossing her arms. "You just want to stare at me naked." Her cheeks were stained red and her voice was cold as ice.

Clenching his hands into fists, he shoved them in his pockets. "That's not true. I already told you it wasn't. I admit I may have glanced at you, but I didn't stare, nor did I have you remove your chemise for my amorous pleasure. There's no need to be embarrassed or upset."

"Oh really?" she said sarcastically. "All right, take off your clothes and I'll glance at you a few times, then you can tell me if you're embarrassed."

"That will not be happening."

"That's what I thought." She inclined her chin.

He crossed his arms. "Emma, me taking my clothes off has no connection to me seeing you without yours. There was a medical reason for yours to come off. My thigh isn't bleeding."

She pursed her lips, and he could have sworn she grumbled something about arranging for his thigh to be bleeding. "All right," she said, turning away.

"What's this about?" he demanded, clutching the sash tied around her waist before she could walk away.

"Nothing. Just let me go."

"You think it's not fair, don't you?"

"No, it's not fair," she burst out. "You got to look your fill at me and I—I—. Never mind."

"You want to see a man undressed?" An odd sense of understanding came over him. As bizarre as her unusual desire might seem to some, he understood. "Sit down," he said, then walked across the room. He bent down and glanced over his shoulder, to make sure she'd sat down and not run off.

"Don't trouble yourself, Marcus. I'm past my embarrassment."

He nearly snorted again. That was a lie if he'd ever heard one. "Just sit still. I vow, before you leave this room, you'll know exactly what a man's form looks like."

Emma sat down and readjusted the tie on his robe.

"Aha," he said as he flipped through *Lady Bird's Ladybird Memoir* to the page he was looking for. He stood up and walked over to her. "Here." He handed her the book opened to the picture on the second to last page. The picture was a simple drawing, really. Just a man alone on a rumpled bed. His eyes were shut, his body completely relaxed, giving off the impression he'd been sated by all the activities he'd been portrayed doing during the previous few pages, and his clothes strewn all over the floor. When Marcus had first received the book, he'd looked through all the pictures in the back before reading the stories and was rather confused as to why there was an image of a naked, content man. After he'd read the book, looked at the pictures again, and gained some maturity with the years, he still wasn't certain why it was there, but just now, he was glad the illustrator had included it. It would give Emma what she was looking for without seeing anything too distasteful.

Emma blinked at the picture then handed him the book back. "That was enlightening," she said sarcastically, standing up.

He frowned and took the book from her. "I don't know how much more enlightening it could have been. Everything's there."

She gestured to the book. "That picture is ridiculous."

Marcus glanced down at the picture. "No it's not. The man is naked. That's what you wanted, wasn't it? Your curiosity should be satisfied."

"It's not," she said with a pointed look at his groin.

Sighing, Marcus closed the book. "That picture has all the same parts I do; I can assure you of that."

"Not hardly." She snorted. "I doubt any man truly looks like that."

He opened the page again and glanced down. "Yes. I'm fairly certain we all do."

She held out her hand and he gave her back the book for another peek. "While I still have my doubts a man's...er...whatever you wish to call that thing, is that size, I do wonder why you have a book with a naked man in it," she mused, cocking her head and looking at him curiously.

Embarrassment and perhaps a tinge of shame flooded him. "My father gave me that book. He was a rather temperate man and claimed it would give me all the experience of a brothel with none of the diseases."

She blinked at him. "When?"

He knew she hadn't meant to ask it aloud, but he answered her anyway. "Before." It was an answer he was sure she could deduce his meaning from, seeing as there were so many possibilities. Before his accident. Before his broken engagement. Before, during a time in which the knowledge of how to properly bed a woman would have actually been useful. Now it was just a book he kept stashed away partly because it had been a gift from his father and partly because from time to time he liked to read it. If that made him an immoral person, then so be it.

She sat back down on the edge of the bed and looked at the picture again, a dubious expression on her face. She grabbed the corner of the page and flipped it backward.

He quickly reached out and took the book from her grasp. "You've seen quite enough." He closed the book with a snap and tucked it under his arm.

Pursing her lips, she reached forward and tried to take the book from him. "No, I have not. I don't for one minute believe that picture was correct. I want to see the others."

Marcus moved out of her grasp. "In comparison to the rest of his body, I would say that was a fairly accurate depiction."

"I doubt that," she said, shaking her head. "I imagine a man drew that and embellished it greatly."

He shrugged. "Think what you wish, but you're not seeing the other pictures."

"And why is that? Are they just as exaggerated?"

"I'll admit the male part in the other pictures appears a bit larger. However, I stand by my earlier statement. For that man's body, his penis is drawn accurately," he said as smoothly as he could while striving to ignore the heat creeping up his face. "Why are you rolling your eyes? It's true. And for a woman who hadn't seen one until two minutes ago, I wouldn't think you'd have any basis for doubts."

Her face turned crimson and her gaze fell to the floor.

"You've seen a naked man before." He wasn't sure if he meant his words as a question or a statement.

"Curiosity satisfied," she croaked, still not looking at him.

Marcus stared at her, fighting the urge to ask who she'd seen without his clothes on. The only person he could think of was that reprobate her sister married. And while it wouldn't surprise Marcus that Hampton had exposed himself to Emma, he hated the idea so much his stomach lurched and bile rose in his throat. "Good," he clipped, walking across the room to put the book away.

"Marcus?"

"Yes?"

"Why did you show me that book?"

"Because I thought you were curious about what a man looked like under his clothes. Since I know you're relentless, I decided the easiest thing to do was to satisfy your curiosity."

"You could have done that without the book," she pointed out.

Marcus ground his teeth. "My anatomy is not for display."

She twisted her lips. "Of course not. I'm not Louise."

He didn't respond. He couldn't do anything more than stare at her. What had or hadn't happened between him and Louise all those years ago was not up for discussion. "Get some rest," he barked, walking stiffly to the door. "I'll have a dinner tray sent to you."

Chapter 6

Emma stared blankly at the door Marcus had just gone through. Most young ladies would be berating themselves if they'd just had that conversation. She snorted. No, most young ladies wouldn't have even *had* that conversation. Nor would any of them have even *suggested*, let alone thought to suggest, he take off his clothes. She sighed. Not only that, but they wouldn't have accused him of denying her request because she wasn't her sister. That usual crushing pain which settled in her chest when she thought of Marcus and Louise together, suddenly hit her like a smithy's hammer.

Only two weeks after Louise married Gregory, she became very ill. When Louise's physician in London examined her, he announced she'd miscarried. Emma had been in the room and asked Louise who the father was. Emma might have been young, but she was no fool. She'd seen the way Louise had behaved with both Marcus and Gregory prior to her elopement with Gregory, only days after Marcus' accident. Louise hadn't given Emma an actual answer on the father's identity. Instead, she just smirked and said, "Who do you think?"

That was the only time they'd ever spoken of it. It was enough to confirm the notion in Emma's head that Marcus and Louise had been intimate. Though she'd known that Marcus and Louise would marry and they'd be intimate, she'd always chosen to push that hurtful truth from her mind. But when Louise had miscarried and all but claimed Marcus was the father, the knowledge of how close they'd been had become a reality. For some reason Emma couldn't justify, she was hurt.

Now, thirteen years later, she was still a bit hurt when she thought about it. Marcus had been so badly injured at the time; she wasn't sure how he'd learned of the miscarriage. It was all immaterial now, though. As the hurt feelings should be, too. She had no right to be hurt, and yet she still struggled to overcome it.

She carefully slid out of the bed, determined not to think about it any longer. Marcus and Louise hadn't married. That should be good enough.

Emma hadn't paid much attention to where Marcus had gotten the book he'd shown her, but she'd been paying attention when he put it back. She was seven-and-twenty, well past the blushing debutante age, and she was curious. So why not satisfy her curiosity? She knew if anyone, especially Marcus, were to ever know what she was doing; they'd be shocked to the core. But nobody would find out. She'd just flip through the book to see the pictures, then put it back.

She took her first tentative step and winced. Her leg hurt. Badly. She widened her stance and took another step, taking care not to let her legs rub together as she padded over to the box he'd put that naughty book in, then frowned. He'd locked it! Her eyes quickly scanned the shelves and the vanity for the key. She didn't see it anywhere. She sighed and reached up to her hair. She'd used a hairpin to pick a lock before; she just have to do it again. Pulling out a pin from the top so as not to compromise her entire coiffure, she bent the pin to make it straight and jabbed the end into the keyhole. She jiggled the pin for a second and smiled when the click of the lock broke the silence.

For good measure, she threw a glance over her shoulder before opening the lid. "*Lady Bird's Ladybird Memoir*," she read aloud. She hadn't caught the title earlier. The shock over Marcus even owning a book with naked pictures was too much for her to care about such a trivial matter as that. Then Emma knit her brows. There wasn't a single mention of a Lady *Bird* in all of *Debrett's*. And she'd know—she'd memorized the entire dratted thing, after all. Not to mention the fact that she'd spent countless Seasons in

London without ever encountering a single mention of such a person. Who was this Lady Bird?

No matter. She carried her treasure back to the bed. Careful to climb in so she wouldn't bump that extremely painful cut on her leg; she adjusted the covers and ran her fingers over the lettering on the front. Nervous excitement raced through her. Taking a breath, she opened the cover and used the tip of her index finger to flip past the first few pages. She got to the table of contents page and blinked. "'Chapter One, The Differences Between a Lord and Lady'. I'd sure hope she'd know the difference," Emma muttered, dropping her eyes down to the title for Chapter Four. "Hmm, 'A Man Versus a "Gentle"man'. Interesting."

Impatiently, she flipped the page to chapter one and thought her eyes might pop out as she started reading. The author of this book had written real stories about her lovers, using enough hints for just about anyone to recognize who she was talking about.

Emma devoured the first page, and then the second, followed by the third and fourth. Before she knew it, she was sprawled out face-down on the bed, face flushed, heart racing, nearing the end of the fifth chapter. When she'd first started, she'd occasionally glanced at the clock that hung just above Marcus' vanity to make sure it wasn't nearing dinner and she wasn't about to be interrupted. Now she was too enthralled to care.

Taking a quick break, she put her finger in the book to mark her page and flipped through the rest to see how much further she had. She sighed. There was too much there to read in an hour's time. She'd have to get as far as she could today and sneak it back out again later.

Keeping her place marked, she went to that page Marcus had shown her earlier. The night Gregory had decided to show up naked in her bed was not the first time she'd seen him naked. Thankfully, it was the last. As a double reason to rejoice, she hadn't actually seen that specific part of him that night. It was either covered by the sheets or his hands after she kneed him. However, she hadn't been so lucky a few months back when his robe "accidentally" came untied just as he entered her room to ask if she'd like him to stoke the fire. She cringed. For years she'd had to endure his subtle hints and uncomfortable innuendo. It wasn't until about five months ago he'd become more bold with his advances.

Pushing the image of Gregory and his unattractive body out of her mind, she looked down at the drawing of the man in the back of the book. Perhaps Marcus had been right. From the five chapters she'd read, "Lady Bird", who Emma was convinced now more than before was a fictional name, had described in detail many male members. Some long, some short, some thin, some wide, all different. She blushed. These were *not* thoughts for proper young ladies. Then again, neither was reading such a scandalous book. She sighed. She was an old spinster governess now. She'd never have a chance to be with a man anyway, so what was the harm in reading the book? Nobody would know, and after she finished, she'd just put it back and pretend to be the naive girl everyone thought her to be.

Curiosity urged her to flip back a few pages and look at all the pictures. She'd read enough stories to have an idea of what she'd find. Just as her finger grabbed hold of the paper and had it nearly flipped back, two sharp knocks sounded at the door.

"Don't come in!" She didn't know how long she could keep her guest outside and dared not take a chance walking across the room to return the book. Instead, she crawled up to the head of the bed, shoved the book behind the mountain of pillows, then turned around and sat with her back leaning against the pillows. "All right, you may come in now."

The door opened and a frowning Marcus walked in. "What were you doing in here that I had to wait in the hall?"

"Getting dressed," she said airily.

He blinked. "You seem to be wearing the same thing you had on when I left."

Emma grabbed the edges of the robe and held them closed, trying in vain to scowl at him. "Not that it's your concern, but I had my robe off," she lied.

Nodding, Marcus took a seat in an empty chair. His face looked slightly pink and every time he looked in her direction, he'd shift and jerk his eyes away.

"Did you come in here for a reason?" she asked after he fidgeted in his chair for a few minutes.

"I wanted to talk to you about earlier. Emma, I was only trying to take care of you. I didn't mean to—"

"I know," she cut in. "It's of no account. I was embarrassed then, but I'm not now."

"Are you sure? I don't want you to avoid me because I saw you naked." The intensity of his steely stare was enough to make Emma catch her breath.

"I won't." She didn't think he could do anything that would make her want to avoid him in earnest. "Anyway, it's not like you haven't seen it all before," she added as casually as she could, belying the sharp pang of hurt in her chest. Louise and Emma looked so much alike they could almost be confused as twins. If he'd seen Louise naked, he'd practically seen her naked, too.

Marcus lowered his eyes and stared at the floor for a few seconds. "Would you be interested in having a dinner companion?" he asked, meeting her eyes again.

"Depends on who it is."

"Me."

She grinned. "Hmm, and do you think during dinner you can keep your eyes trained either on your plate or my face?"

"I'll try. But I make no guarantees."

"In that case, you may stay," she said with a sigh. "Oh, wait, I have another condition."

"Too late." He stood. "You already agreed to let me stay. You don't get to change your mind now."

"Oh please, Marcus," she cried, feigning distress. "You used to let me change my mind all the time when we were children."

His gaze fell from her eyes and settled on her chest. "But you're clearly not a child anymore," he remarked, making heat crawl up her face and her breasts swell at his compliment.

Trying to act unaffected by him, she shrugged. "No, I'm not, but are you?" she goaded, leveling a stare at his groin. Earlier she really wasn't so interested in seeing his parts. She'd merely wanted to even up the score, so to speak. Now that she'd read that book, her interest was sincere. She truly wanted to know what he concealed behind those buckskin trousers.

"That had better not be your condition, or you'll find yourself eating alone," he said, twisting his lips into what she assumed he intended to be a sneer.

"It's not." She waved her hand dismissively.

He relaxed. "All right, what's your second condition?"

"Could you bring me back a book from the library?"

"What do you have in mind?"

She shrugged. "Surprise me."

Marcus rolled his eyes. "Be more specific," he ground out.

"A romance should do."

His jaw tightened and his eyes took on a cold look. "I'll be right back with your book. Don't take that robe off while I'm gone. I'll not be made to stand in the hall of my own house again."

She watched him leave and smiled cheekily at his back. If she were a braver, younger woman who thought she had an honest chance of catching his eye, she'd do exactly that. She'd take that robe off, stuff it under the bed and lounge on the bed in the seductive way Lady Bird had described in her book. But Emma wasn't that daring and brave. She was the younger sister to the woman who'd ruined his life.

Emma put the book away and resumed her spot on the bed, just in time to watch Marcus carry a giant wooden box into the room.

"Here you are. Every romance book I own." Marcus set the crate on the bed.

Emma blinked at him. "I can only read one at a time."

Marcus' grey eyes pierced her. "I know. I don't play games, Emma. You can pick your own book."

"Right," she murmured, picking up the first book her fingers found. "This one should do." She should have named off an author or a book she knew he had, rather than do something like Louise would do. Louise would ask him to buy her something every time he went as far as the village. She'd never tell him what she wanted or give him any idea of what she had in mind. She'd be as vague as could be. Then when he came back with something, she'd find fault with it and pout. Emma had little doubt if Louise had done these things before Marcus had offered her marriage, he'd have moved away from her faster than a man walking barefoot on a bed of hot coals. Unfortunately for Marcus, Louise hadn't started her childish games until just after the ink was dry on the contract. By then, it was too late for him to end the relationship without a scandal and a breach of contract suit, at the least.

"Very well," Marcus said, putting the crate on the floor.

Emma put the book on the nightstand and looked at Marcus. "If you don't mind, I'll return your dressing robe to you in the morning," she said for lack of anything else to say.

"There's no hurry." He sat down and stretched out his long legs. "I won't need it tonight." He crossed his arms and leaned his head back to rest on the back of the chair.

"That's a relief to hear," she said a bit sarcastically. "After dinner, I'll go up to my room."

His eyes popped open. "No, you won't. I told you earlier, that cut of yours needs to heal, and the best way for it to do so is with you lying in bed with your legs spread." When they both flushed crimson, Marcus said, "You know what I meant."

She knew exactly what he'd meant. But after reading that book, she couldn't help getting the unintentional innuendo and mental image that went with it out of her head. "I can heal just as well upstairs."

"I agree. However, by the time you get upstairs, you're likely to have reopened it with all that walking and rubbing together of your thighs. Best not to chance it. You can sleep in here."

"And where will *you* be sleeping?"

"Don't worry, it won't be in here," he said roughly. "I'll push the two settees in my study together and sleep there."

"No. I'll go upstairs. You need your bed. If you sleep on those hard settees, your leg will be paining you in the morning."

"It already is," he retorted.

"I told you not to carry me." She crossed her arms. "I told you

I could walk and take care of myself, but no, the almighty Lord Sinclair had to step in and be the hero of the day and carry me down the hall."

His sharp eyes pinned her. "Are you finished?"

"No, I'm not. It's your own fault you hurt your leg this afternoon, and you're so thickheaded you're willing to do it again. But I have something to say that might come as a shock for you, my lord. That will not happen. After dinner, I will return to my room."

He shook his head. "No. You're going to stay tucked up nice and warm in this bed, and if you suggest otherwise again, I'll tie you to it."

She snorted. "You're just looking for an excuse to tie me to your bed, aren't you?"

"No, I'd rather you stay here willingly. But if you won't—" he shrugged— "then I'll make sure you do one way or another."

Emma scooted to the far end of the bed. She wasn't so terribly hurt she couldn't walk down the hall and up the stairs to her room. She'd prove it to him. Right now. She clenched the edges of his robe together, then put her feet over the edge and lowered them to the floor.

"What the deuce do you think you're doing?" Marcus barked.

"Leaving." She stood up and carelessly started walking toward the door. After a step, she realized her folly. In her haste, she'd forgotten to widen her stance. She clenched her teeth together to hide her grimace as she readjusted her gait.

"Get back here," he commanded, standing.

She steeled her spine. "No. I've imposed on your generosity enough today. I thank you for helping me earlier, but I think I'm well enough to leave now."

"The devil you are." He moved closer to her. "Emma, get back in the bed before you start bleeding again."

She shook her head. "You're not my father or mother, nor my nursemaid, nor my husband. I do not have to do what you tell me."

Marcus' fists clenched and he shoved them in his pockets. "You're right," he said softly. "I cannot make you do anything, but

I am asking you to get back in the bed, please."

"No." She shook her head vigorously. "Marcus, I know your leg hurts and I know it will hurt worse if you sleep anywhere other than your own bed. I'll not be the cause of any undue pain."

"You won't be."

"Yes, I will. You've already carried me today. You can't deny that made it hurt worse than it already did. And don't think for one minute I believe it didn't hurt earlier. I know better than that. You came up the stairs a few nights ago, and though I may not have been a frequent or welcomed guest at Ridge Water in the past, I've been around enough to know you don't walk up the stairs unless you absolutely must." She smiled at his blank face. "I also know, like nearly every other house in this country that has more than one floor, there is not another room with a bed on this level, which means you'll either have to hurt yourself again by walking up the stairs or sleep on a stiff settee. You'll have your bed."

"Emma," he said quietly. "You were always a welcomed guest here."

She paused and stared at him. Her heart was torn. She'd always longed to be welcomed at Ridge Water, and not just because she was visiting Caroline or Olivia. She blinked away the thoughts. "That's all you heard of that?" she asked in disbelief.

"That was all that was important." He shrugged and raised what was left of his eyebrows. "The rest was a bunch of nonsense I chose to ignore."

"You're impossible," she muttered, pushing past him.

His hands shot out and grabbed her shoulders to stay her. "You're not leaving."

"Yes, I am." She pushed on his solid chest.

"Not until I've determined that leg of yours is better." He wrapped his arms around her midsection and carried her back to the bed.

"And when will Marcus the Physician decide I'm well enough to go about my day without his acting as my guardian angel?" she asked sardonically.

He chuckled. "In a day, perhaps two," he said, laying her on the bed.

As soon as he'd put her down and removed his hands, she tried to roll to the other side of the bed. He reached forward and grabbed her about the waist. "Let go," she squealed as he pulled her back toward him.

"No," he answered, climbing on the bed and kneeling while still holding onto her.

"Please, Marcus. Let go of me. I know you think I'm being a pain in your hindquarters, but I'm really not trying to be. I don't want you to hurt unnecessarily."

He flipped her over. "We're at a crossroads, then." He placed a knee on each side of her to keep her firmly down on the bed. "I don't want you to hurt, either."

"My injury is hardly an injury at all," she protested, wiggling her shoulders to get free.

"It's an injury just the same." His voice was silky and rich.

She blinked up at him and stilled. In his pale eyes she could see the things he didn't know how to put into words. He wasn't trying to control or hurt her, he was trying to protect her the only way he could.

"Can we make a compromise?"

He groaned. "I don't think so."

"You haven't even heard it."

"I don't need to. I already know what you're going to say."

Emma frowned. "No, you don't."

"Yes, I do." He grabbed her hands and pushed them back to rest above her head, his fingers slipping in between each of hers. He leaned his head down, bringing his forehead to rest against hers. "You're going to tell me you'll only sleep in this bed if I sleep in it, too."

"How did you know?" she whispered, her breathing hard and labored.

The pads of his thumbs lightly caressed the outsides of hers. "Because I know you, Emma. And while I know your thoughts are completely pure and naive, mine are not. If we share a bed tonight, you might not be so happy with that decision in the morning," he whispered before pressing a sweet kiss on her lips

Emma couldn't help the gasp that passed her lips when he pulled his face away. "Marcus, stay. I won't regret it, I promise."

"Yes, you will," he said savagely. "I might have enough honor left in me not to ruin you, but I cannot guarantee I'll be gentleman enough to keep my eyes shut and my hands to myself if your robe gapes open again."

"Again?" she gasped, trying to pull her hands from his.

"Again," he confirmed in a broken whisper. His strong fingers held her hands in place, and his lips brushed hers once more.

She shivered. If he had been any other man, she'd have been appalled, but not Marcus. Never Marcus. "You don't scare me," she said softly.

"I'm not trying to scare you. I'm trying to warn you."

Emma curled her fingers until her fingertips rested against his knuckles. "Warning heeded. Now promise me you'll stay."

Marcus shut his eyes and exhaled. "Do you promise to keep your clothes on?"

"Yes," she snapped. "Do you?"

He scowled. "That will not be a problem."

"Right, because you're shy," she teased.

"Forget it." He released her fingers and pulled away.

Emma wrapped her arms around Marcus' neck and didn't let go, keeping him as close to her as she could. "Stop, I was only teasing. I promise I'll keep my clothes on at all times. Now, will you stay?"

"You'd better, because heaven help you if you don't." He ducked his head and pulled it out of her embrace.

"Does that mean you're staying?"

"Yes, I'm staying. Now close the top of that robe and retie the sash."

Emma looked down and nearly shrieked when she saw both of her breasts were completely exposed. "How long—" She broke off, clenching the fabric tightly.

"A while," he answered her raggedly.

She nodded curtly and stood up, turning her back to him so

she could adjust the robe and retie the sash. "I think that should hold," she said brightly as she turned to face him again.

"It had better, because next time I'll not be a gentleman and pretend not to notice."

Chapter 7

After supper, Marcus excused himself for a few minutes to attend to some personal business before bed. He walked down the hall and went into his study, sat in his chair with his elbows on his desk and dropped his head in his hands. Why had he foolishly agreed to sleep in that bed with her? He'd not be able to sleep as long as she was next to him, and *if* he did, he would only dream of her. And after seeing her naked today, he had no doubt what kind of dreams those would be.

He groaned in frustration. The reasons against him pursuing Emma were far greater than the one in his favor. He may love her to a distraction, and had for a long time, but it would never be enough. Emma wasn't a shallow woman, she never had been. He'd never gotten that uncomfortable sensation that started in the pit of his stomach and branched out to the rest of him while in her presence. She didn't stare at him or make sly remarks about his physical appearance or folly. She was one of the few people on this planet he didn't feel like hiding from, and that's what drew him to her. The comfortable air she had about her. The way he could easily forget what he looked like and why while in her presence. The problem was her sister. Specifically the past he shared with her.

Being a mature man of one and thirty, Marcus had long ago realized he'd never loved Louise like he once thought. He'd been infatuated with her. His infatuation had been so great, he'd impulsively asked her to marry him and quickly realized what a mistake it had been. Within what seemed like moments after their betrothal contract had been drawn up, she'd changed. She became possessive and vindictive—nearly impossible to stand. That's when he realized while he thought he'd been charmed by Louise, he'd actually been charmed by her family.

Sir Charles Green and his wife, Lady Green, were good, honorable, sincere people, as was their other daughter, Emma. Sir Charles was born an ordinary commoner who was knighted for his bravery during the early years of the Napoleonic Wars and was one of the most intelligent and friendly men Marcus had ever met. Lady Green, was as sweet as she was beautiful. How two of the nicest people could have two daughters with such opposite personalities was nearly impossible to understand.

When Marcus first met Louise, he'd been seven, she'd been six, and Emma three. For several years the three were playmates. They'd fish and swim and climb trees together. He'd even partnered each of them a few times when they'd pretend to waltz around in his parents' ballroom. As the years went by, he'd gone to school and only saw the girls in the summers.

The summer he was seventeen, Louise turned sixteen and her parents continuously invited him to do things with the family. Emma had been only thirteen, which consequently meant, she held no interest for him at the time. He didn't want to run around or play games anymore; he was interested in Louise and her womanly attributes.

As the summer grew to a close, he'd impulsively proposed to Louise in front of her family, thinking the fun they'd had that summer was just a prelude of the life they'd share together. What a fool he'd been. If he'd looked carefully, he'd have seen that the only three who seemed to be having any fun were Sir Charles, Lady Green, and Emma. Louise's demeanor had been prompted only by her mother and sister's presence. They hadn't been alone together enough for him to fully realize that though.

Once he'd proposed and the contract was signed, he saw the real Louise.

Marcus buried his fingers in his hair and wished yet again his father had talked him out of his rash decision. Being only seventeen, his father could have said no, and since Marcus hadn't reached majority yet, his offer would have been rendered null. Unfortunately, Louise's false charm had also fooled Father. And so began the nine months of torture.

While he was away for his final year at Eton College, Louise had taken to writing to him. She'd send letters explaining how all the village boys admired her and brought her tokens of their affections. She'd ask him to send her something with his allowance, and he'd send her something only to receive a letter back saying how it wasn't what she'd expected or how it paled in comparison to whatever one of the local boys had given her. During his leave in mid-December, he brought her several trinkets to give her throughout the month he'd be home. She'd acted disinterested in his gifts and even openly flirted with some of the local men.

By the time he went back to school in the middle of January he was irritated with himself for not realizing how immature they both had been planning to marry.

But it wasn't until March he realized the full extent of his impulsive actions.

A few days before he was set to go home for break, he'd heard a rumor Louise had been seen in London with the Duke of Hampton. Marcus brushed it off at first since Hampton had to be in his early to mid-thirties. It was unlikely a man of that age would find interest with a girl who wasn't quite seventeen. When he arrived home, he went to her house where her parents seemed uneasy and gave him stilted answers. He later ran into Emma outside and for the first time, he really noticed her. He blinked at her as she walked up. The entire summer before she'd seemed so young, and she still was, he reminded himself as she smiled at him. She was only fourteen, far too young to think of in any way except as a younger sister. It had been Emma who had told him the painful truth. She didn't do it to be cruel. She told him because he asked and she wasn't one to lie.

She'd told him Louise had gone to stay with some relation they had in London and the relation confirmed the duke had been paying Louise attention. To Emma it must have looked like Marcus' heart was breaking because she'd naively tried to console him. He'd shrugged off her efforts and left. His heart was the furthest thing from breaking, it was hardening as fury pumped through him. They may not be married yet, but Louise had no business entertaining other gentlemen.

The following day Louise returned home and came to visit him at Ridge Water. She'd done her best to smooth over the rumors he'd heard and promised him it had only been coincidence she'd been seen with the duke and claimed she was looking forward to their wedding. Not many other choices open to him, he accepted her words and tried his best to keep her content. He soon learned keeping her content while being present was more difficult than it had been when he'd sent her letters and gifts through the post.

His last week at home before returning for his final term of school, Louise approached him, eager with the idea of eloping. He'd been apprehensive at the idea. He couldn't return to school if he eloped with her. After explaining to her he couldn't marry her until he was done with school in July, Louise employed tactics that could rival an experienced courtesan. Several times her bodice "accidentally" slipped down, causing her breast to conveniently fall out, and he'd kindly turn to look the other way while she righted her gown.

When she realized he wasn't going to give into her ploys, her actions became more bold. She'd intentionally position herself so parts of her body touched his in ways she'd somehow known would make his body react. By midweek he was giving serious consideration to hauling her off to Gretna Green, but then he'd remember how close he was to finishing school and convince himself they could both wait. For goodness' sake, they were both young enough to wait a few months—life wasn't going anywhere without them.

On the final day before he was to return to school, Louise came to him while he was fishing by the stream that ran through the back of Ridge Water. She once again pleaded with him to whisk her off to Gretna Green, and after he explained his reasons for not, instead of trying to use seduction like he thought she might, she'd become angry and they quarreled.

By the time they finished arguing, she informed him she was off to London to see Hampton, claiming the duke was a better man than Marcus because he'd have already carried her off if she'd have asked him. Marcus' first instinct was to let her go. She'd break their contract, not him. They'd both have a scandal on their hands, of course, but at least it wouldn't be of his creating and his family wouldn't take the brunt. But a few minutes later pride won and Marcus made the worst decision of his life. Yes, even worse than asking her to marry him in the first place.

Cursing himself for ever being ensnared by her in the first place, he threw down his fishing rod, and heedless to his current state of undress, which included his lack of shirt due to the tendency of the cuffs to get in the way, he ran to the stable to grab the first horse he could find. One of the scruffy grooms offered him a shirt. He refused. It would take him too long to put it on, and this would only take a minute. He just needed to catch up with her before she reached the main road. In his rush, Marcus saddled the horse himself. After a light nudge with his heels, the horse took off like a shot and Marcus found himself riding at a hell-for-leather speed in an attempt to catch up to her carriage.

At the end of the drive he turned to go down the lane that led to the main road. Less than a minute later, Louise's carriage came into view down near the end of the lane, too far for the coachman to hear him if he hollered. Marcus gritted his teeth and urged the horse on, barely registering the minor shifting of his saddle on his horse's back. A few strides later, the horse abruptly bucked. Marcus' hands tightened around the reins and his legs squeezed together as he fought to maintain his balance and position on the back of the beast. Still, the horse kept running. Marcus willed his body to relax and loosened his grip on the reins. This horse wasn't yet broken, he didn't want to spook the horse again. "Come on, boy," he crooned. "Just a little further."

The words barely escaped his lips before the horse reared back on his hind legs with such great speed and force that the reins slipped from Marcus' hands and he fell to the ground with a painful, rib-cracking, leg shattering thud. Gasping for the air which had just been knocked from his lungs, he tried to pull his right foot free from where it was still stuck in the stirrup. Each second became more painful than the last as the horse continued to run, dragging the left side of Marcus' body over every sharp rock, stick, tree root, and any other debris that littered the lane.

Intense pain and stinging shot through him as his flesh ripped from being dragged over the jagged surface beneath him. He jerked his foot harder, more frantically. He tired again and again to free his boot from the stirrup. It didn't budge even a fraction of an inch. Without warning, Marcus' body rolled over on its own accord from the velocity created when the horse changed his direction to follow the bend in the lane, twisting Marcus' right knee in an unnatural way in the process. Unable to so much as feel his right leg anymore, Marcus was powerless to do anything else in an effort to escape his excruciating torment as the horse continued to run, dragging Marcus' limp, bloodied body twisting and rolling behind him.

The beast of a poorly trained horse Marcus had been riding only stopped when out of nowhere, a young boy grabbed the reins and pulled the horse to a stop. The abrupt stop jolted Marcus one more painful time before leaving him to rest face down in the middle of the lane. Through the fog of the severe pain and blood loss making him fade in and out of consciousness, he heard Louise's high-pitched screams and the sound of a young man yelling directives to her coachman. Though he'd never know for certain, he could have sworn Louise went into hysterics about them using her family's coach to carry his bloodied body back to Ridge Water.

The next months were painful and trying, as the cuts that covered his upper body were tended with brandy and gauze. His leg had to be set and the chances for his survival looked grim as he struggled to recover. Other than his parents, his only company had been that fifteen-year-old boy who'd bravely stopped his horse: Patrick Ramsey, Lord Drakely. As much as Marcus tried to make the lad leave, the sense of responsibility which had been instilled in Patrick from a young age wouldn't let him leave. Instead, the insolent boy stayed despite Marcus' nasty behavior toward him and became the greatest friend Marcus would ever have.

By the time Marcus was well enough to attempt walking again, he was well past wanting to hear the name Louise ever again, and nearly throttled Olivia when she'd had the nerve come to see him and make up silly rhymes about trees and fleas and falling on one's knees in front of a fair maiden named Louise. And if that nonsense wasn't bad enough, he really did almost throttle her when she took it upon herself to inform him the Duchess of Hampton was expecting.

He wasn't a fool, he knew who the Duchess of Hampton was. That was the only positive thing surrounding his accident: he hadn't made the mistake of eloping with Louise and been forced spend the rest of his natural life miserable with her. He might spend the rest of his natural life miserable with scars covering his upper body and a limp because, like the besotted fool he'd been rumored to be, he'd tried to run down his intended's carriage to beg her to take him back. all the while, he'd been riding a poorly saddled (and trained) horse. But at least he could endure his misery better without her around.

It was nearly three years after his accident before he saw Emma again. He'd known she'd been coming to visit Caroline and Olivia. also had known her real reason for coming had only been for Caroline. She had tolerated Olivia—only because she had to, in order to see Caroline. Emma had formed a strong connection with Caroline ever since Father had brought Caroline to stay with them after her mother had passed. It was as if the two had become the sisters which neither of them had in a biological sense.

When he first saw Emma after three years, he'd been nervous about how she'd react to seeing him and how he'd react to her. As soon as she walked through the door he had his answer. She was stunning. Everyone said Emma and Louise were almost interchangeable. Not to him. Where Louise's eyes were a dull moss green, Emma's sparkled like emeralds. Louise's hair was a few shades darker blonde than Emma's. But the biggest difference was their personalities. Louise had been full of brittle and forced smiles, and Emma's smiles were real, full of love and laughter. Emma was just as beautiful inside as she was out and it made his heart ache. If only he hadn't proposed to Louise and had gone to Cambridge and on Grand Tour before turning his eyes to the female sex. Then he'd have never gotten tangled up with Louise and her web of deceit. Instead, his eyes would have passed her up and landed on the biggest prize in England: Emma.

But as it was, he could never have Emma. She'd forever wonder if he still secretly loved her sister. Who could blame her for thinking it? He'd acted besotted with Louise for almost a year before falling off the horse while chasing her down. He'd heard the rumors Louise spun and didn't care enough to try to disprove them. In a sense she was right, he was running her down to resolve things. But it wasn't because of any great love for her or jealousy she'd broken their engagement in order to marry the duke.

In the ten years since he saw Emma for the first time since his accident, he'd fallen further and further in love with her. Every time she came to Ridge Water, he'd try to talk to her before remembering who he was and who she thought him to be. She'd always been kind to him and was one of the only people who'd never grimaced or flinched when first seeing him.

He sat up straight and rested his head against the back of the chair while he stretched his legs out and his hand idly massaged the muscles in his upper thigh. They always seemed to knot up when he used the stairs or walked around more than usual, which was exactly what he'd been doing since Emma had come to stay with him. He sighed. He'd been gone from his room so long he knew if he didn't get back in there soon, Emma would come looking for him and hurt *her* leg.

Marcus stood and lumbered over to the door. He may have been fool enough to agree to sleep in the bed, but that was as far as it would go. She'd sleep under the counterpane; he'd sleep on top. She'd have his robe on; he'd have all his clothes. Nothing would happen between them.

When he entered the room and saw her beautiful face lying with her cheek on the pillows, he briefly entertained the idea of stuffing a wall of pillows between them to help him keep his distance but dismissed it as going too far—childish even.

Sitting on a plush ottoman, he took off his boots and pushed them off to the side before removing his coat, cravat, and waistcoat. He hung the unneeded clothes over the side of his dressing screen and walked to the edge of the bed. With a hard swallow, he climbed into the one place he'd only dreamed about every night for the past ten years: his warm bed with Emma at his side.

She stirred next to him, and he tried to be as still as possible so as not to wake her completely. A second later, she moved closer to him and threw her left arm across his chest. His heart picked up speed, and he swallowed as his blood fired at her touch. It had been years since he'd been touched in such a way, and never by anyone he cared for so greatly.

Marcus brought his hand up and used his fingertips to trace the outline of her arm from her elbow to her wrist and back again. Her skin was soft and smooth beneath his rough hands.

"Marcus," she sighed, pushing her face to rest closer to his.

He turned his head slightly and stared at her beautiful face. She wore the same smile as she had the other night when he'd walked in the drawing room and caught her dreaming. He nudged her with his shoulder, hoping she'd accidentally mumble something so he'd know what she was dreaming about that could bring such a beautiful smile to her delicate lips.

Her fingers crept up his chest to wrap around his shoulder, and she sighed his name again.

"What is it?" he whispered softly.

"Kiss me again," she murmured.

He blinked at her. Was she talking to him or the man in her dream? "Hmm?"

She sighed again, and her fingers dropped from his shoulders to the buttons of his shirt.

Marcus brought his hand up and wrapped his fingers around

her wrist before she could undo a button. "Emma?" he whispered loud enough to wake her, but not completely startle her.

Her sleepy eyes opened and she blinked at him, then looked to where his hand was holding hers on top of his chest. "Forgive me," she said, trying to pull her hand from his.

He tightened his grip. "You don't have to move your hand away." Before he could think better of what he was about to do, he took his fingers from her wrist and pushed her hand palm-down on the center of his chest, keeping his hand on top of hers.

Emma didn't pull her hand away or fight him when he curled the ends of his fingers around her palm. Her face rested right next to his and ever so lightly, her lips brushed his cheek before she whispered, "Goodnight, Marcus."

Chapter 8

Emma struggled to fall back asleep after Marcus woke her up. Though she'd been exhausted before, his mere presence now kept her wide awake.

She had no idea how her hand had ended up on his chest. She'd been dreaming of kissing him again when suddenly the real him said her name, and she discovered the top half of her body was draped over him with her hand on his chest and his fingers wrapped around her wrist.

Beneath her fingers, his heart beat fast and strong. The warmth of his skin radiated through his clothes. If she moved her fingers, she'd probably feel the grooves of the scars she was certain he hid under his shirt.

A sudden itch on her right shin caught her attention. Carefully, she moved her left foot up to rub the side against the itch and froze. Bending her knee to scratch her itch must have disturbed the bandage, and now the knot was slipping free.

Panic seized her. When Marcus had left earlier, she had assumed it was so she could have time to attend her personal business. She'd taken the time to change the gauze on her leg and reapply some of the salve. She hated to admit Marcus had been right earlier. It was not the minor scrape she had claimed it to be. Not only had the blood soaked through the gauze and the strip of cloth, it had also started bleeding again while she was changing the gauze. Fortunately she'd been able to contain the mess and had found another, smaller piece of cloth to tie around it.

And now that cloth seemed to be loosening and slipping off

her leg. She abruptly pulled her hand from Marcus'. He wouldn't be pleased about this if he found out. He'd likely claim she'd reopened it when she'd stubbornly been trying to leave. Which was probably an accurate claim, she conceded in her mind. But it did nothing to solve the problem she had right now.

"What's wrong?"

"Nothing," she lied, edging to the side of the bed. "I need to go use the necessary, that's all."

He frowned. "I was gone more than an hour. You didn't do it then?"

She shook her head. "I'll be right back."

"No," he grumbled. "I'll go wait in the hall. Just use the chamber pot that's in there." He pointed to what she presumed was his dressing room.

"No, no. I'm already nearly up. I'll just go down the hall."

"What's going on, Emma?" He sat straight up in the bed.

"I've a female problem," she rushed to say. "I require a bit more privacy, please."

He snorted. "The only female problem you're suffering from is stubbornness. Is something wrong with your leg?"

She bit her lip. "I'm sorry. While you were gone I changed the gauze, and I don't think I got the linen secured right, and now..."

Marcus turned to light a few candles and fetch another towel. "Here, lie on this and I'll look at it again." He turned around and left for a minute, coming back with several clean cravats.

Emma got onto the bed and positioned herself on the towel. She looked down and nearly screamed in frustration. Her leg was bleeding just as badly now as it had when she'd first come into the house.

Marcus glanced over and muttered an unsavory expression under his breath. "I'll be back. Don't move." A few minutes later, he came back with the suture she'd seen him with earlier in the day. "I didn't think it looked bad enough for this earlier," he explained, bringing his chair up close to the bed. "But perhaps that's why I'm not a physician."

She smiled weakly at his jest and relaxed her thighs as he once again spread them enough to attend to that dratted cut. She closed her eyes and leaned her head back, willing herself not to be embarrassed that Marcus was once again seeing more of her than she'd ever planned to show anyone.

"I'm not looking," he whispered, giving her hand a light squeeze.

She nodded uncomfortably.

Marcus continued to wipe off the blood and use the rag with liquid fire on it to clean the cut. "Emma, this is going to hurt. Badly, I'm afraid. If I had something to give you to numb the pain, I would. But I've just used the last of the alcohol to clean it and as you know, I don't drink, so there isn't any more in the house."

She nodded again, fisted her hands in the sheets, and made her mind focus on why Marcus had no alcohol in his house rather than on the pain of what he was doing. She frowned. She didn't know why Marcus didn't drink alcohol. She only knew he took lemonade with most of his meals and drank tea at various times throughout the day. "Marcus?"

"Hmm?"

"Why don't you drink?"

He weakly smiled. "Would you like the boring reason I usually give or the real one?"

She flinched when he pressed the sharp tip of the needle through the tender skin on one side of her cut, then the other. "Both."

He pulled the suture through and tied a knot in the end before clipping it. "Well, I usually tell people it's because my father was a real Holy Willie who preached about temperance and over indulgence so much I heeded his teachings and stayed away." He made another painful pass through her skin with his needle and tied another knot before clipping the suture again. "But the real reason is alcohol gives a man courage to do or say the things he otherwise wouldn't *and* gives him the stupidity to do the things he knows he shouldn't."

She knit her brows. "What did you do that you shouldn't?"

He pushed the end of the needle through her skin again and

didn't pause in his work to answer her. "That's not so important anymore," he said dismissively.

She blushed and glanced away briefly. He had to be talking about the night he'd proposed to Louise. They'd been at a local assembly hall and he'd been indulging in some champagne.

She watched his face as he continued to sew. The muscles tightened and ticked every time he pressed the point of the needle through her skin. It was almost as if he was hurting just as much as she was. Her heart squeezed at the simple gesture. "Marcus, I think the real reason you don't drink is a bit of both," she said, trying to strike up *some* sort of conversation to take her mind off the severe pain she was feeling.

One of his shoulders went up. "You're probably right. But it really doesn't matter. I'm one-and-thirty and haven't developed a taste for it yet. I doubt I will, and I really don't give a hang."

She smiled at him. He was certainly not your typical titled gentleman; that much was obvious.

"Either way," he continued after he clipped another tag, "I'll have to send out for some tomorrow in case this comes open again."

"Let's just hope that doesn't happen," she said dryly. "Although, I must admit I'm surprised you're out of brandy."

He looked at her and blinked.

She waved him off. "I meant for your sister. She used to injure herself at regular intervals. I thought perhaps you'd keep an extra bottle on hand for her."

He laughed. "Actually, I did. For a while, anyway." He stopped and frowned.

"Where is she?" Emma had heard rumors Olivia had gone off to America, but the details had been very hushed up—even Caroline didn't know why.

Marcus swallowed. "She's in America."

"What is she doing there?"

He shrugged. "Living, I'd wager."

She rolled her eyes and poked him in the shoulder with her toes. "You're being awful cheeky, Marcus. What happened? Why did she go to the 'Land of the Savages,' as she always called it?"

He grinned. "She did always call it that, I quite forgot. All right, I'll tell you why she went, but please do not repeat the story. I wouldn't wish to give anyone digestive troubles."

She giggled and watched him as he picked up the little jar of salve.

He uncorked the lid and dipped his finger inside. "Just remember, I warned you," he said, looking into her eyes, his full of laughter. "She's going to be a mother."

"What?" Emma squealed before she could stop herself. "When? How? With *whom*?" She clamped her hand over her mouth. "Forgive me," she said against her fingers. "That was most rude of me to burst out that way."

He chuckled. "Don't worry, those were all the same questions I blurted, too." He grinned at her and rubbed the salve on her leg. "Do you remember old Mr. Saxon in the village?"

"The smithy?" Images of missing or black teeth, a purple nose, and hands the size of hams floated through her mind.

"That's the one." Marcus nodded his head. "Say, didn't his son fancy you when you were younger?"

Emma grimaced. "Unfortunately."

He frowned. "Why unfortunate? If you'd accepted his offer, Olivia could have been your mother-in-law."

"How can you even think such a thing?" she asked with a groan.

Marcus flashed her a smile. "Actually, if you're interested in the truth, the baby isn't his, or at least that's the story she tells. She claims my former valet, Robinson, is the father. I would have doubted her claim if he'd stuck around and told me otherwise. But, since he ironically disappeared earlier that day, I couldn't ask him."

Emma thought her eyes were about to pop from their sockets. She remembered Robinson. The man had to have at least sixty years in his dish. Not to mention he was what she always thought of when someone described a whale. She had no doubt Olivia and Robinson suited each other just right. "Then why did she marry the smithy?"

Marcus shrugged. "Because he asked."

"You mean he knew she was carrying someone else's child, and he wanted to marry her anyway?"

He nodded again. "Don't worry; it wasn't for any great love he had for Olivia. It was her dowry he was after."

"And you gave it to him?" Emma asked, shocked.

"Yes. I didn't want Olivia to be completely without funds. I gave Saxon a bank note for five thousand pounds and put the rest into a trust for Olivia in the event he should desert her."

Emma stared at him. So many thoughts—several rather unkind, but nonetheless true—were running through her head just now. It wasn't an *if* the man deserted her; it was a matter of *when*. Olivia took pleasure in treating people poorly, and sooner or later that smithy was not going to be able to tolerate her any longer. If Emma had to guess, that time had come before the boat docked in America. But she wouldn't be so unkind as to voice such a thought to Marcus. He was her brother after all.

"When was this?" she asked, partly out of politeness, but mostly out of the shock of all this new information.

"Two months ago. The day after she told me she was expecting. Saxon approached and requested her hand. I told him no and showed him the door. The next day Olivia was gone. Two weeks later, she showed up and presented me proof she was Mrs. Byron Saxon, married by special license." He put the cork in the jar and put the salve on the table. "I wasn't overly pleased, but I couldn't do anything else about it, so I gave them part of her money. A day or two later, she came by to inform me they were going to America. I didn't argue with her about leaving. By going to America, she could save herself a lot of embarrassment, and that's something I could understand."

Emma nodded, her brain still too muddled to think.

"Over there, nobody would know how long she'd been married before she had her child. And over here, nobody will know the daughter of an earl slipped from grace and married a smithy old enough to be her grandfather."

She grinned. "You're a good brother, Marcus."

"I tried," he said, twisting his lips. "She was actually betrothed to Alex at one time, but as you know, I played a large role in his courtship of Caroline."

"I know," Emma said softly. "Don't blame yourself for Olivia's fall. She made her own decisions. Your helping Alex and Caroline had nothing to do with what she did. She didn't want to marry Alex in the first place, and Caroline did. Nor did Alex wish to marry Olivia; he wanted Caroline. It all worked out like it should."

"Thank you," he said softly. "I've partially blamed myself for her exile because of my meddling."

Emma shook her head. "You can't." She'd learned long ago everyone makes their own decisions. That's why Louise hadn't listened to Emma and had run off with the duke instead of seeing things through with Marcus.

"I think we'll leave the gauze and wrap off it this time," Marcus said, looking at her leg. "Those stitches should hold. I'm sorry I hurt you."

"It's all right," she assured him. "It wasn't so bad. The talk of your drinking habits and the shock of Olivia's whereabouts kept my mind off the pain until the salve soothed it."

"Well, I'm glad Olivia could finally be of some use to someone," Marcus said dryly. He stood up and walked into his dressing room before coming back in with what appeared to be a very old nightshirt. He threw it down next to her. "It's all I have that will fit you. Tomorrow the seamstress is coming; I'll have her make you a couple nightrails in addition to the chemise and two gowns I owe you."

"I couldn't."

He grinned. "That was the weakest protest I've ever heard pass your lips. You'll accept those nightrails, or you'll have to sleep without them," he said with a wink.

A shiver skated down her spine and she nodded dumbly. Well, if *those* were the terms, she'd better accept.

He turned around to face the wall so she could take the now stained robe off and put his nightshirt on. "I'm dressed," she said, rolling the robe and towel up and putting them behind the dressing screen.

Marcus turned around and frowned at her. "Quit cleaning and get in that bed. If you're not careful, you'll burst one of those stitches, and I'll tell you right now, that hurts far worse than having them put in."

She climbed back into bed and returned to her previous spot, waiting for Marcus to join her. He walked over and blew out the candle before climbing in.

"Do you plan to fall asleep in all those clothes?" she asked, settling in beside him.

"Yes. Because if I don't, there won't be any sleeping going on in this bed tonight."

Chapter 9

The night was pure torture for Marcus. As soon as the first rays of light came in the window, he moved to get out of bed and realized he couldn't. He was stuck. Emma's head was in the middle of his chest, with her soft breasts pressed against his side. Her left arm was slung across his chest at a diagonal with her fingers curling over his shoulder.

As much as he wanted to get up and end this torture, he couldn't. He didn't know if or when he'd have her in his arms again. He sighed and brought his arms up around her again. The feel of her so close made his heart ache. He wanted her, and here she was in his arms, but only because he'd forced her to stay and not because she wanted to be here.

He closed his eyes. "Emma," he whispered against her hair. "I need to get up."

She wiggled against him in a way that would have hardened him instantly if he hadn't been already. "So soon?"

He nodded. "Yes. I have things to do before the seamstress gets here."

"What am I to do while we wait? I cannot walk around in your nightshirt."

Marcus groaned. He hadn't thought of that. "I'll send someone up to the attic to see if a suitable gown can be located. In the meantime you can have breakfast in here and read your book."

Her eyes lit up. "Excellent idea."

He shook his head and stepped into his dressing room to change. A few minutes later, he emerged.

"That was fast."

"Doesn't take long when you don't have to shave," he commented, sitting down to put on his boots.

She cocked her head to the side. "You don't shave?"

"No." He laced his boot. "Hair doesn't grow through scarred skin."

"Oh." She dropped her gaze to her hands.

He finished tying on his boots and stood. "It might take a while to locate a gown for you. If you need anything, just pull the bell pull. It's over there." He pointed to the long gold velvet cord hanging by the door.

Two hours later, Marcus anxiously knocked then burst through the door of his room. Emma was on the bed lying on her stomach with her bare feet high up in the air, crossed at the ankles. Her head was by the pillows with her book in her hands. "Goodness, Marcus." She closed the book with a snap and shoved it beneath the pillows.

He chuckled. "You don't have to hide the book from me. I already know you're reading it." He handed her a thirty-year-old day dress that once belonged to his mother. It was the nicest thing he could find that would pass as somewhat fashionable by current standards.

"You do?" she squeaked, her eyes wide.

Marcus shook his head. "I'm the one who brought it to you, remember?"

She nodded and swallowed.

"For goodness' sake, Emma, it's not a crime to read a romance novel."

She giggled nervously. "I know." She shifted her eyes from his and looked to the dress, stockings, and slippers he'd brought with him. "Is there a shift?" she asked, her cheeks turning a light pink.

"I knew I forgot something," he muttered, setting the clothes down on the bed. "Do you have to have it?"

"Yes. Otherwise I'll have to be measured naked."

He smiled at the mental image her comment conjured up and only stopped when a pair of balled up stockings rapped his knuckles. "Sorry. I'll be right back."

Ten minutes later, he returned with a shift he'd borrowed from his fifty-year-old housekeeper. "Here you are." He handed it to her. "I see this time you were anticipating my arrival?"

"What do you mean?" she asked, eyeing the ripped seam in the shift.

"You weren't reading your book this time." He gestured to the rumpled bed.

She blushed. "No, I put it away."

He glanced down to the nightstand where *Moll Flanders* lay right out in the open before looking at her again. "Are you feeling all right today?"

"Yes," she said with a frown. "Why do you ask?"

Marcus shrugged. "Not ten minutes ago when I came in here you shoved your novel under the pillow and blushed furiously when I mentioned it, and now it's lying in clear view and you look as calm as an autumn's day."

She grabbed the book and jammed it under the pillows. "There."

He shook his head and left her to get dressed.

"Marcus?" she yelled through the door a few minutes later.

He opened the door slightly. "Is something wrong?"

"I can't get the hooks in the back of my dress." She turned her back to him.

Marcus walked in and shut the door behind him. He'd been fending off awkward stares all morning from his staff because of the sleeping arrangements last night, no need to give them something else to gossip about. Not that it mattered a great deal. He was the master of Ridge Water, after all, and anyone who dared question his actions would find himself seeking new employment —without a reference, naturally.

The back of Emma's gown gaped open, and he went over to do the clasps for her. A minute or so later he finished and squeezed her shoulders. "You're all ready."

Emma turned around, and he couldn't tear his gaze away from where her breasts were threatening to fall out of her bodice. "Was this all you could find?" She aggressively tugged her bodice up, giving Marcus quite a show as her plump breasts bounced and jiggled.

"Stop fussing with it before you spill out the top." He scowled at his hoarse tone.

"I'm fussing with it so I *won't* spill out the top," she retorted, giving the fabric a hard yank.

"I have an idea. In the hall is a shawl that used to belong to Olivia or Caroline or someone. I'll get it for you." Marcus found the shawl and came back into the room. "Wrap this around you."

Emma reached out for it and stilled. "I think I'll survive without it," she said coolly. "Once the seamstress arrives, I'll have to take my dress off anyway."

He walked up to her and wrapped the shawl around her shoulders, noting how she stiffened when he touched her with the fabric. "Emma, I know you don't like borrowing other people's things, but the owner of this shawl will not mind. I promise."

"Yes, she will," Emma countered bitterly. "The owner of that shawl never wanted to see it again."

"I don't think so. She just forgot about it."

Her right hand let go of her bodice, grabbed the shawl, and jerked it off. "She did not forget about it. She discarded it."

"Was this yours?"

"Yes. It was mine, and though I never brought it across the threshold of Ridge Water, I bet I know who did."

"Where did it come from?" A knot formed in his stomach. He probably wasn't going to like her answer.

"Hampton," she said tightly. "Out of spite for you having ruined her impending marriage, Olivia wrote to Louise, to ask her to come to Caroline's wedding. The day before the wedding, a letter arrived from Louise with her regrets. It included a small package with something for me to wear to the wedding. When Olivia showed me the letter, I recognized the writing as his, not Louise's. While I was reading the note, Olivia took it upon herself to open the package and pull out the shawl. I took it from her and ordered it destroyed immediately. I honestly thought it had been."

"Are you sure this is the same one?" he asked, his throat dry.

She nodded. "It's the same. He always has gifts embroidered with that." She pointed to the corner.

Marcus grabbed the fallen corner of the silk shawl and brought it to his line of vision. "Does he often give you gifts?" he asked harshly, running his thumb over the dark red threads that embroidered a bold heart shape with GT & EG inside it.

"From time to time," she admitted. "All but that one have found their way to the rubbish bin or a large flame."

Scowling because there was no roaring fire in the room, he balled the shawl up. "I'm sorry she did that," he said on his sister's behalf. Olivia couldn't go a day in her life without making at least one person miserable. Poor Mr. Saxon.

Emma snorted. "She wouldn't have had the chance if Louise hadn't married such a degenerate," she muttered, then started. "I'm sorry." She blushed, presumably at realizing what she'd said and who she had said it in front of.

"I'm not," he said honestly.

She smiled sympathetically at him. "Marcus, I know she hurt you—"

"No, she didn't." He sat on the edge of the bed. Against his better judgment, he pulled her to him and settled her on his lap. "Emma, not a day has gone by these past thirteen years that I'd wished I'd married her. Yes, I've wished I hadn't been hurt. And yes, I've regretted that I was unable to finish school or go on the Grand Tour. But not once have I regretted that I didn't marry Louise."

"But I thought you were riding after her," Emma said, her eyes uncertain.

"I was," he admitted. "But not for the reason you think. She wanted me to haul her off to Gretna Green, but I refused. She left and said she was going to Hampton because he'd take her. The reason I was chasing after her was to talk her out of running to Hampton and creating a scandal. I'd proposed to her, and though I didn't really want to marry her, I would have. As a gentleman, I was bound to honor my proposal. And I would have—in July. I rushed after her because I wanted another chance to persuade her to wait until July when I'd be finished with school."

Emma looked at him oddly. "She couldn't have waited that long, Marcus. Even you had to have understood that."

"She could have waited three months," he scoffed. "She just didn't want to."

"Surely you didn't expect her to be exposed to the censure and rumors that would have surrounded her once news of her condition was made known."

"*Her* condition?" Marcus said with a sneer. "I wasn't aware *she* had a condition. I was the one lying abed being tended for broken bones and infected lacerations."

Emma frowned. "Marcus, you do know the reason she was in such a hurry, don't you?"

"Yes. So she could prove once again she could control me." He forced a thin smile to offset the bitterness in his tone.

"You don't know," Emma said quietly, blinking at him.

"Know what?"

"Nothing." She scrambled off his lap.

He wrapped his arm around her waist and pulled her back to settle on his lap. "Tell me."

She glanced at the floor for a minute then back at his face. He squeezed her waist affectionately to encourage her to speak. She sighed. "Just so you know, I do not think this justifies her behavior, but it does explain it. The reason she ran off with Gregory three days after your accident was because she was expecting."

Marcus' stomach clenched as if he'd just been punched. If he'd not been hurt, he'd have had quite an eventful year ahead of him. First, a wedding in July, then another man's bastard that winter, followed by the beginning of a parliament-granted divorce in the spring. Unlike some men of the *ton,* he would not have accepted her bastard, and if that brat had been born any sooner than nine months after their wedding, he'd have sought a divorce immediately—no matter what kind of shame and scandal it might have brought on him to do so.

"I'm sorry, Marcus," Emma went on, her eyes glistening with

tears. "I thought you knew all this."

He shook his head numbly. Why was she so upset?

"Then I suppose you didn't know she'd miscarried?" she asked, brushing back a tear.

"No," he said softly. "And to be frank, I really don't see why I should care."

She sucked in her breath and jumped from his lap so quickly he couldn't stop her. She marched over to the door and wrenched it open.

"Where are you going?" He came up behind her and held onto the edge of the door before it hit him in the face.

"To the seamstress," she exclaimed, picking up her skirt and moving quickly down the hall.

With a grimace, he walked as fast as he could and snaked an arm around her, hauling her back against his chest. "What was that about?"

"You're heartless," she snapped.

He laughed bitterly. "Pray explain yourself."

"You act as if you haven't a single care in the world about Louise's miscarriage."

"Why should I?" He tightened his hold. "That has nothing to do with me."

She turned around in his hold, her eyes flashing fire. "Doesn't it?"

"No. Louise and her brats are none of my concern."

"How can you say that?" She choked on a sob, and two tears slipped from the sides of her eyes.

He stared at her dumbfounded. Just because he'd been engaged to the chit didn't mean he held her in any great esteem, then or now. "What are you looking for from me, Emma? A little sympathy? Very well. I'm sorry she had to suffer the pain of a miscarriage. Is that good enough?"

"No," she snapped. "You and your black heart don't understand. I don't want you to feel sympathy for Louise. She's the second least deserving person of sympathy I know—right behind her brute of a husband. However, a little emotion on the behalf of *your* child that was miscarried isn't too much to ask, I shouldn't think."

Marcus gaped at her. "That wasn't my child," he said flatly, loosening his hold on her. "I don't know what she might have told you, but there is absolutely no chance that child could have been mine."

She took a step backward. "P—pardon?"

"I think you understood my meaning." He exhaled and raked a hand through his hair. "Tell me something, Emma. Is the only reason you've bothered to come to Ridge Water these past years because you felt sorry for me about what happened with Louise, the broken engagement, and the supposed miscarriage of a child you were told I had sired?"

She recoiled at his bitter words. "No, Marcus, those are the reasons I gave myself for why I *shouldn't* come to Ridge Water." She spoke in a tone he couldn't identify. "Now, if you'll excuse me, I have an appointment with the seamstress."

"Wait." He reached out and grasped her wrist to stay her. "What reasons do you give yourself for why you *should* visit?" He ignored the raggedness of his voice and hoped she would, too.

She pulled her wrist from his hold and took a step back. "Because I love you, Marcus," she said, turning to walk away, leaving a stunned Marcus with his heart hammering wildly in her wake.

Chapter 10

Emma couldn't climb those stairs fast enough. She'd just bared her heart to Marcus, and if he rebuffed her, she'd never recover.

When he'd denounced Louise's insinuation that the two of them had been intimate, her heart had sung for joy, only to be silenced by his cruel question that followed. Why she had decided to be honest and tell him the truth of her feelings following that, she'd never know.

Entering the pink salon, Emma paused and caught her breath. This room had been transformed from a quaint little sitting room to a beautiful dressmaker's shop. A large screen and a dais stood in the middle, with three mirrors surrounding the dais to offer a reflection of all angles. Bolts of beautiful fabric were draped over every surface and hanging from the top of the screen. She swallowed. This was far too much for just two simple gowns. She hadn't planned to let Marcus commission the nightrails and chemise he'd suggested. All she'd won was the gowns, and that's all she would accept.

"Good afternoon, miss," Sarah Cole,   said, not meeting Emma's eyes.

Emma sighed. Sarah Cole was a village girl who had become a seamstress. Though Marcus' staff could be trusted not to start rumors, and Caroline had likely instructed her staff to keep quiet, too, nothing short of a row of a dozen sutures would keep Miss Cole's mouth closed. By tomorrow, the whole shire would know she was staying at Marcus' and he was buying her wardrobe. Which would also mean everyone would assume what her sister already had: Emma was Marcus' mistress.

"Miss Cole," Emma greeted, looking at the fabric.

Sarah pulled a sheet of paper out of her apron and pursed her lips as she read it. "It seems his lordship has quite a large list of gowns planned for you." She stuffed the paper into her pocket. "Why don't you go behind the screen and take off your gown. You may leave on your shift. If you're even wearing one," she muttered.

Emma's cheeks flushed, and she went behind the screen to disrobe. She and Sarah had once been friends, but that had ended shortly after Emma discovered Sarah had only been pretending to be her friend to her face while speaking poorly of her behind her back. Ever since Emma confronted her about this, Sarah had dropped all pretenses and said whatever scathing remark she had about Emma to her face.

"Could I get a bit of help?" Emma called when she realized she wasn't able to undo the clasps by herself any easier than she'd been able to fasten them in the first place.

Sarah walked behind the screen and methodically undid the clasp. "I do wonder, Miss Green, who helped you into this dress?"

Embarrassment flooded Emma. "That's none of your business," she snapped. "Your job is to make me a gown, not speculate on who helped me into my clothes."

Sarah laughed. "And what about speculating on who will be helping you out of your new gowns and nightrails?" she asked condescendingly.

"That is also none of your concern, Miss Cole," Marcus boomed from the doorway. "As Miss Green told you, your job is to sew her gowns. Now, I suggest you get to it or you'll find yourself sorely lacking patronage."

"Yes, milord," Sarah said, fidgeting with the clasps on Emma's gown with far more force than necessary.

When Sarah was done unhooking her metal clasps, Emma stepped out of the dress and tossed it over the screen.

"What are you waiting for, Miss Green?" Sarah called impatiently from the platform.

Emma frowned and peeked around the side of the dressing

screen to see if Marcus was still in the room. She didn't see him and released a deep breath before walking out.

Sarah rolled her eyes. "I don't know why you're acting so modest when he's seen you in much less before." She walked up to Emma with her measuring tape and wrapped it around her waist. "Twenty," she murmured. She grabbed the pencil tucked in her bun and jotted the figure down in her little notebook. She moved tape up to her bust and grimaced. "Thirty-six. If you weren't practically naked, I'd think rolled-up stockings accounted for six inches of that."

Emma ignored her. Sarah had a way of getting under everyone's skin, rather like Olivia. In fact, she probably rivaled Olivia with her beastly personality. She blinked away the thought and picked up a stack of fashion plates. "I'll take two gowns in this pattern." She handed the card to Sarah. "One in blue muslin, the other in green."

Sarah clucked her tongue. "Mighty plain, don't you think?"

"No," Emma said smoothly. "I think the gowns are just right for a position as governess."

Sarah snorted. "Is that what you call it? I believe the correct term for what you are is a mistress, and I highly doubt his lordship will want to take you out looking like a ragamuffin."

"And I believe the correct term for what *you* are is unemployed, Miss Cole," Marcus said from the doorway. "You have ten minutes to pack your things and be out of my house. You'll have twenty-four hours from then to clear out your belongings from Mrs. Crofter's store."

"You cannot do that, milord," Sarah said, raising her chin defiantly. "I work for Mrs. Crofter, not you."

"Ah, but Mrs. Crofter rents her building from me," he pointed out in a tone full of authority. "Therefore, as the person she answers to, I approve who she allows to work in her shop, madam. And I have no doubt she'd rather keep her business and lose you, than fight me on this and lose her shop."

Sarah clamped her mouth shut and stormed out of the room.

"You didn't have to dismiss her," Emma said with a frown.

"Yes, I did. She had no business saying those things to you."

Emma shrugged. "It's no different than what others have already said or thought." She went behind the screen and stepped back into her dress.

"Who?" Marcus peeked over the top of the screen.

She ignored him. "Now, I'll never get those new gowns." She sighed and put her arms through the sleeves. "I'll just write to Caroline and ask to borrow one of hers," she said, resigned. She'd borrowed a dress from Marcus' only female staff members, already this week. She'd sent Caroline's dress back to her on Thursday, and now she was borrowing the housekeeper's shift. Could things get any more uncomfortable?

"You'll do no such thing," Marcus countered. "Just before I sacked Miss Cole, I sent word to Mrs. Crofter saying I required her services post haste. I assume she'll be here sometime early this afternoon."

"Why?"

"Because I had a feeling trouble was in the making when Chapman told me who Mrs. Crofter sent in her stead."

"You're familiar with Sarah?"

Marcus nodded. "You forget, I had a younger sister, a cousin, and a mother who have been fitted by Mrs. Crofter's apprentices in the past ten years. I'm familiar enough with Miss Cole's personality to know she and Olivia used to use each other to sharpen their claws."

"Then why haven't you sacked her sooner?"

"Because usually her comments are directed solely at or about me, not about the woman I love."

Emma's breath caught and she stared blankly at him. Had she heard him right?

"Come on." He extended a hand in her direction. "Let's go for a walk."

She put her shaky hand in his. "My gown," she croaked.

"Right." He released her hand and went to her back to make quick work of closing her gown for her. When he was done, he took her hand again and led her from the room. "You shouldn't be swimming with those stitches, but perhaps we could walk by the water and put our feet in."

Her heart raced. "I'd like that."

"Good. Let's make a quick stop by the kitchen. That new cook who started today is fantastic, and she's made up some treats."

"Something small, I hope," Emma said dryly. "I fear if I eat anything larger than a biscuit, the seams of this dress will rip."

Marcus chuckled and picked up a new shawl he'd hung over a chair in the hallway. "Not to worry. No one but me will be around to see anything."

She blushed. "That's plenty enough reason to worry."

"Not at all," he assured her, handing her the shawl. "Here, wrap this around yourself. It'll keep you covered well enough until we get outside, then you can misplace it somewhere." He winked at her as he said those last words.

Emma wrapped the shawl around her shoulders and positioned it just so to cover the exposed part of her bosom. She adjusted her pace to match Marcus' as they reached the stairs. "I hope you didn't hurt yourself going up and down two flights of stairs today," she said, wagging her finger playfully at him. She really was worried, but didn't want to ruin the moment by scolding him.

"I'd have done it twice more to be rid of that awful woman."

After a quick stop at the kitchen to grab a hamper, Marcus led her outside and down to the creek.

Marcus put the hamper down on a grassy area near a giant fallen log. "I wonder what's in here."

Emma's curiosity matched Marcus', and she opened the hamper while Marcus sat on the log, stretching his legs out. "I have no idea what this is," she murmured, pulling out a little covered dish. She lifted the lid and sniffed. "A candy of some sort, I believe." She handed it to Marcus, who nodded his agreement.

"Is that jam?" Marcus wondered.

"It is," Emma confirmed, picking up a jar of jam that the new cook must have brought with her when she came to Ridge Water.

"Curious," he said with a shrug, watching her intently as she pulled out a plate of biscuits and another of some sort of tarts.

ROSE GORDON

Marcus patted a spot next to him. "Come sit with me, Emma.
If you don't wish to get the back of your dress dirty, you can use
that shawl to sit on." He grinned at her in a way that made her
heart skip a beat.

"Now, now, Lord Sinclair," she began in teasing tones, "just
because we're all alone does not mean you should be allowed to
view my nearly naked breasts."

His grin held in place. "Would you rather I view your
completely naked breasts?"

She blushed. "That's quite enough of that talk," she scolded
playfully, taking a seat next to him.

His silvery grey eyes darkened a bit, and he leaned closer to
her. "Just so you know, a man likes a hint of mystery. Therefore,
viewing your nearly naked breasts holds a bit more excitement for
a man than if you come right out and show him." His silky voice
sent a shiver down her spine.

Emma licked her lips. "Are you telling me men don't enjoy
seeing women completely naked?"

"They do. But they also like the thrill of the unknown and
enjoy being teased a little."

Turning her head so he couldn't see her smile, Emma sat down
and mentally put a lot more credit in Lady Bird's words of wisdom;
she'd practically said the same thing in chapter three. "I'll have to
remember that."

"Don't overdo it, you minx," he warned. He picked up the
plate of biscuits and offered her one.

She took the biscuit from him and slathered some strawberry
jam all over the top before eating it. She had to admit this cook
was much better than the last, and her mouth watered just thinking
of what her tarts might taste like. "What kind of tarts are those?"
she asked, unable to hide her interest any longer. She should have
looked when she was pulling them out.

"Apple, I think." Marcus handed one to her.

Greedily, Emma reached forward to take the tart from Marcus.
As their fingers brushed, her hand stilled. She liked touching him.
His skin was warm and sent a thrill through her body when he

touched her. "Thank you." She took a bite and sighed in delight as the flaky crust and sweet apple filling melted in her mouth.

Marcus watched Emma and swallowed. "You've a little..." he said raggedly. Not letting her have a chance to wipe her mouth, or even indicating where the crumb was, he leaned forward and pressed his slightly parted lips to the corner of her mouth, slipping his tongue between his lips to lick off the stray crumbs.

Emma froze and a tingly sensation washed over her. She liked feeling his lips on hers and hoped he wouldn't ever remove them. Being as subtle as she could, she turned her face just a little so his lips would find hers, taking a measure of pride when he responded as she'd hoped and brushed his lips across hers. She sighed his name.

His right hand came up to cup her face as he held his lips against hers. "You taste so sweet," he murmured against her lips.

Being bold, Emma pressed her lips back against his and opened her mouth enough to let the tip of her tongue pass. She brought her hand up to rest on his jaw as her tongue traced the edge of his bottom lip.

Marcus groaned and sought to deepen the kiss by opening his mouth and sucking her bottom lip between his. He let his tongue lightly slide over her lip until she opened her mouth just a fraction further, allowing him to slip inside and taste her. "Emma," he groaned against her mouth.

Emma's fingers clutched his lapels as his tongue continued its exploration of her mouth, her fingers twisting the fabric so hard it was likely his collar could never be ironed straight.

Withdrawing his tongue, Marcus' lips pressed a series of sweet, soft kisses on hers before he pulled back to look at her, his breathing ragged and his eyes several shades darker than before.

Emma's fingers went to her tingling, kiss-swollen lips.

In silence, they both finished their tarts, neither taking their eyes off the other.

"Would you care to wade?" he asked, brushing the crumbs off his fingers. "You could wear your chemise and I'll roll up my trousers. We can go as deep as your knees, I believe."

She blinked at him in shock. Not only had he just suggested she take her gown off in front of him, he'd also offered to roll up his trousers. Which, while not the most intimate and daring of actions, was quite unusual for Marcus. Since his accident, she'd never seen anything more than his face, part of his neck, and hands. Even last night, he'd insisted on wearing almost all of his clothes. His suggesting he'd bare his feet and expose his legs was quite shocking. Then again, those weren't areas his skin had suffered. "How about we just put our feet in like you said before," she said timidly. She really wasn't sure if she should continue taking her gown off in front of him. He may have seen everything already, but still she deserved some modesty.

He cocked his head to the side. "Is there a problem? Nobody's here to see but me."

"I know," she agreed. "But it would be remarked upon if I was found wading in the stream wearing only my chemise."

"You did it the other day. You even swam."

"But I was alone. You're with me this time. It's different."

"Suit yourself," he said, leaning down to untie his boots. He kicked them off and drew one of his trouser legs up far enough to reveal the top of his stocking.

Emma stood still, watching him as he slid his stocking down his leg and off his foot. She'd seen Marcus barefooted many times as a child, but never as a man. She glanced at his broad foot before shifting her eyes and catching his gaze. "I was just—"

"Curious about my toes?" he teased, digging them into the thick grass.

She shook her head and bent down to remove her own slippers and stockings. "I wasn't staring," she murmured in her defense. She didn't want him to think she had a foot obsession.

"I was only jesting," he assured her softly. "I know your experience with the male form has been highly limited. I don't fault you for being curious."

Removing her stockings, she nodded mutely.

"No need to be embarrassed," he continued, watching her peel off the last bit of her stocking. "I'm rather interested in seeing yours, too."

She rolled her eyes. "Didn't you see enough of my feet and ankles yesterday?"

"A man can never see a woman's anatomy enough." He swept her entire body from head to toe with his intense eyes.

Emma's skin heated under his gaze. "Yes, well, all right, you caught me. I was curious. Are you satisfied now?"

He grinned. "I'm glad I have something that fascinates you."

That's the least of what you have that fascinates me. "Don't give it too much thought," she said with a grin of her own. "I may have been a bit curious, but my curiosity has been satisfied on that score."

"Hmm," he said, slowly standing up. He took off everything except his shirt and trousers. "I suppose then I have nothing left for you to be curious about?"

"No, I don't believe so," she said pertly, standing up next to him. She might still have other curiosities. He just didn't need to know what they were.

"Well, Miss Green," he began, leading her to the water, "I've seen far more of you than just your feet, and I'll gladly admit my curiosity is nowhere near satisfied where you're concerned."

His words caused her heart to race. "And what about me do you find yourself curious about?"

"Everything."

Emma swallowed and used one hand to hold up her skirt so as not to get the hem wet as they stepped into the shallow water. "Everything?" she croaked, the cold water doing nothing to cool her simmering blood.

"Everything," he confirmed. He interlaced their fingers. "See that rock over there?" He pointed to a large rock positioned in the middle of the water with just enough of it above the waterline to allow one person to sit on top of it.

"What about it?"

"We'll walk over there, and you can sit on it."

She frowned. "But the water is too deep between here and there. My skirt will be soaked."

"Then perhaps you'll take it off next time," he said, scooping her up in his arms.

She considered protesting since she knew it must hurt his leg to do so, but instead, she kept her protests to herself and enjoyed the way his strong hands held onto her as he carried her to the rock.

He set her down on the top of the rock and started lifting her skirt up, bunching it around her waist. "What are you doing?" she squeaked, trying to pull the fabric from him.

"Making sure it doesn't get wet." He moved to stand between her parted thighs.

"What of you?" she asked, giving a pointed look to where the water was up to the waistband of his trousers.

He shrugged. "I'm already wet. No use in taking them off now." He positioned her skirt behind her to rest on the rock, exposing a generous amount of her thigh for his view. "You're beautiful," he whispered, bringing his lips to meet hers.

Emma sank her hands into the back of his thick, brown hair and pulled him closer as he deepened the kiss. She was vaguely aware of his hands caressing her thighs before moving up to her face. His tongue brushed the inside of her cheek, and she groaned in response as his fingers found the back of her hair.

Feeling daring, Emma shifted in a way that pressed her swollen breasts more firmly against his chest and her nipples hardened. A second later, she felt a slight tug on her hair and pulled her lips from his.

"Sorry," he murmured, pulling a pin from her hair. "I didn't mean to jerk it so hard." His voice was thick with desire.

"Would you like me to take it down?"

"No." He dropped a series of kisses along her forehead and cheeks. "I'll do it."

She nodded and placed her hands on his broad shoulders. She brought her lips up to kiss along his jaw, and he tensed for a brief second before turning his attention back to her hair. She followed the hard edge of his jaw line with her lips from one side to the other. Slowly, she moved her fingers to the button at the top of his shirt. She slipped it through the hole and pressed a kiss to the part of his throat she'd just uncovered. She darted her tongue past her lips and licked the hollow at the base of his neck where his shirt had once hidden it. He groaned and rested his forehead against her hair at the gesture.

Marcus' palms moved to Emma's cheeks and carefully pulled her face away from where she'd been kissing and tasting the base of his neck. "Let me see you," he rasped, tipping her chin up toward him. His fingers gently combed through her hair and splayed it along her back and over her shoulders.

Emma's breath caught. This was just how she'd imagined he'd look when he took her hair down in her dreams. She reached for the front of his shirt to pull him back closer to her.

He didn't respond the way she'd expected. Instead of stepping closer so she could continue her exploration of his chest, he leaned his head forward and buried his face in her thick hair, using his fingers to massage the back of her scalp. His head lowered and he brought his lips down behind her ear, dropping kisses along her hairline until he reached her neck.

She rolled her head to the side, allowing his lips greater access to her neck. He took advantage and left a trail of hot, openmouthed kisses along the side of her neck until he reached the column of her throat. His lips descended south until they found the plane of her chest, where they greedily moved over every inch of exposed—or only slightly covered—skin her chest had to offer. She sighed as his tongue ran under the edge of her bodice, leaving a warm path in its wake along the swell of her breast.

"Emma," he groaned, his face pressed into the valley of her breasts.

Arching her back, she squeezed his muscled shoulders to keep from sliding off the rock and into the cool stream. "Marcus," she sighed as he brought his right hand up to cup the underside of her breast. To further steady herself, she brought her legs up and wrapped them around Marcus' abdomen, crossing her ankles for support.

His thumb brushed across her swollen breast as his mouth

continued to feather kisses across the top of her chest until he reached her clavicle. Leaving her breast, his hand moved to support her back while his tongue traced the ridge of her collar bone all the way to the ball of her shoulder. His eyes met hers. "We should probably get off this rock."

She nodded and allowed him to pick her up once again to carry her to the soft patch of grass they'd left behind earlier. He set her feet down on the ground and let her go, allowing her skirt to fall back into place. Her gaze slid down his body, noting how his wet trousers clung to his legs in a most revealing way. She took a step toward him, then came to an abrupt stop. "Marcus, is something wrong?"

"No," he said, shaking his head. "Not yet anyway. We need to get you inside and into the drawing room, and quick."

Emma peered over her shoulder and sucked in a sharp, nervous breath when her eyes collided with Drake's carriage rolling up the drive.

Chapter 11

Marcus' mind raced as he prodded Emma toward the house. What was Patrick doing here? He was supposed to be in London. What if Emma accidentally said something about the girls' lessons? He groaned. That would be no accident. Emma was bound to say something to Patrick about the girls and their lessons. She thought she was their governess.

"How long will it take you to put your hair up?" he asked, silently praying she'd say an outrageous amount of time.

"Fifteen minutes," she replied, picking up her pace. "I'll hurry, I promise."

"No need to hurry." Unease settled over him. Fifteen minutes didn't offer him much time to make himself presentable and beat her to the drawing room. "You take your time. I'll talk to him and keep him busy. I've wanted to talk to him about drainage ditches anyway."

She stopped walking and looked over her shoulder at him. "Drainage ditches?"

"You know, those shallow ruts in the ground that run downhill and away from the tenants' houses," he explained as if it were the most fascinating thing in existence.

"I know what they are." She nudged him playfully with her elbow. "But why would he wish to talk about them?"

He waved a hand through the air. "Believe me, he'll be intrigued. He's a viscount, remember? He has tenants just like I do. He likes to talk about this kind of thing."

"If you say so." She stepped aside to let him open the door for her.

He followed her inside and went down the hall to his room, Emma right at his side. "Perhaps you should use a different room just now," he suggested when she stopped outside his bedchamber door and looked as if she was waiting for him to open the door for her.

She blinked up at him. "Why?"

"Because I have no mirrors in there," he said quickly. "I think you'll be all right to walk up the stairs now."

She nodded somewhat sadly and climbed the stairs. He would have stopped to watch her as she went if he hadn't needed to change out of his wet clothes so badly.

As quickly and haphazardly as possible, Marcus put on another pair of trousers. His shirtsleeves, however, were not wet enough to bother changing. He put his stockings on and slipped into his boots before gathering his coat, waistcoat, and cravat. Walking down the hall, he slid his arms into his waistcoat and then his coat. He was certain he looked as disheveled as his friend Alex usually did, he just didn't care. Entering the room, Marcus glanced around to make sure Emma wasn't there yet as his fingers worked a knot in his cravat.

"Patrick, I need a favor," he said without ceremony. "When Emma comes down, she's going to want to talk to you about the girls and their lessons. Please humor her and ask questions."

Patrick blinked his brown eyes at him. "Why?"

Marcus glanced over his shoulder to make sure Emma wasn't in the hallway then closed the door. "In order to get her to stay, I told her you needed her to act as the girls' governess."

A grin broke out across Patrick's face. "That's why she's willing to watch them five out of the ten days she's here? Wait, a governess is supposed to teach every day. I believe I'm being cheated."

"Stop it. There's no time to argue about this. She'll be coming in here in a moment, and she truly believes she's their governess. Please treat her as such."

"Doesn't she find it strange she's tutoring *my* girls at *your*

110

house without ever talking to me directly about it?" Patrick wondered, cocking his head to the side.

"Yes." Marcus sat down and bent forward to tie his bootlaces. "She also found the schedule you set for her odd. However, I've convinced her that's the way you want it because it's only temporary and she believed it, so please keep up with the charade."

"All right. I can do that."

Marcus nearly groaned at Patrick's tone and the mischief in his eyes, but was glad he hadn't when the door suddenly opened and Emma strode in.

Patrick's eyes widened in surprise at the way Emma's bosoms nearly fell out of the front of her dress. "Miss Green, do you often dress that way?" he drawled.

"Patrick," Marcus snapped, sending his friend a warning look.

"Right, well, Miss Green, I've come by today to discuss my daughters." Patrick steepled his hands below his chin. "Would you care to tell me how you feel they're faring with their sums?"

"We haven't gotten that far, my lord," Emma said, biting her lip. "And I should tell you—"

"Don't bother," Patrick said, cutting her off. "Please have a seat." He gestured to an open spot on the settee. "Mathematics was never their mother's chosen academic. I'd hoped they'd have inherited my way with numbers, but it's of no account really. How are they doing with their musical lessons?"

Emma's brows knit together. "Musical lessons?"

"You know, the pianoforte or flute or some other instrument. You have been instructing them on how to play, haven't you?"

"Once," she said, shooting Marcus a curious look. "But Lord Drakely, I should tell you—"

He dropped his head and held up a hand. "Don't," he said, shaking his head. "Let me guess, they cannot play a single note, can they?"

"Well, no. But that's not—"

"I should have known," he interrupted. "I must confess they get that from me. I tried to play the trumpet like Marcus here, and I never could get the sounds to come out right."

"Well, their letters and numbers are good," Emma said softly, clearly trying to make him feel better. "However— "

He groaned loudly. "Don't tell me, they haven't a clue about fashion."

"I don't think that's a problem," she said slowly.

"Phew." He wiped his sleeve across his forehead. "I was afraid I was going to have to fire the maid who dresses them if you were going to criticize the way they dressed."

"Lord Drakely," she said, catching his attention. "You do realize they are only four, eight, and nine, don't you?"

"I know. I even know their birthdays." He smiled as if he were the proudest man on Earth.

"That's good."

"You bet it is. Ask any other lord of the realm, and he'd have trouble. But not me."

Marcus couldn't help noticing the pride showing in the man's face. There was no mistaking the love he had for those three little girls. Emma must have noticed it, too. "That's very nice," she said smoothly. "However, I'd like to talk to you about my post."

"I'd like to, as well," he agreed, sending a wave of dread to wash over Marcus. "Miss Green, I believe my girls would benefit from more of your tutoring, and I'd like to hire you permanently. You may start immediately. Girls," he called. The three girls Marcus hadn't noticed in the corner came over to Patrick. "How would you like to see Miss Green every day?"

Three girls squealed with excitement.

"It's settled then," Patrick said, smiling broadly. "Girls, Miss Green is to be your governess and you shall be staying here at Ridge Water until I'm done in London."

The three little girls ran over to a stunned Emma and clung to her as if she were their saving grace.

Emma swallowed and smiled at them. Marcus could be wrong, but he thought he detected a hint of worry and possibly insincerity in her smile. "Lord Drakely," she said stiffly. "May I speak to you privately?"

"There's no need." He waved his hand in the air. "I've no

doubt about your ability to give my daughters the best education. Although, I mean no offense, but I'd like to contract a seamstress for you."

Emma's eyes went wide and red crept up her face, irritating Marcus to no end.

"Patrick, I need to speak to you for a moment in my study please," Marcus nearly barked.

Patrick stared at him for a moment before gaining his feet. "I'll be back to say goodbye, girls."

"What are you doing?" Marcus demanded once the study door closed.

Patrick smiled. "If she wants to be a governess, I have no problem letting her."

Marcus scowled. "You know full well she wouldn't have stayed with me otherwise. Why did you have to go and do that? Now, when you're done in London she's going to insist on going with you."

"No, she won't," Patrick countered. "She has no desire to leave."

"What makes you so sure?"

"She tried to quit on me half a dozen times in there. Not wanting my girls to suffer Mrs. Jenkins' company alone for a week, I wouldn't let her."

Marcus' jaw dropped. He raked his hand through his hair and tried to remember the previous conversation. Had Emma tried to resign? He honestly couldn't remember. Patrick had interrupted her so much, it was hard to tell. Anyway, what would happen in a week if she didn't go with Patrick? Would she go back to Caroline's? She'd have to. She couldn't stay here. His heart sank. She could never stay here. "Thank you," he said solemnly, falling into a chair.

"For what?" Patrick asked, crossing his arms.

"Securing me another week with her," Marcus replied, mentally planning what he'd do with her for that week.

"A week?" Patrick echoed in disbelief. "I think it'll be longer than that. Besides, I should be the one thanking you for letting my girls stay here for a week."

Marcus nodded, not really listening to his friend's words. His thoughts were filled with more days like today. Perhaps tomorrow he'd take her for a picnic—

"You're not planning to expose my girls to anything inappropriate, are you?" Patrick asked, breaking into Marcus' thoughts.

He sighed. With three little girls underfoot, he'd not get more than five minutes alone with Emma to *do* anything inappropriate. "I'll be on my best behavior," he lied to Patrick, once again his mind trying to think up situations where he could have Emma all to himself.

"Good. I need to say farewell to the girls then leave for London." Without waiting for another word from Marcus, Patrick left.

*****

Emma tried to smile as the three girls bounced around, asking her what lessons she had planned for them. It was odd they were interested in lessons when just two days ago they appeared dreadfully bored. She'd tried to tell Drake she'd not be available for the post after all. Now that she'd told Marcus she loved him and he admitted the same feelings for her, it was just a matter of time before they married. She shouldn't get too attached to Drake's girls. She sighed. It was only for a week. When he returned from London, she'd resign. Just not verbally, of course. She'd have to write him a letter of resignation if she actually wanted him to let her go.

"All right, young ladies," she said, standing up. "Let's go see what's in the nursery, shall we?"

"I imagine it's full of dust and old books," Drake offered from the door.

Emma whirled around and faced the smiling man. She stepped back as he told his girls he'd see them in a few days and reminded them to be on their best behavior for Miss Green.

"Actually, they'll need to be on their best behavior for me," Marcus intoned. "Emma, Mrs. Crofter is here to see you now. I'll take Celia, Helena, and Kate to work on their first official music

114

lesson."

Drake chuckled. "Do you have some cotton for your ears?"

"No, and I don't believe I'll need any," Marcus said smugly. "The other day I let them make merry with several of the spare instruments around here. You'd be surprised at the skill these three possess, especially, little Katie over there."

Drake shot a disbelieving look at his youngest daughter, who smiled like a court jester.

"Say, why don't we put on a performance for you when you come back next weekend?" Marcus suggested, an amused grin on his lips.

Emma nearly choked on her laughter. What she remembered from the time Marcus let them play those instruments, those girls were awful. Not that she was musically inclined, but one didn't have to be in order to identify others who weren't.

Drake nearly growled but then smiled at his girls. "Very well," he agreed, shaking his head ruefully. "I suppose I deserve that."

Emma didn't know what he was talking about. However, Marcus did, because he said, "Excellent. I shall work with them an hour a day so they can play the perfect song for their papa upon his return next weekend."

Nodding, Drake agreed and said one more quick goodbye to his daughters before leaving.

Marcus slipped out of the room for a minute and came back in with Mrs. Crofters. "Miss Green," he said, looking at Emma. "Mrs. Crofters is going to do your fittings in here while I practice music with the girls. I hope that's all right."

"That's perfect," she said with a grin, stepping back so two footmen could bring a dressing screen into the room. It wasn't appropriate for Marcus to be alone with the three young girls, nor alone with her. It was an odd situation, but if they all stayed in the same room with Mrs. Crofters present and able to go to both sides of the screen, it made the whole situation as acceptable as it could possibly be under the circumstances.

The girls ran over and each grabbed an instrument they fancied. Celia chose Olivia's old three-stringed violin (the fourth one was broken, of course). Helena decided she wanted to plunk out an awful tune on the pianoforte. Kate thought it necessary to pierce all their eardrums with the flute, while Marcus accompanied them on the trumpet. Emma slipped behind the screen and disrobed with the help of Mrs. Crofters.

An hour later, all three adults were ready to quit the room and see Cook for a tonic for headaches then take a nap; all three little girls, on the other hand, only left the room after having their chosen instruments pried from their little fingers and receiving a promise of a double portion of dessert if they didn't so much as play or sing another note until this time tomorrow.

Chapter 12

Getting time alone with Emma proved harder than Marcus originally thought. Following her fitting, she'd taken the girls up to the third floor to become familiar with Ridge Water's nursery, and he didn't see them again until dinnertime.

After they ate, she helped them bathe and dress for bed before retiring to her room for the night.

Much to his dismay, on Monday he only saw her at breakfast and dinner.

At nine that night, his arms ached to hold her, his lips yearned to kiss her, and his eyes longed to see her so much so that his feet set out to find her.

By ten, he'd nearly given up his search when the door to the drawing room creaked open and a tired Emma stepped out. "Good evening, Marcus," she said, looking slightly surprised, but mostly tired.

"Why aren't you in bed yet?" He put his arms around her and pulled her to him.

"I had to come up with a lesson plan for tomorrow." She rested her head against his chest and closed her eyes.

He rubbed her back with long, even strokes, slightly swaying her. "Do you need any help, or do you have it all done?"

"It's done," she said with a sigh.

He bent his head lower and kissed her soft lips. She responded instantly and opened her mouth to allow him entry. His hands tightened their hold on her as his tongue tangled with hers. She sighed against his mouth and he pressed his hard body against her soft, yielding one.

Her hands reached up and found his hair, twirling her fingers into the back. He groaned as she boldly pressed her hips into him, slowly grinding against his erection. Where had she learned to do *that*? "Emma."

"I love you, Marcus," she whispered as his lips trailed kisses from her lips down to her ear.

He parted his lips and lightly nipped her skin. "I love you, too," he replied, dying to show her just how much, even though he knew he couldn't.

"Miss Green," a four-year-old Kate called from somewhere on the stairs, startling them both.

"Yes." Emma stepped back from Marcus. Her face was flushed and her hair was all out of sorts.

Kate walked further down the stairs. "I had a bad dream." She wiped a tear from her eyes.

Emma walked up to the girl and picked her up. "How about we go to the kitchen to see if we can find something to eat, and you can tell me all about it," she said, holding the girl against her breast.

"Mind if I join you?" Marcus asked.

"Only if you carry me." Kate reached out to him.

Marcus smiled and took the little girl from Emma. "Lead the way, Miss Green."

Emma flashed them a smile and strode down to the kitchen. Marcus put the little girl down in one of the chairs surrounding the small round table. He took a seat next to her while Emma dug through the pantry until she found some treats for them to eat.

She set them down in the middle of the table and took the seat directly across from Kate. Marcus took one of the biscuits and handed it to an anxious Kate. She took the treat from him and ate it without another word.

Marcus grinned at her then turned his gaze to Emma. She was looking down at Kate, her brows knit in worry. Under the table, Marcus extended his foot in her direction and brushed her calf with his.

She looked his way and he immediately turned his attention to Kate. Though he wasn't looking at Emma, he could feel her eyes on him—he continued to brush her leg with his.

Emma reached out and took a biscuit. His gaze trained on Kate, he nearly jumped out of his skin when the side of Emma's foot touched his ankle and made a slow, provocative trail up to his knee before descending back to his ankle.

His eyes shifted to Emma. She wasn't looking at him now. Her foot was still resting on top of his, but her eyes were resting on Kate. "Would you like to talk about your dream?" she asked, reaching forward to push a stray lock of Kate's hair off her forehead.

The little girl shook her head.

"All right," Emma said slowly. "Do you need anything to drink? Some water or milk, perhaps?"

"Milk," Kate said, snatching another biscuit.

"Milk it is." Emma left the room then came back with a little container of milk. She poured the little girl half a glass. "Will that be enough?"

Kate eyed the glass for a second before nodding. "It should do."

Marcus and Emma both chuckled at her expression. "Would you like some, too?" Emma asked him.

He shook his head. He wasn't much of a milk drinker. Water, tea, and lemonade were his preferred drinks.

Emma sat back down, and the three sat quietly while the little girl finished her snack. After she was done, Marcus watched as Emma escorted Kate back up the stairs to put her to bed. It would likely be tomorrow night before he got to see Emma again, he thought sadly, walking to his bedchamber.

Fortunately for Marcus, it wasn't an entire day before he saw her again. After breakfast the next morning, she asked him if he had any mounts which would be suitable for the older girls. He closed his eyes and inwardly cringed. Ever since his accident, he'd been wary of horses and had only ridden when absolutely necessary, never for pleasure.

"I believe so," he said at last. He had a few old nags which were so slow, Kate could move faster than they could.

Together the five went to his stables, and he informed Larson, his head groom, that Celia and Helena would like to learn to ride. Larson ordered a groom to have two horses saddled. "Wot about the lil one?" he asked, glancing down at Kate.

"She's too young," Marcus said automatically.

"Fer a big hoss, pr'aps. But we gots tat pony," Larson said with a grin.

"A pony?" Kate shrieked excitedly.

Marcus rolled his eyes. "She's only four. I don't think it's wise."

Emma touched his arm. "Can we speak for a minute?"

Marcus followed her over to the fence and thought up his defense. He knew what she was about.

"Now, Marcus," she said, squeezing his arm affectionately. "I don't see the harm in letting her ride."

"You wouldn't," he muttered.

She frowned at him. "I know about your accident. Everyone here does. But that horse you were riding wasn't trained, and you were riding much faster than you should have been. I've seen Polly. She's harmless."

"Polly?"

"The pony," Emma answered offhandedly. "The point I'm trying to make is that she's not going to get hurt."

"How do you know?" he countered, pinning her with his stare.

She dropped her gaze. "Caroline and I have let Celia and Helena ride Polly before."

"When?"

Emma's eyes came back up, and she suddenly found something just beyond his left shoulder very fascinating. "I don't know," she admitted at last, hesitation and uncertainly evident from her tone to her stance. "It's been a while. Two years or so. Polly is perfectly harmless."

He continued to do nothing but openly stare at her. He couldn't hide the agitation that filled his voice when he finally spoke. "Then if you've made this kind of decision before, why did you even bother to ask my permission today?"

"I'm sorry, Marcus. Caroline assured me it was all right."

Pursing his lips, he said, "Well, it wasn't. In the future, nobody gets on a horse at this estate without my knowledge, understood?"

"Yes, my lord," she agreed with a mock salute. "But what about Kate riding Polly today?"

He glanced off into the distance for a moment before turning his attention back to her. "That's why you asked about suitable mounts for the others. You'd already planned for Kate to ride Polly," he stated flatly.

She blushed at his accusation. "I won't deny it."

Marcus clenched his fists and ground his teeth until his jaw hurt. He unclamped his jaw and blew out a deep, pent-up breath. "She can ride Polly today. But Larson is going to hold those reins, and if something happens to her, Polly's off to the glue factory, Larson's sacked, and I've yet to think of your punishment."

Grinning and nodding, she said, "Agreed. But no need to think up a suitable punishment for me. Nothing's going to happen."

"I hope not." Turning to Larson with a resigned expression, he said, "All right, saddle her up."

***

Emma glanced at Marcus and bit her lip nervously. Perhaps she should have left Caroline's name out of it when she told him Polly had given the girls rides before. She shook her head. Nothing for it now. She watched as Larson helped Kate mount Polly. The little girl turned back to smile at Marcus with a playful grin only a four-year-old could have. He had to soften at that expression of joy, she thought as she reached over and rubbed his forearm affectionately.

"She'll be all right, Marcus," Emma whispered. Marcus had extreme reservations where horses were concerned, and rightfully so. But he couldn't be so worried all the time. It wasn't good for him.

He sighed and wrapped his arm around her. "I'd never forgive myself if something happened to one of them."

"I know." She pressed closer against him.

"Would you like to go sit over in the shade while we wait?" He gestured to some chaises and a table that were set up in viewing distance of the stable yard.

"I'd love to." She let him escort her over to the table and frowned down at the table top. "Is this a chess table?" Of course it was a chess table. She may not know how to play, but she did recognize the black and white squares.

"Do you like to play?" He dropped into his chair and stretched a leg out.

"I don't know how," she admitted, tracing the grooved outline of the chess table with the pad of her index finger.

He slid a drawer in the side of the table out and started picking up the pieces. He handed her the white pieces and set the black pieces in front of him. "Put yours in the same position I put mine. When we're done placing them, I'll show you which two you'll need to switch, then I'll explain the rules."

She knit her brows. Switch two? She shrugged and put her pieces down to mirror his. When they were done she said, "All right, now what am I switching?"

"Your king and queen." He pointed to the pieces in question. "Your queen needs to be on her color." When she furrowed her brows again, he explained, "Since you're playing white, she needs to be on white."

"Oh, I understand now," she said, feeling like an imbecile. "Now what?"

He quickly explained how each piece could move and a few of the basic rules. "White always goes first, so you may start, and if you have any questions, just ask."

She glanced up and waved to the three girls who were making their way around the yard. She placed her fingers on the smooth pawn in front of her queen and moved him two places forward, thinking to free her queen for game play. Apparently, besides the king, the queen was the most valuable piece.

Marcus grinned and moved the pawn that was in front of his queen's bishop forward one.

She frowned. What good did that do? Refusing to dwell on it, she moved her queen to rest on the white square right behind her pawn. There. Now her queen was out in a position to move side to side or diagonally to take any of his pieces she wanted to!

In one second, her joy ended when he grabbed his bishop and slid it across the board. "Check," he said, nudging her foot with his under the table.

"Check?" she echoed. "How can you already have cornered my king?"

He used his finger to show her the line that went straight from where his bishop sat on a black square on the side of the board to her king.

"Drat," she said. "I can move my queen back a space and he'll still be safe, right?"

"You could," he acknowledged.

Without another thought, she moved her queen back once space, then watched completely dumbfounded when he slid his bishop from the side to capture her queen, informing her she was once again in check. She sighed. "This isn't looking very good for me."

"No, it's not. But I'll give you a hint—"

"No, thank you," she said, cutting him off and using her bishop to capture his.

He grinned. "Very good."

Five minutes later, Marcus set his queen down and grinned at her. "Checkmate."

"I have no idea why Caroline likes this so much," she muttered in defeat.

"It's fun if you know how to play. You're just learning. One day, you'll think it's fun."

"I doubt it," she argued, glancing to the girls who appeared to be having too much fun to stop.

Marcus picked up the pieces and put them back into the drawer. Inside the drawer were thick, circular chunks of rocks she recognized as the pieces for draughts. "Would you like to play?"

"Not really." Board games never seemed to end in her favor.

"What if you could win?" he asked, an unusual gleam in his eyes.

She waved her hand through the air. "Don't bother. It can't be any more fun for you to play against someone you can so easily beat than it is for me to play against someone so much more advanced than I am." She was speaking mainly about her lack of skill at chess, but her skill at draughts was just as bad.

"You make a good point. However, I was going to suggest we play a little differently." He winked at her.

"What did you have in mind?"

He leaned back in his chair and crossed his arms. "Before I tell you, you have to either agree to play or not."

A shiver skated down her spine at the expression on his face. "All right, Lord Sinclair, I'm game. What are the rules?"

"A boon," he said simply, placing his twelve pieces down on the black squares.

"You mean, for every time you capture one of my pieces, you get to request a favor from me?" she asked. She was certain to get the bad end of this arrangement.

"No. Quite the opposite, actually. If I capture your piece, you get to ask me for a favor. And if you capture one of mine, I get to ask a favor of you."

A sly smile took her lips. "You're scheming. I just know it. All right, we'll play."

"Excellent. You go first." He grinned and stretched his legs out under the table, his ankle brushing hers.

Startled, she looked up at him and couldn't decide if he'd done it on purpose or not. She inwardly shrugged off the notion and moved one of her front pieces forward.

Still leaning back in his chair, Marcus reached a hand out and mirrored her move.

She frowned. What was he about? She reached her fingers forward to move a different draught.

He grinned at her and moved his draught in a way that gave her an easy jump without leaving her piece in a position to be jumped in return.

Emma cocked her head to the side and looked at him curiously. He was definitely planning something. Moving her piece to jump his, she glanced up at him and asked, "Now what would you like me to do?"

"A kiss."

Her eyes grew round. "But we're in public," she protested weakly. She wanted to kiss him. Badly. But not in front of others.

"You took my draught, Emma. You owe me."

"I know," she admitted with a sigh. She leaned forward and pressed a quick, chaste kiss on his cheek.

He grinned. "I'll accept that. My move." He rested his elbow on the table and leaned his cheek against his hand, studying the board. Under the table, the side of his foot slowly brushed the side of Emma's calf. "Hmm, I just don't know where to go," he drawled, trailing his foot all the way to her knee.

"Marcus," she warned. "People can see."

He flickered a glance to the stable yard. "They're too busy to notice."

Emma looked over to the girls and the grooms. They did look busy. She turned her gaze back to Marcus and tried to appear as casual as possible while she stared at him. His foot on her calf was driving her to a nervous distraction, and the more he continued to touch her thus, the more she wanted to squirm in her seat. She blew out a breath and a devious thought entered her mind.

Keeping her left leg in place where he could continue to brush his foot against it without realizing what was going to happen, she kicked off her slipper and raised her right foot slowly into the air until it connected with Marcus' knee.

Marcus jumped slightly and his eyes shot to hers. "What are you doing?"

"Nothing." She twisted one of her blonde locks around her fingers in a horrible display of mock tedium.

"Well, stop it."

She smiled at him and kept her foot resting on his knee. A minute later, he put his finger on one of his pieces, ready to move it. Catching him unaware, she slid her foot forward along the inside of his thigh.

He let go of the piece mid-slide and grabbed hold of her foot. "Emma," he warned. His eyes looked different, but she couldn't decide how.

"Yes?" she asked, wiggling her toes under his grip.

"I've warned you."

She shrugged. "I know. I chose not to heed it."

"Typical," he muttered. "Now, move your foot, so I can take my move."

"I don't think so," she said airily, bringing her left foot up to rest on his other thigh.

His head jerked up from where it had been resting on his hand and his other hand went down to grab her second foot. "I can't play like this."

She wasn't sure if he was talking about with having her feet on the inside of his thighs, or because his hands were occupied holding her feet. "Let go of one of my feet then," she suggested with a sweet smile.

He groaned. "That will not be happening."

"Suit yourself." She pushed her foot against his strong hold.

His grip tightened on her feet, not hurting them, but firm enough she wasn't able to move her feet further up to her goal.

She frowned at him. "Are you going to move your piece? I don't believe this current position is very fitting for a military man," she teased, glancing pointedly at the piece that was occupying the corners of four different squares, because Marcus had stopped moving it in order to grab her wandering foot.

"You can move it for me. I want him to be at B-5, please."

"Excuse me, what?" She frowned at him. She had absolutely no idea what he was talking about.

He sighed. "Sorry, I forgot. That was a chess term." He rolled his eyes and frowned. "You know where I want him, Emma. Just move him, please."

Her eyes widened and she shook her head.

"Why not?"

"First, I know how sensitive you are about people touching

your game pieces while you're playing," she said sweetly. "Second, I'm not going to do all the work in our game."

He swore under his breath. "You'll never forget that, will you?"

"No. I shall go to my grave forever remembering how angry you got with me when I was eight and straightened one of the pins before you rolled your ball in skittles. However, to be fair, your ball was nowhere near that pin. You wouldn't have knocked it over whether I'd touched it or not," she informed him primly.

"Perhaps. But all the same, you distracted me."

Emma hid her grin at the memory of how red his face had gotten when he lost that day. "All right, I take full responsibility for your losing skittles that day. Now, would you please move your piece?"

He scowled. Releasing her foot and squeezing his thighs together as quickly as he could, he finished pushing his draught to the desired square.

"Not fast enough," Emma taunted, pushing her foot closer to his waist.

"You do know they can see you?" Marcus used his head to point in the direction of the stable yard while he moved his piece.

She shrugged. "As you said, they're too busy having fun to notice a couple of dullards like us."

Marcus gritted his teeth and grabbed her wayward foot. "Move your piece."

Right. She'd forgotten it was her turn. Carelessly, she moved a piece and flashed him a smile. Her interest in the game on top of the table was nothing in comparison to the game going on under the table.

Frowning, Marcus looked at the board. "Did you even pay attention to where you were moving?"

"No." She smiled and gently rubbed both of her heels against the inside of his muscled thighs.

"Clearly," he replied with a snort. He moved another piece. Emma didn't know where; she was too busy pushing her foot all the way up until her toes rested against his groin. "You'd better be careful." His low, deep voice mixed with his serious expression gave her pause.

"Don't worry; I know what I'm doing." After having read Lady Bird's memoir, she had a very good idea of exactly what she was doing, and she had every intention of using her newfound knowledge to torment him as much as he tormented her in her dreams.

"I don't think you do." His voice was still unusually low and husky. "Now, move."

"Yes, my lord." She pressed her foot more firmly against his undeniable arousal, and moved her foot slowly up and down, once, twice. "I moved. Now it's your turn," she said, smiling coyly.

"You little minx," he said raggedly. He leaned forward and reached under the table as his eyes looked over the board. A second later, he leaned back in the chair and being just as careless as she had been earlier, he thoughtlessly pushed one of his pieces to a vacant square.

She knit her brows. Did she really have to move again? She hadn't even moved a piece last time. She leaned forward and moved one of her currently unimportant pieces forward. What did she care if she won or lost? She just wanted to prolong the game as long as possible, and making inane moves was the best way to do that.

"My turn."

Slightly disappointed that Marcus' voice had returned to normal, she sat back and waited for him to make his move while using the side of her foot to lightly stroke his erection.

Suddenly, something touched the insides of both of her thighs. Her eyes jerked to Marcus, and she clamped her legs together. "What are you doing?"

"Moving." The roguish grin he wore left no doubt that he wasn't going to stop moving his foot between her legs until he reached the top.

"Stop," she said with a squeak. "You can't put your foot up my skirt."

"Why not?"

"Because it's not proper."

He laughed. "And it's proper for you to have your feet on *my* privates?"

A blush stained her cheeks and she started to remove her feet. His hands grabbed her feet and stopped their descent.

"What are you doing?" she asked.

"I like them there," he admitted. "Now, leave them and I'll return the favor."

Her eyes grew wide. "This isn't a good idea."

"No," he agreed. "It's an excellent idea."

A slightly shocked, and certainly unladylike, noise escaped Emma's mouth when Marcus' foot reached its intended destination. "Marcus," she began, her voice unusually high-pitched, "you must stop."

He chuckled, presumably at the way her voice squeaked at the word *stop*. "I don't think so. You tortured me. Now, I'm going to do the same to you. It's only fair."

Since when had Marcus given a fig about being fair? "This is definitely not fair," she protested as his foot pressed boldly against her tender flesh, only the thin layers of his stockings and her drawers separating them. Even after reading that book, she hadn't realized how sensitive and pleasurable intimate touching could be for a woman.

"I think it's fair." He motioned to the board. "Your move, I believe."

She clenched her teeth, willing herself not to sigh at sensations he was sending through her body. She swallowed and looked down at their game. She couldn't concentrate even if she wanted to. Steeling herself the best she could, she glanced at his rigid face and moved her foot against him. She'd nearly forgotten her power over him. A smile took her lips as she increased the pressure and used the sides and bottom of her foot to move up and down his rigid erection.

A moment later, his foot stilled and his eyes locked with hers, his jaw clamped tight. "You'd better stop," he whispered harshly, taking hold of her foot in a tight, stilling grip.

Her eyes searched his face, and she realized right then she'd almost driven him to the brink Lady Bird had described in her little tome. She smiled to herself. That little book was invaluable. If this simple action was accurate, chances were the rest of that rather detailed book was, too.

She slowly removed her feet, reveling in the knowledge that she could affect him so.

His foot, however, was not so quick to retreat.

"Marcus, move your foot," she insisted.

He shook his head. "Not yet."

"Marcus, not like this." She pushed at his foot.

He brought his foot out from under her skirt and set it on top of her thigh. "Since when did your thinking become so depraved?"

Her face burned and she couldn't think of a single thing to say.

Marcus cleared his throat and gestured to the board. "It seems you're in a position where your only move is to jump my man." He pointed to the two pieces in question. "And once you do, I'll ask for my boon, which consequently, involves my foot being in your lap."

She rolled her eyes and moved her draught. "Your boon?"

"Rub that foot, would you?"

Chapter 13

Marcus won draughts. Of course. Emma had always been terrible at board games. He walked through the hall on the way to his study. He opened the door to the dimly lit room, fell into the comfortable chair behind his massive desk, and breathed a sigh of relief. Thankfully none of the girls had been injured on the horses today.

He couldn't believe Emma and Caroline had taken it upon themselves to allow those little girls to ride Polly without his permission. He twisted his lips in agitation and sighed again. It was little wonder they'd done that without consulting him. He had hardly been involved with much of anything over the past years. Between not wanting to leave the estate and dealing with Olivia and her antics, he'd been distant. Everyone had learned to make decisions without him.

He leaned forward and picked up his account ledger. One thing that hadn't gone on without him was estate business. He reviewed the numbers and made notes of which tenants were in debt. He didn't like throwing people out. Usually he'd find an alternative way for them to pay their rents. It looked like tomorrow was shaping up to be a busy day indeed. He needed to visit three different tenants to make arrangements for their past due rent.

Closing his ledger, he spotted a stack of missives Chapman had left for him on the corner of his desk. Chapman was an interesting sort when it came to certain tasks. Marcus snatched them up and leaned back to flip through the stack. Marcus may not have a lot of butler-type tasks for the man to do, but the ones he did have, Chapman accomplished far better than most. Including how he arranged Marcus' correspondence, always putting the newest letters at the bottom of the stack instead of the top so Marcus would read them in the order they'd been received. Which was the way they were meant to be read, wasn't it? He smiled at the man's strange tendency then scowled down at the letters. He hated letters. He hated reading them. And he abhorred writing them.

Dropping the top two to the floor in disinterest, he recognized the writing on the outside of the third as Olivia's. Not sure whether to be relieved she had written or to groan at what the missive might contain, he turned it over and broke the seal.

Dear Marcus,
America is beastly. I hated the voyage here. It was absolutely miserable. I was sick every single second of every single day.

He rolled his eyes. She'd have been sick every single second of every single day had she been on land or sea with her condition.

Anyway, I am here now and I do not know how long I shall stay. Besides the bizarre way things are done here, Mr. Saxon is not at all what I expected in a husband. He is loud, rude, insensitive to my sensitive needs, and to be honest, his looks are quite lacking! If it weren't for that horrid trip across the ocean, I'd board a ship tomorrow and return home at once.
Perhaps after this creature removes itself from my innards, I shall do just that. Actually, that is an excellent plan. Please book passage for the first week of December. I should be well enough to travel by then, I should think.

Marcus ground his teeth. She hadn't changed a bit. She was just as selfish as ever. She didn't have to come out and say it, but he'd wager every pence to his name she meant passage for one. Well, she was about to learn a hard lesson. If she wanted to return, he'd pay her passage. But she was not coming back without Mr.

Saxon and her child.

I suppose that is all I have to say for now. I'll be sure to write you more regularly now that I'm settled.
Yrs,
Olivia

Marcus scowled and put the paper down. He frowned when his eyes fell on the next letter in the stack. It was another letter from Olivia. He tossed it on the floor with the others he had no desire to read. He turned his eyes back to the next letter and his frown deepened. Olivia again. He tossed it on the floor. Olivia again.

He sighed. Using his thumb and forefinger, he went through the stack. Olivia. Olivia. Olivia. Olivia. He tossed more than twenty letters on the floor before finding one from Alex. He quickly scanned the missive and jotted a note in response.

Sighing, he glanced down at all the letters on the floor and bent to pick up the most recent letter from Olivia. Perhaps she'd changed her mind and was willing to accept her new life.

Marcus,
I'd say I'm worried about your safety due to your lack of response. However, I know that's not the case. You're probably just dandy, enjoying your perfect life while I'm left to suffer the sickening attentions of Mr. Saxon in the wilds of a place called Virginia! I tell you, it's horrid here. People are so rude and barbaric they make Mr. Saxon appear refined. Which, as we both know without question, he is not! He is nothing but a filthy commoner who makes me cringe whenever I have to so much as glance in his direction.
But not to worry, I shall return, Marcus. With or without your help. I demand you forward me the funds so I may book my own passage since you're so unwilling to book it for me.

He crumpled up the paper without reading the rest and threw it in the direction of the rubbish bin. He'd read enough of her stupidity.

Taking out a piece of paper, he inked a quill and positioned himself to write a letter.

Dear Olivia,

My situation has changed. I'll not be able to send you the funds to book your passage. If you truly must return, then ask Mr. Saxon to pay for your passage from the generous dowry I gave to him. Otherwise, learn to accept the consequences for your actions and be content with a husband and the impending birth of your first child. There are many people in this world who envy you and your situation.

He jerked his hand away from the paper. What was he doing? She'd never get past his lie about not having the money to send her passage to read the rest. He tossed the paper on the floor and grabbed another sheet.

Dear Olivia,

I'm glad to hear you're faring well and your husband is treating you as he ought. Please be sure to write again after the birth of my niece or nephew.

Yrs,

Marcus

He smiled thinly as he sealed the paper with hot wax and stamped it with his signet ring. Olivia wasn't likely to take kindly to his response, but for the life of him, he couldn't seem to force himself to care. After all the rotten things she'd done to others in her lifetime, a little misery was her due.

"You look rather pleased with yourself," Emma said from the doorway.

His head snapped in her direction. "I am."

"Why do I get the impression you're doing something naughty?" She took a seat on the settee by his desk.

"Perhaps because you want me to do something naughty," he suggested, wiggling his eyebrows at her suggestively.

She shook her head. "No, not really. I was worried about you when you didn't make it to dinner tonight."

His eyes shot to the clock on the mantle. How had he missed dinner? Had he spent that much time in here with his accounts and useless correspondence? He shrugged. "Was it good?"

"I'd say so." She looked down at the scattered letters at his feet. "What have you been doing in here?"

"Wondering how exactly Olivia and I are related."

She giggled. "You know, it's interesting you say that. I've always wondered as well."

He shook his head. "I once overheard Caroline mumble something to that effect, too."

Emma grinned. "I've heard her openly question it on more than one occasion."

"Do you and Caroline talk much anymore?" he asked, letting his gaze travel down her body, lingering at her breasts for a moment before dropping to her hips.

"I suppose so. I try not to bother her too much though."

"Because she's married?" They'd obviously talked at some point since Caroline had married or else Emma wouldn't have known how to tease him in such a manner earlier this afternoon. He hardened instantly at the memory. Who knew her foot could get him so excited? But then again, it was just a part of Emma; no matter what, Emma could always get him excited. He shifted uncomfortably in his chair.

Emma looked curiously at him. Obviously he'd missed her answer.

"Did you like staying with Caroline?"

"Of course. We rub along very well. It was kind of like having a sister," she said easily, then froze and bit her lip. "Sorry, I didn't mean that how it sounded."

He smiled at her. "Emma, it's all right. I know you have a sister. I may not personally care for her, but I know she exists. I also know, from experience unfortunately, that sometimes our sisters behave poorly, but because they're our sisters, we forgive them and love them anyway. I don't hold your love for Louise against you in any way."

She swallowed and met his eyes again. "Between Louise and Olivia, I don't know who's worse," she teased with a thin smile.

He knew. Louise was worse by far. But perhaps he was biased. Olivia said and did dastardly things, but she'd never gone nearly as far as Louise. Well, perhaps that depended on who one asked. Putting aside everything Louise had done to him in the past, her actions still outdid Olivia's. Marcus had no doubt the reason Emma was living with Alex and Caroline had something to do with that ugly bruise he'd seen on the underside of Emma's breast. Unfortunately, he knew she'd never confide in him what had happened. It was just as well she wouldn't, because he couldn't do a thing about it.

If he confronted Hampton, who he had no doubt was the filthy bastard who'd put it there, he'd have just as good as admitted to having slept with Emma. For how else would he have seen it? Then her reputation would be shredded, and he'd have condemned her to a life of shame and embarrassment, all because of his temper. A sharp crack suddenly rent the air, and Marcus flinched.

"Gracious, Marcus, must you break all your quills?"

He glanced at the broken quill he'd forgotten was in his hand then to the quill he'd broken last week when Patrick had been over. With Patrick, he'd been able to pretend not to notice, but with Emma's laughing green eyes staring at him, he couldn't. Tossing the two pieces on his desk, he forced a smile. "I forgot I was holding it."

"I bet you did." She stood up and walked up behind him. "You're awfully tense," she muttered, placing her hands on his stiff shoulders.

Willing his body to relax and let go of the mounting tension he felt when he thought of Emma's poor treatment at the hands of her only living family member, he allowed her to rub his tight shoulders and neck. "That feels good," he said inanely as her thumbs and fingers rubbed his tense muscles.

Wordlessly, she rubbed him until his muscles were relaxed and loose. "Do you like your head scratched?" Her fingers sank into the back of his hair, and she used her nails to lightly scratch his scalp.

Who *didn't* like their head scratched? He closed his eyes and leaned his head back to give her better access. He heard her smile. "There's nothing you can do that I wouldn't enjoy."

"Hmm, I'll have to make a note of that," she whispered, leaning forward to kiss his forehead. Her lips stayed against his skin for a few seconds before she moved them ever-so-slightly to the right and kissed him again.

Marcus reached up behind him and grabbed hold of Emma's hands. He used his thumbs to trace the ridges of her knuckles. "Come around," he said gently, lightly tugging on her wrist. After she stepped out from behind his chair, he pushed it back to allow enough room between his legs and the edge of his desk for her to sit on his lap.

Emma looked uncertain when he tried to pull her into his lap.

"I'm not going to hurt you, I promise," he said quietly, pulling her down to his lap.

She nodded once and took a seat, allowing him to wrap his arms around her and pull her against his chest. She smiled at him before bending forward and pressing a quick kiss on his lips.

"You're beautiful." He reached up to pull the pins from her thick hair. While his fingers worked to loosen her hair, he bent his head forward and pressed his lips against hers. He slightly parted his lips and ran his tongue along the seam of hers.

She sighed against his mouth and parted her lips in response. His tongue pushed past her lips and brushed over the sweet inside of her mouth.

Her fingers dug into his shoulders as his tongue tangled with hers. Marcus moved his hand from where it was splayed across her back and slowly moved it around to cup the underside of her thinly covered left breast.

Her body jerked at his touch and she moved back slightly.

"I'm sorry. I didn't mean to push the boundaries."

"You didn't." She averted her gaze.

Understanding dawned as he realized he'd just touched her where she'd been hurt. "I'm sorry," he repeated. "I forgot about..." He looked into her eyes and knew she understood what he was saying.

"It's nothing. I was merely caught off guard."

"Don't lie to me, Emma." He moved his fingers to the buttons on the back of her gown. "I know you're hurt. I didn't think it would still be tender, though."

"It's not. As I said, I was merely surprised."

His fingers stilled and he looked at her. "What happened?"

"What do you think happened?"

"Hampton."

She nodded. "But it's not as bad as you're thinking," she rushed to add.

"Not as bad as I'm thinking?" The man had touched her when he had no right. That alone made it bad enough.

"I mean—" she took a deep breath and clenched her hands— "I'm still a virgin," she whispered at last.

His eyes went wide. He hadn't even thought of the possibility that she wasn't. But the reality of her whispered words came crashing down on him. Emma had always been a strong girl. Always. When they were children, he'd seen her demonstrate the strength of her will many times. He'd just assumed she was still just as stubborn and strong. That was a stupid assumption for him to have made. Hampton was bigger and stronger than she was. He could have easily overpowered her and forced her to submit to him. Marcus squeezed her tight, hating Hampton all the more for what he'd done.

"Marcus, you're hurting me," she whispered. "I promise, nothing happened. I'm perfectly all right. It was the best thing that could have happened."

"That degenerate putting his hands on your breasts was the best thing that could have happened?" His voice could only be classified as a harsh bark.

"Yes and no." She trailed her fingers along the row of buttons that went down his shirt. "As much as I didn't like him touching me, it did provide an escape."

"That's why you went to live with Caroline," he reasoned, rubbing his hands up and down her back.

She nodded once.

"Louise didn't like it, I take it?" He bit the inside of his cheek so as not to grin at the mental image of Louise's world crashing around her ears when she realized her husband's affections no longer were directed at her.

Emma's fingers slipped his top button through the buttonhole. "She didn't care. He's been unfaithful to her for years."

"Then you left on your own," he stated, perplexed. He'd always suspected Emma's living conditions at Louise's were unfit. It just wasn't his place to say anything. He wasn't in a position to offer her help. Until a year ago when Caroline married, there had not been anyone else to whom Emma could turn. That left her with no choice but to stay with Louise and Hampton. He also knew now that Caroline had married, Emma would be reluctant to ask her for help, even if Caroline would do anything in her power to assist Emma. Sometimes it was easier to live with an unpleasant situation than to ask for help. He could understand that. Thankfully, she'd finally reached a breaking point and had gone to Caroline. How unfortunate that had come at the price of being mauled by Hampton.

"Actually, no," she said after a minute.

He took hold of her fingers that were undoing the buttons on his shirt and brought them to his lips. Kissing the tips, he asked, "Then whose idea was it?"

"His." She grinned at him so brightly he forgot if he'd just kissed that fingertip already or not, so he did it again.

"Excuse me? Do you mean to say that after you refused to do what he wanted, he tossed you out?" Not that he was complaining she'd gotten away, but he couldn't help wondering where in the blazes was Louise when all this was happening.

She coughed. "Well, yes, in a manner of speaking that's what happened."

"How so?"

"Does it matter?" A pale blush crept up her cheeks.

He nodded.

Her checks turned redder before she blurted, "I kneed him there." She pointed to Marcus' waist then quickly turned her head.

A bark of laughter broke the air. "Good girl." He squeezed her again. If it had been any other man and for any other reason, he'd have winced and advised her against doing such a thing in the future.

She turned her head back to face him. "You're not scared of me?" A teasing grin was on her lips.

He glanced down where her right knee was nestled right up against his unmentionables. "Not at all. I have no reason to be. I'll never hurt you, nor do I have any intention of forcing myself on you."

She licked her lips. "You wouldn't have to."

Marcus looked into her eyes and saw the truth of her words. His heart clenched. She wasn't his, and she never could be. The pain of that harsh reality hit him like a blow to the heart. He forced a smile in her direction. "Emma, you should probably go up to bed."

She blinked at him. "Pardon?"

"It's getting late. You should go to bed." He forced himself to say it as evenly as he could.

"Oh." A crimson blush stained her cheeks. "All right, I'll go." She gracelessly got off his lap and walked to the door. Was it his imagination or was the sway in her hips more pronounced? She got to the door and stopped. She rested her right hand on the doorjamb and turned her face back to look at him. "Goodnight, Marcus," she said, winking at him.

He shook his head at her odd behavior. Then he enjoyed the view of her backside as she continued to sway her hips while leaving the room.

Once she was down the hall and out of sight, he folded his hands and leaned his head back. For a moment he stared blankly at the ceiling before closing his eyes and thinking what he should do about Emma. He loved her, and for some bizarre reason, she loved him, too. Sadly, that only made things harder.

He clenched his teeth and scrubbed his face with his hands before raking his fingers through his hair. With a huff, he put his hands back on his knees and waited for a solution to present itself.

As the clock struck midnight, the perfect, blatantly obvious solution crept into his head. Satisfied, he shoved to his feet and numbly walked down the hall to his room.

He opened the door and stood frozen in the doorway when his eyes fell on the sight of Emma lying in his bed.

Chapter 14

"What are you doing in here?"

Emma jumped at least a foot in the air at Marcus' shout. Trying to regain her composure, she sat up and clenched her fists together under the counterpane. "Nothing." She swallowed hard, pretending she hadn't just stammered.

"This isn't nothing," Marcus pointed out, crossing his arms.

Clearly she wasn't doing *nothing*. She'd been sleeping. However, Marcus' rigid face and disapproving tone suggested she had better have a better reason for being here other than she was passing by and decided she needed a little nap before heading upstairs to her room.

"Why did you come here?" he asked more softly, taking a seat in the chair close to the door.

She swallowed convulsively. "You told me to go to bed."

"I didn't mean *my* bed."

"But we were..." she shrugged. "Then you said..." Unease settled over her. Not only had she misunderstood his words, but it would seem that Lady Bird's book had been incorrect on the part about a man being unable to resist a scantily clad woman in his bed. Not that she'd been planning to try out that suggestion so soon, but when he'd told her to go to bed...

His unblinking eyes stared at her, making her squirm.

Raising her chin a notch, she slipped out of bed. "I can see that I was clearly wrong."

"Emma," Marcus whispered. He reached out for her hand to stop her before she could leave. "I didn't mean to make you think I intended for you to shame yourself."

She winced at his words. Her parents had always stressed the importance of the wedding before the bedding, but she'd known Marcus nearly her whole life and knew he'd not take her virtue then desert her. That was the only reason she'd not been offended or appalled when he'd told her to go to bed. Though he'd not made a formal proposal to her, she knew he intended to marry her. He loved her. It was that simple. The way she'd reasoned it as she left his study was that his word was as solid as stone. If he'd said he loved her, he did. Since he loved her, he'd marry her. Therefore, she'd been willing to go against everything she'd ever been taught about virtuous young ladies and join Marcus in bed this once before their wedding. And now he'd forever think she was a woman with loose morals.

She pulled her wrist from his hand and angled her blushing face away from him. "I merely misunderstood."

"I do want you that way," Marcus admitted after she'd crossed the threshold. "I desire you more than you'll ever know, but I—"

"Want me to be a virgin on my wedding night," she finished for him, blinking back the tears of mortification that stung her eyes.

"Exactly. You deserve that, Emma."

"Yes, I do," she agreed stiffly, then walked down the hall to the staircase.

Marcus hollered for her to stop, but she didn't; she sped up. She was too mortified by his rejection to stop and listen to whatever it was he was hastily spouting behind her. Of course all proper young ladies were virgins until taken to the bridal bed by their husbands, and as much as she'd always planned to be one of those proper young ladies, Marcus' rejection of her just now hurt far more than any censure she might have endured had she been known as a fallen woman.

Reaching the top of the stairs, she glanced over her shoulder and glimpsed Marcus down at the bottom, struggling to climb the stairs. She pushed away the pang of guilt she felt for running away from him and darted into her room, sliding the lock as soon as she was safely inside.

Uneasily, she walked to the vanity and picked up the silver hairbrush Marcus had given her on her first night here. She brushed her hair and hummed loudly, drowning out the muffled words Marcus was saying when his fist wasn't pounding on the door.

Ten minutes and a hundred strokes later, Emma laid the brush down, blew out the candle, crawled into bed, and pulled the covers high above her head. She instantly felt like a fool. What was she doing? Why was she hiding from him?

With a sigh, she threw back the covers and forced herself to walk to the door. Now that she'd not only presented herself to him like a prostitute, but had also acted childishly, she needed to put her insecurities behind her and face him.

Hand shaking, she unlocked the door and flung it open, causing Marcus to literally fall into her room. "What were you doing?" she asked, narrowing her eyes on him.

"Picking the lock," he explained, grabbing the penknife that had stuck into the wooden floor when he'd fallen inside.

She shook her head. Good thing she'd not been directly in front of the door when she'd opened it. "Were you leaning on it?"

"Yes," he bit off. He used a nearby chest for leverage to push himself to a standing position.

Emma fought back the urge to giggle. Marcus had always intrigued her. "All right. Now, what was it you wanted?" She lit the five candle candelabra that sat on the table next to the bed.

"If you'd not run away from me, you'd know." He sat down the chest and groaned as he simultaneously stretched out his leg.

Guilt flooded her. She should have stayed and listened to him instead of running up the stairs like a ninny. Now, because of her pettiness, his leg hurt. She threw her hair over her shoulder and knelt down in front of him. "Where does it hurt?" She placed her hand just above his knee in the place she usually saw him rub when he was in pain.

"There."

She nodded and rubbed his leg, taking note of the large, hard knot under her fingers. "Is this always there?" she asked even though she had a feeling she didn't want to know the answer.

"The knot is always there, it just gets bigger when I use the muscle too much," he answered with a grimace.

She bit her lip. "I'm sorry."

"It's just as much my fault as it is yours." he said with a grunt. His head rolled back and he closed his eyes. "I'm the one who chose to chase you up the stairs even though you clearly had no intention of speaking with me."

She leaned forward and rested her forehead against his thigh. "I was embarrassed."

"I can understand that. My reaction to finding you in my bed wouldn't have inspired any other reaction, I'm afraid."

At least he had that right. "Once again, I'm sorry, I—"

He reached his hand forward and pressed his fingers against her lips to stop her. "Don't. I can see now how my words in the study weren't very clear. I had intended we go to our respective bedchambers, but when I found you—" he shrugged— "I should have handled it a bit better."

That was an understatement. She didn't comment though. Instead, she refused to look at his face as she continued to massage his knotted thigh.

Just as her hands were getting tired, his fingers encircled her wrist and gently tugged.

She looked up. His grey eyes had softened considerably.

"I love you," he whispered with a hint of a smile.

"I love you, too."

"Emma, I'm sorry about our misunderstanding tonight."

Emma closed her eyes. "Can we please not mention it again?"

"Done," he agreed, his body visibly relaxing. "I ought to go back downstairs now."

Nodding, Emma stood up and took a step backward. Suddenly feeling shy about only wearing a chemise, she folded her arms across her breasts and waited for Marcus to stand.

Marcus braced his hands on either side of him and pushed up to gain a standing position. As soon as he was on his feet and tried to take the first step, he stumbled. Muttering an unflattering phrase under his breath, he tried to regain his stand while Emma grabbed onto his arm and shoulder to steady him.

"You're not fit to go back down the stairs."

"I'll be all right." He disengaged himself from her hold and tried to take another step, nearly collapsing as he did.

She shook her head and held onto him again. "No, you're not. Here, you can stay in my bed and I'll go downstairs."

"No. I'll not kick you out of your bed. I said I'll be all right. Just let go of me, please."

"Absolutely not. You'll get in that bed and stay there until morning if I have to tie you there," she said with a smile.

He grinned back. "Touché."

"So we're in agreement, then?" She urged him in the direction of the bed. "Marcus, I've never seen you limp so badly. Do you need me to go get something for the pain from downstairs?"

"No," he said with a wince as he took a step. "I knew this might happen." He closed his eyes tightly and clamped his teeth together as he continued to slowly lumber over to the bed. "I've been doing too much this past week."

She was surprised he'd admitted what she'd known. Since she'd come last week, he'd gone up and down several flights of stairs, carried her around repeatedly, and even playfully wrestled her to the bed. There was no denying he'd been using his leg too much. "Lie down. I'll be back in a minute."

"Where are you going?"

"I'm going to see if there's anything for pain in the kitchen."

He scowled. "There's not."

"How do you know?" She put her hand on her hip.

Marcus shifted against the pillows. "Allow me to rephrase. There's no pain medicine in this house I'll take without it being forced down my throat."

"You've taken a strong dislike to laudanum. I take it you were given enough of it after your fall."

"You're correct. The only reason I ever allowed that vile concoction into this house is because Olivia demanded it on a weekly basis to alleviate whatever was ailing her at the time."

Emma turned her face so Marcus wouldn't see her snicker. "All right, no laudanum. What about a poultice? Would that help?" She turned her gaze back to him and watched as he idly rubbed his leg.

"Don't bother. The pain usually goes away by morning. And if it doesn't, then I'll do something about that unpleasant possibility when the time comes."

"Goodnight, then." She took hold of the door handle to shut it behind her on her way out.

"Wait."

She turned her head slightly in his direction. "Yes?"

"Could you help me first?" He jiggled his foot slightly to draw attention to his boots.

"Right. Can't sleep with your boots on, can you?" She walked over to him and sat down on the end of the bed. "Put them on my lap, it'll be easier to unlace them that way."

He obeyed and watched her as she untied the laces and pulled his boots off. "Thank you."

"You're welcome. Is there anything else you need?" She couldn't force herself to look at him as she asked that question. The only other thing left for her to do was help him remove his clothes, and he'd made it quite clear on several occasions now that he'd not require her help on that score.

"Just one more thing." He removed his feet from her lap so she could stand.

She stood and clasped her hands together in front of her. "What can I help you with?"

He held up his hand and crooked his finger at her. "Come closer," he urged, his face expressionless.

She took a step closer. "What would you like me to do for you, Marcus?"

"You're not close enough yet. I think three big steps should do the trick."

Humoring him, she took three steps in his direction. "Yes?"

Marcus slipped both his hands under his head, interlocking his fingers before looking back up at her. "I don't think I'll sleep very well without a goodnight kiss."

"You're impossible."

He frowned. "Not at all." He reached his right hand out from behind his head and took hold of her hand in his. "Emma, I thought we'd agreed to forget about earlier."

"I didn't say anything."

"You didn't have to," he countered. "Your refusal to kiss me and the tension in your hand told me more than your voice ever would."

She cracked a smile. It would seem she was rather obvious. "All right. One kiss." She leaned forward to kiss his cheek, but his quick hands reached up and framed her face before she could pull away.

"Not yet," he whispered. He pulled her lips back to his and kissed her again. "Don't go back downstairs. Stay here. With me."

Emma shut her eyes. She didn't want to make herself look like a tart again by making assumptions. "It's best I go downstairs."

"No," he said, shaking his head adamantly. "Stay. I'll not dishonor you, I promise."

She smoothed a lock of his hair back from his brow. She knew he'd not dishonor her. The problem was she could very easily dishonor herself if she stayed in the same room with him tonight.

Before she could voice another protest, however, he wrapped his right arm around her waist and pulled her on top of him. "I love the way you feel against me," he murmured before he kissed her again.

Emma's breasts swelled and her nipples hardened against his muscled chest. As Marcus deepened their kiss, she reached up and threaded her fingers through his thick brown hair. Twirling her fingers in the silky strands, she allowed him to roll her onto her back. "Marcus," she sighed.

Marcus' lips left her mouth and left a hot, searing path to her ear then to her neck. She arched her back, granting him better access.

He groaned. Lowering his lips to her shoulder, he used his

thumbs and pulled both straps of her chemise over the crest of her shoulder. His fingers let go of her chemise and his hand moved over to gently cup the bottom of her right breast.

She sighed as his fingers seared her flesh and made it tingle through the thin fabric. Wanting to touch him as intimately as he was touching her, she reached between his arms and quickly undid his waistcoat and attempted to shove it, along with his coat, off his shoulders.

Reluctantly, Marcus removed his hand from the underside of her breast as she pushed his coat and waistcoat off his shoulders, immediately putting his hand back when she was done. Emma settled her hands on his shoulders then lingered down to the hard muscles in the tops of his arms. She marveled at the feel of him. He felt hard as stone, and yet as warm as freshly baked bread.

Marcus' body shifted and his lips traced the top edge of her chemise, bringing her excitement to the next level. She pressed her breast more firmly into his hand and moved her fingers to the front of his shirt to undo the buttons.

Slipping the first three free with great ease, Emma reached her hands inside his shirt to connect with the bare, rough skin of his chest. Marcus pulled back as if she'd touched him with a branding iron. "Did I hurt you?"

He shook his head. "No. They're not sensitive to the touch. A bit itchy at times, but not tender."

"Then why did you jump back?" She looked down and watched as Marcus propped himself up on the bed on one forearm and used his other hand to close his shirt. "Marcus?"

He looked at her, his grey eyes full of uncertainty. "I just prefer not to be touched there."

"That's not an answer."

"Well, it's the only one you're getting."

She closed her eyes and refused to sigh. "Marcus, I know they're there. I don't care."

He looked as if he didn't really believe her. "I care."

"Well, I don't," she said flippantly. "It's a part of who you are."

"Yes, I know." The bitterness in his voice was unmistakable.

"Then what's the problem? They're on your face, too, but you don't go around insisting on wearing a mask. What's the difference?"

His eyes grew hard. "Emma, leave it alone."

She shook her head. "I don't understand you. I love you, Marcus. I always have. Before your scars and after. They mean nothing to me. Why can't you accept that?"

"I have accepted them," he countered, rolling off her and onto his side of the bed.

"I wasn't talking about your scars. I was talking about my love."

"I've accepted that, too." He glanced away as he said it, and she couldn't be sure, but she thought she picked up on a trace of sadness in his tone. "But that does nothing to change the way I feel about..." He shrugged as if that were a sufficient way to finish the sentence.

Trying not to groan in aggravation, she shook her head against the pillow and stared up at the embroidered flowers in the top of the canopy.

Why did he have to be so difficult? She knew the scars were there and didn't find them repulsive the way most would. She loved him, so why should he have insecurities around her?

She rolled on her side, ready to demand some answers from him when she noticed the soft set of his slightly unhinged jaw and heard his soft snores.

Refusing to act like Louise would in this situation by waking him up to argue, she rolled over onto her back and once again studied the needlework on the canopy. Tomorrow was a new day. She'd get her answers then. Even if it meant she had to take a few minutes to consult with Lady Bird's naughty book to determine a sneaky way to have him at her command, she would.

Chapter 15

Marcus was relieved that Emma had believed his act. There was no way he could sleep after everything that had just happened between them, not to mention the horrific pain in his leg.

To Emma it seemed immaterial for him to remove his shirt. She was right. He had nothing to hide. She knew as well as anyone about the scars that covered his arms, chest, stomach, and back. The scars themselves weren't the real reason he had refused to remove his shirt and let her touch him. They only served to remind him once again of what he could never have: Emma. She may say she didn't even see the physical scars that covered the upper half of his body, but she'd care about the rest. That was why the plan he'd developed last night had to work.

He grabbed one of the two pillows under his head and shoved it under his thigh for support. His leg hadn't hurt this badly since right after his accident. He'd certainly been taxing himself too much. Starting tomorrow he'd stay off his leg more, and in the process, put more distance between Emma and himself. Getting too attached to her or allowing her feelings for him to continue would only lead to more heartbreak in the end. He wouldn't avoid her altogether; that would be too obvious. But he'd keep his hands and lips to himself from now on.

Shutting his eyes, Marcus counted forward to one hundred, then backward to one twice before finally losing track of where he was and falling asleep, his hand loosely holding hers.

Emma's stirring woke Marcus just before dawn. Blinking his eyes to get accustomed to his surroundings, he realized Emma was once again lying on his chest and his arms were wrapped tightly around her. He loved the way she felt against him. Since she was asleep, he could fully enjoy her closeness one last time, so he didn't push her away.

"Marcus," she whispered against his chest some time later.

"Hmm?"

She shifted against him to make herself more comfortable, making his discomfort increase tenfold. "I was wondering if you'd take me horseback riding this morning before the girls get up."

His heart thudded in his chest. Why did she want to go horseback riding with him? Did she think him getting on a horse would magically make him forget his past and let go of any ill feelings she assumed he had because of his scars. Pushing his thoughts aside, he said, "Don't you have to see to getting the girls up and ready?"

"No." She rolled off of him and propped her head up on her hand. "Molly's been attending to their needs before breakfast and after dinner."

The smile on her face made the feeling of loss she'd created when she'd rolled off him disappear. "I don't know if I should." He patted his left leg.

"Oh, I forgot," she said with a blush. "How terrible of me. How about on Friday, then? Do you think that will be enough time for your leg to recover?"

Against his better judgment, he nodded. "I think so. But you need to know something." He rolled on his side to face her and tucked a golden hank of her hair behind her ear. "I don't gallop. I rarely ever canter. The most I normally do is a trot. Do you still want me to take you?"

She nodded. "I know it's asking a lot of you. Not that I think you're afraid of horses, mind you. I just thought we could have some time together outside and since I didn't think you'd enjoy walking through the forests overmuch, riding horses seemed the only choice left." She paused and her face lit as if she'd just made some great medical discovery. "Oh wait, I bet you'd rather fish, wouldn't you? You can still stand long enough to do that, can't you?"

"Yes." He reached forward to untwist the thin strap of her chemise that had somehow turned over in the night. "I wouldn't mind taking you fishing one bit. We could go now if you'd like."

Her green eyes lit with excitement and a grin split her beautiful face. "Yes. I just need to put something else on first."

"Just wear that," he said, turning his face away so he wouldn't give into the temptation and kiss her soft lips. He forced himself to stand and immediately clamped his jaw shut as tightly as he could. It wouldn't do to scream the string of vile curses that were sounding in his head from the crippling pain he was feeling in his leg just now. A night's rest had not improved the soreness in his leg one bit. Now, instead of it feeling like a smithy had taken his hammer to it, it felt like the whole bloody smithy's shop had fallen on it. He took a step and winced. Thankfully, Emma had scurried over to the vanity and was braiding her hair. She couldn't see him in pain.

He hobbled over to the door and leaned against the frame. "Emma, I'll meet you out there. I need to make a stop first."

She smiled. "Perfect. I need to do something, too. Just go on and I'll be out there when I'm done."

Nodding, he left the room. He didn't really have a stop to make. He just said that to allow himself some extra time to limp out there without her getting suspicious about what was taking so long and insisting she nurse him back to health. Bitterness washed over him. If he was in a position to marry her, that's exactly what he'd do. He'd lie in bed and let her fuss all over him whether he needed it or not. When he'd been recovering from his accident, nobody had fawned over him, not that he'd wanted them to. But now he understood why the men sent out in the Napoleonic Wars encouraged the troupe of women who followed them. When injured, the attentions of a beautiful and sweet woman could do wonders for a man, physically and in other ways.

By the time Marcus exited the side door of his house, he feared Emma had beaten him to the fishing spot they'd always used in the past. If she had, he'd just make up some excuse about stopping to see if another spot was better for fishing this morning. He pursed his lips. Emma wouldn't believe him if he said that. From the first time he'd brought her out here, he'd always touted the same spot, claiming the position of the trees made the spot ideal any time of the day to go fishing because it was always in the shade. Of course, as any good fisherman would do, he'd walk around and fish other places, too. But as a force of habit, he always started out and ended in the same spot. He highly doubted Emma would have forgotten this fact.

"I'm coming!"

Marcus' head snapped around and his eyes beheld the most beautiful sight a man could see: Emma with pink cheeks and flying hair, wearing nothing but a thin slip of a chemise as she ran barefoot straight to him. He smiled. "Slow down or you'll run right into the water."

She slowed and came to a stop right next to him. "Did you forget something?"

He blinked at her. Damn. Between his limping and thoughts of Emma's tender touches, he'd forgotten to get the fishing gear. "No," he said as evenly as he could. "I thought you were bringing that."

"Oh. I didn't realize. All right, you scout out a good place to stand, and I'll be right back." She turned to walk away, then turned back to him. "Oh, and take off those nasty stockings, would you?"

He glanced down at his stocking-clad feet. He'd been in no position to bend over and put his boots back on in Emma's room and hadn't had time to stop by his room to find a pair of shoes that didn't require bending over to put on. He sat on a rock and effortlessly removed his right stocking before scowling at the left. Perhaps he should have asked Emma to remove his stockings last night when she'd taken off his boots. Now *that* would have been romantic, he thought with a wry smile.

Grinding his teeth to keep from calling out in pain, he bent forward and tried his best not to touch his thigh any more than was necessary. Whoever invented these offending things should be shot. A man shouldn't have to wear a garment that's made to cover his foot, but actually covers his foot, ankle, calf, knee, and then two to six inches of his thighs. It just wasn't manly. At least he wasn't like some men, who wore garters to keep their stockings in place so they wouldn't slip down and look wrinkled, or heaven forbid, fall below the bottom of their breeches and expose part of their knee. Marcus grimaced. That was the advantage of wearing trousers. One's stockings could slip down and roll up around one's ankle (which, to be honest, sometimes they did), and nobody would be any the wiser about it.

"I've got it all, I think," a breathless Emma said. Her flushed face and full arms made him feel like such a cur for making her go fetch the equipment.

"Good. Why don't you bring it over here and I'll get our rods strung."

She nodded and put the creel—or little wicker basket as nearly everyone who wasn't a fisherman liked to call it—down by his feet before handing him the two rods. Taking a seat next to him on the log, she pushed her braid back behind her shoulders. "I'd help, but it's been a while."

He flashed her a smile. "Not to worry. I didn't expect you to remember. Besides, I'll get to redeem myself by rigging it up for you."

"It was never my responsibility to go get the poles, was it?" she asked laughingly as she lightly elbowed him in the side. "I didn't think so."

Grinning, he attached the reel to her pole and pulled the fly line through the guides. "Pick a fly." He handed her his fly box.

She opened it and frowned. "You don't have very many."

He shrugged. "I can only use one at a time." He glanced over at the fly box and counted the flies inside. "The way I see it, we each have three to lose."

"I don't plan to lose mine," she said, raising her nose in the air.

He chuckled. "We'll see about that. Just pick one."

"Hmm," she said as she looked down at the six pathetic flies. She held one up and turned it to the side to inspect the hair and feathers. He'd combined them to make what he considered his best mayfly. "This one." She handed it to him. "If you don't mind, that is."

"Not at all." He took the fly from her and tied it onto the end of her line. "There you go, Miss Green. Go see if you can beat me."

She grinned at him. "You know I can't."

"You never know," he encouraged with a wink.

Emma and Louise had always made a game of trying to catch Marcus' perfect fish while he was still rigging up his pole. Only once had either of them actually gotten a fish on their line in the amount of time it took him to get his rod set up. And though the fish wasn't anything special, it had been to Emma. She'd been ten at the time. He'd rigged her pole first and let her go while he got Louise's ready. As soon as Louise's was ready, she'd snatched it from him and run to the bank to compete with Emma while he tied the fly he'd hidden in his pocket on his line. Just before he'd pulled the last knot, Emma had run back up the bank with the smallest, ugliest fish he'd ever seen.

Upon closer inspection, he'd realized the fish was dead and had been for quite some time by the smell of it. But Emma wouldn't hear a word of it. She'd dangled that stinky fish in his face for a good ten minutes before he'd agreed she was the best angler he'd ever seen.

Marcus grinned at the memory and grabbed a shabby looking fly out of his fly box. It had been more than thirteen years since he'd had the urge to tie any new ones. Even though he'd gone infrequently over the past thirteen years, he'd managed to lose several and hadn't bothered to replace them. He really ought to make more. He'd have more time next week after Patrick reclaimed his spawns. Perhaps he could spend a few afternoons replenishing his selection of flies.

"Finally. I was beginning to think I'd have to hire a Bow Street Runner to track you down," Emma said when Marcus leisurely limped down to the bank and leaned against a tree.

"How many have you caught?"

She shot the worst scowl he'd ever seen in his direction.

Chuckling, he pulled out his line and got ready to cast. "Emma, I've been meaning to ask you something."

Emma started and visibly swallowed. Hard. He squinted his eyes at her. Was she worried? He shook his head and waited for her to look at him again. "Yes?" Her eyes were shiny with what looked like tears but couldn't possibly be. Marcus might be tall and rather unsightly, but he'd never hurt a fly—except maybe the ones he fished with, that is. She had no need to be scared of him.

He cocked his head then shook off the thought. "Just how did you manage to get that dead fish on your line?"

Her mouth fell open and he ducked his head so she wouldn't see his smile. "Oh. Papa caught him the day before, and I hid him in my reticule. Then while you were getting Louise's pole ready, I pried his mouth open a little and shoved my hook inside."

He scrunched his nose and felt the tug of his top lip attempting to curl up in disgust. That was actually a rather gruesome tale. Perhaps next time she pulled a trick like that, he'd not ask for the details. "You wanted to win that badly?"

She nodded. "If you remember correctly, the only person who seemed to ever catch anything was you."

"That's not true." Or was it? He couldn't really remember either way. The only reason he'd ever allowed them to fish with him was because they'd begged to go, and sometimes they'd actually turned out to be good company. He'd once taken his friend Alex and learned what bad company while fishing was all about. Alex had insisted on examining the outside—and inside—of every fish Marcus caught. After that horrific day, he had willingly taken Emma and Louise and hadn't breathed a word of complaint about anything they had done. "It doesn't really matter, does it?"

"I guess not. Perhaps I'm not doing it right."

"Your form looks right to me," Marcus said without even looking at her. If he watched her, then he'd see what she was doing wrong. If he saw what she was doing wrong, he'd want to help her, and helping her would only lead them both into trouble. He'd have to stand behind her and press his body against hers so he could help her bring the rod back and forth; which meant not only would her perfect derriere be pushed up against him, but there was a chance, albeit a small one, that his arms might brush her plump breasts. He shifted his right leg forward in case she glanced over at him. The last thing he needed was another intimate encounter with Emma. He was trying to put distance between them, not get closer to her.

"Are you sure?" she asked with a frown.

He started. "Hmm? Oh, yes. Your form is as it should be." He blew out an aggravated breath. He needed to concentrate on fishing and stay focused on the conversation, not think about her luscious body. Such thoughts only led to trouble.

"I don't know," she said, casting in a way that would make the early pioneers of the sport cringe. "It's been a long time. Can you come help me?"

"No, no, you're doing everything right." Before she could protest again, he cast his fly into the stream and fished it as slowly as possible. He scowled. She'd pulled all her line in and appeared to be waiting for him to bring his line in so she could demand he help her. Taking as much time as he dared, he popped and jerked and slowly pulled in his fly, until he was afraid it would get caught on some weeds. "All right. I'll help you. Once. That's it."

"Excellent!" She pulled out more than enough line and let it pool at her feet while he leaned his rod against the tree and came to her side. "Do I hold it like this? Or this?"

He scowled. "Neither." Covering her hand with his, he positioned it where she should hold the rod. "All right, now come back with it, then snap it forward. Very good. Do it again." He took his hand off hers and watched her, narrowly escaping being impaled by the sharp hook on the end of her line as she slung her pole around without an ounce of care or grace. "Very good. Do it just like that and you'll catch a fish in no time."

"You're lying," she called to his back as he hobbled away.

He couldn't deny her words, so he ignored them. "I'm going to miss my perfect fish." He picked up his pole again.

"Heaven forbid that happens." Her brows knit together in a most innocent way as she tilted her head to the side and studied him with an intensity that almost made him squirm. "Hmm, you're holding the rod differently and casting it differently than I am."

"Of course my stance is different. I'm leaning against a tree." He elbowed the tree behind him to prove his point. "I have to do a side cast or I'd either break my rod on the tree or get my hook stuck up in the branches."

"Can you teach me the side cast?" she asked excitedly.

He groaned. "No. You're doing just fine with the cast you're using."

"But I'll never catch a fish."

"Oh, for goodness' sake, Emma." He leaned his pole against the tree again and started doing his best to walk toward her in a dignified manner despite how badly his leg hurt. "I'll help you catch one. That's it."

She grinned and a burble of laughter passed her pretty pink lips.

"I know I said I'd only help you cast once, but I mean it this time. One fish."

She sobered. "Very well, one fish. But I get to net him."

"And would you like to pull the hook out of his mouth, too?"

Emma's face scrunched up in disgust and she adamantly shook her head. "No, thank you. You can do that. I just want to hook him and scoop him up with the net. You can take the hook out and throw him back."

"All right, this time I'll have to hold onto your hands the whole time."

She let him close his hands around hers and leaned her back against his broad chest.

Forcing his concentration on fishing, he brought their hands back and forward three times before letting the line go and watching the fly land in the stream. Praying they'd catch a fish—even if it was only a little minnow—on the first cast, he gently tugged on the line, hoping to entice a fish to bite their fly.

"Can I work the line?" she asked in a voice that made his resolve crumble.

"Of course." He waited for her to take the fishing line before letting go.

She tugged on the line, and he shoved his hands in his pockets so he wouldn't yank the rod from her. "I've got one! I've got one!" Her sudden excitement surprised them both.

"Are you sure?" He tried to mask the doubt in his voice, but knew he hadn't done it well enough when she turned her hurt-filled eyes to him.

"I believe so, yes," she said, inclining her chin an inch.

"Go get the net." He reached for the pole. He tugged the line and realized what she thought was a fish on her line was actually a large hunk of weeds, or some other non-breathing object. "Emma, it's—"

"Don't worry, I'll get him," she yelled, hurrying to the bank, waving the net high in the air like a battle flag. "Don't reel him in anymore, Marcus. I want to scoop him right out of the water."

Why she wanted to do that, he had no idea. "I'll leave the line just where it is," he said, trying to contain his laughter. She was going to be dreadfully disappointed when she learned her catch of the day wasn't what she thought it was.

Emma stepped ankle deep into the stream and leaned forward with the net. "He must be deeper than I thought. Just hold the pole still, and I'll pull up on the line."

He bit the inside of his cheek. She wasn't going to pull that line anywhere. It was stuck. "Emma, darling, I think we should let this one go."

"Let him go?" Her eyes grew wide and the hand not holding the net went to her hip. "Marcus, this might be my only catch. Ever. I must net him."

He ducked his head and grinned like an idiot. "He's all yours."

She stepped further into the water until it came almost to her knees and tugged on the line again. "I need some help."

"No, I don't think you do."

"Yes, I'm fairly certain that I do," she countered with an unfeminine grunt as she impatiently pulled on the line.

Marcus winked at her. "He's all yours."

"But he's not cooperating." She yanked on the line so hard he was certain it was about to break any second now. Her face was so full of admirable determination as she struggled to get that elusive fish he couldn't help but feel a small twinge of compassion for her, knowing her struggles were in vain.

"Be careful or you'll snap it off."

"Snap it off?" she repeated. Her hands instantly stopped pulling on the line and her worried eyes searched his.

He nodded. Truth was they'd have to snap the line off anyway. But letting her think she'd been fighting the catch of a lifetime and lost the battle rather than telling her the dull, disappointing truth wasn't going to hurt anything, so he stood quietly and watched as she bit her lower lip and struggled once again to yank her wayward fish up out of the water.

"All right, Emma, come out of the water before you get your stitches wet. We'll let him go and get another."

She shook her head. "No, I've almost got him. I can feel it."

"Oh? And is he squirming around a lot?" He couldn't resist asking.

She responded, but he couldn't make out her words through her shrieks and grunts.

He stepped closer to the water. "Emma, I think you should come out of the water."

She looked at him with narrowed eyes. "Not until I get this fish. He's coming with me if I have to dive under the water and scoop him up myself."

"I wouldn't do that."

"But you're not me," she retorted, clutching the handle of the net so hard her knuckles and fingertips were turning white, then dunking it into the water, presumably trying to blindly net the fish.

Marcus stared at this beautiful and highly unusual woman he loved more than all others. Nobody else he'd ever met was stubborn enough to go this far to catch a phantom fish. Of course she didn't know that. Perhaps it was time for him to be honest. "Emma, there is no fish."

She stilled. "Yes, there is. Just give me another minute and I'll get him."

"No, you won't," he said gently. "Your hook is caught in a tangle of heavy weeds or maybe even a log. I don't really know which, but whatever it's stuck on isn't breathing."

Blinking at him and opening and shutting her mouth like the fish she'd been so eager to net, she dropped the net in the water. "You knew that this whole time?"

He nodded.

"And you still let me get in the water and act like a Bedlamite knowing it was all for naught."

He nodded again. "If it helps, you're a very beautiful Bedlamite."

She groaned and shook her head. "What am I going to do with you, Marcus?"

He grinned. "Snap off the line and let me help you catch another fish?"

She shook her head. "No, not today. I have to get inside and bathe before the girls' lessons."

Disappointment flooded him. He needed to keep his distance and it was unwise to keep helping her fish, but knowing it was for the best did nothing to alleviate his desire to be near her. "I'll put this away if you'd like to go on inside."

She nodded and reached down for what he assumed was the net. But when her hand came back up, it was filled with thick, slimy, dark brown mud. Without so much as a slight pause, she flung it all over him—his eyes growing wide with shock. "That was for making me look a fool," she said sweetly.

He used his thumb and forefinger to wipe the mud from his lips and stared at her, determined to keep a straight face. "Is that so?" he drawled, walking closer to her. "Don't worry, Emma. I'm not going to sling mud on you. I'm just here to snap off the line." He grabbed the clear line and gave it yank hard enough to break the fly off the end. He smiled at her worried face. It appeared as though she was rethinking her boldness.

"I must be off," she announced airily, walking toward the bank.

His hand snaked out and caught her about the waist. "Before

you go, could you hand me the net?"

"Of course." She turned around to grab it and sighed. "Perhaps not."

He hummed a merry tune and walked out of the water, pretending not to hear her. "I'll just be over here taking apart the poles."

"Marcus, I can't reach the net."

"Sure you can. Just lean over those low branches and grab it. It shouldn't be too tangled."

With a slight groan, Emma leaned over and, like he knew she would, leaned over too far. Her chemise got caught in the low-lying cluster of branches which had an uncommonly large number of sticks and twigs growing off of them, almost like a nest of sorts. He stood and enjoyed the view of her derriere swishing as she twisted and turned, trying in vain to free herself but only managing to get more tangled.

"Marcus," she hollered.

"Yes, sweet? Is something the matter?"

"Come help me."

"I'm afraid I can't come just now. I seem to be struggling with my own problem."

Emma grunted and wiggled again, only catching more of her gown on the spiky twigs and branches. "Put down the pole, Marcus, and help me."

"What was that?" he called, winding the reel right next to his ear so he purposely couldn't hear very well over all the clicking noise his reel was making from him spinning it.

"I said, you'd better get over here and help me out or I'll—I'll —"

"You'll what?" he cut in. "I don't believe there's a single thing you can do to me in this situation. I, on the other hand, can stand here and enjoy this view all day if I wish."

A sound of agitation accompanied her frenzied wiggles. "I mean it. I have to go teach Drake's girls. Please come help me."

"And what do I get?"

"Whatever you want. You can have whatever you want. Just

come help me, please."

"Oh, all right." He dropped what was in his hands, and waded out to her. "You're more tangled than I thought," he mused as his eyes did a sweep of her snagged chemise.

"Just get me free," she said through clenched teeth.

Snapping the sticks and pulling them off her as quickly as he could, Marcus murmured, "I'm sorry, Emma. I didn't mean for you to get this stuck."

"Yes, you did."

"No, I meant for you to get stuck, just not quite like this," he corrected. "I didn't realize there were stickers here, too. If I'd known that, I would have waited until later to exact my revenge." He pulled off what he thought was enough to free her without ripping her chemise or scratching her skin and put his hands on her hips. "All right, I'm going to lift you straight up. Try to stay still." Very slowly, Marcus lifted her away from the tangle of branches and sticks.

"Thank you," she mumbled, brushing a broken twig off her shoulder. Her back was still facing him, and he grabbed her shoulders to turn her around.

"Emma, I'm sorry," he said honestly. "I hope you're not hurt."

"Just a scratch or two. I'm sure I'll live."

"Good." He scratched his jaw and looked over her shoulder for the missing net.

"Is something amiss?" Emma asked, sidestepping him and walking toward the bank.

"Just looking for th—" His words stopped abruptly as a net full of thick weeds, mud, and who knew what other kind of sludge suddenly came down on his head.

"Thank you for taking me fishing," Emma called, running out of the water as fast as her bare feet could take her.

Mud dripped from Marcus' hair and down his face as he lifted the net-acting-as-hat off his head and grinned at her retreating form. She may have gotten the better of him this morning, but the day was still young.

Chapter 16

Emma spent the rest of the day peering over her shoulder. Marcus wasn't one to let the mud incident of the morning pass, and she didn't want him to. She was rather looking forward to whatever he thought was suitable punishment. Within reason, of course.

But he never sought retribution.

Not that day, nor the next, nor the day after that.

Several times throughout the rest of the week, she thought he was up to something only to discover he wasn't. That was when she realized *that* was what he was about. He was trying to make her paranoid. Or was he? She sighed. She had no idea what he was or wasn't up to.

Accepting help from Molly, she dressed in the blue gown Marcus had commissioned for her and went downstairs to rehearse once again for the dreaded musical performance they were to put on for Drake. Why Marcus insisted they do this, she'd never know. Those girls were awful. Even after an entire week of patient instruction, they were still awful.

Repressing a groan and contemplating sneaking a little sip of laudanum, she walked down the hall and to the stairs. At the bottom of the stairs, Marcus' big frame leaned against the doorjamb of his room.

"Everything all right?"

He nodded and smiled. "Yes. The girls are in the kitchen with Cook making something special for Drake."

Emma's eyes narrowed. Marcus' eyes were full of mischief.

"You're scheming something naughty, aren't you?"

"Of course not." He gestured for her to come closer.

She walked over to him and came up on her toes to plant a kiss on his lips. "All right, Marcus, what's going on?"

"Nothing." One corner of his scarred lips tipped up, belying his innocent statement.

"Mmmhmmm." She pursed her lips and looked at him thoughtfully. "I know you're scheming when you do that."

"Do what?"

"What you're doing right now."

"And what am I doing right now?" He leaned closer to her and pressed his forehead against hers. "Furthermore, what, pray tell, would I be 'scheming' about anyway? You seem to have been a bit preoccupied with my plans these past few days."

"Well, wouldn't you be?" she demanded, trying not to laugh.

Marcus brought his hand up to cup her cheek and pulled his face away so he could look down on her. "What has you so out of sorts?" he asked soothingly, stroking her cheekbone with the pad of his thumb.

"Oh, stop the act," she scolded playfully. "Something's off here, I can feel it."

He brought his hand back to her cheek to stroke it again. "What makes you so sure?"

"Because all week you've been—you've been—I don't know, I can't explain it. You've been something."

Marcus chuckled. "Yes, I've been something all right."

Emma groaned. "You know what I'm talking about. Quit playacting like you don't. You're up to some sort of mischief, Lord Sinclair. I may not know exactly what you're about, but I do know you've something up your sleeve."

Marcus' hand dropped from her face and he used the fingers of one hand to unbutton the cuff of the other sleeve before looking up, then repeated the process with the other. "No, nothing up there except my arm."

"You're ridiculous," she said with a snort. "You've been up to something since I dumped that mud on your head earlier this week.

I just know it."

"Don't you think if that were true, I'd have already done something?" he wondered, wrapping his arm around her shoulders and pulling her close to him.

She looked up at his impassive face. "I suppose so." She cocked her head to the side. "But I don't know for sure. I mean, you've had several days and haven't done anything. But you couldn't, either. Not with the girls around all the time, that is." She frowned. "Oh, I don't know what to think of you right now, Marcus."

He shrugged. "Think what you will."

"You're impossible. But I love you anyway."

"Good," he said before pressing a quick kiss on her lips. "After Patrick leaves with his clan this afternoon, I'd like to talk to you in the drawing room."

Emma nodded and tried not to let her excitement show. Two days ago, Marcus had left before breakfast and hadn't returned until well after dinner. Everyone in the house had been speculating on where he'd gone and what he'd gone for. The most common opinion was that he'd made a trip to London to select a betrothal ring. Emma wanted to ask him about it, but assumed he wanted to keep it a surprise and did her best to hold in her excitement. But now that the time was so close, she could hardly contain herself.

"Miss Green, Lord Sinclair, we're ready for you," Celia called, walking down to the hall to them.

Marcus let go of Emma's waist and took out his pocket watch. "You're papa should be here in fifteen minutes. Let's go get ready for him."

Celia giggled and grabbed both Emma's and Marcus' hands. The trio walked down the hall and into the drawing room where the other two girls were already waiting. Four chairs had been set up in a semicircle with another chair about ten feet away facing the small cluster of chairs.

"Was all this necessary?" Emma asked Marcus.

"Absolutely," he said with an excited nod. "Now, girls, take your seats and let's get ready for when your papa gets here."

The three girls took their seats and grabbed the instruments they had finally decided upon. One had an out of tune three-stringed banjo his father had brought home for Olivia after traveling to Africa, another had a cracked flute, and the last piece to this band was a tambourine. At least Marcus, who had what appeared to be the loudest instrument, could actually play, and with any luck, he could drown out the other three. Once again Emma was in charge of keeping beat by clapping her hands, just like every day during practice.

"Presenting his lordship, Viscount Drakely," Chapman said from the doorway, an unusual look on his face.

Drake waltzed in and waved to his three girls who were bouncing in their seats at seeing him. They stood up to greet him, and Marcus put on the sternest face he could and told them to stay seated.

Emma smiled. He was truly intent on torturing poor Drake.

"All right, Miss Green, we're ready when you are."

Emma took her place behind the quartet to set the beat and count them off.

Marcus reached for her wrist. "Not so fast. You're the conductor. You need to be in front conducting."

"I think not," she said with a horrified glance at Drake. She wasn't going to stand with her bottom directly in front of him and conduct those four while they played horrible music.

"What do you think, girls? Shouldn't Miss Green stand in front and conduct?" Marcus asked, grinning when the three girls squealed in agreement.

Resigned, Emma sighed before murmuring a quick apology to Drake then took her spot in front of the musicians, ready to conduct. Clapping her hands together in a somewhat steady beat, she said, "One, and two, and here we go now."

As soon as the word "now" escaped Emma's lips, four very eager musicians began tooting, strumming, banging, or blowing their instruments, resulting in an outrageous amount of noise filling the air and causing anything that wasn't nailed down to bang and clatter, only adding to the fracas.

For five painfully long, headache-producing minutes, Emma clapped her hands jovially, pretending to keep time and conduct the group at the same time. Sometimes she'd stop clapping and give a rolling hand gesture in the direction of one of the girls who'd stopped playing. Other times, she'd force a smile and try not to grimace in pain when the flutist hit an extremely high note.

When Emma was sure they'd all suffered enough, she quit clapping her hands and made a quick slicing motion through the air to cut them off.

"Very good! Very good!" Drake lied, accepting hugs from his girls as they abandoned their chosen weapons of ear-torture and ran to his open arms.

Emma smiled at the happy foursome. Those three little girls might not have a mother, but there was no doubt in her mind they were loved no less than any child with two parents. She glanced at Marcus, who was quietly putting away his trumpet. He'd make as good a father as Drake. All week, he'd been patient with the girls, even when they'd called Emma's attention away from him. He'd either tag along or warmly surrender her to them without complaint.

"Drake...er...I mean, Lord Drakely," Emma said with a blush. Though they'd been friends for a long time and she'd always called him Drake before, she was still in his employ, and needed to remember her place. A broad smile spread her lips. She wouldn't be in his employ much longer. "I need to talk to you in private for a moment."

Drake's dark brown eyes met hers. "Is there something I should be concerned about?"

Emma bit her lip. "No."

"Did one of the girls do something beastly to you?" He looked at the girls with an overdone look of reproof, complete with his eyes narrowed to slits, lips pursed, and head cocked to the side.

She laughed. "No. Nothing like that. They were perfect angels. I just need a moment alone."

Drake sighed. "Is this one of those conversations every parent dreads?"

"Pardon?"

"You know, where the governess hems and haws and shifts from foot to foot biting her lip then blurts out she thinks one of the children is better suited for the workhouse or a foundling hospital than the nursery."

Emma blinked. "I have no idea what you're speaking of. I would never suggest such a thing."

"Phew." Drake used the back of his hand to wipe a nonexistent bead of sweat off his forehead. "You had me really worried about Helena over there." He dropped his voice to a stage whisper. "Mrs. Jenkins is scared to death of her. She once confided in me that she feared for her life because of Helena's unusual attachment to her pillow."

"What?" Emma asked in exacerbation.

"I don't know all the particulars," Drake said with a shrug. "All I know is Mrs. Jenkins feared a death by suffocation at Helena's hands—and pillow, naturally."

Emma shook her head. "I still have no idea what you're talking about. There is nothing the least bit wrong with Helena. She suffers no unusual fascination with her pillow, and I would highly recommend you look for a replacement if Mrs. Jenkins has suggested such a thing."

"Don't mind him," Marcus grumbled, walking up to her side. "Patrick never could carry off a jest."

"That was a jest?" Emma asked.

"Sadly, yes," Drake said sheepishly. "As Marcus here pointed out, unlike him, I'm terrible at pulling one over on a person."

"I'll say," Emma agreed, flashing him a weak smile. "At any rate, I would like to speak with you in private."

"Absolutely. But first, perhaps you should think about removing the sign hanging in front of your bottom. It doesn't exactly exemplify the professionalism of the governess you're striving to display."

"Excuse me," Emma exclaimed, her hands flying to her bottom where sure enough a piece of parchment was loosely pinned to the bow just above her bottom. Snatching at the piece of paper, she scowled at Marcus. "You!"

His eyes widened in the worst display of innocence she'd ever witnessed. "Me what?"

"I knew you were up to something, you rascal!"

Marcus grinned. "Perhaps it was me. Perhaps it wasn't."

"It was," she said, still trying to free the paper without ripping her dress or untying her bow.

"You don't know that. Apparently little Helena here has a penchant for dastardly deeds." Marcus rested one of his hands on Helena's shoulders. "You should just be thankful she didn't attack you with her pillow."

Emma shook her head and managed to get the paper free without causing any harm to either her dress or the paper. She knew Marcus wouldn't pin a blank piece of paper to the back of her dress. It said something. What, she didn't know. But she'd soon find out.

Turning the paper over so she could read it, Emma let out a horrified shriek. "Marcus Sinclair, that is not funny."

"Yes, it is," Marcus said with an easy grin.

"If it's any consolation, Miss Green, I didn't believe the message," Drake said, his lips twitching.

Repressing a groan borne of embarrassment, Emma shook her head. "Well, thank you. I'm glad you realized it really *was* Marcus' trumpet you were hearing."

Drake shrugged. "I might have put more credence into it had I not recognized Marcus' handwriting."

"Drat," Marcus said, clicking his tongue. "I knew I was overlooking something. Next time I'll get Celia to write it out for me."

"There will not be a next time," Emma retorted. "Not if you wish to live to see another day, that is."

"All right, children," Drake cut in before Marcus could reply. His gaze shifted between Marcus and Emma, letting them know exactly who he thought to be the children in the room. "I need to be going soon. Miss Green, I'll be happy to meet with you in the library."

"I'll be right there, my lord." Emma balled up the offending piece of parchment and threw it at Marcus' chest. "I'll be right back to talk to the girls. While I'm away, you had better not tell them anything." She gave him a pointed look that even a blind man could interpret.

"Not to worry, Miss Green. I'll not tell them the story as to why one should suspect anything but the trumpet playing when you're present for a musicale," Marcus laughingly assured her.

Emma scowled. Apparently more than fourteen years later, Marcus still remembered one of her most embarrassing moments. She turned to walk to the door and paused in the doorframe. "Just so you're aware, that noise wasn't what you think it was."

"I know," he admitted quietly. "It's just more fun to pretend otherwise."

Emma rolled her eyes. "As long as you know." She shook her head and went down the hall to the library to tell Drake she was resigning her post.

"I hope everything is all right," Drake said easily when Emma walked through the door.

"It is." She licked her lips. "Actually, I lied, it's not. I know I haven't been in your employ very long, and this is most rude of me, but I must resign."

Drake blinked. "Resign? Already? Did Helena try to smother you?"

She laughed. "No." A big grin took her lips and she bit her lower lip to help her regain her composure again. "See, umm…" She fidgeted and looked to the side to make sure nobody could hear. "Marcus and I are going to marry."

"Really?"

"Really," she cried, grinning like a simpleton and nodding her head just the same.

"Congratulations to you both," Drake said with a chuckle. "Clearly you two will be very happy together."

"I know," she chirped, clapping her hands merrily in front of her. "Excuse me. I mean, thank you, my lord. I'm sure Marcus and I shall rub along well enough."

Drake grinned and shook his head. "No need to contain your excitement. I'll just gather my urchins and be on my way."

"Thank you for being so understanding," Emma murmured before moving out of his way so he could leave the room.

He waved her off. "No need. I knew it was only to be for a week."

"You did?"

"Yes. Now don't think another thing of it and start planning that wedding of yours."

Emma walked with Drake back down the hall and said an emotional goodbye to the three girls she'd grown so close to over the past week. She kissed them each and promised she'd come to see them soon. She also promised she'd bring candy and hair ribbons with her when she came to visit them and would leave the quills, paper, and history tomes at Ridge Water.

After they were done, Marcus and Emma walked them to their waiting carriage and went through the whole process again.

"I thought they'd never leave," Marcus remarked, waving to the carriage making a slow crawl down the drive.

"Oh, stop. You know you think of Drake as the brother you never had and you love those girls as much as—if not more than—you'll love Olivia's spawn."

"That may be, but still a man needs peace every once in a while."

"You're the one who suggested the musicale."

"And it was well worth it," Marcus replied, turning to take both of her hands in his. "I know you couldn't see Drake's face, but trust me, the look he sported throughout that performance was worth the headache I have now."

"If you say so."

"Oh, it was. I've never seen a man grimace one second and form an overdone grin the next. I wager at least four of his teeth turned to dust from him grinding them."

Emma shook her head. "What was it you wanted to talk to me about?" She couldn't contain her eagerness about his impending proposal a second longer.

An unusual shadow crossed Marcus' face. "Why don't we go inside?"

"I'll be right there." She pressed a quick kiss on his cheek, then ran up to her room to get the cufflinks she'd once had commissioned for him but had never actually given him. They were one of those few precious things she always kept with her in her reticule. Just now, to celebrate their engagement, was the perfect time to give them to him.

Chapter 17

Marcus lumbered into the drawing room and sat down in the chair closest to the settee to wait for Emma's return. He ran his hand through his hair and rehearsed the words he'd say to her when she came back. Where she went, he'd never know. But he was thankful all the same she'd gone somewhere. It gave him a few minutes to prepare what he'd say to her. His heart hammered in his chest as nervous excitement coursed through him. In a matter of minutes, their lives would change.

He forced an overdone smile to his lips as she breezed into the room. The sight of her excited face made his heart squeeze. There was no doubting how much he loved her. That was why this had to work. He wouldn't be able to bear it if it didn't.

"What's in your hand?" he asked when she sat down and idly jiggled something in her left hand, making a little pinging noise fill the air.

Her hand stilled. "Nothing." Her grin tattled her lying hide.

Marcus smiled thinly as a little knife of regret stabbed his heart. "Emma," he said roughly, sitting down across from her. He swallowed and cleared his throat. Twice. "I wanted to talk to you about something."

"Yes," she squealed, her level of excitement rivaling that of a little girl being taken into a confectionary for the first time.

"I want you to know I love you."

Emma's grin widened. "I know that already. And I love you, too. But go on." She favored him with a smile that would put one of the king's chandeliers to shame.

"I wanted to talk to you about something serious. Emma, I—"

"Yes! Yes! Yes!" she burst out, jumping to her feet, dropping whatever was in her hands and throwing her arms around Marcus' neck.

Marcus blinked. Emma was still hugging him tightly and kissing him anywhere she could fit her lips. "Emma darling," he said, trying to pull her off him. He cupped her face. "You haven't even heard my proposal."

"I don't need to. I accept."

"You accept?"

"Yes."

"But you don't know what you're accepting."

"Yes, I do. You."

"Me?"

She turned her face to kiss his palm. "Yes, you, you clodpole. I accept your suit."

"My suit?"

Emma corralled her excitement and briefly raised her hands in the air as if she were surrendering. "All right." She sighed, and climbed off where she'd perched herself on his lap. She stood straight in front of him. "If you wish to be formal about this, then do so. I'll listen to every word of your proposal. But please don't get on your knee."

"I wasn't planning on it." Taking her hands in his, he looked into her deep green eyes and rubbed mindless patterns on her knuckles with his thumbs. "Emma, I want you to go to London."

"What?"

His fingers involuntarily tightened around hers for a brief second before relaxing. "I think you should have a Season."

Emma's lower lip trembled. "Wh—what?"

"I want to fund a Season for you."

"Why?"

Marcus frowned. "I just told you. I want you to have a Season."

"I don't want one," she said, shaking her head to prove her point. "I'm perfectly happy as things are."

"You won't be," he said tightly.

"What's that to mean?"

"It means you won't be happy in the future."

"And another Season in London is going to change that?"

Marcus nodded slowly. "It'll help you find a husband."

"I've already found one," Emma said in a tone Marcus couldn't interpret.

"You have?"

Emma closed her eyes and shook her head. When she opened her emerald orbs again, she looked him square in the eye and said, "Have you been indulging in Olivia's opium?"

"No. Why?"

"You are acting most strange."

Ignoring her, Marcus pulled her to his lap. "Let's start over. Emma, I want to give you a Season."

She shook her head and looked a little dumbfounded. "Why all of a sudden do you have an interest in going to London?"

"I don't," he stated firmly. "I'm not going. You are."

"Marcus, you're not making a whit of sense. Why am I going to London? I already told you I don't need a Season. I'm ready to marry you now."

Her words nearly knocked the air straight out of his lungs. "I don't recall proposing."

"You haven't. But you were about to when I took a temporary leave of my senses and jumped on you like a madwoman."

"No, I wasn't," he said solemnly.

"You weren't what?" Her brows furrowed together.

He used the tip of his index finger to smooth out the wrinkle between her brows. "Emma, I can't marry you."

"Pardon?"

The shock and hurt in her voice made his heart constrict in a most painful way. "If I could marry, I'd marry you tomorrow. But I can't. I can't do that to you."

"Pardon?"

"I can't marry you."

"Pardon?"

"Have you temporarily forgotten all other words in the English language?"

Emma scrambled off his lap at his jest. "What are you talking about Marcus?" she demanded, the porcelain skin on her face stained with pink blotches.

"Emma," he said slowly. "I cannot marry."

"What do you mean you cannot marry?"

He scratched this suddenly uncontrollable itch that had developed on the back of his head. Well, not really. He was just scratching his head frantically in an attempt to stall for time. But no amount of time would make this any easier. With a deep exhalation, he met her eyes. "All right, you caught me. I can marry. I choose not to."

With hard, unyielding eyes, Emma stared at him. "Would you care to elaborate?"

"No."

"Elaborate."

He sighed. "Emma, I love you. And because I love you, I can't marry you."

"Are you sure you've not indulged in something?" she demanded, her voice not full of the humor it was the first time she'd suggested it. "What you just told me does not explain anything. If you love me, then you'll marry me. That's what people who love each other do."

"No, they don't," he corrected, momentarily forgetting she'd been born of a lower station. One which made love matches very common. She might have been the daughter to one of the lower gentry and had witnessed the social scene among the nobles, but that didn't mean she understood it. To her, people married for love. That was the way of it for the commoners. Money and connections had little to do with it.

"They can," she amended, bringing him back to present. "Look at Alex and Caroline."

"Yes, they can," he allowed, ignoring the part about Alex and Caroline. They were not a good example for his cause. "But the point is I am a lord of the realm. As such, I'm not expected to marry for love."

"Who cares?" she burst out. "Who cares if you have a love match or an arranged marriage? Likely nobody will care. You're such a recluse as it is, the majority of them won't even know who you are when you're gossiped about for having a love match."

"I don't care about the gossip. I've been subjected to more than most. That's irrelevant. The point is you'll not be happy if we marry."

"Yes, I will," she said with a sound of frustration.

"No, you won't. I can't give you the life someone else can."

"What are you talking about?"

Marcus sighed and closed his eyes. "I can't have children."

Emma's mouth opened and shut several times, never a sound coming out.

Standing up, Marcus cupped her face and tipped it up toward his. "I love you too much. I can't subject you to a life without children. That's why I want you to go to London. I want you to marry a man who can give you what I can't."

"No," she said fiercely. "You're lying."

"No, I'm not. After my accident there was some soreness and swelling." He grimaced. "You don't really need all the details. The physician was rather certain I'd not be able to reproduce."

Emma's cold hands suddenly grabbed his and pried them off her face. "You liar!" she spat. Tears coursed down her cheeks and a sob wracked her body. "You don't want to marry me and you're using this as an excuse. Be honest, Marcus. Just tell me you don't want me. Tell me my morals are too loose for you and your ilk. Just tell me the truth!"

"I do want you."

She shook her head. "No, you don't. If you did, you'd marry me. But instead, you're making up some excuse."

"No, I'm not." Marcus fisted his hands at his side. He did want her. But he also wanted her to be happy, and he knew she could never be fully happy with him. She might pretend otherwise, but he knew just like all other women, she craved motherhood. "Emma, be rational. You know I want you. But you'll not be happy here."

"Yes, I will," she countered. "But it doesn't matter. You're lying."

"About what?" What could she possibly think he was lying about?

"Your inability to have children," she said plainly. "You think I'm so naïve I'll not question something like that. But you're wrong. I know more than you give me credit for."

"And what would that be?" Exactly what did she think she knew about his body better than he did?

"Your male anatomy is perfectly functional," she said flippantly. "You just think I'll not question what you say."

"What has that to do with anything?"

"I know your...your..." She waved a hand in the direction of his waist— "works quite adequately, if the other day is anything to judge by."

He blinked at her.

"I may not be as educated on the subject as Alex or Caroline, but I know enough to know the basics of how babies come about, and to be quite frank, your wedding tackle seemed to be in working condition the other day."

Marcus sighed. "Yes, that's correct. But there's more to a man's part in procreation than his member." He swallowed and tried to push past his embarrassment of talking so candidly about such a private part of his anatomy. "And while I admit that part does work as it should, the rest does not."

She stared at him for a minute. "I have no idea what you're talking about."

"I know," he whispered. "But that's the way of it."

"No, it's not the way of it. You're just making up excuses and hoping I'm too dull-witted to know the difference."

"That's not it at all. I've been told by three different physicians the trauma I sustained makes it impossible to have children."

"And yet you stiffen right up at a second's notice," she retorted, doubt filling her voice.

"As I said earlier, the two matters are unrelated. While I'm grateful I was not completely unmanned, I was still injured."

"I don't see how. Nor do I understand why you'd lie to me about this."

Marcus ground his teeth. "It's difficult to explain."

"Try."

"No," he snapped. "If you're so curious, ask Caroline. I'm sure she's a never-ending stream of information on the topic."

"I don't want to ask Caroline," Emma said, her gaze boring into him. "I asked you. Now answer."

"I already have. Now, enough on that. Let's speak of your Season. I've made arrangements with Alex for you to stay with them so you don't have to go back to Hampton and Louise."

"You what? When? Why?"

"The other day when I went out."

"That's where you went?" she asked, a sob caught in her throat, making her voice crack mid-sentence.

Nodding, Marcus moved his hands to her shoulders. "Yes. I spoke to Alex to arrange for him to act as your sponsor for the Season."

"My sponsor?" she repeated sharply. "I don't need a sponsor. I am seven-and-twenty, Marcus. I can do as I please."

"I know that. But I know you don't have any other option but to stay with them, and this way it'll be seen as a favor to me, not as you asking to stay with them again."

"I don't believe it." She shook loose from his grasp. "You really intend to send me away."

He nodded solemnly.

"But why?" she burst out.

"I've already told you."

"I don't care about that, Marcus," she cried. "Even if it's true and you cannot father children, I don't care. I love you."

That was the crux of it. She might love him today, but how would she feel month after month, year after year when the cold reality finally sank in for her and she realized it would always just be the two of them? Would her love change to resentment when she finally understood? Would she seek out a lover to console her,

181

or worse yet, in hopes of producing a child with him? The possibilities were limitless and painful just to think of. "I know you love me," he said at last, his voice ragged and raw with emotion. "And I love you, too. That's why you need to go. I want you to be happy, and you're not going to find that happiness with me."

"You're wrong. I'll be content just to be your wife."

"Exactly. Content. Not happy—content. I want you happy."

"And I will be, if you'll stop behaving this way and accept that I love you."

Marcus flickered a glance outside to where his carriage was waiting. "No, you won't. I know right now you don't see it, but one day you'll be glad you didn't marry me. I expect that time will come shortly after you hold your child in your arms for the first time." He smiled thinly at her and tore his gaze away as she shook her head and swiped at her tears.

"Why are you being so cruel to me? You've never acted this way before. Never. Is this because of Louise?"

"No," he said bitterly. "This has nothing to do with her. This is about you, Emma."

She crossed her arms and stared at him in a way that made him feel like the biggest cad in England.

A moment passed with only the sounds of his pounding heart and her quiet sobs breaking the silence. "Did you intend to send me away *now?*" she asked, catching sight of the carriage through the window.

"Yes."

"You're heartless," she said with a bitter laugh.

"No, I'm not. I have a heart just like yours. It beats just like yours. It loves just like yours. And just now it's breaking, just like yours."

"I don't believe it," she whispered. "You couldn't possibly possess a heart if you think by sending me away, you're showing me you love me."

"Oh, but I do. I love you that much. Now go."

She shook her head and crossed her arms. "No. We're not finished here."

"Yes, we are."

"No, we're not. I'm not satisfied."

He snorted. "Arguing about it any longer isn't suddenly going to make you satisfied, either. The fact remains, I refuse to marry you. And nothing you can do or say will change that."

"You don't mean that."

"I do, too."

"No, you don't. You're just uncertain, that's all. You were afraid I'd reject you because of your secret, and now that you've told me and I still want to marry you, you're scared."

He snorted at her ridiculous reasoning. "That's not the least bit true. I meant what I told you earlier. If I were able to give you children, I'd marry you tomorrow. But I can't, and I won't make you suffer because of it."

"Tell yourself what you wish. Your lies won't work with me. I don't care what our future would be like. As long as I'm with you, I'll be happy."

"I don't think so," he said sadly after a brief pause. "And even if you were able to feign happiness well enough, I'd never be happy knowing I'd made you give up the life you could have had. Just go, Emma. Caroline's expecting you."

"Make me." She put her hands on her hips and stared at him with a look of absolute defiance.

Marcus nearly smiled. That was the Emma he remembered. The headstrong and stubborn one. The one full of determination. Only this time, all her determined energy was being channeled at a battle she had no chance of winning. He wasn't going to budge. Wrapping one arm around her shoulders and the other around her legs, he swooped her up and limped straight out the door.

"Put me down," she protested, kicking her feet wildly.

"No. Now be still before I drop you."

She kicked her feet more violently.

Marcus scowled at her. "I'm serious. Stop kicking."

"No." Now she was not only kicking, she was wiggling and squirming.

Grinding his teeth, Marcus set her down as soon as he stepped outside.

"You're impossible," he said with a huff.

"No. *You're* impossible."

"No. I'm realistic. There's a difference. Now, get in the carriage and go to Caroline."

Emma wiped her eyes and sniffled once more before clearing her throat. "Marcus," she began brokenly. "I love you. I always have. I never dreamt you'd return my love and I even accepted that you were going to marry my sister, but now to know you love me, too, and you're willing to give it all away hurts far more than if you'd never loved me at all." She cleared her throat, and when she spoke again, her tone was much firmer and clearer, almost cold and distant. "I understand your hesitancy. I really do. But I love you, Marcus, and part of loving someone is accepting them exactly how they are. I've never cared about the scars, and I don't care if we're not able to have children together. That's not why I love you. I love you because of who you are. But right now, I don't recognize you.

"I've never seen this side of you before, and I don't care to again. I'll go to Caroline's and give you some time to regain control of your brain. Don't make me wait forever, because I won't." Her last words felt equivalent to the hard punch in the gut he'd received from one of the older boys at Eton, when he'd thoughtlessly accused him of cheating at cards.

Marcus tried not to blink his stinging eyes as he helped her climb up into the carriage. This would likely be the last time he'd ever see her, and he didn't want to miss one second. Once she was in, he leaned his head in. "I'll have your things sent," he said quietly, sweeping imaginary dirt out the door of the carriage.

He glanced up and quickly shifted his eyes back to the floor. The hurt in her eyes was more than he could bear. Then with one final glance in her direction, he whispered, "Goodbye, Emma," then slammed the carriage door shut and rapped on the roof.

Standing motionless as the carriage drove away, getting smaller and smaller with each passing second, Marcus realized what true pain was about. It wasn't being dragged a quarter mile behind a horse; it was watching the one you loved above all others roll away from you forever.

Chapter 18

He didn't come.

Emma waited for him, and he never came.

She hadn't expected him to repeat the same foolishness he'd shown with Louise and try to chase her down only five minutes later. But she had expected him to realize his mistake and come to Watson Estate. But he didn't.

She'd waited up for him that entire first night. Then the next. And the next. And the next. Until finally, she couldn't wait any longer. Or, until Caroline *wouldn't* let her wait any longer, to be exact.

After two weeks, Caroline had insisted Emma go to London for the start of the Season to start looking for gentlemen who'd make her a good match. But she didn't want to make a match and get married. Not with any of the London gentlemen, anyway. She still wanted Marcus, and she was certain he'd come around, if only she waited a little longer. She tried to stall going to London by using her age as an excuse. Caroline wouldn't have it though.

"Your age won't be a problem," Caroline assured her, pinning a brooch on her dress. "Marcus dowered you so well it wouldn't matter if you were two-and-seventy instead of seven-and-twenty."

Bile rose in her throat. He was willing to pay a stranger forty thousand pounds just to have done with her. It was sickening. "Why are you so excited to go to London, anyhow? Last year you couldn't even dance."

Caroline's blue eyes met Emma's. "I'm going to let that pass."

"I'm sorry. I didn't mean it how it sounded."

"I know. But since you brought it up, I'll tell you. Alex taught me to waltz!"

"Alex? As in Arid Alex? As in Lord Watson?"

Caroline nodded. "Yes! The very one. And despite what you and everyone else thinks, he's not arid. He's a lot of fun. Besides, he's my husband."

"And *that's* why you think he's fun. You love him."

"I suppose," Caroline agreed. "But I thought he was fun even before I loved him."

Emma snorted. "No you didn't. You were angry at him for tossing you out of that biological society he runs when you fell in love with him."

"And your point?"

"My point is you fell in love with him long before you really got to know him. Don't you dare cut me off. I was there that night. I saw the way you looked at him when you walked into the drawing room. A little drawing room chitchat does not make someone fun, and yet I could tell you were already in love with him."

Caroline shrugged. "Does it really matter? Wait, I understand now. We're not talking about me and Alex at all, are we?" She came to sit beside Emma and wrapped her arm around her. "I never thought of it that way before. Marcus is your Alex, isn't he?"

Emma nodded. Caroline was a smart woman. She was probably the only person in the world who understood that to Emma, Marcus was the same as Alex was to Caroline. Both men were usually only seen at a basic, superficial glance. Alex was considered boring and arid due to his unusual interest in science and nearly pristine reputation, and Marcus was seen only for his scars and former folly. But just as Caroline was able to see past Alex's awkward exterior to find the man who lurked beneath, Emma was able to do the same with Marcus. She didn't care about his past or the scars that marred his body; she didn't even care about his inability to have children. When she looked at him, all she saw was *him*. The sweet and caring man she loved. The same one who apparently didn't return her love.

"Caro," Alex said, coming into the room. "We need to be going."

"We'll be right down."

Alex nodded and left. "Could I just stay here?" Emma suggested weakly.

"I don't think so," Caroline said, shaking her head wildly to emphasize her answer. "I know you may not believe this, but I've overheard Marcus blister Olivia's ears a time or two, and I have no desire to take her place. You're going."

Emma smiled thinly. She, too, had overheard Marcus rail at Olivia for something foolish. She certainly understood Caroline's hesitancy to go against his wishes and leave her behind at Watson Estate when he'd practically demanded they take her to London to shop for a husband.

* * *

Two miserable days later Emma found herself looking around the ballroom at the massive crush. She fought the urge to run far, far away. Tonight, Caroline had dragged her to a ball given by the Duke and Duchess of Gateway. Emma had met them the year before at Caroline's wedding. They were some relation to Alex, however, knowing this did *nothing* to settle her nerves.

She hated ballrooms before, and now with her excessive dowry, she hated them even more. Before her parents had died, they'd insisted she come to London for a Season, but her heart wasn't in it. It was back in Dorset—with Marcus. Now, more than ten years later—three uneventful Seasons followed by another seven missed (but not sadly so) Seasons—she was right back where she didn't want to be: having another Season. When she was younger, she'd just acted disinterested in the gentlemen. Not cold or rude, mind you. Just disinterested. That, coupled with her pitiful dowry, had kept them exactly where she wanted: in someone else's drawing room.

But now it was different. Now she had a dowry and gentlemen were continuously asking her to dance, often while she was still on the arm of another gentleman. Several tried to get her to go off alone with them into the gardens, and a few had been so bold as to offer a marriage proposal during a waltz. It was humiliating and disgusting, and she wanted nothing more of it. It was time to do something to force Marcus' hand.

Since she wasn't dancing at present—not for lack of being asked, but because she'd sent her partner off to the refreshment room yet again—she peered around the room in hopes of finding the perfect man for her task. She needed one who had a reputation so dark even Marcus would have heard of him.

She didn't see a man who would fit her purposes right off, so she decided she'd excuse herself from the knot of gentlemen who'd surrounded her and stand with Caroline and Alex until she spotted a good candidate. Even if Alex and Caroline could barely go five minutes without talking of science, which was preferable to the torture she was currently enduring. Besides, it was easier to ignore them and let her eyes search the ballroom than it was to be whirled around the room and proposed to while trying to locate the most rakish, scandalous, and unsavory man in existence.

"May I have this dance?" a familiar voice asked when she was halfway to Caroline.

"Drake," she said, turning around and flashing a smile at him. "Fancy seeing you here."

He chuckled. "That is a sentence I never thought I'd hear escape your lips."

She smiled thinly. "I'm trying."

"I know. Is your dance card full?"

She blinked at him. Though she was stunned to see him at a ball, she was more stunned he'd asked her to dance. She'd never seen him dance with anyone but the late Lady Drakely, and the look in his eyes suggested he'd like to keep it that way. "Sadly, yes, my card is full."

His face softened remarkably. "Would you be too terribly disappointed to miss the next waltz or two to walk with me?"

She placed her hand on his proffered arm. "Not at all. I've heard from about fifteen sources that the gardens are very nice."

"Then let's explore, shall we?" He led her to the far wall and through the double doors that led to the gardens. "How have you been?"

She shrugged. "I guess you've heard about everything?"

"No. Not everything. But enough."

They found an empty bench and sat down. Emma grabbed the ends of her pink shawl and twirled the fringy tassels. "Have you been to talk to him?"

Drake shook his head. "He won't see anyone."

"Of course not."

"It's just his way," Drake said casually. "That's the way men are."

"Stupid," she muttered.

"That may be, but it doesn't change anything."

Digging the toe of her pink slipper into the soft soil, Emma stared into the moonlit distance. "What am I to do, Drake? I thought he'd come back, but he hasn't."

"What do you want to do?" Drake asked carefully.

"I don't know. I always dreamed of growing up to marry Marcus. But then he was engaged with my sister and—" she closed her eyes— "I let the dream die. Even after Louise ran off with Hampton and Marcus recovered, I never dared dream of marriage to him again."

"Why?"

"I was always afraid he'd spurn me the way my sister did him."

"That's not what he intended to do."

Emma blinked back her tears. "I know. He's not like that. He'd never intentionally play with my affections."

"No, he wouldn't," Drake agreed. "He's never held your sister's transgressions against you, either. You do know that, don't you?"

She nodded. "I know." A wobbly smile took her lips. "But the end result was still the same, wasn't it?"

Exhaling, Drake leaned forward and placed his elbows on his knees. "As I said, I don't know everything. But yes, the result was the same. What do you plan to do now?"

"I don't have much choice." Her voice was flat, resigned. "I have no living relatives who I can stay with, and I can't impose on Caroline forever. That only leaves marriage. And since marriage to Marcus isn't shaping up like I'd planned, I have to pick one of those toads in there."

"Is that really what you intend to do?"

Emma broke eye contact with him and developed a strong interest in the beadwork on her skirt. Could he tell she was reaching the end of her wits and was about to try one last attempt to force Marcus into action?

"Emma?"

She met his gaze and bit her lip. "Yes."

"That was the weakest yes I've ever heard."

Unable to stop herself, the corners of Emma's mouth tipped up. "What are you thinking?" she asked, trying to avoid telling him too much in case he didn't guess right.

Crossing his arms and leaning back, Drake shook his head. "I'm not sure what I think. You're here in London at a ball like Marcus wanted, and not sneaking into Ridge Water and using whatever female tactics you can think of to get Marcus to change his mind, but for some reason, I think I'm missing something. Almost like you're taking a more subtle approach by complying with his demands, but your motives are still focused on getting Marcus to the altar, not one of these gentlemen."

"Drat you," Emma said with a sigh. Was she that transparent?

"Don't worry," Drake assured her with a wave of his hand. "Marcus is so secluded in the country he'll not get wind of what you're doing. But, I must ask, exactly what is your plan?"

Emma eyed him skeptically. Could she trust him? He was Marcus' closest friend. Surely he wouldn't approve of her methods. What if he told Marcus what she was doing and Marcus became angry with Caroline and Alex for not being better sponsors? Or what if Drake tried to stop her? She shook her head. No, she couldn't tell him anything. There were too many ways he could ruin her plans. It was better he didn't know.

"Emma?" he prompted again.

"I'd rather not say."

He nodded once and a moment of silence passed between them. "Do you remember my wife?"

Emma started. "Yes."

"When she was scheming some silly antic, she acted the same way you're acting right now. Luckily for you, Marcus isn't here to see you just now and shake you. Alex probably wouldn't notice if he were here, and Caroline would probably join you. But, I'm the one here right now, and I want some answers. What are you planning to do?"

"I'm going fishing," she said cryptically.

Drake didn't even blink at her. He just stared at her. Hard. "You're going to try and lure him out of Dorset by having rumors spread to the effect that you're courting someone he wouldn't approve of, aren't you?"

Emma gulped in a most unladylike fashion. "Yes."

"Who are you planning to include in this scheme of yours?"

"I—I don't know yet," she stammered. "The idea just came to me."

"I just bet it did," Drake muttered. "And just when did you plan to start this—this—this nonsense?"

"Whenever I find a man with a black enough reputation. Care to make a recommendation?"

Drake snorted. "No. Our host has a pretty black reputation, but he's married. Besides, even if he wasn't, he's probably not the kind you would want to associate with, anyway."

Emma knit her brows. She'd heard some terrible things about the Duke of Gateway and knew he'd even been called the Dangerous Duke, but the few times she'd been in his presence he hadn't been *that* bad. "Know of any others?"

He shook his head. "Viscount Bonnington is the only other man I can think of who could court you and have Marcus here by nightfall. But he's the worst sort of man there is." He exhaled sharply. "Does it have to be a hardened rake with a reputation that matches his black soul?"

"I think so," Emma said sincerely. She may like to think of Marcus as a warm and caring man, but she knew he had a will that couldn't easily be bent. It would take something drastic to get him to act. Unfortunately, that meant being "courted" by a scoundrel.

"You do understand your pretend courtship might lead to a real marriage, don't you?"

Emma swallowed. That was certainly a possibility. One she didn't like to think about, but one that couldn't be ignored. If her plan didn't work, she'd still have to marry someone, and chances were he'd be whichever scoundrel she was about to be courted by. Slowly, she nodded. She had to do this. She knew it didn't make a lot of sense and she knew most would think she was daft for scheming in such a way when it seemed rather clear Marcus didn't want her. But she had to do this. And if it didn't work the way she wanted, she'd marry the scoundrel.

Drake threaded his fingers through his black hair. "What if I give you another choice? One that doesn't include marriage to a blackguard."

Emma's blood stilled. He wasn't going to offer himself as a substitute, was he? She couldn't even contemplate the idea of marrying him. He was Marcus' closest friend. If she accepted his proposal, not only would Marcus not voice a complaint about her choice, he'd probably encourage the match. Then she and Marcus would be devastated far more than they were already, and poor Drake, who'd once had a love match, would be married to a woman who'd never love him. What a coil! "Drake, I can't accept your suit."

"I'm sure Marcus will be pleased to hear that," he said casually, a grin on his lips. "However, I hadn't offered it."

Embarrassment flooded Emma. Twice now she'd accepted an imaginary proposal. "I'm sorry, it's just you said…"

"I know. I have something else in mind. I have this cousin you might like. He's a baronet, so if rank is of no accord—"

"It's not," she blurted.

"Good. What of age?" He flickered a glance at a tree just behind her shoulder, then met her eyes again, a pale pink on his cheeks. "I'll be blunt. He's younger than you. Not a lot, mind you."

"How young?"

"Four-and-twenty."

Emma sighed with relief. The way Drake was acting, she'd have thought this fellow was still in leading strings. "That is not a problem."

"Good. There's one other thing, he's...er...he's a little different, if you will. But don't worry; he'll make a good match for someone like you."

"Someone like me?"

Drake nodded. "Someone in love with someone else."

"Oh."

"His name is Sir Wallace Benedict. If you'd like, I can introduce the two of you."

"Wait." Now that there was a chance of this becoming real, she needed to know a few things. "If he's not a blackguard, what good will he do me?"

"A lot," Drake said with a triumphant smile. "Believe me; a man doesn't have to be a blackguard to get Marcus' attention. Besides, if you do wind up having to marry him, he won't make you a bad husband." He paused a few seconds to let Emma think about his words. "Are you sure this is what you want to do?"

Emma bit her lower lip in nervous excitement. What would this Sir Wallace be like? What would it be like being courted by him? Or what if she did end up married to him? Was that what she really wanted? She took a deep breath that did nothing to calm her nerves. "Yes."

"You don't sound very convinced," Drake teased. "How about we make a bargain? You meet Wallace, and if you don't find him to your liking by the end of the Season, you can come to Briar Creek to work as governess—for real this time."

She smiled weakly. "Agreed."

"Excellent," Drake said, flashing her a weak smile. "Are you ready to meet him?"

"He's here?" Emma squeaked with uncertainty.

"Just over there." He jerked his thumb to the right. "He's the one inspecting the duke's brick over by the wall sconce."

Emma's gaze followed Drake's thumb to collide with a man

who appeared to be as cracked as he was handsome. The man wore buckskin breeches and a white coat. The profile of his face was breathtaking with hard lines and a strong chin. It was too dark to see any of the finer details, but it was easy enough to tell he was devastatingly handsome. However, there was something strange about him. She couldn't name it exactly, just an air about him. He was by himself now, and she'd seen him by himself earlier this evening, too. He had been standing by the refreshment table, counting the glasses, and now he appeared to be counting the bricks on the exterior of the duke's house.

Ducking her head so as not to give away her thoughts about this unusual man Drake had suggested, Emma said, "How about tomorrow, when he's…uh…less distracted."

"As you wish," Drake said with a chuckle. "I told you he was a bit different."

"Yes, just a bit."

***

Marcus tilted his head and shoved his clammy hands into his pockets then balled them into fists. He hated London. He hated balls. He hated watching couples dance. But most of all, he hated watching Emma be twirled around the floor by a man who wasn't him.

Right now she was in the arms of Lord Wray, a young, attractive lord who had everything he needed to give any woman the type of life she deserved, including children. Marcus nearly snorted. Not only was it suspected, it was proven he could do that. At Eton he'd gloated when a chambermaid was dismissed from her employ for reasons undisclosed. Nobody had to guess what that meant; they all knew, and they even knew who'd put her in that condition. Wray had made sure of it.

Marcus scowled and sagged against the wall, doing his best to stay hidden in the shadows of the ballroom. He'd sought admission for the sole purpose of seeing Emma just one more time. When he'd made arrangements to come, he hadn't considered the fact he'd have to watch her dance with every man in attendance. All men in attendance, except Patrick, he amended. With him she hadn't danced. Instead, they'd gone to the gardens for what felt like an eternity. A bitter taste filled Marcus' mouth, and the sick feeling already in his stomach intensified tenfold. What had those two done together in the garden?

"Hard to watch the woman you love in the arms of another, isn't it?" Benjamin Collins, Duke of Gateway and the host of this ball, commented, coming to stand next to Marcus. Gateway offered him a glass and together the two stood in silence for a minute, their eyes fastened on Emma.

"Yes, it is," Marcus acknowledged at last. He didn't know a lot about Gateway's relationship with his wife, but he did remember Alex telling him the duke had a love match. Likely, Gateway must have spent his share of dances watching his wife in the arms of another man. But at least she was his wife, Marcus thought bitterly as he let his eyes scan Emma's figure.

Silence enveloped the two once more as the orchestra played the final bars of a waltz. "I can ask the musicians to play one more waltz at the end, if you'd like," Gateway offered, turning his ice-blue eyes back to Marcus.

Marcus shook his head. "No, thank you." He didn't want to watch her dance with yet *another* man. He'd seen enough already tonight to give himself an ample amount of jealous feelings to last a lifetime. One more dance would only add to his torture.

Gateway cocked his head to the side. "It wouldn't be an imposition. I'd rather enjoy an extra waltz with my wife."

"It's your ball. Do as you wish." After the words were out, he gave a stiff shrug he hoped Gateway would take as his indifference, though he doubted it.

The duke sighed. "You're not being very forthcoming, Sinclair."

"Nor do I need to be."

"No, you don't." Gateway glanced over to his wife, who was talking to one of her sisters. "Sometimes it's up to us to make the hard choice which will gain us what we want more than anything else."

Marcus nearly snorted. The only reason he stopped himself

was because he might draw attention to where he was lurking in the corner if he did. "Some might disagree with your methods."

"No, not some. Most," the duke said easily, his lips twisting into a brittle smile. "But you forget—my actions weren't so she'd marry me. Quite the opposite. I just wanted her happy. Even if that meant with someone else."

"Then I think we understand each other better than I originally thought."

Chapter 19

As agreed, Drake came by the Watson townhouse the next day with his cousin in tow.

"Emma." He gave her a light, emotionless kiss on her knuckles. "I'd like to introduce you to Sir Wallace Benedict. Wallace, this is Miss Emma Green."

Emma curtsied to the man and smiled warmly as he did a low bow. "It's a pleasure to make your acquaintance, Sir Wallace."

"The pleasure is mine," he returned with the widest grin she'd ever seen.

"Shall we sit?" She took a seat and waited for both the men to join her before pouring their tea. Caroline had just come back in from the garden only a few minutes before Drake's arrival, surely she'd be down soon to help with this awkward conversation.

"I hear you're in the market to catch a husband," Sir Wallace said frankly.

Emma nearly choked to death on her own tongue. She was certainly interested in a husband, but she'd hoped Drake would have explained the situation to him and he didn't think she was interested in *him* becoming her husband.

"Wallace, your manners," Drake murmured, casting Emma an apologetic glance.

"I apologize," Sir Wallace said, looking shamefaced. "I was too forward."

Tucking a tendril of blonde hair behind her ear, Emma smiled weakly. "It's all right. It's the truth, in a manner of speaking."

"Very good, then." Sir Wallace snatched a biscuit off the

platter. "I should like to court you. If that's acceptable to you, of course."

Emma interpreted his wink to mean he understood the situation better than she originally thought. She nodded slightly and swallowed hard. "I accept."

"Good. Good. Do you like horses?"

Emma waved off Drake's blatant cough at Sir Wallace's question. "I do like horses," she said, stretching her lips as wide as she could. If these two were to give off the appearance of courting, it was the least she could do to show him some encouragement. Besides which, she did like horses; furthermore, there was no reason the two of them couldn't have a good time together.

"I have tickets tonight to go to Astley's. Would you like to join me?"

"Only if her chaperones are allowed to come, too," Caroline informed him, stepping into the drawing room.

Sir Wallace blinked rapidly. "Of course they are. Why wouldn't they be? I have absolutely no intentions of spending any more than a second or two alone in Miss Green's presence."

And that night Emma—and everyone else in their party—realized he meant to honor those exact words no matter the cost.

At precisely six o'clock that evening, Sir Wallace brought an annoyed-looking Drake—and Drake's carriage, naturally—to Watson Townhouse to collect Emma, Caroline, and Alex to go to Astley's.

"I don't believe Drake's carriage can transport us all," Sir Wallace said in a gravely serious voice. "We each need our own cushions optimum comfort and his coach only has four cushions. That will not do. How many cushions does yours have, Lord Watson?"

Emma tried not to giggle as Alex, who Emma had always thought was the most unusual person she'd ever met until her introduction to Sir Wallace, stared at Sir Wallace unblinkingly. "Four, I think."

Caroline turned her head in Emma's direction and cast her a queer look, leading Emma to cough delicately and turn her head away. "Why don't we just split up, then?" Caroline suggested.

"How could we possibly divide?" Sir Wallace asked. His eyebrows rose so high they were almost lost in his hairline.

"What if you ride in Lord Watson's carriage with him, Caroline, and Emma and I'll just go home," Drake suggested pointedly.

Sir Wallace's face tensed. "No."

Drake groaned. "Are you sure? You do realize if I left, it would not only create an even number, but everyone's arse would be able to rest upon its own cushion."

"That won't do," Sir Wallace said, frowning. "Five is prime. Nothing can divide it. We need to be indivisible. We need to be five."

Emma's body stiffened. Was this what her life would always be like if Marcus didn't choke down his foolish pride? Caroline's arm looped through hers, her hand lightly squeezing Emma's arm for assurance. "You don't have to do this," Caroline whispered. "Perhaps we could go to Lady Vessey's ball and look for a more suitable match there."

"Let's hire a hack," Alex suggested quietly. "Most of them are larger than regular carriages. Surely a hack will have enough cushions."

"Excellent idea," Sir Wallace cheered. "I knew a scientist like you would be able to solve this terrible conundrum."

"I'm glad to know my brilliance could be of assistance," Alex said dryly before walking off to find a hack stand.

"Miss Green, I do hope you don't mind us taking a less fashionable way to Astley's. I just *cannot* be comfortable sharing a cushion, nor would I wish to impose that travesty on another." Sir Wallace grimaced as he spoke.

"It's no trouble," Emma assured him with a stilted smile.

Sir Wallace's returned smile lit his entire face. He really was a handsome man. He had high cheekbones and rich brown eyes with arching brows the color of coffee. His nose was slim, yet rigid, as were his chin and lips. His face reminded her of a statue she'd once seen at the British Museum.

His clothes were absolutely flawless, too. Emma's eyes did a quick sweep from his perfectly polished shoes all the way to what she could see of his hat. Not a single piece of lint could be found anywhere on him. Even his walking stick looked perfect. There wasn't a scratch on the shaft, and what she could see of the handle looked like a perfectly smooth and polished piece of ivory.

"Twelve," the object of her survey murmured, and Emma blushed lightly at being caught staring at him.

"Pardon?" Caroline asked as Drake rolled his eyes up toward the sky.

"I said twelve. It took twelve strokes with the hot iron to get the pleats perfect," Sir Wallace explained as if everyone in the group were extraordinarily interested in his pleats.

A hack drove up and Alex opened the door from inside. He climbed down and helped his wife in first, then stood and waited for Sir Wallace to help Emma. Sir Wallace, however, stood fidgeting and looked to Drake then to Alex with pleading eyes.

"I don't need any help," Emma said. She stepped closer to the carriage.

Drake's hand reached out and grabbed her arm. With a murmured apology, he helped her into the carriage then followed her in. "He's just nervous. Give him a little time."

Emma nodded and straightened her skirt. She could understand his nervousness. She was nervous, too.

Sir Wallace and Alex came into the carriage with a rigidity Emma couldn't place. Sir Wallace took the seat across from her, right next to Drake. Alex, who seemed unusually perceptive this evening, cast Sir Wallace an odd look, and then took the last vacant cushion, which just happened to be on the end next to Emma.

The ride to Astley's was rather uncomfortable as Caroline tried in vain to strike up some sort of conversation. Unfortunately, her attempts were met with indifference or brief answers.

Drake, being the highest ranked gentleman in their party, grumbled as Wallace nudged him to use his rank to get better seats.

"I like this box," Sir Wallace explained to the group as they walked down the hall to their box. "It offers the best view of the stage, and five chairs can be repositioned to form one row instead of two."

Behind her, Emma heard Caroline making an unusual choking sound. Twisting her neck a little, she tried to see what was wrong with her friend.

"Here we are," Drake said, opening the door to the box. "Wallace, why don't you and Emma take the front row and I'll sit with Lord and Lady Watson."

"Oh no," Wallace exclaimed, pausing right inside the door. "I wouldn't wish to bring shame on Miss Green that way."

"What are you talking about?" Drake asked through clenched teeth. "There are three other people in the room. Nobody is going to think a thing of you and Miss Green sitting next to each other at a circus performance."

"No," Wallace said. "It only invites trouble. Someone across the room may not see you three, and start nasty rumors about Miss Green. I'll not have it. Let's just rearrange the chairs."

Everyone but Sir Wallace stood back and waited while he arranged the five chairs to his satisfaction. Emma closed her eyes and tried to remind herself that Sir Wallace was a relative of Drake's, and Drake had been the one to suggest him as a potential match. She may not be overly close with Drake, but she did trust he'd not deliberately cause her harm. Besides, Sir Wallace was handsome and seemed to be more interested in preserving her reputation than any of the other men she'd met since coming to London. That was certainly a point in his favor.

Taking the chair next to Caroline, Emma arranged her skirts and waited for Sir Wallace to sit on the other side of her.

"I hope I'm not making you uncomfortable," Sir Wallace whispered with a swallow. "I...uh...a few years ago, I inadvertently ruined a young lady's reputation. Since then, I've become more cautious."

Emma nodded. How in the world does one inadvertently ruin a girl's reputation? What was more, how did he manage not having to marry her? "I thank you for your thoughtfulness."

"Think nothing of it," he said with a shrug. His brown eyes

left her face and looked to the stage where an announcer was taking his place in the middle of the stage.

The first half of the performance was filled with performers doing tricks on horses, humorous skits, and the occasional bawdy jest. Next to Emma, Sir Wallace chuckled a few times, but most notably, she noticed he *hadn't* been counting like she thought he might do when a juggler came out or when a person holding a lighted candelabrum took center stage. Actually, he was perfectly relaxed. Perhaps Drake was right and he'd just been nervous earlier.

"Why don't you two go get some refreshments," Caroline suggested when the curtain dropped for intermission.

Wallace's face tensed again. "Will you be joining us?"

"No," Caroline said. "I'm in no need of refreshment. Are you, Alex?"

Alex shook his head.

"Well, I am," Drake mumbled. He stood and quit the room.

"You don't need anything, do you?" Sir Wallace asked Emma, two beads of sweat racing down his forehead.

"No, I'll survive until I get home," Emma murmured, licking her dry lips. She could really use a glass of lemonade. Her heart twisted in her chest. Lemonade was Marcus' drink of choice. She clenched her fists and steeled her spine. Why was she even thinking of him when it was becoming more and more clear he didn't want her?

Sir Wallace visibly relaxed in his chair. "Good. It's settled then."

"And people think I'm obtuse," Alex muttered, dropping his head and digging his fingers in his hair.

"Did you say something?" Sir Wallace asked.

Alex sighed. "Old chap, you were just given an opportunity to be alone with a beautiful woman, and you passed it up. Take her down to the refreshment area and find her something to eat and drink."

"But she said she wasn't in need of anything," Sir Wallace argued.

"She said that because she thought that's what you wanted her to say," Caroline pointed out.

"Oh." Sir Wallace turned quizzical eyes on Emma. "Are you thirsty?"

"A little."

"All right. You stay here with your chaperone. I'll be back in a minute with something for you to drink." Sir Wallace stood up and righted his coat, then picked up his walking stick.

"Take her with you," Alex said as Sir Wallace walked in front of him.

"Pardon?"

"You need to take her with you." Turning to his wife, Alex said, "Please tell me I did not miss so many subtle opportunities during our courtship."

"I did not miss so many subtle opportunities during our courtship," she repeated flawlessly. She winked at him. "You didn't miss so many, either. In fact, you seemed to take advantage of just about every opportunity you could."

"Good. Now, Sir Wallace, take Emma downstairs, walk as slowly as you can, and engage her in some sort of conversation."

Sir Wallace looked at Emma and shifted from one foot to the other. "I would not like to damage her reputation. I think it best if Lady Watson joins us."

Emma shook her head. It wasn't going to ruin anyone's reputation to walk downstairs with a gentleman at a performance. "It's all right, Sir Wallace."

"No, it's not," Caroline butted in. "Nobody is going to think anything improper is happening."

"Yes, but I promised I'd not be more than just a few seconds alone with her," Sir Wallace said. "I cannot in good conscience break that promise."

"Yes, you can," Caroline said flippantly. "Now, you two go downstairs and don't come back up until you have a tray of drinks for Alex and me."

Emma smiled. She'd never seen Caroline so assertive. She rather liked it. She'd finally learned to speak her mind. After years of putting up with Olivia and her rotten demeanor, Caroline deserved to command some respect. "Let's go," Emma chirped. She walked to Sir Wallace and placed her hand on his arm.

Taking a minute to wipe the sweat off his brow with his handkerchief, Sir Wallace led her out of the room. In the hall, Emma sighed. Her escort was counting all the wall sconces they passed.

Rounding the corner to go down the stairs, Sir Wallace froze, and his face instantly went as pale as his cravat.

"What's wrong?" Emma whispered.

"Wallace," a shrill voice trilled.

Emma snapped her head around to see a beautiful woman with dark black hair piled high atop her head. She wore a sparkling red dress and had the face of an angel. Tearing her eyes from the beautiful woman, Emma looked once again at a deathly still Sir Wallace.

"Won't you introduce me to your light-o-love?" the woman asked, batting her eyelashes at Sir Wallace.

Sir Wallace tried to clear his throat. Then again. And again. Finally, on the fourth try, he cleared it enough to form a few uneven words. "Lady Silverton, this is Miss Emma Green. Miss Green, this is Lady Silverton."

Emma tried her best to do a perfect curtsy in front of the marchioness. She'd heard of Lady Silverton before. She had several characteristics in common with Louise. One of which was the fact she was known among the *ton* for being engaged to a gentleman and jilting him in favor of a man with more wealth and a higher title.

Emma's head snapped back to Sir Wallace. He was the man she'd jilted! A wave of sympathy for Sir Wallace washed over her. She squeezed his arm.

Lady Silverton looked Emma up and down then pursed her lips. "I guess I shouldn't be surprised you finally found my replacement. Though I admit I still dream of the day I can marry you after Silverton cocks up his toes, but I suppose an affair will have to suffice."

205

Emma's eyes grew wide. "Excuse me?"

Lady Silverton flashed her a superior smile. "You didn't think Wallace would be faithful to you, did you?"

Emma didn't answer. She just stared at the addled woman in front of her.

"Oh, you did," Lady Silverton said in mock sympathy. "Dearest, you must understand those vows men take at their wedding mean nothing. After you produce the heir, they won't mean anything to you, either, I expect."

Looking to Sir Wallace, Emma realized he still hadn't found his voice. She stiffened her spine. "Lady Silverton," she began in a sharp whisper so nobody would overhear, "your husband might stray from you regularly and you may cuckold him with anyone you please, but I have no intention of being untrue to my husband, and I honestly believe he'll keep his vows to me."

Lady Silverton took in a sharp intake of air. "Is that so?" she asked nastily. "Well, you have a lot to learn. I suspect Wallace will be out of your bed and into mine before midnight on your wedding night."

"I don't think so," Emma said proudly. "Why would he want an old, tired woman like you, when he could have me?" Emma's eyes nearly popped out of her head when she realized exactly what she'd just said and to whom.

Not three feet behind Lady Silverton's shoulder, Drake stood with an odd expression on his face, as if he, too, realized she had just as good as publicly announced she was engaged to a perfect stranger.

Chapter 20

"I'm sure Sir Wallace will release you from the engagement," Caroline said, sitting down on Emma's bed. "He knew this was all a charade from the start, didn't he?"

Emma shrugged. "It doesn't matter. He may count everything, but at least he's better than some of the other men I could have become engaged to." She shuddered just thinking of who else she might have been forced to marry.

"You're just saying that. I know you're still hurt about Marcus' rejection, but that doesn't mean you need to make yourself miserable for the rest of your life."

Whirling around to face her friend, Emma put her brush down with a hard clank on the bureau. "What makes you think I'm going to be miserable?"

Caroline crossed her arms. "Don't pretend with me, Emma. I'll admit I had no idea you ever had feelings for Marcus—I mean at one time I thought you might, but I'd convinced myself otherwise..." She shook her head. "What I'm saying is, just because Marcus seems to have some misguided notion regarding your future doesn't mean you need to make yourself suffer more than you already are by being denied the one you want. Pick someone else. You and Sir Wallace are not a good match."

"I can't pick someone else. I've already become unofficially betrothed to Sir Wallace."

"Yes, that's what I heard," Caroline said dryly. "You just couldn't ignore her, could you?"

Emma sat down on the bed next to Caroline and smiled

ruefully. "No, I couldn't. But that matters naught. I would have accepted his suit anyway had Marcus not come to his senses, which, we both know was doubtful to begin with."

"You really would have accepted his proposal?" Caroline asked. "He's a little odd, don't you think?"

Nodding, Emma brought her knees up to her chest and rested her feet on the edge of the mattress. "That he is. But if you look on the positive—and slightly ironic—side, we'll both be married to very logical men. That'll be helpful when we get together for house parties and such."

Caroline tucked a long lock of her dark hair behind her ear. "I suppose that counts for something,"

"Anyway," Emma cut in as she hugged her knees tighter to her chest. "I don't think he'll always be so stiff."

Caroline snorted.

Sighing, Emma shook her head. "You know what I meant."

"Yes, I did," Caroline admitted. "But I hope for your sake he *is* stiff after the wedding."

Emma twisted her lips. That was probably the worst thing about marrying Sir Wallace. She had no desire to go to bed with him. Though he seemed nice enough, she didn't relish the thought of performing the acts described in *Lady Bird's Ladybird Memoir* with him. With Marcus, yes. Absolutely. Without question. With Sir Wallace? Not really. Likely he'd be nervous and start counting his movements. She grimaced. *That* would certainly kill any enjoyment she could possibly have with him. Not that she anticipated any in the first place.

"Caroline," Emma said softly after several minutes of uninterrupted silence.

"Yes?"

"Do you think Marcus will change his mind now?"

Caroline's blue eyes held her gaze, but in them, Emma saw the same uncertainty and doubt she feared herself. "I don't know," Caroline whispered. "Since you won't tell me the reason he sent you away, I cannot give an honest opinion."

Emma swallowed. "I can't tell you. It's his secret, not mine."

"I know," Caroline acknowledged. "And I don't expect you to break his trust by telling me. But that's the problem, Emma. If I don't know, I can't give you advice. I'm sorry."

"It's not your fault," Emma mumbled. She leaned her face forward to rest her forehead on the soft blue fabric of her nightrail that was stretched across her raised knees. "Do you think Alex could talk to him?"

"He could." Caroline reached her fingers over to brush a lock of hair out of Emma's eyes. "But don't expect anything to come of it. Marcus can be just as stubborn as you sometimes, and even though I love Alex more than anyone, he's not exactly the most convincing man who ever lived."

Emma smiled. "He's not going to treat it like an experiment, is he?" Caroline had the right of it when she claimed Alex wasn't the most convincing man there ever was. He was the kind who conducted a courtship like a science experiment rather than just being straightforward and spending the lowly fifteen minutes it would have taken for him to convince Caroline to marry him.

Shrugging, Caroline flashed her a lopsided smile. "Perhaps he should. Last time produced some rather favorable results, if I do say so myself."

"I just hope it works out just as favorably this time."

"I'll ask Alex to speak to him the day after tomorrow."

Emma's arms instinctively tightened around her knees. She'd temporarily forgotten the breakfast Caroline was hosting on the morrow. Sir Wallace would be there, naturally. Perhaps she could persuade him not to ask Alex to make a formal announcement until after Alex had a chance to speak with Marcus.

As if reading her thoughts, Caroline delicately placed her hand on Emma's wrist, and said, "I'll ask Alex to refuse to make the announcement tomorrow. Balls are so much more fun to announce engagements anyway. Perhaps next week at the Townsons' ball we can have the formal announcement."

"Thank you, Caroline." She sorely hoped at that ball next week the announcement of the engagement between her and Marcus would be made instead, but even if that wasn't to be, at least she was given a small reprieve.

"Caroline," Emma said abruptly as a thought popped into her head.

"Hmm?"

"Please tell Alex not to mention the only reason I went with Sir Wallace to Astley's was to get Marcus' attention, I don't think he'd be very happy to know that."

Caroline grinned. "Don't worry. Alex doesn't even know that was your plan. For once Alex's obtuseness is to someone's advantage—particularly yours. He thought you genuinely wanted to be courted by the man. And that, Emma, is a good thing. You wouldn't want Alex to know the truth. He's an awful liar and Marcus would know the whole tale in less than five minutes." She shook her head as a slow smile spread across her lips. Just thinking of Alex seemed to cause that reaction in Caroline. "I'll just send him to tell Marcus you've made your selection and ask what needs to be done about your dowry."

With a dull ache in her heart, Emma nodded.

***

Sir Wallace was the first guest to show up at Watson Townhouse the next day. His clothes were once again pristine and sharp. From his mustard yellow coat to his bottle green breeches and waistcoat to his white shirt and cravat, not a piece of lint could be found. His boots were so polished they could almost pass as a mirror.

"I hope I'm not overdressed," he teased when he caught sight of Emma staring at his clothes for the second time in as many days.

"Not at all." Emma flashed him a smile. Now that she had hope Alex would talk sense into Marcus, she wasn't so nervous around Sir Wallace. Truly there was no reason the two of them could not be friends after all this was over. "Would you like to…" She tried to quickly think of something of interest in the house for them to look at. "Go for a tour?" she finished dully.

"That would be most excellent. I heard this house has recently been redecorated."

Emma tried not to giggle. "Yes, it has. The former baron had a rather unusual sense of humor and decorated this house in such a fashion that was considered…um…unsettling, if you will. When Alex first brought Caroline here after his father's passing, the first thing she did was order the place redecorated."

"I must humbly admit my townhouse is twelve hundred thirty seven square feet smaller than this one, but I still think you'll have just as much entertainment redecorating it as Lady Watson did redecorating this one."

Emma nearly tripped over her own feet. How in the world did he know his townhouse was precisely twelve hundred thirty seven square feet smaller than Watson Townhouse? Never mind. She really didn't want to know the answer to that. "I'm sure your townhouse isn't as badly in need of redecoration as this one was," she said to end the discussion. With any luck, Marcus would come to his senses and she'd be decorating *his* house.

Sir Wallace chuckled. "No, it's not as beastly as this house was once rumored to be, but I do know how you ladies are. You're welcome to redecorate anything you wish." He grinned at her in a way that made Emma begin to feel uneasy about her plan to send Alex to talk to Marcus.

Clearing her throat, she gestured to two chairs that were perfectly in view of the others working around them, but still allowed them some privacy. "Sir Wallace—"

"Just Wallace," he cut in.

"Pardon?"

"Now that we're engaged, you may call me Wallace."

"Right," Emma said slowly, absentmindedly biting her lip. "About that…" She fidgeted in her seat and used the fingers of her right hand to mindlessly pull on the loose thread on her left sleeve cuff. "W-were y-you…" She cleared her throat. "Excuse me. Were you set on the announcement being made today?"

Wallace's lips twitched. "You're really in love with Sinclair, aren't you?"

"Yes," Emma said as evenly as she could, ignoring the fact that her word came out as little more than a squeak.

"Very well." Wallace stood up and removed his hat. Holding it in his hands, he fingered the brim for a minute before looking at Emma again. "What are your plans?"

Emma stared at him, dumbfounded. His words, though not said unkindly, had caught her off guard. "What do you mean?"

He smiled and shook his head. "I mean, do you still plan to just ignore all the gentlemen who dance attendance on you in hopes he'll be struck by lightning and run back to your side?"

"No. Alex is going to speak to him tomorrow." She didn't know why she'd told him that, but she had, and now a horrible feeling of dread and unease washed over her as she realized just how bad this all must look to him.

"Ah." He put his hat back on his head and shoved his hands into his coat pockets. "What then?"

"Hopefully, he'll..." She trailed off and waved her hand vaguely, hoping he'd get the unspoken message. She really hated looking so desperate.

"And if he doesn't?" Wallace asked softly, his dark brown eyes full of tender concern that made her heart ache.

She swallowed. "Then I'll seriously pursue a husband."

He nodded slowly and exhaled. "I know I haven't made the most favorable impression on you thus far, what with my annoying habit of counting everything in sight when I'm uncomfortable or nervous, and all. But I think with time, I'll be more comfortable with you and I'll stop."

Emma smiled weakly at him. She'd suspected he only counted because he was nervous. "Are you saying your offer of marriage will stand next week if I have need to accept it?" she asked warily.

"Yes."

"Thank you." Overwhelmed with gratitude, she surged to her feet and wrapped her arms around him in a close hug. "I know this is a rather unusual arrangement, and I thank you for your indulgence. But I give you my word, if I formally accept your suit and our engagement is announced, I'll marry you. I promise it. I'll not jilt you."

"Good," he said, stiffly patting her back and softly rattling off numbers under his breath.

Emma stepped back. "You're uncomfortable. I'm sorry. I shouldn't have hugged you."

"It's just as well." He shoved his hands back into his pockets. "I'll get used to it, I promise. I…um…" he reached up and tugged jerkily on his cravat, "after the mess with Lady Silverton when I was younger, I've been a little wary when it comes to those of the female persuasion."

"I understand." And she truly did. "I promise I'll not cause you any undue embarrassment or hurt."

"That's all I ask."

"Sir Wallace," Alex called, walking in their direction.

"Lord Watson," Wallace greeted with a bow.

Alex didn't bother to return his bow. "I was hoping to speak to you. Privately."

"No need. Miss Green and I have already reached an understanding."

Alex blinked. "You have."

"Yes. We'll wait to announce our engagement until next week."

Staring blankly at Emma, Alex blinked a couple of times. "Very well." Giving them each one more strange glance, he shook his head and without another word walked away to stand by his wife.

***

Emma couldn't fall asleep. No matter how hard she tried to stave them off, thoughts of Marcus and Wallace both spun around in her head. A tear slipped from her eye and she quickly wiped it away. Marcus really didn't love her. He claimed he did and wanted her to be happy, but she could never be truly happy. Not without Marcus, anyway.

She could try to force herself to have an amiable marriage with Wallace. She may not truly be happy being married to him, but perhaps she could learn to be satisfied. That would be enough, wouldn't it? She lay there trying to convince herself that it would be. Earlier today, he'd been much more relaxed around her than he had been before. He'd escorted her around and told her several

213

amusing stories about people he knew, or pranks he was involved in at Harrow. He'd laughed at her weak attempts at jokes and even asked her questions about growing up in Dorset.

Though they barely knew each other at the beginning of the day, by the time he left, she was much more comfortable with him than she thought she could have been. He seemed more comfortable, too. She'd only caught him counting twice during the whole four hours they were at Caroline's breakfast.

He really wouldn't be a bad husband, she thought, turning over. He might be a bit unusual and awkward, but if she couldn't have Marcus, he'd be perfect.

That guilty knot she was becoming all too familiar with formed in her gut. She hated openly treating Wallace like nothing but a *spare*. It wasn't fair to him. He may not have voiced a complaint, but that didn't mean she had any right to treat him as if his feelings didn't matter and all he was good for was to be a replacement, if Marcus truly didn't want her. Bile rose in her throat. Marcus *didn't* want her. He'd plainly told her so the day she left Ridge Water, and his lack of trying to contact her since she'd departed only confirmed it. A new round of tears flowed from her eyes as the harsh reality washed over her that the man she'd always loved didn't love her back.

By the time the clock struck midnight, Emma knew what she must do. She needed to apologize to Wallace for being so careless with his feelings, beg his forgiveness for being so callous in her treatment of him, and accept his suit if his offer still stood. There was no use in waiting for Marcus. Alex might be uncommonly smart, but all the intelligence in England wasn't a match for Marcus when he'd made up his mind.

Decision made, Emma rolled over and used the edge of her lacy pillow sham to wipe her tears for what she hoped would be the final time that night. Tomorrow she'd tell Alex she'd made her decision to marry Wallace.

Chapter 21

Marcus fought back the miserable sadness that had begun swamping him the moment he heard Chapman announce Lord Watson was here to see him. He knew what that meant: Emma had decided on a husband.

Hardening his facial features so as not to give any hint at the turmoil he was inwardly fighting, Marcus stood up and waited for Alex to be shown to his study.

"Afternoon," Marcus greeted gruffly.

Alex took his hat off and carelessly tossed it in a vacant chair before plopping down in the chair next to the one currently holding his hat. "What are you doing?"

Marcus' gaze dropped to his desk where he had an entire array of snippets of animal feathers and fur scattered all over his desk. "Don't worry, the animals were already dead," he grumbled, sitting back down in his chair. He brushed the clippings to a little pile on the far side of his desk.

Blinking, Alex said, "I wasn't talking about that. I may not care much for the sport of fishing, but I'd recognize your 'fly tying' attempts anywhere." He reached forward and picked up a dark brown creature Marcus had made that was supposed to resemble a mouse. "It seems you've lost your touch," he mused, turning the loosely tied bug over in his hand.

Marcus reached his fingers forward and plucked the fly from Alex. "That was the first one I'd attempted in more than thirteen years, thank you." He picked up one of his more recent attempts and tossed it at his friend.

Alex turned the Goddard Caddis over in his hand and quietly inspected it. He put it back down and looked over at a giant piece of thick leather Marcus was using to hook his finished creations on. He whistled and shook his head. "Hell's afire, Marcus. Is this all you've been doing?"

Marcus yanked the piece of leather off the top of the desk. "I don't question you about your enjoyment of conducting bizarre science experiments, even though I find them dull. I expect the same courtesy." In all the years he'd known Alex, he'd never been quite so irritated with the man. "Now, tell me why you're here."

"No need to be sharp. I came to inform you that you have exactly three days to let go of whatever is holding you back and declare yourself to Miss Green."

"What's that to mean?" Marcus barked. Three days? What would happen in three days? And why did his heart lurch at Alex's silence.

Folding his hands in front of his stomach and leaning back in his chair, Alex sat quietly and looked around the room. Finally, his brown eyes met Marcus'. "In three days, her engagement will be announced."

A large lump formed in Marcus' throat, threatening to choke the life out of him. He looked down at his hands as they tightened and released. Tightened and released. Tightened and released. He knew this was coming. He'd sent her away so she could make a match. Alex's news wasn't anything he hadn't expected. So why did it feel like his heart was being ripped straight from his chest?

He closed his eyes and leaned his head back to study the ceiling. She'd done it. She'd found a match. A man who could give her what he couldn't. He closed his eyes and pictured her heavy with child. Someone else's child, to be exact. A bitter taste filled his mouth. Another man was going to get to hold her, and kiss her and spend his nights in bed with Emma. Another man would make her a wife and mother.

A cracking sound rent the air. Marcus casually released the armrest he'd just inadvertently broken and put his hands on his knees, never opening his eyes or tearing his thoughts away from

Emma and the realization he was losing her forever.

"There's still time," Alex said quietly.

Twisting his lips, Marcus lowered his head and met his friend's gaze. "No, there's not. There never was. It's for the best she marry another."

"But that's not what you want, now is it?"

Marcus laughed bitterly. "No. It's not. But it's what's best for her."

"Are you sure about that?"

Pushing away from his desk, Marcus stood up and walked to the closest window. Emma wouldn't be happy here. She'd be lonely with only him as company. Even that was conditional. She needed a gentleman who'd race with her on Rotten Row or take her to London for the Season. The same gentleman could provide her with the kind of home young ladies dreamed about. The kind full of love and laughter, friends and family, nieces and nephews, and most of all children of her own.

He made a fist and slammed the side of it against the windowpane. As much as he'd like to blame this unhappy circumstance on Louise, he couldn't. It had been his decision to run after her for the sake of his pride. Unfortunately, that one ill-made decision not only hadn't saved his pride then, but it had also cost him dearly. He'd lost the friends he'd had at Eton, he'd lost his intended (which, in and of itself, was actually for the best), he'd lost his pride, but worst of all, in the end he'd lost the only woman he'd ever loved.

"I'm sure," he croaked. "She'll be happier this way."

Alex snorted. "I think she'd argue that."

"She'd argue with Lucifer himself if she thought he'd bother to listen to her."

"You truly mean to let her go, then?"

Nodding his head, but not moving his eyes from where they were fixed on the tree just outside his window, Marcus whispered, "Yes."

"All right. How do you think I should handle everything?"

"Everything?"

"Yes, everything," Alex said stiffly. "You seem to have appointed me as her sponsor, but I have no idea what you're expecting of me. Do you want me to contact the duke and duchess and let them help her make the announcement and wedding arrangements?"

"No," Marcus barked in annoyance and frustration. He didn't want Louise or Hampton within a half-mile radius of Emma, let alone planning her wedding. He sighed. He really had no choice. Louise was her sister and Hampton her only living male relative. She couldn't plan a wedding without them. And as much as it pained him to even think it, Hampton would be the one to walk her down the aisle. Fury pumped through him at the mere thought of that reprobate touching her. He blew out a breath. "Do not tell them. They may find out by reading the announcement in the newspaper."

Alex nodded. "What of her dowry?"

Marcus raked his hand through his hair before tightening his fingers around the locks and pulling them. Hard. He'd nearly forgotten her dowry. He'd wanted her to make a good match so he'd set up an impressive dowry. He didn't mind parting with the money—that wasn't the problem. He'd pay every last shilling he had and then some to see to Emma's happiness. What he didn't like was the fact he would have to sit across the table from the man who'd get to claim her as his wife while Marcus not only signed over a small fortune, but his own happiness right along with it.

"Perhaps I can have Abrams arrange for separate signings," Alex suggested after a minute, as if by some not-so-small miracle he'd miraculously been cured of his obtuseness and was able to distinguish the subtle undertones of the conversation.

Clearing his throat, Marcus nodded slowly. "I'd appreciate it if you could arrange that." He pulled away from the window and flopped carelessly down in his chair. "Arrange it so I can sign first, please," he added as an afterthought. It was bad enough he was losing Emma to another man; it was best he didn't know exactly whom he'd lost her to. Not that it would be possible to live out the rest of his life not knowing, of course. But that was one advantage to being a recluse. It would be a long, long time before the news of who her husband was reached his ears. Hopefully by then, he'd be indifferent when he heard the announcement. He nearly snorted. He'd never be indifferent, and he knew it. But at least he'd have a little longer to prepare himself for the news.

"I'll see what I can do," Alex said. He leaned forward and reached his hand across Marcus' desk. "Say, these are nice. Wherever did a recluse like you find—"

"Don't touch them," Marcus barked, knocking Alex's hand away from the little dish that held a set of silver cufflinks. He'd found them in the drawing room a few days after he'd sent Emma away. It had been nearly a week after she'd gone away before he had been able to go into that room again. And then it had only been because he needed a cushion to prop his leg up on. When he'd stepped inside the room, his eyes had immediately caught on two little pieces of sparkling silver lying on the rug. Since then, he'd not gone back into that room but had kept the set of cufflinks in a dish on his desk as a reminder of what would never be. Because he wasn't suffering enough already, of course.

Alex shrugged. "I just thought they looked rather dapper. Especially for someone who thinks going to town means a ride to the village once a year to search for some pathetic looking feathers and fur because he's too lazy to either go gather the material himself or go to London and have a look about."

"Emma left them," Marcus informed him curtly, ignoring Alex's other senseless remarks.

Making a big show of removing his spectacles and cleaning them, Alex mused, "Now, I wonder why she'd leave a perfectly good set of cufflinks with *you* when she could have saved them and given them to her new husband on their wedding day?"

"Because they have my initials on them, you dolt," Marcus said gruffly. Since when had Alex become so perceptive or annoying? It must be Caroline rubbing off on him. "Now that we've discussed everything, perhaps you should go."

"I'm in no hurry." Alex stretched his feet out in front of himself.

Marcus nearly groaned in aggravation. Just his luck, Lord Perceptive was gone and the usual Alex had once again taken his place. "Alex, why are you still here? Go home. Go kiss Caroline and hold your son."

A slow smile spread across Alex's lips. "Marcus, old chap, that is exactly what I'd love to be doing. I want nothing more than to walk through the doors of my house and feel Caroline's arms wrap around me, and I'd wager you'd like to come with me and feel Emma's close around you, too. But it seems I haven't convinced you to put aside your stubborn pride. Therefore, I cannot go home yet."

"Why not?" Marcus growled, fury bubbling inside him.

"I just told you. I cannot go home until you're with me."

Marcus clenched his fists and ground his teeth. "Did Caroline put you up to this? Did she threaten to refuse you entrance to her bed until you dragged me to your house?"

A muscle ticked in Alex's face and he jerked to a standing position with record speed. "Marcus, that is my wife you're talking about. She may be your cousin, but she is *my* wife. You have no call to talk about her that way. If you do so again we'll be naming seconds. Clear?"

Marcus blinked at his friend. Alex was never one to get into a temper. He must have touched on a particularly sensitive spot where Alex was concerned. He nodded. "I'll be sure to watch my tongue around you in the future as long as you do the same."

Alex tersely nodded his agreement. "I'll say no more to you about Miss Green. I'll handle everything from here, starting with announcing her engagement to Sir Wallace next week at Andrew's ball."

"Sir Wallace," Marcus thundered. "You mean the one who—"

"The very one."

Chapter 22

"What the devil do you think you're doing?" Marcus shouted, bursting through the door of Patrick's study, heedless to the fact that the three young girls were playing in the corner.

"Girls," Patrick said slowly, piercing Marcus with his cold stare. "Why don't you go see if Mrs. Jenkins is ready for afternoon tea?"

Marcus crossed his arms and murmured a halfhearted apology as the three girls walked past him. Once little Helena shut the door, his tirade immediately continued. "What have you done? How could you have paired those two together? Emma deserves a chance at a real marriage—"

"She'll have a real marriage," Patrick cut in sharply. "Wallace is a man."

"Barely," Marcus bit off.

Patrick shrugged. "I fail to see the problem. She'll have what you seem so reluctant to give her."

"No, what she'll have is a cold, loveless marriage without children. I could have given her that."

"Then why don't you?" Patrick's shrewd eyes searched Marcus' for the answer he'd never say aloud.

Jerking his gaze away, Marcus angrily shoved his hands into his trouser pockets. "That's not what we're discussing. We're discussing your interference. Why did you do that?"

"I want her to be happy as much as you do," Patrick admitted. "I didn't see any other way."

"No other way? No other way, you say. So instead of leaving

her alone to have a Season and find a suitable husband, you suggest she marry your molly of a cousin!"

"He's not a molly."

"Isn't he?" Marcus countered sourly. "Let's see if I recall correctly what you told me. Oh, yes, it goes something like this: 'Marcus, can you ask Caroline to entertain my girls for the next two afternoons? I have to make take a quick trip to London to play the sympathetic cousin for Wallace tomorrow when his bride jilts him.' Bewildered that you knew she was going to stand him up, I inquired as to how you could know she was going to jilt him and why you were going to let him suffer the embarrassment. To which, you replied, 'She's not really standing him up. Well, she is. It's complicated. See, Wallace has always been a little off. His family seems to think he might have…different interests, if you take my meaning.' Then you cleared your throat about half a dozen times and had a hard time meeting my eyes as you finished by saying, 'The plan is to have a woman break his heart at the altar and let everyone assume his subsequent devastation made him the way he is.'"

"You have a surprisingly good memory. You remember more of the situation than I thought you might. However, I need to correct you on one point. Wallace doesn't have any unusual interests like the one you're implying. Nor is he a limp lily. At least I don't think he is." He shook his head. "The unusual interest he has revolves around his need to incessantly count and other such odd behaviors that I'm not entirely certain of."

"Don't flick your wrist in nonchalance," Marcus snarled. "That's the woman I love. I want her to experience every happiness available. Not for her to be trapped with a man who walks around the world thinking everything he sees is a substitute abacus."

"Cool your heels. He only does that when he's nervous."

"I don't care. He's not good enough for her. Go back and persuade her to cry off."

"No," Patrick said tightly.

"Why?"

"I don't see a reason to interfere."

222

Marcus stared at him unblinkingly. He clenched his fists in rage and willed them to stay in his pockets where they belonged. Though punching Patrick might be satisfactory for the moment, it wouldn't solve the problem. "You interfered before. Do it again."

"No."

"Why not?" Marcus demanded angrily. "She'll be miserable."

Patrick shrugged. "You're likely right. But she'll be less miserable with him."

"Than with who?"

"Just about anyone else."

Closing his eyes, Marcus leaned his head back and took deep breaths, silently counting in his head. He got to fifteen and snapped his eyes open, no less angry than he was before. "Patrick, you had better pray there is no wedding."

"Then you had better act."

"No, you'd better do as I suggested and convince her to find another match before the announcement is made."

Reaching forward to smooth out a wrinkle in one of the pages in his account ledger, Patrick casually said, "She'll have to cry off on her own. And you'll have to be the one to give her a reason to do so."

Marcus closed his eyes and, as usual, an image of Emma flashed before him. This particular image was what she'd looked like wearing her chemise in the river right after she'd flung mud at his face. The smile on her face was so bright and full of joy. He squeezed his eyes tighter, willing the picture to evaporate. Would he forever be tortured with images of her whenever he closed his eyes?

"Just go to her Marcus," Patrick said softly.

"I can't."

"Yes, you can," Patrick countered. "Whatever foolish thing you've done, she'll forgive. She loves you. She always has. Just go to her before it's too late."

Sadly, Marcus shook his head. "Are you sure your cousin Wallace is…er…able?"

Patrick nodded once. "I can't verify from firsthand knowledge, but we had a talk or two about his activities at Oxford."

Marcus twisted his lips bitterly at the thought. This was what he'd wanted, he reminded himself. What he'd planned, even. Patrick was right when he said Emma would be happier with Wallace than with the other gentlemen who pursued her. At least Wallace, with his bizarre tendencies, wasn't likely to hurt Emma in any way.

"You know, Marcus," Patrick said slowly, resting his elbows on his desk and leaning forward to rest his chin on the little bridge his hands were making. "Even after five years, I still miss Abigail as much as I did the day she died. There's no land or estates or possession I own that I wouldn't give to go back in time and change the outcome that day. And while I love my girls more than anything, nothing quite replaces the feelings I had for her."

Marcus stared at him. It all seemed so easy for Patrick. He'd had a wife, however, ill-suited for Patrick Marcus may think she'd been. And though Patrick had lost her through childbirth, at least he'd been able to give her those children. Marcus shut his eyes again and thought about Abigail. She'd been so happy and full of life around Celia and Helena. She'd take them outside and laugh and play with them in the sunshine, abandoning the norms of society right along with her slippers.

But that's what had made Lady Drakely so happy: her girls and being able to play with them. Before she'd had them, she was a different person entirely. She'd been quiet and reserved, barely even noticeable. Quite odd really, her sudden transformation. He shrugged uncomfortably. Emma would be the same way with her children. Except, while Abigail used her children as an excuse to indulge her inner child, Emma would see them as a gift to be truly loved. That's why she needed to marry Sir Wallace, even if he was considered a bit of a pansy.

"You're certain he can perform?" Marcus asked again, startling both of them with the roughness of his voice.

"He has a duty to his title, meager as it may be," Patrick said easily. "He may not be rumored to enjoy the activity as much as most men, but he does know his duty. Though why you're so eager to know Emma will be bedded by another man is rather odd, don't you think?"

Jerking his eyes away, Marcus clenched his teeth together so tightly his jaw hurt and he thought at any minute one of his teeth might crack. He *didn't want* to think about Emma being bedded by another, he just wanted to make sure she'd have a child, even if it was just one. That's what he wanted to think about, not her warming another man's bed.

"Just make sure he fulfills that particular duty, or it'll be your neck I throttle."

Patrick shrugged. "I already told you he would. Besides, I think he just might have a sincere interest in Emma. Perhaps she's just what he needs to indulge himself, so to speak."

Marcus growled and shot to his feet so fast a casual observer might have thought he'd been tapped on the bottom with a hot branding iron. "Not another word about that, Patrick. In the next six months I had better read in a scandal sheet that she's retired to the country to await the birth of her babe. No other details are necessary."

"I have no control over her breeding," Patrick said tightly, an unmistakable sadness filling the man's eyes. "You know, Marcus, as much as I love my daughters, I would have still loved my wife just as much had we not had children. Perhaps, Emma feels the same."

Swallowing hard past the lump in his throat, Marcus gave one final glance at his forlorn friend and stalked from the room.

Patrick was wrong. Emma would be happier with a man who could give her the life he couldn't. Patrick wouldn't have loved his wife just as much if they hadn't had children. It was the children who brought out the fun, lovable side of Abigail. That's what all women wanted. What made them come alive.

And that was what he was determined Emma would have, no matter what he had to do to get it for her.

Chapter 23

Today was *the* day. The day Emma would become Lady Benedict, making her a real lady, a baronetess, and a wife, all at the same time.

Closing her eyes tightly to keep the tears pricking her eyes inside where they belonged, she scooted to the edge of her bed, swung her legs over, and let her bare feet fall into the thick crimson rug. She squeezed her toes together, making a sad mental note of the soft fibers of the carpet. This would be the last morning she'd get to wake in a familiar house with familiar surroundings. Tonight she'd go to Sir Wallace's house and wake up tomorrow in a bed that she was nearly certain she'd never be able to feel comfortable in. She swallowed and stood. She needed to get ready for her wedding.

"May I come in?" Caroline asked a moment later, opening the door a crack and peeking inside.

Emma smiled. "Please."

Caroline's blue silk nightrail swished as she walked into the room and over to Emma's side. Impulsively, Emma gave her a quick hug.

"You can stay here as long as you'd like, you know."

"Thank you, Caroline. But I cannot. I must marry. Wallace really isn't as bad as you think he is."

"I know," Caroline admitted with a slight laugh. "I don't know if it's because I've gotten used to his odd tendencies, or if he simply doesn't do them anymore. I'm sure he'll be a good husband."

Silence filled the air as both women stared at each other, an unspoken message passing between them. A message filled with unanswered questions, curiosity, pain, sympathy, and more than anything, confusion and hurt. It had been more than five weeks since Emma had last seen Marcus. He truly wasn't coming back.

The day Alex had gone to speak to him, Emma had tried to intercept him before he left, but found she'd slept too long, thus reverting her back to her original plan—to let Alex talk to Marcus before publicly accepting Wallace's proposal. She'd once again dared to dream he'd return to his senses and would come to collect her. But once again, he hadn't.

Alex returned home alone that next night, his solitary presence silently confirming what she'd already known in her heart: she'd marry Wallace and do her best to put aside any feelings she held for Marcus. She may never come to love Wallace, but she could do her best to make their marriage work.

"Let's get you dressed," Caroline said with feigned excitement. She stood up and walked to Emma's vanity. "These are awfully nice. Why haven't I paid them any mind before?" She picked up the silver-plated brush Marcus had given her.

Emma frowned. She really shouldn't have those combs and brushes. They belonged to Marcus, not her. "I'm glad you like it," she said, walking up to the vanity. "It's yours."

"Pardon?"

"Marcus gave it to me. I think it belonged to his grandmother or something like that. I really shouldn't have kept it, and since his grandmother is also yours, you should have the brush. You can take the comb and mirror, too, if you'd like."

Caroline gently set the brush down. "I think he wanted you to have them."

"I don't think so." Emma fought to keep control of her emotions. "He only let me use them when I came to stay with him. I hadn't brought anything with me."

"I disagree. He wanted you to have them. If he didn't, he wouldn't have given them to you in the first place. Heaven knows Olivia required so many brushes and combs to manage that nest of hair she had, she could keep an army properly groomed."

Emma's rebellious fingers reached out and traced the intricate designs on the handle of the brush. She closed her eyes and yanked her fingers away as if she'd been burned. "I can't keep them."

"All right," Caroline said softly. "I'll take care of them for you. Why don't you go find your gown, and I'll help you put it on."

With a quick nod, Emma walked to her wardrobe and withdrew a silken pale blue dress. Caroline had commissioned one of the most experienced modistes in England to make this dress— at Marcus' expense, of course, Emma reminded herself bitterly; unaware her fingers were squeezing the fabric so hard they were leaving marks. Loosening her grip, she laid the garment over the back of her dressing stool and weakly smiled at Caroline.

Anxious feelings welled up inside Emma as she watched Caroline wordlessly loosen the fastenings of the blue gown to get it ready for wear. Maria, the maid who had been attending Emma the past five weeks, would be in shortly to attend Emma's hair, because Caroline declared only a large mound of overflowing curls would be acceptable. Caroline, however, had made such a big to-do about helping Emma get ready for her wedding, Emma knew better than to argue about it. Maria may be allowed in to fix her hair, but *Caroline* would help Emma put on her dress.

Three hours and two burns with the hot curling tongs later, Emma was a vision of beauty with a stilted smile and salve-glistening skin as she walked out the front door of Watson Townhouse to Alex's carriage.

"You look very lovely, Emma," Alex murmured, giving her a hand up into the carriage.

Emma looked down at him and smiled a genuine smile. Caroline had been very fortunate to find him. He might be unusual and rather awkward at times, but next to Marcus, he truly was the kind of husband girls dreamed of. "Thank you, Alex." Sitting down on the red velvet squabs, Emma watched as Alex handed Caroline up into the carriage, determined not to get jealous at the loving look the two of them exchanged.

"I wonder if Wallace is already there," Alex mused aloud,

presumably just trying to fill the awkward silence.

"I'd assume so. He's probably counting the pews," Emma jested playfully.

Caroline grinned. "That or the tiles on the floor."

"Oh, anything but that." Emma shook her head. "We may never get to the ceremony if he's doing that."

"Don't worry," Alex said. He stretched his long legs out in front of himself and removed his black top hat. "If he insists on doing that, I'll just suggest for the sake of time he just counts all the tiles going in each direction and multiply them. That should give him a rough idea of how many tiles are in the church."

"But what about the missing tiles around where the altar upfront?" Caroline asked as if this topic of conversation was the equivalent of ferreting secrets out of Napoleonic spies.

"That's why I said it would give him a rough idea, Caro," Alex said gently. "If he really must know, he can do as I suggested by finding the number of all the tiles, and then walk around to all the little areas where the tiles are absent or covered and deduct the number that should be there from the whole."

Emma leaned her head back and closed her eyes, trying as hard as she could to block out Alex and Caroline's rather disturbing conversation. To quote Caroline, *Good grief!* She was about to marry a man obsessed with counting and numbers.

Barely aware her fists were clenched so tightly the seams of her white satin gloves were about to burst, Emma relaxed her fingers and took a deep breath through her nose. Exhaling, she tried to think of the good things about Wallace. He was…he was… he was…he was nice. Yes, that was a start. He was a nice man. He was also kind. Wait, that's the same thing. She clenched her hands tightly again. He was something else besides nice, she knew it. He had to be. Everyone had more than one positive attribute to recommend themselves to others.

Squeezing her eyes even tighter, she desperately tried to think of another adjective for Wallace. What else was he? Boring. That's what he was. He was boring and bland. Dull, even. She sighed. The undeniable truth was that awful tea Marcus' temporary cook made was more interesting than Wallace. Drat! Drat! Drat! There she went thinking of dratted Marcus again.

"Emma, calm down," Caroline murmured. She picked up one of Emma's tightened fists and unfurled her fingers. "Wallace will not really insist on counting the petals of all the flowers. Stop scaring her, Alex."

Emma's eyes widened and a little strangled sound from deep in her throat escaped her lips. Though Alex and Caroline might have been jesting, Emma wouldn't so easily dismiss the idea that Wallace would think to do such a thing.

"You weren't even listening, were you?" Caroline asked, cocking her head to the side.

Shaking her head slightly, Emma just stared at her friend.

"You were thinking of Marcus, weren't you?"

She nodded sadly. "I promise I'll stop. Right now, I'll stop. I won't think of him again."

"I'm sure Wallace will be glad to hear that." Alex picked up his hat from the cushion next to him and with a fluid motion put it on his head. "If you want to cry off, now is the time."

The anxiety showing in his face urged Emma to swallow her own unease. Last year, Alex had quite a scare when Caroline was nearly late to the start of her wedding and Alex thought she was jilting him. That was yet another reason she had to go through with her promise to marry Wallace, she didn't want to force Alex into the uncomfortable position of cleaning up her mess. He didn't deserve that any more than Wallace deserved to be jilted.

The carriage came to a jolting stop, or perhaps the jolting of the carriage was caused by Gregory pounding on it, causing it to shake violently. Emma shook her head. That was absolutely the most favorable aspect of marriage to Wallace: she'd no longer have to have contact with Gregory or Louise in any manner if she didn't wish it. And she didn't wish it.

Ever since her engagement was announced those two had been like vultures on the hunt, trying to manipulate Emma for the sake of appearances. Reluctantly, she'd agreed that Gregory could walk her down the aisle. But that was it. She continued to live at Watson

Townhouse with Caroline and even allowed Alex to make decisions as if he truly were responsible for her.

"Come, Emma," Gregory clipped as soon as the carriage door swung open merely an inch. "We're to wait in the back chambers until it's time."

A chill skated down Emma's spine at the sight of Gregory's leer. Biting her lip so as not to make a scene, Emma went to the door of the carriage and warily reached her trembling fingers out to connect with Gregory's palm.

As soon as her fingertips made contact with his gloved palm, he curled his fingers around hers in the most painful way she'd ever felt.

Wincing, she slowly walked down the steps before trying to pull her hand back from Gregory's vise-like grip.

Alex was down and helping Caroline descend only seconds later. Caroline walked over to Emma and looped her arm through hers. "Excuse us, Your Grace. I need to have a talk with Emma."

Gregory's sharp eyes impaled Caroline, who, much to Emma's surprise, stood firm with her chin lifted and confident. Despite herself, Emma smiled. Being married to Alex had given Caroline the starch and polish which growing up being ignored had not. Very quickly, Emma flashed Alex a slim, thankful smile, which he returned with a quizzical look.

"I'm sure you understand the need for Emma to have some alone time with another woman right before her wedding. We have things to discuss."

"Things to discuss?" Gregory echoed coldly. "I'm sure she knows enough about what you mean to 'discuss' with her that she could teach you a thing or two."

Emma's face burned. Gregory was right. Emma probably *did* know far more than Caroline. But that was because she'd read that memoir, not because of the reason Gregory was insinuating. Swallowing her nerves, she steeled her spine and looked Gregory straight in the eye. "Your Grace, I'd like some time with my friend."

"And I'd like some time with you."

"Whatever for?" she asked irritably. "You made it rather clear to me that you never wanted to see me again that night you tossed me out without anything more than a few coins to my name and a thin scrap of fabric for a wardrobe."

"Yes, well, nothing has changed. I still have no desire to see you again after today. But, for today, we shall play nice and give off the impression of a loving family. Now come."

Irritation, anger, and even a shred of hatred ran through Emma as she yanked her hand from Gregory's tight grasp so fast and hard, her glove slipped half of the way off. He didn't wish to play nice, he had other ideas. Ideas she didn't even want to *think* about. "I think not. I'll spend my time before my wedding alone with Caroline. You can send someone to collect me when it's time for you to do your final duty and walk me down the aisle."

Gregory's strong hand reached forward to grab her elbow, but just before he was able to close his bruising fingers around it, Alex's hand reached forward and, using the edge of his hand to hit the inside of Gregory's wrist, knocked Gregory's hand away.

Gregory grimaced and rubbed his wrist. "Very well. I'll be waiting for the blasted event to start in the back of the church. Don't dawdle. The sooner you marry that madman, the sooner nobody will associate my grace and title to your debauched ways."

Emma gasped at his words. Why did he insist on being so cruel to her? "Have no doubt, Your Grace; I am looking forward to no longer being associated with your lecherous ways just as much as you are looking forward to being rid of me."

Sneering, Gregory stalked off.

"Come, let's go inside," Caroline said, flashing a disgusted look at the back of Gregory.

Together the trio strolled inside. Alex took a seat on the end of a church pew being occupied by some of his cousins while Caroline walked Emma back to her bridal chambers.

"Were you nervous?" Emma blurted as soon as Caroline shut the door.

Caroline grinned. "No. Well, yes. But my nervousness was different I suppose. I was afraid Olivia would show up and make one final attempt to ruin my wedding."

"Yes, that is reason enough to make anyone nervous," Emma admitted with a giggle. The night before Caroline's wedding, Olivia had made ribbons out of Caroline's dress just to spite her for marrying a man Olivia hadn't given a fig about. "But as you said, your nervousness was completely different from mine."

"Are you nervous about tonight?" Caroline reached forward to tighten the pins holding Emma's curls in place.

Shaking her head, Emma tried not to let her expression tell too much. "No. I certainly know what to expect on that score."

Caroline's hands froze, and she cast an amused glance at Emma. "Is there something you want to tell me?"

"No, I can't say there is."

Chuckling, Caroline raised her brows.

"It's not what you think," Emma said softly. "I found this book...and...I'm sure you get the idea."

"You read a naughty book?" Caroline exclaimed, her blue eyes positively alight with laughter.

Emma shrugged and took a seat. She knew she shouldn't continue to sit or her dress would wrinkle, but truly, it had probably already wrinkled from the ride. Besides, perhaps it would give Wallace something to count. She nearly snorted at the thought. Adjusting herself on the seat to get more comfortable, she glanced back up at a quizzical Caroline. "To be fair, I only read half of it. But it was enough to know what to expect tonight."

"Well, that's what's important," Caroline said in a flippant tone. Smiling, she took a seat close to Emma. "You do know all men are different, and though I have no idea what you read in that naughty little book of yours, nor what you did with Marcus, you cannot expect Wallace will be the same."

"I know," Emma said airily. "Lady Bird explained about how all men are different and each time was a different experience. Some good, some not-so-good, and some, well, some to be remembered for a lifetime."

Caroline's mouth fell open, and Emma did the best she could to stifle her laughter. "And did Lady Bird explain these three different outcomes?"

"In the greatest detail imaginable."

"And just where did you get such a book?"

"From Marcus."

The look that came over Caroline's face was beyond price. Unfortunately, Emma wasn't given the chance to shock her further because a series of loud thuds rattled the wooden door.

"It's time." Caroline stood up and offered Emma a quick hug.

Swallowing convulsively, Emma stood still as Caroline unlocked and opened the door before coming back to her side and giving her shoulder an affectionate squeeze.

Silently, they left the room and walked down to where Gregory was waiting with the darkest look on his face she'd ever seen..

"Get going," he barked at Caroline. "The sooner you get down to your spot, the sooner Emma will be married."

Caroline looked like she was about to whack him over the head with her bouquet of white roses, but must have decided he wasn't worth the bother and walked down the aisle to her spot.

Now it was time for Emma and Gregory to walk.

Closing her traitorous eyes so she wouldn't give into the temptation and glance one last time at the closed doors of the church, Emma rigidly walked forward down the aisle to her immaculate groom.

Without ceremony, as soon as Emma and Gregory reached Wallace, Gregory disengaged Emma's arm and placed her hand in Wallace's with all the love and grace an adder would express to a mouse.

Mumbling a few words about giving his permission for the match, Gregory walked off, leaving the priest with his mouth opening and shutting as he fruitlessly tried to form words. "We have not gotten to that part yet." Or so one would presume that's what his gibberish meant.

Emma just shook her head. "It's all right. Now that we all know we have his permission, and dare I say blessing—" she sliced a quick glance at her scowling sister and husband— "we can continue to the vows."

"A—a—all right," the priest stammered. Shifting his Bible from one hand to the other, he said in a loud, even voice, "Does anyone see any reason these two should not be joined together in holy matrimony?"

Emma held her breath. Now was the time. This was the last time anyone could object. The last time for Caroline or Alex to intervene. The last time Louise or Gregory could try to ruin her life. The last time for Wallace to back out. The last chance she'd have to put a stop to this. The last time Marcus would have a chance to stop the wedding.

The moment seemed to last forever as the silence engulfed the room. Not a single objection. None from Caroline or Alex, nor Louise and Gregory. Not a sound from Wallace. Not a protest among anyone in the church. And certainly not a word from the absent Marcus.

"Very well," the priest said at long last. Opening his Bible, he flipped to the passage he'd marked then started prattling on about love, the meaning of marriage, and whatever else he thought necessary.

Emma looked up at a very pale Wallace. He appeared to be just as nervous as she felt. His lips were moving and anytime the priest paused, he said a number in the barest whisper.

To take her mind off her own bit of nerves, she started making a list in her head of *what* Wallace could possibly be counting just now.

In the not-so-distant distance, Emma listened as the preacher continue to prattle, occasionally his words breaking her from her concentration and she'd have to start forming her list all over again.

The minister cleared his throat, and both Emma and Wallace started. She smiled thinly at Wallace, then the minister. But her thin smile froze in place, becoming brittle and forced when she caught sight of the little red book in the man's hands. It was time to take their vows.

In what couldn't possibly be more than a minute from now,

she'd officially be his wife, belonging to him, and only him, for the rest of her life. She forced herself to stand up straighter and willed her lungs to keep breathing as the vicar turned to talk to Wallace.

"Wilt thee, Sir Wallace George Benedict; take this woman, Emmaline Harriet Green, to be thy wedded wife, to live together after God's ordinance in the holy estate of Matrimony? Wilt thou love her, comfort her, honor and keep her, in sickness and in health: and, forsaking all other, keep thee only unto her so long as ye both shall live?"

Wallace's Adam's apple bobbed as he swallowed then parted his lips far enough to slip his tongue through and lick his dry lips, "I—"

"No," boomed a loud voice as the two wooden doors in the back of the church swung on their hinges with enough force to make them collide with the wall, resulting in a noise that resembled a clap of thunder. "He doesn't, but I do."

Chapter 24

Marcus struggled to choke down the nauseating sensation that was quickly spreading from the pit of his stomach throughout the rest of his body. He hated groups of people. Especially when they were all focused on him. And no doubt about it, they were all looking at him.

Willing his disobedient heart to stop hammering in his chest, he started walking down the aisle toward Emma, trying fruitlessly to ignore the gasps and whispers as he went.

Only five or six feet from her, Hampton jumped to his feet. "What's the meaning of this, Sinclair?"

Marcus ignored him. He had no desire to talk to Hampton; he'd come for Emma. These five weeks of being separated from her had been the hardest weeks of his life. He had no idea how he hadn't gone mad, but somehow he hadn't. He knew now what he must do: he must claim her as his. He loved her more than anything, and somewhere deep down he had finally begun to believe their love for each other *would* be enough. She'd said she loved him despite his inability to make her a mother, and though he hadn't believed her then, he believed her now.

"Emma," he said hoarsely, searching her vivid green eyes for any signs that she may still love him and call off this sham of a marriage to Sir Wallace.

Emma blinked at him. The look in her eyes was uncertain, scared even.

Impulsively, Marcus reached his shaking fingers up and pushed a wisp of hair that had fallen across her forehead back behind her ear. "Emma, I'm sorry," he whispered unevenly. "I shouldn't have done this to you..." His words died off as his face flushed with unease, embarrassment, and even shame. He cleared his throat. Then again. "I'm ready now," he said softly.

"Ready for what?" He almost didn't recognize that cold, brittle voice as belonging to Emma.

Pushing past his uncertainty at the chilling look in her eyes that matched the tone and meaning of her words, Marcus said, "I'm ready to be the man I should have been. I'm ready to marry you now, Emma."

"How convenient of you," she said, blinking away what looked oddly like tears. "Now that I'm taking vows to another man, you're suddenly ready to marry me."

Marcus' hands clenched as he glanced over to that other man she spoke of. He'd never seen Sir Wallace in person, but he'd heard enough to know he'd have recognized this unusual, but also very handsome man anywhere. "It's not too late." Marcus turned his gaze back to Emma.

"Yes, it is. Just as I warned you not to, you waited too long."

Marcus shook his head. "No, I haven't. The groom takes his vows first, and he hasn't."

Emma pursed her lips and looked at him with one of the saddest expressions he'd ever seen. "That doesn't matter any longer. You've missed your chance, Marcus. I've made a promise and I cannot break it."

Marcus exhaled. "What do you want? Do you want to marry Sir Wallace or me?"

"Don't," she snapped. "Don't do this."

"Don't do what? It's a simple question. Just answer it."

A tear slipped out of her eye, and she took one of her gloved hands from Sir Wallace's grasp to wipe it away. "You cannot expect me to answer such a question. Not now. It's too late, Marcus. I'm going to marry Sir Wallace."

Marcus closed his eyes. He'd gotten here too late. He should have ridden his horse faster. He still would have missed being able to speak to her at Watson Townhouse yesterday, but he could have confronted her about this in her bridal chamber. Instead, he'd put her in an awkward situation by having all these onlookers privy to their discussion. Perhaps if he could get her to agree to talk to him privately, she'd let go of her stubbornness about having made a promise to Sir Wallace and agree to marry him. "Can we talk in private?"

"No," she said flatly. "I'm sorry, Marcus. You know how I feel about you, but I cannot break my word."

Jaw clenched, Marcus took Emma's hands from Sir Wallace. "Emma, I know this isn't the ideal situation, and I know you'd prefer not to be embarrassed nor embarrass Sir Wallace by such a display, but it's the only option left now. Please, call off the wedding and marry me."

"Why?" she asked in a voice that bordered on hysterical excitement. "Why now? You've had more than five weeks, and I've heard nothing from you. Why now? Why today when it's too late? Why?"

Marcus squeezed her hands and stroked the back of her knuckles with his thumb. How many times in those weeks had he started writing her a letter only to never finish it? How many times had he wanted to come for her but stopped himself? If only he'd posted one of those letters or given in to the temptation to come for her. His heart hurt anew at the realization of how much easier it would have all been for them if he'd done *something* sooner. He swallowed convulsively. His new understanding of just how he could have done things differently was immaterial. He hadn't acted soon enough, and now he needed to be honest and bare his soul to her in hopes she'd forgive him.

"I realized what a fool I'd been," he began softly. "I know it took me a while to sort things out, but I did. I finally realized that maybe your love for me could be enough. And if it's not..." He trailed off and swallowed hard. "If it's not, I don't know what we'll do, but the time we can be happy together is worth the risk."

Staring down at their hands, Emma slowly pulled her fingers from his. "You cannot just come in here, profess to all of a sudden believe I truly love you, and expect me to marry *you* today instead of Wallace. It doesn't work that way. I'm sorry, but I cannot marry you now. You've waited too long."

"No, I haven't," he said more fiercely this time. "You're not married yet, and until you take your vows you can change your mind. Now, who will it be? The man you love or the man you don't?"

Emma's emerald eyes flashed fire. "How dare you! How dare you just march in here in the middle of my wedding and tell me you've decided I do love you enough, and then push me to jilt my groom in front of all of our guests due to your sudden, but-slow-in-the-making grand revelation? Just who do you think you are to do such a thing?"

"A man who loves you very, very much," he said simply. "A man who didn't know what he had until it was gone. Wait. That's not true. I knew what I had. I—"

"Then why did you relinquish it?" She clasped her trembling hands together in front of her.

"Because I thought—"

"That's just it, Marcus. You thought. You didn't believe me when I told you I loved you, you thought I couldn't truly love you enough. You also thought it would be the easiest course of action to send me away so I'd marry someone else to have whatever happiness it is you *thought* you couldn't give me. But that's where you were wrong, you didn't really think. Not about me anyway. You thought only about yourself."

"I did think about you. That's why I—I—" He waved his hand around the room as if to indicate what he'd tried to do for her without exposing everything about their past to this room full of curious and gawking guests.

"No, you didn't," Emma said sharply. "You were thinking of yourself when you sent me away. You couldn't accept that I loved you in spite of your scars and your past with my sister. You couldn't accept that I would love you whether or not we could build a family together. Instead, you thought only of yourself and sent me away, so I could marry another man and not grow to resent you for the things you couldn't accept about yourself—the things that I loved you in spite of. But do you know what? I did love you. And I still do. But I've made a promise to Wallace to marry him, and if you're angry with anyone in all of this it should be yourself."

Swallowing, Marcus reached his hand forward to once again hold one of hers but she pulled away from his grasp. He blew out a deep breath and closed his eyes, waves of emotions swept through him. She was right, of course. She'd told him she still wanted to marry him even after he'd told her of his inability to have children. And yet, he'd sent her away. He'd sent her away with the direct order to find a man to marry. And she had. She may not love that other man, nor he her, but she had made him a promise, and she'd be no better than Louise if she were to break her promise now.

"Very well, then." He leaned forward to brush one final kiss on her tearstained cheek, fighting the impulse to accidentally let his mouth graze hers. He pulled back and turned to Sir Wallace. "Take care of her," he whispered brokenly before spinning around and facing her small group of wedding guests.

He shoved his hands in his pockets, his right fingers curling around that blasted ring he'd found while digging in that chest the first time he'd tricked Emma into staying with him. Optimistically, he'd foolishly brought it with him to London. A tidal wave of regret and remorse washed over him as he squeezed the ring so tightly the prongs cut into his fingers. Blinking rapidly so as not to give in to the emotions he was inwardly fighting, he placed one foot in front of the other and slowly walked down the aisle, trying to look anywhere but at the faces of the wedding guests. Coming here today would result in a bit of scandal and nasty gossip, no matter which way the outcome fell. Nobody actually interrupted a wedding. Ever. It wasn't done. It went beyond scandalous. It was indecent!

But he'd still wanted to try. He wanted to make one final appeal and beg her to forgive his foolishness and take him to be her husband.

He no longer cared about the scandal this would produce, and he anticipated hearing whispers about his past with Louise as he walked down that carpet-covered stone aisle that would take him to the door of the church. But nothing prepared him for the deathly silence that greeted him as he walked that seemingly never-ending trek. About halfway through, he glanced up just in time to glimpse the sympathetic faces of Drake and Alex. He nodded curtly to each of the men before averting his eyes.

Reaching the wooden doors at the back of the church, his hand closed around the door handle. He spun it and gave the door a slight shove. Stepping through the doorway, he froze when he heard loud and clear the words, "I don't."

Chapter 25

Emma's heart literally stopped for a few seconds when she heard Sir Wallace start to speak. He didn't what? "Pardon?" she asked weakly, the priest echoing her word.

"I'm sorry, Miss Green, but I don't and he does," Sir Wallace said as if that was all the explanation necessary.

"Pardon?" she repeated, her heart now beating wildly inside her chest.

Sir Wallace shrugged, and for some odd reason, he looked decidedly more comfortable. "Miss Green, I relinquish all rights. Go on, marry him if you wish."

"Pardon?" she said again, realizing, but not caring, that she sounded like that colorful parrot Olivia used to keep until Marcus gave it away when he found out she was plucking the feathers to wear in her hair.

Sighing, Wallace gave her hands a gentle, affectionate squeeze before letting them go and shoving his hands in his pockets. "Miss Green, it doesn't take a great mind to know where your affections lie."

Emma licked her dry, cracking lips. "Wallace," she said quietly, so quietly she almost didn't even hear her own voice.

He shook his head. "You don't love me, and quite frankly, I don't love you. That's the way of it. This isn't a love match. I didn't expect it to be, and neither did you."

"I know." It was no use lying to Wallace, or herself for that matter. She'd always love Marcus—even if she married Wallace.

"Then marry him. I'm giving you my permission."

"No," Emma said with a quiver. "I'll not embarrass you the way Lady Silverton did." Closing her eyes to dam up the tears forming in her eyes, she swallowed the sob that lodged in her throat. "Please continue," she croaked at the priest.

"No." Wallace turned back to look squarely at Emma. "If Lord Sinclair had come yesterday, would we be standing here just now?"

"I—I—don't know," she stammered, her face flushing at her lie.

"Yes, you do." His warm brown eyes were as calm and gentle as his voice.

Not daring to chance a look at Marcus, who was standing rigidly in the back of the church waiting for some sort of final answer, Emma swallowed as hard as she could to push down the lump that had lodged itself in her tight throat. "That matters naught, now. I've given you my promise, and I mean to hold to it."

Grinning, Wallace shook his head. "You're rather stubborn, aren't you? Emma, I'll go through with this ceremony and marry you if you wish it. I have no problem making you my wife. But I don't think you want it, do you?"

"No," she whispered, searching his eyes for any condemnation or reproof, and found none.

"Then marry him."

"I can't," she protested weakly. Regaining some of her earlier starch and stubbornness, she further explained, "I'm betrothed to you. I'll not be known as a woman who gives her word to one man then turns around and marries another."

Wallace sighed. "Emma, this is one of those moments in life when you have to put your foolish pride aside and do what's best for you, even if you break a number of rules along the way. Now, I'll save you the exact number of rules you'd be breaking, but I will tell you that if you marry me today, you'll be stuck with me a long, long time. Not only are all of my grandparents still alive, most of their parents are, too."

Emma tried not to smile despite herself. "But—"

"No buts. A good portion of my relatives are octogenarians.

244

Not too many young widows, I'm afraid. Are you prepared to be married to me for at least the next fifty-three years?" He idly scratched his jaw for a minute. "I know you're angry with him for what he's done to you, and he deserves nothing less than to see your fury, but you cannot punish yourself, too."

Emma bit her lip and risked a glance at Marcus. She did love him in a way she could never love Wallace. Even if Wallace was the father of her children, she couldn't love him as much as she loved Marcus.

"It's your decision," Wallace repeated softly. "I'll marry you right now if that's what you want. But you have to choose. You have to be the one to decide everyone's fate."

Her lip trembled and she tried in vain to bite it enough to keep it steady as she looked over the crowd of people who had come to witness her wedding. Several of them looked like they could hardly wait to leave the church to start spreading this tale. Others looked at her with disgust and contempt that she'd even entertain the idea of jilting her groom this way. Some, mainly her sister and Gregory, looked furious. She glanced at Drake and saw an unusual gleam in his eye, then turned her gaze back to Wallace. "I—I—I'm so—sorry, Wallace. I pick him."

"Then what are you doing still standing here with me? Walk back down the aisle to your rightful groom."

Flashing him a watery, apologetic smile, Emma ran down the aisle and straight into Marcus' waiting arms.

He lifted her off the ground and spun her with excitement. "Oh, Emma, I'm so, so sorry," Marcus whispered against her hair as he held her tighter than ever before. "I love you so much and... and...I shouldn't have let you go. Every day you were gone was pure torture for me."

"I know," Emma said. She wiped away her tears when he set her back down in the corridor of the church, out of view and earshot of the wedding guests.

"Will you marry me?"

Emma blinked at him. Did he mean in general or right now?

"Right now," he clarified. "I don't want to go another day

without you."

"But we can't marry today," she objected. "We have to post the banns or at least get a special license."

Marcus grinned. "No we don't. We'll just scratch Sir Wallace's name off the license," he teased.

"We will do no such thing. It is bad enough we've humiliated him and made him the object of gossip, I'll not go so far as to—to... I can't even put voice to it."

"No matter," Wallace said, coming up behind her. He handed Marcus a piece of parchment. "I already took care of it."

"You what?" Emma questioned, her voice squeaking a note.

"I already scratched out my name and wrote his."

"Is that legal?"

"Probably not," Wallace confessed with a lopsided smile. "But you'll always have this paper to show in the circumstance someone questions it."

Marcus grinned and shoved the license in his breast pocket. "Thank you, Sir Wallace. Thank you for everything."

"No need to thank me. I truly never wanted to marry. I would have, of course, but my heart wasn't in it, just like Emma's wasn't. As you've probably heard, I enjoy being a bachelor. That's why my family paid Lady Silverton's father so handsomely to convince her to jilt me all those years ago."

Emma gaped at him. "Pardon?"

Sir Wallace shifted uncomfortably. "I didn't really wish to marry her, but after I inadvertently ruined her reputation at a garden party, we quickly became betrothed. Fortunately, another man had an interest in her..."

Emma blinked at him. "You knew she was going to jilt you?"

"Yes. It was planned," he admitted with a simple nod. "She didn't enjoy the company of the man who was pursuing her, so she found a way out by following me into Lord Flannigan's back gardens."

"Oh." Emma blushed. Lord Flannigan was rumored to have some very naughty statues hidden throughout that very overgrown garden behind his house. A young lady's reputation could be ruined just by being seen stepping through the doors that led to that garden. No telling what would happen if she were caught, especially alone with a gentleman.

"Indeed. Lord Silverton found us and threatened to expose her fall from grace if she didn't accept his suit. She didn't, of course. She would gladly accept mine, instead." He shifted uncomfortably again, then rocked back on his heels. "I didn't accept her suit though. Perhaps I should have, but I was far too interested in someone else at the time and I foolishly thought—" He broke off and waved his hand dismissively. "The details aren't so important. I didn't wish to marry her, so my family bribed her father to persuade her to marry Silverton instead. She didn't want to, but her father's lack of funds coupled with whatever he might have said to her in private changed her mind, and she followed through with the plan to leave me at the altar and marry Silverton instead."

"Then why did she—" Emma broke off abruptly and clapped a hand over her mouth. "Forgive me, it's not my business."

He waved her off. "She was just trying to bait you into saying something rash in an effort to rankle me. Lady Silverton and I shared no love for each other whatsoever, but if she could ensure I ended up in the parson's mousetrap after all, she'd be satisfied."

"You're truly not disappointed?"

He shook his head. "No. I know I must marry some day to procure an heir. I would have married you to do my duty, but I'm still young. Surely another will come along." He shrugged carelessly again. "And if not, then I'll continue to enjoy my bachelor freedom."

"One cannot be divided," Emma quipped with a watery smile.

"Well, actually it can," Wallace corrected. "But I won't bore you with decimal points or fractions. I know what you meant."

"Thank you," Emma said.

Wallace tipped his hat and was gone.

"We cannot marry here," she said after Sir Wallace's carriage rolled away. "That would be very awkward for me."

"It would be awkward for me, too."

"Emma!"

Emma jumped, and her hands fisted at the sound of Gregory's roar.

"You get out there and—"

Crack!

Emma's eyes widened and her mouth dropped open in surprise, but she felt not a bit of sympathy. At least none for the vile man moaning in pain and spilling blood—and teeth—at her feet. Her eyes swung to Marcus. His knuckles were red with blood and his face hard as stone.

"Hampton," he barked.

Gregory moaned.

"To your feet."

Gregory groaned.

Marcus reached down and fisted his fingers in Gregory's clothes, then jerked him to a standing position and pulled him close. "Don't so much as *think* of her again, or I'll kill you." The rancor in his voice was so sharp everyone within earshot froze.

Except Gregory. He whimpered.

A second later, Marcus loosened his hold on Gregory's clothes and brought his knee up just in time to connect with Gregory's bloodied face once more on his fall to the floor.

Marcus turned back to Emma, his eyes growing warm yet again. He lowered his lashes and when he spoke again; his voice was thick and rough. "I should have come sooner."

"Yes, you should have," Emma agreed.

"I'm sorry. I can't change the past, but I want to make a future with you. A future filled with love and happiness."

"And you doing everything I ask to make up for your stupidity?"

"That, too." He swallowed. "You never answered my question. Will you marry me?"

Emma smiled at him. "I'll marry you, Marcus. Tonight even." At his wide, broad grin, she amended, "But only if you can hunt down a special license. We're not using that." She patted the outside of his breast pocket so he couldn't feign a misunderstanding later like she knew he would probably try to do.

"All right, we won't use that one," he said with a chuckle. He reached into his other breast pocket. "What about this one? Will it suffice?"

With shaking fingers, Emma reached forward and plucked the paper from Marcus. Unfolding it, she gasped. "You..." Her voice faded as her eyes scanned the page.

"I would have been here sooner, Emma," Marcus said solemnly. "But I've spent the last week riding across the English countryside trying to hunt down the Archbishop of Canterbury to get this special license."

A fresh wave of tears flowed from Emma's eyes. "Why didn't you send me a message?"

"I did. It just didn't reach you in time."

"No, but you did," Emma said, leaning up to kiss him.

"With a stroke of luck, I sure did. A moment later, and I'd have had one hell of a time trying to get Sir Wallace to agree to annul your marriage."

Emma laughed and shook her head. "Good thing you made it here, then."

"Yes, it is. Now let's get married."

Chapter 26

Alex clapped Marcus on the back as he walked through the door of Watson Townhouse. It had been a long, long time since he'd been inside this house. If he remembered right, the events that led up to his coming to Watson Townhouse the last time were not nearly as favorable as they were just now. He cast a glance over at Caroline and smiled. Who knew the young girl with the bleak future would have ever found the type of love that lasted a lifetime?

"This scene looks rather familiar," Emma said lightly, allowing Marcus to intertwine his fingers with hers.

"Yes, it does," Marcus agreed with a chuckle as he looked around and noticed that with the exception of Alex's mother and deceased father, this was the exact same group who had assembled last year for Alex's wedding. Even Drake's three little girls were present.

"Come along, you two," Mr. Grimes, the replacement vicar, called from the drawing room.

Marcus walked in and blinked. "It's different."

"Thank heavens," Brooke, Lady Townson, one of Alex's cousins, said with a bright smile. "It seems Caroline actually has taste."

Caroline smiled sadly. "I do miss Edward and his unusual ways. However, for as much as I miss him, I'm glad Alex allowed me to redecorate. I cannot imagine holding a wedding in this house if it had still been decorated so wildly."

"I can," Paul and Liberty Grimes said in unison, eliciting

several chuckles from the group.

"Our wedding was held in the foyer just below the stairs," Mrs. Grimes explained.

"Gads," Marcus said with a shudder.

"Exactly," Mr. Grimes commented.

"Well, enough reminiscing," Marcus said, hoping they'd all take the hint and Mr. Grimes would progress with the ceremony. He was ready to be married and carry Emma off to his freshly aired townhouse.

Mr. Grimes took his spot in front of Emma and Marcus and, without any further ado, began the ceremony.

Marcus barely paid attention to the vicar's words. He just nodded and mumbled when he thought he was supposed to. The majority of his attention was focused on Emma. She was so beautiful, standing across from him as she recited her vows. He was mildly surprised she'd agreed to marry him today. But thankful, nonetheless. He'd made a terrible mistake sending her away, and he was more than prepared to spend the rest of his life making it up to her. Starting tonight.

He shifted and sent the vicar a pointed glance. He might have been displeased last year when Alex made a remark at his wedding to Caroline about what would be happening later that night, but now he knew the excitement of wanting everyone to vanish and leave him alone with his wife.

Mercifully, Mr. Grimes kept it short, and Marcus was able to think up an excuse to leave without staying for a meal. He'd wasted far too much time away from Emma; he didn't want to wait another minute to have her in his arms again.

"Someone's awfully anxious for his wedding night," Emma teased when he sat next to her inside the carriage.

Marcus grinned. "Yes, I am," he stated proudly. He wondered if Caroline or Louise had spoken to her about what to expect. He frowned. Either source was likely to overwhelm her with information, Caroline's information being too scientific, while Louise would probably make marital intimacies out to sound like something one would find in a brothel. "About tonight," he began uneasily.

"No need to discuss it," she said. Her cheeks turned pink. "I know in detail what'll happen. Or what you'd like to happen, rather."

"Pardon?" He wasn't sure which part of her words he was responding to, the part about she already knew in detail what to expect, or the cryptic statement he took to mean they may not be sharing a bed tonight.

Tucking a tendril of her blonde hair behind her right ear, Emma licked her lips. "I...uh...I've been informed."

"Good," he said slowly. "Do you have any questions?"

"None," she said pertly, not meeting his eyes.

He wanted to ask who'd informed her so he'd have an idea of what she might have been told, but didn't want to press. He sighed. "Are you still angry with me?"

She met his eyes again, and in those emerald depths, he knew the truth: she wasn't angry, she was furious.

It was a few minutes before he spoke again. "Why did you marry me today if you're still angry with me?"

"Because I love you, Marcus. I may not be overly thrilled with what you've done, but I do love you."

"We could have waited," he told her softly, exhaling sharply.

She shrugged. "Today, tomorrow, it doesn't matter. My feelings for you won't change. I'll still love you. I'm just hurt by what you did." She turned her face away, but not before he glimpsed the tears shining in her eyes.

His heart clenched. He knew he'd have a lot to make up for, but he hadn't realized just how much he'd hurt her. "Emma," he whispered hoarsely. He gathered her into his arms and froze, unable to say another word as her body trembled and shook with sobs.

***

Trying in vain to stop her onslaught of tears and sobs, Emma sat on Marcus' lap as the carriage rolled down the streets of London to his townhouse. She was just as ready to leave Caroline's as Marcus had been, but she wasn't ready to be alone with him.

Not yet anyway.

This morning she was convinced he truly wanted nothing more to do with her, and then he had turned up, stopped the wedding, and married her all in one day. It was too much. Of course she still loved him. That was why she had married him right away. But it didn't mean she wasn't still hurting. For some reason, as soon as she'd climbed up into the carriage and looked at him, all the feelings of uncertainty, hurt, confusion, betrayal, and loss she'd dealt with for the past few weeks swamped her and threatened to choke her until he gave her some answers.

"I'm sorry," she murmured, trying to scoot off his lap.

He held her firmly on his lap. "Don't be sorry for having emotions. I'm the one who ought to be sorry for being such a cad."

Yes, he should. He could have spared them both a lot of heartache if he'd just accepted her love five weeks ago. Instead, they'd both suffered unnecessarily. "Why did you come back?" she whispered. He'd said something in the church, but she couldn't really remember what it was. Now that they were alone, she'd get her answers. The real ones this time. The ones he'd be hesitant to voice in front of a large group of people.

Though she knew it was a remarkable gesture that he'd come to her wedding and stopped it that way, she didn't think that cleared him of his past transgressions.

"I told you, I realized my folly," he said simply, squeezing her tighter.

She looked up at him and noticed his scarred jaw ticking. She reached up and ran the pad of her thumb over the puckered, uneven skin. "How? How did you realize your mistake?"

He sighed. "I'd rather not say."

"Why not? I'm your wife. Don't hide things from me."

"You're right," he acknowledged with a quick nod of his head. "It wasn't any one thing, really. It was a combination of many things."

"Such as?"

Marcus closed his eyes. "I've had nothing but time since you've been gone. Of course you know Alex came to visit, and I was none too happy about who he said you were going to marry. But instead of coming to London and claiming you then like I should have, I went to see Patrick. Between those two and Gateway, I don't really know what stuck and what didn't. But then--"

"What?" Emma interrupted abruptly, her brow furrowing in confusion. Usually Marcus talked sense, but his last sentence didn't make a bit of sense.

He sighed. "Three nights before Alex came to see me, I bribed Gateway to help me find a way into his ball without having my presence announced. He and I chatted a bit in the corner while we watched you dance with every blasted man in England. I came back home the next day, then later that week I had two more frank conversations—one with Alex, and the other with Patrick. One of those three—I'm not sure which—put in my head the kernel of a belief that you could still love me whether or not I'm capable of giving you the things other men can. From there, I spent another near month in solitude, not daring to attempt another trip to London to spy on you.

"During those weeks, I spent most of my day reflecting on the letters I continued to receive from Olivia describing her miserable life, and all I could think was she could have all the happiness she wanted if she'd just take a good look at everything she has." He paused and shook his head. When he looked at Emma again she saw the truth of it: he'd been hurting just as much these past months as she had. He cleared his throat.

Still and silent, Emma almost groaned in vexation when the carriage came to a stop. Of course she would have liked him to keep explaining his reasons, but they could finish the conversation inside. They would be married for the rest of their lives, after all.

"Would you care to join me?" Marcus asked as soon as he descended the carriage and reached up to help her down.

She smiled. "I may not be persuaded yet to share your bed tonight, but I don't have any intention of sleeping in the carriage."

"Good. I shudder to think of how much my leg would hurt if I were to try to cram in here next to you."

She allowed him to help her down, then turned back to look at him. "Where will I be joining you?"

"My bedchamber."

"This isn't some sort of seduction, is it?" she asked, coming to a halt.

Marcus shook his head. "Not unless you want it to be."

"You've a lot to answer for." She gave him a stern look.

"And I intend to answer anything you ask," Marcus said. He reached his hand over and gave hers a gentle squeeze.

As soon as Emma crossed the threshold of his downstairs bedchamber, she dropped her hand from his arm and took a seat on the plush, green velvet chair that was positioned by the window. She was nearly certain he would have preferred she sat on the settee at the end of the bed, or even on the bed, but at least she was in the room. That was as much leeway as she was willing to give him just now.

"I'm listening," Emma said at last, prompting him to get about explaining his sudden change of heart.

Marcus sighed and fell onto the settee at the end of his bed. "Emma, I've loved you for years. Far longer than I can remember, really. Perhaps even when we were children, I loved you and just didn't know. But what I do know is that I love you, but I've never felt worthy of you."

"Worthy?"

"Yes, worthy." He reached up and ran his hand through his hair. "To me, you're perfect. You always have been. I thought...I thought...I thought, you being perfect, that you deserved the perfect life. A life I cannot give you."

"But I told you I didn't care." Her eyes stung with tears at the memory of the last time she was at Ridge Water with him and he couldn't get her out of his house fast enough, followed by five miserable weeks of longing for him.

"I know," he acknowledged softly. "I know." Shifting in his seat, his eyes never left hers. "I know what you said, but I thought I knew better. I thought you'd grow to resent me."

"But why?"

"I've already told you why. I didn't want to condemn you to a lonely existence, which is exactly what you'll find with me." A self-deprecating smile took his lips that made Emma shake her head.

"You may be a recluse, but you do have a personality. One I happen to like as a matter of fact. I just don't understand your thinking," she continued, shaking her head. "I told you I loved you anyway. I told you I didn't care about having a house full of screaming brats. All I care about is you, Marcus."

"I know—"

"Then if you know, why did you not accept it? Why do you doubt my love for you at every turn?" she burst out in frustration.

"I don't," he argued, crossing his arms. "I know you love me."

"Do you?"

"Yes."

"Then why do you constantly close yourself off to me? How can you possibly know that I love you, but you don't accept it?"

Cocking his head to the side, he stared at her for a moment. "I'm not sure I know the difference, but I do know you love me, and I accept it. I might have been a little slow to truly comprehend that you'd be happy—not just content, but happy—with spending the rest of your life with just me, but I did realize the error of my ways and acted before it was too late."

"Barely," she reminded him with a slim smile. "Another second or two, and I would have been married to Sir Wallace."

"That's not true," he countered with a grin. "The way I see it, I still had a good thirty seconds to spare. Just because he was about to make his vows didn't mean anything. You hadn't made yours yet."

"I don't find your observation nearly as entertaining as you do."

"Sorry," he murmured. He picked up a nearby pillow, and put it on his lap. "But I did come. Please, remember that. I might have been a fool to send you away and I might have almost waited too long to come back for you. But I did. I did come back."

"I know that." Emma's throat clogged with tears. "We've been over why you came back. We don't need to discuss it further. I just want to know the truth of why you sent me away. And don't you dare say it's because of your inability to have children. That's not the real reason, and you and I both know it. I've known you for as long as I can remember. You always struck me as a sensible person who understood such a thing as the existence of a foundling hospital. So leave off the inability to father children excuse and tell me the truth."

Silence filled the room, choking them both. Emma bit the inside of her lower lip to keep it firm and steady.

"I already told you," Marcus said softly.

Closing her eyes in frustration, Emma stood. "I believe I've heard enough. Goodnight, my lord."

Before she made it to the door, Marcus was off his seat. He closed his fingers firmly around her wrist, holding her in place. "You didn't let me finish."

"You were finished. You were once again going to remind me of your 'condition'," she said irritably. "Quite frankly, I don't want to hear of it again. Goodnight."

Marcus' fingers didn't relax their hold in the slightest. "I didn't feel I was worthy of you," he said softly. "Not only can I not give you children, but what I can give you is a constant reminder that I'd once foolishly proclaimed myself to your sister."

Emma swallowed and stared at him. "You mean…"

He nodded. "I mean as much as I like to pretend I never knew Louise as anything other than an old childhood friend who I encounter in passing from time to time, that doesn't make it true. I also like to pretend it doesn't mean anything to you that she and I were once engaged. But I know it cannot be easy for you, especially when there's a constant reminder of it printed on my face for the entire world to see."

"I've never cared about your scars," Emma said quietly, hardly believing what she was hearing.

"I know you don't care about their physical appearance. But you have to care about the reason they're there. I know I do."

"Why? You never really loved her. I know that."

"You do?"

Emma nearly laughed at his expression. "Yes. I realized you weren't marrying Louise for love but for honor the day you came to our cottage and asked if the rumors about Louise and Gregory were true. I may have only been fourteen, but I recognized the difference in you that day from the day you proposed. You weren't the same. You didn't really wish to marry her and were only planning to marry her because you'd given her your word." She did laugh now. "I'd wager that forty thousand pound dowry you bestowed upon me that if your father and mother hadn't been such champions of the match, you'd have tried to use your age as a reason for reneging."

His nod confirmed her suspicion.

"Marcus, I've become more convinced as the years have passed, you didn't even love her when you proposed, but you gave your word and you had to honor it." She briefly paused and smiled as he continued nodding his agreement. "Then the day of your accident, she put you in a difficult position and you had to do something. I may not have been there that day, but I do know my sister. I can only imagine what she said to you that made you act so foolishly, if for nothing else than to save your pride. That's the reason I shoved aside my feelings for you and encouraged her to keep her promise to you. Not because I thought you loved her or she you, but because she owed it to you. Keeping her promise and not bringing scandal and shame to you was the least she owed you for all she'd done."

"You had feelings for me then?" he asked, blinking owlishly at her.

She gave an exaggerated sigh. "Marcus, I've fancied myself in love with you since the day we met and you pulled those dratted thorns out of my skin after Louise tripped me and I fell into your mother's rosebush."

He blinked. "I remember that day." His eyes danced with amusement and the corner of his lips tipped up. "I can honestly say, though, I didn't share the feeling at the time."

"How romantic," she quipped.

"Yes, well, what can I say? You weren't a tin soldier, a fish, or a chess piece; therefore, you were not on the list of loves in my life at the time. I do love you now, though."

"I know you say you do, but your actions suggest otherwise."

Sighing, Marcus pulled her to the settee he'd been occupying. Wrapping his arms around her, he brought her down to sit on his lap. "Can you honestly tell me it bothers you naught that everyone thinks I was so besotted with your sister I ruined my body and future to run her down?"

"No," she answered with a slight hitch in her voice. "I don't care about what others think. You're far more important to me than their opinions."

Marcus swallowed audibly. "I'm sorry," he said thickly.

"Don't be sorry." Emma pierced him with her eyes. "Just accept that I love you. I love everything about you. From your scarred skin to your scarred past, I love you." She raised her hand to stop him from breaking in. "You say you know, and you claim to accept my love, but you don't. If you did, we wouldn't be having this conversation. Again."

Marcus' grey eyes shifted from Emma's for a moment before meeting them once more. "Let's start fresh. Let me show you that I do accept your love."

"And how do you propose to do that?"

"You'll see." He loosened his arms around her waist and, with a slight pat on her bottom, encouraged her to get up. He stood and offered her his arm. "Come along."

Without argument, Emma walked with him out to the entrance hall and waited while he went off to speak to some servants. A few minutes later he came back, a smile on his face that would rival the width of the Thames.

"Your carriage, Lady Sinclair," he said as he opened the front door for her to see their carriage waiting at the end of the walkway.

An excited chill skated up her spine at the way he'd called her Lady Sinclair. "And where are you taking me, my lord?" she asked with a hint of a smile.

"You'll find out soon enough."

Chapter 27

"Where are we?" Emma asked an hour later when they'd pulled up to a little cottage only a few miles outside of London.

Marcus climbed out of the carriage and helped his beautiful wife descend. "Hideaway. It's a cottage that belongs to Patrick. He told me I could bring you here if I wanted."

"Why?"

"Because I thought this cottage could allow us the freedom my townhouse couldn't. Anyway, Ridge Water is too far away to reach today."

"There are no servants here, are there?"

"Not one," he confirmed, pulling her to him. Without giving her a second to protest, he covered her mouth with his.

Beneath his, Emma's lips softened and parted as his tongue traced her lower lip. Slow and gentle, he pulled her bottom lip in between his lips and traced the bottom edge with his tongue.

She sighed, and he pushed his tongue past her parted lips to taste her. Her hands came up to rest on his shoulders, her fingers digging into his flesh as his tongue slid over hers.

Without thought, he brought his hands up to her face and ran the pads of his thumbs over her cheekbones while his fingertips tangled in the soft hair that rested behind her ears.

"Oh, Emma," he groaned against her mouth. He pulled back and stared at her flushed face. She was beautiful. Of course, she was always beautiful, but seeing her flushed from his kisses made her all the more stunning.

She blinked at him. "You're not planning to seduce me into

submission, are you?" The worried wrinkle that creased her brow belied her light words and airy tone.

"No. I already told you I have no intention of seducing you to do my bidding. We're here to start over. Start fresh."

"And just how do you suggest we do that?"

He grinned. "I think we should start by spending some time together down at the pond."

Emma clapped her hands together in what he could have sworn was sarcastic excitement. "Oh, Marcus, you are *so* romantic. I do believe I shall be the envy of all my friends when I tell them I got to catch a fish on my wedding night."

He frowned at her. "You used to like it when I helped you catch a fish. In fact, just a few weeks ago you practically begged me to help you."

"We're not children anymore. Helping me catch a fish is not the way to go about mending what you've done."

"I know that." He cleared his throat. "Would you just give me a chance and meet me down at the pond in half an hour?"

"And what shall I do until then?"

He grinned at her. "Practice your cast, of course."

With an odd look and a shake of her head, Emma walked off.

Marcus waited for her to be out of sight before he hobbled about his business.

Glancing out the window to make sure they still had just enough daylight for his plan to work, he set out about getting everything perfect.

***

"You want me to what?"

"Take off your clothes," Marcus repeated with a roguish grin.

"You're cracked," she proclaimed, her eyes doing a slow perusal of Marcus' nearly naked body. Just as she knew it would be, the skin that covered his arms and chest was covered in rigid pink and white scars. She tried not to stare so he wouldn't feel uncomfortable, but it was horribly difficult for her to keep her eyes off him. She let her gaze travel down to his waist where he wore a simple pair of smalls and nothing else. His legs, for the most part, looked like they had escaped injury and had smooth skin covered in light brown hair.

"All right, now that you've looked me over, remove your gown," Marcus told her, instantly concluding her perusal of his body.

Her eyes met his. "I—I—I don't think so."

"Why not?"

"I'm not fishing in my chemise, that's why not!"

Marcus shifted the weight off his injured leg the best he could. "I didn't ask you to. Now, why don't you turn around and I'll undo the buttons on your gown."

"Marcus, answer truthfully. Have you suffered some sort of brain fever recently?"

He shook his head. "No. Have you?"

She wasn't even going to dignify his ridiculous question with an answer. "Are you sure you haven't? Perhaps you fell and hit your head on something."

"I did no such thing." He took four steps toward her.

She stood still and looked out over the pond as he walked up behind her and began untying the strings on the back of her gown. "Wh—where are the poles?" she asked a moment later when she realized he was truly going to undress her, and more disturbing, she was going to let him.

A low chuckle sounded in his chest before he cleared his throat. "You don't worry about that. On more than one occasion you've expressed an interest in seeing more of me than I was willing to share at the time. This is your chance, my lady."

"What are you about, Marcus Sinclair?"

"Nothing. Just planning to take a swim with my new wife." He unhooked several of the clasps on the back of her dress.

"A swim?"

"Mmmhmmm." His fingers stilled. "Now, would you like me to continue to take your gown off, or would you prefer to swim with it on?"

"You can take it off," she answered, trying not to let him know how much she was enjoying him undressing her.

He carefully undid the remainder of the buttons that went down her back then focused on untying her corset. Loosened just enough, he slipped his hands to the top of the undone fabric and with a slow and steady ease, peeled the dress and corset from her and let the unneeded clothes fall to the ground. Marcus sucked in his breath at the sight of her and clamped his hands on the flare of her hips, his fingers searing her beneath the thin layers she still wore.

She cleared her throat. "Our swim."

His fingers tightened a little before letting go. "Right you are, my dear," he agreed huskily. He walked around to stand in front of her. "You had better finish…" He waved a hand downward toward her stockings then leaned against a nearby tree with his hands clasped together tightly in front of his waist.

A wicked thought popped into Emma's head, and she tried her best to act as if she didn't notice him or his distress as she stepped out of the pool her gown made at her feet and stood next to it. Very slowly, she let her fingers grab for the middle of her chemise and pull up just high enough to expose the top of her stockings. Holding it still, she reached the slender fingers of her right hand down to grab hold of the top of her right stocking, her left hand following suit.

Emma let her fingers slowly walk her stocking down her leg and she subtly peeked through her lowered lashes to glimpse Marcus' rigid face. She inwardly smiled. She was definitely torturing him. Good. He deserved it for all he'd put her through.

With all the skill and finesse of England's well-trained courtesan, learned straight from the word of Lady Bird herself, Emma slowly peeled her stocking off, pausing after she'd lowered it every couple inches for no other reason than to torture her new husband all the more.

She pulled the top edge of the silk down just below her knee. "Would you just take that confounded stocking off," Marcus said in a gruff voice, accompanied by a strangled noise that sounded as if it were ripped straight from his chest.

Emma looked up at him and turned her lips into a sultry smile.

"That's what I'm doing, dear."

"Well, do it faster."

She shook her head, dispelling some of her blonde tendrils. "You're not in a rush, are you?" She nearly choked at the sound of aggravation he made in response to her jest.

Without another word, she slid her stocking to her ankle then raised her foot a few inches off the ground before pulling her stocking the rest of the way off with deliberate slowness and ease. She tossed it to the ground and tried not to smile at Marcus' groan when her fingertips found the top of her other stocking.

With the same slow, torturous movements as before, Emma removed her second stocking and carelessly discarded it in the direction of its mate. "I believe I'm ready now," she announced as she walked closer to the tree Marcus was resting against.

His grey eyes swept over her. "What of your chemise?"

She looked down at the offending garment and tipped one shoulder up in a sensual, one-shouldered shrug. Letting her eyes drop to his waist, she said, "I think we're evenly matched."

He stared at her.

She coughed delicately, but he didn't act.

Shaking her head at his blatant confusion mixed with what she guessed to be desire, she took mercy on him and stepped closer to him, gently placing her hands on his tense wrists. "Relax," she murmured, pushing them away.

Swallowing and simultaneously screwing up her courage, Emma lightly pressed her fingers to Marcus' shoulders and let them trail from his broad but scarred shoulders to just above his waist, touching every inch of his imperfect-to-everyone-but-her skin along the way. Her eyes remained locked with his the entire time. She hooked the ends of two fingers from each hand into his snug waistband and with the barest movement, gave a gentle tug.

He stepped forward to press his body against hers as his hands settled on her shoulders and his lips met her mouth.

"Emma," he groaned, digging his fingers into her shoulders and pulling her as close to him as she'd allow.

She brought her arms up, wrapped them tightly around his

neck, and parted her lips when the warm tip of his tongue traced the seam of her lips.

Deepening their kiss, Marcus' tongue explored the inside of Emma's cheeks and brushed her tongue. She sighed, and sank her fingers into the back of his silky brown hair.

Marcus' tongue continued to plunder her mouth, and holding nothing back from the man she loved, she boldly moved her tongue into his mouth to mimic his actions. Marcus' hands came up to cup her face, his thumbs mindlessly brushing small strokes across her cheekbones.

"I love you, Emma," Marcus said raggedly, pulling his mouth only an inch or two from hers.

"I love you, too," she returned, her voice unsteady. Her eyes met his and in that minute, everything hurtful that had passed between them vanished. There, in the smoky depths of his grey eyes, she could see just how much he loved her, always had, and always would. He may have the power to hurt her more than anyone else, but he hadn't intended to cause her pain. She saw that now. It was his love for her that made him send her away. Her heart swelled at the misguided notion. He didn't need to send her away in order to give her everything she could ever want. All he had to do was give her himself. And just now, nothing stood in the way of him doing exactly that.

"Emma, I—" he started.

She lifted one finger to his lips. "Shhh. Don't talk." Not taking her gaze from his, she trailed a path from his shoulders to his wrists with her fingertips, slow and seductive, taking a measure of pride at watching his eyes grow darker with desire while the muscles in his arms involuntarily flexed under her fingers.

Leaving his wrists behind, Emma wrapped her fingers around the loose knot in the drawstring of his drawers and tugged one of the ends, until the knot slipped and the waistband loosened. Still holding his smalls up to cover him, she walked her fingers around to grab hold of the fabric that hung on either side of his hips.

Her eyes not leaving his, she gave a quick jerk and swallowed nervously when his drawers fell straight to the ground.

"Satisfied?"

"Not yet. She took a step back so she could admire his body. She let her eyes break contact with his and thoroughly sweep his body. Most women would be repulsed or disgusted by his body. But she wasn't. No amount of puckered and scarred skin could dampen her desire. To her, those imperfections ceased to exist. Instead, she saw a broad, muscled chest that she longed to kiss and a firm midsection she itched to touch. Her eyes stopped just above his waist and she licked her lips nervously before letting her eyes continue their southward journey.

She coughed and cleared her throat. "Excuse me," she sputtered inanely, patting her chest and trying in vain not to stare. Lady Bird had used many informative adjectives in describing the male part, but nothing she'd read or imagined compared to what she saw. Long and thick, his erection jutted out from a nest of springy curls. "I just—"

"I was wearing breeches," he teased, one side of his mouth tipped up into a hint of a smile.

She blushed. "I know." With a surge of bravery, perhaps spurred by curiosity, she reached forward and loosely wrapped her fingers around his hard length.

A harsh breath passed his lips, emboldening and empowering her more. Tightening her grip, she slowly glided her hand up and down his shaft. With a pleasure-induced groan, Marcus closed his eyes and sagged against the tree.

Emma tightened her grip a little more and quickened her pace, reeling with excitement as she realized how much power she held over him just now. There was no denying he enjoyed her attentions. A shudder wracked him and his fingers suddenly encircled her wrist. "You'd better stop," he said thickly.

"And if I don't want to?"

"You want to, I promise it."

Emma smiled saucily at him. A virginal young woman who'd never read *Lady Bird's Ladybird Memoir* wouldn't know just how close to the brink he was. But Emma knew. And it thrilled her. "No, I don't think I want to stop," she countered, giving him a

266

brief squeeze.

He groaned. "You little minx, you know exactly what you're doing."

"Perhaps I do." She tipped one shoulder up in a way that made one of the lacy straps of her chemise fall from the edge of her shoulder, her hand still firmly grasping his rigid flesh.

His eyes turned nearly as dark as coal. "Now who's the one trying to seduce the other?"

She lowered her lashes. "And did you think I was really in there practicing my cast?"

He laughed. "No. I know better than that. Besides, no matter how much you practice, you'd still need my help."

"Ah, so that's how you planned to seduce me," she mused, trying to distract him while the fingers of her free hand came up to try and pry his fingers from her wrist.

Instead of letting go like she hoped, his tight fingers kept their grip. "I'm warning you, Emma, you may not like the end result if you insist I let go and you continue."

She glanced down at their hands then let go. He may not be quite as close to losing control now as he was a few minutes ago, but he was still on the edge, and there were other ways she could push him beyond his control. She stepped back and pulled her wrist from his loosened grasp. Licking her lips slowly she took another step back and used her fingertips to seductively play with the straps of her chemise.

Marcus' hand reached forward, and she swayed her body away just in time. "Not yet."

"Not yet?"

"No, not yet," she confirmed.

"And just what must I do for you to drop that chemise?"

"Beg."

"No."

She lifted the shoulder that still had the strap on it just enough to let it slip to the end of her shoulder, then turned around so he could have full view of the back of her neck and shoulders. Holding her chemise in place by the lacy edge that rested just above her breasts, she rolled her shoulder back just enough to let that second strap fall completely.

Marcus' breathing grew hard and labored as Emma used deliberate slowness. She eased her chemise down a few inches to expose another patch of skin to his gaze.

"Do you have anything you wish to say?" she asked when the top of her chemise had just passed the bottom ridges of her shoulder blades.

"Take that confounded chemise off now before I take it off for you."

She shivered at his words. "That's not what I was hoping you'd say."

Before her last word was out, Marcus' warm body was pressed to the back of her, his big hands grabbing the delicate fabric and pulling it from her grasp, then letting it fall to the ground, forgotten. His hands roamed the front of her body, searing her with every touch.

"Was that what you were hoping I'd do?" he asked gruffly, his breath hot against her ear.

"No, I—"

"Wanted me to beg," he finished for her. "I won't beg, Emma. I may be a man, a foolish one at that, but I won't beg. Nor do I think you want me to." He kissed a line from her ear down her neck and to her shoulder, then back up again, making her go weak in the knees and fall back against him. "What do you really want?"

"To be yours." She couldn't believe she'd spoken the words aloud, but she had. And she meant them. That was what she wanted more than anything. More than to hear him beg her for forgiveness. More than hearing him admit once more how wrong he'd been. More than anything, she just wanted to be fully his.

His arms tightened around her and his hands caressed her swollen breasts. "You already are." He pressed a kiss behind her ear. "You've always been mine. Always. I may have been fool enough to let you go for a brief time, but even then you were still mine." His hands slipped under her breasts and tested their weight while his mouth placed hot, searing kisses along the top of her shoulder. "I'll never willingly part from you again. I promise. You're mine."

At his honest declaration, Emma's heart squeezed and thoughts of seduction and torture fled to be replaced with thoughts of love and longing. All she'd ever wanted was to be loved by him. And right then, she knew she was loved and always would be. All the pain and hurt she'd endured at his hands in the previous weeks vanished, never to return again.

She covered his hands with hers and pulled them from her before spinning around to face him. "Show me."

"Come," he commanded huskily, gently tugging her hand in the direction of some trees.

Wordlessly, the pair walked naked through the copse of trees like Adam and Eve until they came upon a little patch of grass where a big blanket had been spread. "You planned this," she accused laughingly.

"I'd hoped for it," Marcus corrected, awkwardly sinking down to the blanket and pulling Emma with him.

She dropped to her knees and looped her arms around his neck, bringing her lips to his for a scorching, soul searing kiss.

"I want to kiss you everywhere," he panted, pulling away.

"Then kiss me everywhere."

Marcus' lips brushed hers once more then feathered kisses across her cheek and down to her jaw. Kissing the edge of her jaw, his hands came up to shape her breasts. Her nipples hardening against his palms, she arched her back and pushed her breasts more firmly against his hands.

Bringing his hands up to her shoulders, he gave her a slight push backward. "Lie down."

She did as he instructed and sighed with pleasure when his hands found her swollen breasts again, his tongue tracing the ridge of her clavicle until he reached the valley between her breasts. Pressing a line of warm, openmouthed kisses down the length of her sternum, Marcus' body moved lower and his large hands continued caressing her breasts.

Marcus' lips kissed a line to her waist, and his fingers found her hardened nipples and gave them a slight squeeze. Emma's body bucked and twisted of its own accord as a quick shot of pleasure coursed through her.

Marcus' mouth covered the point of her left hip and gently nipped it. Then he used his lips and tongue to draw a line to connect to the point of her right hip. Sliding his hands from her breasts and up to rest on her shoulders, he kissed his way back up her body and pressed soft kisses along the underneath curve of her right breast before closing his lips around the rigid peak.

Emma sighed at the sensation caused by his mouth and tongue. Lost in the pleasure he was creating, she closed her eyes and rolled her head off to the side. Very lightly, Marcus sucked, then nipped the peak of her breast, and Emma's hands flew to the back of his head, her fingers tangling in his hair, holding him to her. He circled her nipple with his tongue and she arched her back to offer him more.

A whimper passed her lips as Marcus' lips left her right breast and kissed a path to her left before lavishing that breast with the same attention he'd shown the first. His left hand abandoned her shoulder and made a slow, lingering descent down the side of her body to her hip. Bringing his mouth from her breast, he repositioned himself atop her and whispered something near her ear she couldn't quite make sense of over the excitement coursing through her and the blood thundering in her ears.

Marcus' hand shifted to her thigh and gently pushed her leg to the side just enough for him to settle between her parted legs.

Emma's eyes locked with Marcus'. This was it. They were about to become joined for life in a way she would never be with another. Staring up at the man she loved, she tried to heed his urging for her to relax as he slid himself into her then paused. "Just a bit more," he murmured.

She swallowed, not knowing what fully to expect. Lady Bird had only described sensations she was not feeling at present. Bracing himself on his right elbow and holding tightly to Emma's hip with his left hand, Marcus gave one more push forward and froze. "Are you all right?" His words were broken and his breathing ragged.

She stared at him in shock. Those stories said nothing about pain. She blinked and gave a weak nod, not trusting her voice.

"It'll get better," Marcus promised. He repositioned himself to take as much weight off his leg as he could. "It's supposed to hurt the first time..." He trailed off and scattered kisses across her forehead. "Just relax and you'll get accustomed."

She raised her brows at him. "Mighty knowledgeable for a virgin," she quipped, shifting her hips to get more comfortable.

He groaned. "I may be a recluse who thought he'd never need the knowledge, but I do remember being told that bit of information."

Emma smiled at him and brought her hand up to push back a lock of hair which had fallen in his face and was partially covering her view of his grey eyes. "It doesn't hurt anymore."

Grunting his understanding, Marcus eased his hips forward, then back again, taking time to find a slow, gentle pattern. Placing her hands on his shoulders, Emma closed her eyes and rolled her head back, enjoying the pleasant feeling of Marcus inside her as his steady strokes stoked an inner fire she hadn't imagined would be possible only a few minutes earlier. He bent his head down close to her ear and whispered sweet words of love and admiration. His words were so soft and low, nobody else could have heard them if they were standing right there. And that made them all sweeter. They were meant just for her.

Wanting to feel him deeper inside her, she brought her legs up around his waist and crossed her ankles. He groaned and pushed himself as far in as she could take him. She sighed at the intense spark that shot through her that time, then the next, then again, each time building up to something bigger, stronger, more intense. Then finally, she peaked. She reached the culmination she'd been building up to with each of his strokes and a delicious tension washed over her, one that caused her whole body to stiffen followed by a wave of relief, flooding her with waves of ecstasy.

Just as the final rounds of pleasure started to fade, Emma opened her eyes and met Marcus'. The look in his eyes was one she didn't recognize, but she knew right then she loved seeing that look and always would. A guttural grunt suddenly rent the air, followed by Marcus' body turning hard as stone as he reached his climax.

Collapsing on top of her, he whispered the three words she'd never tire of hearing before rolling off onto his side, taking her with him.

She rested her head on his chest and let her fingers wander aimlessly across his skin until her eyelids grew heavy and she started to drift to sleep.

"Thank you," Marcus whispered, startling her.

She snuggled closer to him. "For what?"

"For loving me in spite of my many flaws."

She stiffened. "Marcus, don't you dare do this. I've told you a thousand times I don't give a hang about your sc—"

"Not that," he cut in. "I know you don't care about those. I was talking about the flaws of my personality. Such as the one that wouldn't allow me to believe your love was real and lasting, or the one that made me send you away."

"Oh, *those* flaws." She walked her fingers down his midsection. "Well, Lord Sinclair, I do believe you have a lot to make up for."

"I do?"

"Yes. Did you think you were forgiven?"

He blinked down at her. "Yes. I mean, we—"

"Oh, you're not forgiven. Far from it."

"And what must I do to be forgiven?"

"I don't know." She twisted in his hold so she could look up and see his face.

Brushing his knuckles across her cheek, he smiled at her. "Just when do you think you'll have an idea of what I can do to be granted your forgiveness."

She shrugged and kissed his cheek. "I don't know that, either. Sometime in the next fifty years, I expect."

The corners of his eyes crinkled and he pulled her back down to him. "I guess I'll just have to wait until then, and in the meantime, I'll just do whatever I can to stay in your good graces."

"That sounds like a perfect plan."

He gave her shoulders one last affectionate squeeze, and together the two drifted off to sleep, all troubles, worries, problems long forgotten. Just the two of them lying in the arms of the one they loved and always would.

Epilogue

Dorset
May 1865

Emma's lips curved ever-so-slightly as she read the scratched out words on the little slip of paper in her hands.

Meet me by the water.

She shook her head. Even as an octogenarian, her husband still had a love for fishing that outmatched even a young boy's. She put the paper down and tried not to dwell too much on the memory from last week when she'd watched his not-so-steady hands push the fishing line through the guides on her pole as he ever-faithfully rigged it up for her. Even after all these years together, she still found it a sweet satisfaction that he enjoyed her company on his fishing excursions, and went so far as to get her equipment ready.

She pulled on her leather half-boots and re-pinned her silver hair, then walked outside to find her husband and see what he had waiting for her. Every year for the past fifty years, on the thirteenth day of May, Marcus would somehow surprise her with yet another letter he'd written to her during those miserable weeks they were apart. She was sure he'd have run out years ago. Truly, what man enjoyed writing letters?

The sun was shining bright that morning, and she brought her hand up to shade her eyes as she walked in the direction of the stream. "Hello Marcus," she greeted when she saw him leaning up against a tree.

"Emma," he said with an easy smile. "It's nice of you to join me."

She shook her head. As if she'd have denied his request. Even after all these years, she loved being near him. Her eyes caught on a little corner of yellow vellum poking up from the top of his suit coat. Smiling up at him, she leaned forward and plucked the missive from his pocket. He didn't even try to stop her. Curious. Normally he grabbed her wrist to stop her, or would hold the paper out of her reach. When they were younger, he'd hide it somewhere in his clothes and make her search for it. That *always* led to some naughty game. A small smile took her lips. She may be an older woman now, but nothing could erase those steamy memories from her mind. Nor would she want to forget a single second they'd shared together in the past fifty years.

"Are you going to open that sometime today?" Marcus asked.

His gruff voice startled her a bit and she jumped. Something was off today. Something about this letter was different than the others. With a slight swallow, she broke the seal. Wait. Her eyes narrowed. None of the others had had a seal. Some hadn't even been folded. Some hadn't even been signed. They'd all been incomplete in one way or another. But not this one. This one had been sealed with wax, and looked as if it'd actually spent some time in a mail coach. Her heart picked up pace. When Marcus had interrupted her wedding to Wallace, he'd said he'd sent a missive that didn't reach her in time. Caroline was supposed to forward it to her when it arrived. But it never came. Weeks and weeks, then months and months, she'd waited to read that letter. After two years, she'd given up hope.

"Is this—" Her voice broke.

Marcus nodded. "In my hurry, I marked the direction wrong. It seems I sent it to America in place of one meant for Olivia. Mr. Saxon intercepted it and kept it. Why he never sent it back, I don't know, but his grandson found it a few months ago and sent it."

"Oh," she said, her fingers trembling as she unfolded the letter. It wasn't important how it came back to her. The important part was it was here now. She'd finally be able to hold the paper in her hands and read his words with her own eyes.

Dear Emma,

As I write this, the sun is rising on the fourth day of May, the year 1815, and I have finally come to terms with what I am: a fool. No. Not a fool. A besotted fool. No. Not even a besotted fool. A broken, besotted fool. The biggest, most broken and besotted fool to have ever walked the face of the earth, to be exact. I know that now.

During the day, I yearn for you. At night I cannot sleep for fear I will dream of you. You are always in my thoughts, and it hurts. It hurts more than anything I've ever experienced. It hurts that you're not here with me, and it hurts to know you're going to walk down the aisle to a man who's not me. But most of all, it hurts to know the reason you are not here with me as my wife is my own doing and nobody else's.

It may be too late for me to make this right, but I want the chance to try. Please give me that much. I love you, Emma. I always have and always will. I was too blind and stubborn to see just how much you loved me in return, but I see it now. I just pray it's not too late...

I understand you are to marry Sir Wallace soon and I may very well lose you forever, but I'm asking one final thing of you. Grant me an audience in Alex's drawing room on Friday. That's all I ask. Give me the chance to show you how much I love you now and always will.

I realize no amount of fancy words, endless groveling, or tearful apologies will undo what I've done. It's too late for those things now, I know that. Emma, I've made many mistakes where you're concerned, and if you refuse me, I will live with my regrets.

All I can do now is ask that you'll wait for me. I'll be there soon.

Humbly yours,
Marcus

Emma used her frantically shaking fingers to swipe at the tears streaming down her wrinkled cheeks as her heart nearly exploded with love.

She looked up and met Marcus' grey eyes.

"I meant it," he said hoarsely. "I remember writing that letter like it was yesterday. Every single word of it has been imprinted on my brain for fifty years now. And I meant every one of them, Emma. I was a broken man during those weeks. As the time got closer—"

Emma put her finger to his lips. They'd never spoken of any of this since the day they'd married, and she didn't wish to now. She was glad to have his final letter, but there was no need to go over the past. "Just tell me this," she said with a slim smile. "You said you remember writing this letter as if it was yesterday. You didn't just write it yesterday, did you?"

Marcus blinked, and his body tensed. "No. Why would you even think that?"

Emma grinned up at him, trying her best to ignore the hurt she'd heard in his voice. "I just wanted to make sure. You did forge Caroline's science experiments for years."

He chuckled and his body relaxed. "Did you have to remind me of that?" he asked, shaking his head. "It took me nearly ten years to push those painful memories from my mind." He shuddered. "How was it you found out about that, anyway?"

"Marcus, you do know even Caroline knew before you told Alex, don't you?"

He nodded. "I know. I didn't know then, but I knew after Alex had his fun saying he'd passed on the title of 'Most Obtuse Man Who Ever Lived' to me. Apparently you and Caroline knew all along."

"Not all along," Emma assured him. "Just most of it."

Marcus moved closer to her and cupped her face with his hands. "Then you should have known all that time just how much I loved you."

Her eyebrows snapped together. "Pardon?"

"E. S. Wilson," he said simply.

She stared unblinkingly at him.

"Think about it for a minute." He brushed a silver curl from her forehead. "Does the name Wilson mean anything to you?"

She blinked then nodded. "It was my mother's maiden name."

He smiled at her. "I know. Now, think about your initials. Specifically your first and last."

A slow smile took her lips then disappeared, and her brows drew together again. "My initials are E. S. now, but they weren't then. Back then I was still Emma Green."

"I know," he conceded, bringing his index finger up to smooth out the wrinkle in between her eyes. "But a man can still dream, can't he?" He grinned at her and used his right thumb to trace her left cheekbone. "When I created her pseudonym I never dreamed I'd ever be able to make you my wife. So I did the next best thing, I changed your initials to reflect my name. Knowing what the E, and specifically the S, stood for, was the brightest part of doing that."

Emma shook her head. He was an odd man, indeed, but he was *her* odd man. "Why haven't you ever told me this before?"

He shrugged. "Why would I have? It really isn't that important, is it?"

"No. But isn't it a little odd to think, in an unusual way, you and Alex both fell in love with and married the same person?"

Marcus chuckled. "No, we did not. We fell in love with two entirely different people. He may have married the woman behind the articles. But I got to grow old with and experience all of life's joys—including the one I never thought possible—with the real E. S."

"Yes, you did!"

If you enjoyed *Her Reluctant Groom*, I would appreciate it if you would help others enjoy this book, too.

Lend it. This e-book is lending-enabled, so please, share it with a friend.

Recommend it. Please help other readers find this book by recommending it to friends, readers' groups and discussion boards.

Review it. Please tell other readers why you liked this book by reviewing it at one of the following websites: <u>Amazon</u> or <u>Goodreads</u>.

Other Books by Rose Gordon

BANKS BROTHERS' BRIDES

His Contract Bride—Lord Watson has always known that one day he'd marry Regina Harris. Unfortunately nobody thought to inform her of this; and when she finds that her "love match" was actually arranged by her father long ago in an effort to further his social standing, it falls to a science-loving, blunt-speaking baron to win her trust.

His Yankee Bride—John Banks has no idea what—or who—waits for him on the other side of the ocean... Carolina Ellis has longed to meet a man whom she can love, so when she glimpses such a man, she's determined to do whatever it takes to have him—Southern aristocracy be damned.

His Jilted Bride—Elijah Banks *cannot* sit still a moment longer as the gossip continues to fly about one of his childhood playmates, who just so happens to still be in her bridal chamber, waiting for her groom to arrive. Thinking to save her the public humiliation of being jilted at the altar, Elijah convinces her to run away with him, replacing one scandal with one far more forgiving. But when a secret she keeps is threatened to be exposed, it falls to Elijah to save her again by revealing a few of his own...

His Brother's Bride —Henry Banks had no idea his brother agreed to marry a fetching young lady until the day she shows up on his doorstep and presents the proof. To protect the Banks name and his new sister-in-law's feelings, Henry agrees to marry her only to discover this young lady's intentions were not so honorable and it wasn't really marriage she sought, but revenge on a member of the Banks family...

Coming July 2013
Celebrate America's independence with the:
OFFICER SERIES

(American Historicals based in Indian Territory mid-1800s)

The Officer and the Bostoner—A well-to-do lady traveling by stagecoach from her home in Boston to meet her fiance in Santa Fe finds herself stranded in a military fort when her stagecoach leaves without her. Given the choice to either temporarily marry an officer until her fiance can come rescue her or take her chances with the Indians, she marries the glib Captain Wes Tucker, who, unbeknownst to her, grew up in a wealthy Charleston family and despises everything she represents. But when it's time for her fiance to reclaim her and annul their marriage, will she still want to go with him, and more importantly, will Wes let her?

The Officer and the Southerner—Second Lt. Jack Walker doesn't always think ahead and when he decides to defy logic and send off for a mail-order bride, he might have left out only a few details about his life. When she arrives and realizes she's been fooled (again), this woman who's never really belonged, sees no other choice but to marry him anyway—however, she makes it perfectly clear: she'll be his lawfully wed, but she will *not* share his bed. Now Jack has to find a way to show his always skeptical bride that he is indeed trustworthy and that she does belong somewhere in the world: right here, with him.

The Officer and the Traveler—Captain Grayson Montgomery's mouth has landed him in trouble again! And this time it's not something a cleverly worded sentence and a handsome smile can fix. Having been informed he'll either have to marry or be demoted and sentenced to hard labor for the remainder of his tour, he proposes, only to discover those years of hard labor may have been the easier choice for his heart.

If you never want to miss a new release visit Rose's website at www.rosegordon.net to subscribe and you'll be notified each time a new book becomes available.

Also Already Available

GROOM SERIES

Four men are about to have their bachelor freedom snatched away as they become grooms...but finding the perfect woman may prove a bit more difficult than they originally thought.

Her Sudden Groom—The overly scientific, always respectable and socially awkward Alexander Banks has just been informed his name resides on a betrothal agreement right above the name of the worst chit in all of England. With a loophole that allows him to marry another without consequence before the thirtieth anniversary of his birth, he has only four weeks to find another woman and make her his wife.

Her Reluctant Groom—For the past thirteen years Marcus Sinclair, Earl Sinclair, has lived his life as a heavily scarred recluse, never dreaming the only woman he's ever wanted would love him back. But when it slips out that she does, he doubts her love for his scarred body and past can be real. For truly, how can a woman love a man whose injuries were caused when he once tried to declare himself to her sister?

Her Secondhand Groom—Widower Patrick Ramsey, Viscount Drakely, fell in love and married at eighteen only to be devastated by losing her as she bore his third daughter. Now, as his girls are getting older he realizes they need a mother—and a governess. Not able to decide between the two which they need more, he marries an ordinary young lady from the local village in hopes she can suit both roles. But this ordinary young lady isn't so ordinary after all, and he'll either have to take a chance and risk his heart once more or wind up alone forever.

Her Imperfect Groom —Sir Wallace Benedict has never been good with the fairer sex and in the bottom drawer of his bureau he has the scandal sheet clippings to prove it. But this thrice-jilted baronet has just discovered the right lady for him was well-worth waiting for. The only trouble is, with multiple former love interests plaguing him at every chance possible, he must find clever ways to avoid them and simultaneously steal the attention—and affections—of the the one lady he's sure is a perfect match for him and his imperfections.

Already Available--SCANDALOUS SISTERS SERIES

**Intentions of the Earl**—A penniless earl makes a pact to ruin an American hoyden, never suspecting for a moment he'll lose his heart along the way.

**Liberty for Paul**—A vicar's daughter who loves propriety almost as much as she hates the man her father is mentoring will go to any length she sees fit to see that improper man out the door and out of her life. But when she's forced to marry him, she'll learn there's a lot more to life, love and this man than she originally thought.

**To Win His Wayward Wife** —A gentleman who's spent the last five years pining for the love of his life will get his second chance. The only problem? She has no interest in him.

About the Author

USA Today Bestselling and Award Winning Author Rose Gordon writes unusually unusual historical romances that have been known to include scarred heroes, feisty heroines, marriage-producing scandals, far too much scheming, naughty literature and always a sweet happily-ever-after. When not escaping to another world via reading or writing a book, she spends her time chasing two young boys around the house, being hunted by wild animals, or sitting on the swing in the backyard where she has to use her arms as shields to deflect projectiles AKA: balls, water balloons, sticks, pinecones, and anything else one of her boys picks up to hurl at his brother who just happens to be hiding behind her.

She can be found on somewhere in cyberspace at:

http://www.rosegordon.net

or blogging about *something* inappropriate at:

http://rosesromanceramblings.wordpress.com

Rose would love to hear from her readers and you can e-mail her at rose.gordon@hotmail.com

You can also find her on Facebook, Goodreads, and Twitter.

If you never want to miss a new release visit her website to subscribe and you'll be notified each time a new book becomes available.

CPSIA information can be obtained at www.ICGtesting.com
Printed in the USA
LVOW10s1615030614

388429LV00022B/1471/P